MODERN NOISE, FLUID GENRES

Modern Noise, Fluid Genres

POPULAR MUSIC IN INDONESIA,

1997–2001

Jeremy Wallach

THE UNIVERSITY OF WISCONSIN PRESS

This book was published with support from
Bowling Green State University,
the Gustave Reese Publication Fund
of the American Musicological Society, and
the Center for Southeast Asian Studies
at the University of Wisconsin–Madison.

The University of Wisconsin Press
1930 Monroe Street, 3rd Floor
Madison, Wisconsin 53711-2059

www.wisc.edu/wisconsinpress/

3 Henrietta Street
London WC2E 8LU, England

1   3   5   4   2

Printed in the United States of America

Library of Congress Cataloging-in-Publication Data
Wallach, Jeremy.
Modern noise, fluid genres : popular music in Indonesia, 1997-2001 / Jeremy Wallach.
p.   cm. — (New perspectives in Southeast Asian studies)
Originally presented as the author's thesis (Ph. D.) — University of Pennsylvania, 2002.
Includes bibliographical references and index.
ISBN 978-0-299-22900-9 (cloth: alk. paper)
ISBN 978-0-299-22904-7 (pbk.: alk. paper)
1. Popular music — Indonesia.   I. Title.   II. Series.
ML3502.I5W35   2008
781.6309598 — dc22
2008011974

FOR

JONATHAN

Nations are mythical creatures, gaseous, and some-times poisonous. But they start to solidify when diverse people have moments when aspirations coincide.

Binyavanga Wainaina

CONTENTS

ILLUSTRATIONS

Tables

Figures

PREFACE

Modern Noise, Fluid Genres is a study of Indonesian popular music and its audiences written by an American anthropologist and amateur musician. The book is divided into two parts. The first half examines the cultural dynamics of particular sites for the production, mediation, and reception of popular music, including record stores, recording studios, video shoots, roadside food stalls, and other public and private spaces where music is performed, consumed, discussed, and debated by Indonesians from all walks of life. The second half of the book investigates specific live performance events as occasions when musical production, mediation, and reception processes occur simultaneously. The chapters in that half focus on three major youth-oriented popular music genre categories: dangdut, pop, and "underground" rock.

Through the book's focus on concrete sites and practices, I attempt to illuminate the complex affective politics of identification and exclusion that characterizes responses to contemporary popular music genres among people from different social classes in Indonesia. I conclude that access to globally circulating musics and technologies has neither homogenized nor extinguished local music making in Indonesia. Rather, I argue that this access has provided Indonesians with a wide range of creative possibilities for exploring their existential condition in a time of political transition and heated debate over Indonesia's future as a multiethnic, democratizing nation in a globalizing world. Moreover, the book posits that the popular, inclusive nationalism implicit in nearly all national Indonesian popular musics provides a viable alternative to the various forms of extremism and exclusivism (religious, regional, ethnic) that continue to threaten national integration, social justice, and democracy in post–New Order Indonesia.

In the acknowledgments to *The Religion of Java*, a landmark study of Javanese village life during Indonesia's last great experiment with democracy, Clifford Geertz (who sadly passed away while I was completing the final revisions of this book) thanks the many ordinary Indonesians who assisted him in his research and wrote of his "hope that in some way [his] book [might] contribute to the realization of their aspiration to build a strong, stable, prosperous, and democratic 'New Indonesia'" (1960, x). I humbly wish the same for the present study, which portrays life in Indonesia once again during a time of cultural ferment, political upheaval, and cautious hope for a more just and democratic future. It is my hope that this book will advance scholarly understandings of Indonesian national culture as it evolves in the current era, and that it will serve as a model for ethnographically grounded popular music research in contemporary urban settings throughout the world. Most of all, I hope it will bring to the attention of the scholarly community the diversity, creativity, and exuberance of Indonesian popular music and reveal how an informed understanding of this music can forcefully challenge ossified, monolithic Western preconceptions of Muslim and Asian cultures.

ACKNOWLEDGMENTS

This ethnographic study, like any other, would have been impossible without the aid and support of a vast number of individuals and organizations. The length of the following list of thank-yous attests to the amount of assistance and encouragement I enjoyed during the long process of researching and writing this book.

First, I am forever indebted to a multitude of figures in the Indonesian music world for their input, gracious hospitality, and boundless patience and generosity with their time and their craft. I wish to thank in particular Edy Singh, Cahyo Wirokusomo, Edo, Donny, Patty, Raymond, Sonny, Pak Cecep, and Pak Hassanudin at 601 Studio Lab; Pak Paku of Maheswara Musik; dangdut artists Oppie Sendewi, Iyeth Bustami, Titiek Nur, Lilis Karlina, and Murni Cahnia; Dessy Fitri; Bagus Dhanar Dana; Mas Puput; Pak Jerry Bidara; Yukie Pas; Richard Mutter, Helvi Sjarifuddin, and Uki of Reverse Outfits; Robin Malau and Arian Tigabelas; Dwiki Dharmawan; Trie Utami; Pra Budidharma and family; Wendi Putranto; Nugie; Adam Joswara; Rully Rohmat; Andy Atis, Amanda, and Anggie; Benino Aspiranta and Titie; Sabdo Mulyo; Melly Goeslaw and Anto Hoed; Ari Lasso; Candra Darusman; Jan Djuhana and Lala Hamid of Sony Music Entertainment Indonesia; George Effendi; Iwan Fals; and the late Harry Roesli. Many thanks also to the following bands and their management: Bantal, Betrayer, Cherry Bombshell, Eternal Madness, Karnaval, Koil, Krakatau, Kuch Kuch Hota Hai, Netral, OMEGA Group, Pas, Pemuda Harapan Bangsa, Potret, Puppen, Ramirez, Samudera, Slowdeath, Soekarmadjoe, Step Forward, Tengkorak, Tor, and Trauma. *Ribuan terima kasih, dan saya mohon maaf sebesar-besarnya kalau ada yang saya lupa untuk menyebut di sini.*

I am grateful as well to Dean Tanete Adrianus Pong Masak, Dean A. Agus Nugroho, and the other members of the Faculty of Business Administration, Atma Jaya University (Jakarta), for their logistical support and intellectual engagement with my project. Thanks are also due to Ian White, an Australian filmmaker creating a documentary on the Balinese underground music scene, for sharing his unreleased film footage with me. I am grateful to the regulars at three *warung* in Santa,

Kebayoran Baru, South Jakarta, for sharing their time, wit, and music. Last, I would like to extend my heartfelt thanks to Ahmad Najib, Guntoro Utamadi, Paramita Prabarathayu, Donny Suryady and family, and Haryo Koconegoro and family for their friendship, hospitality, and invaluable assistance with my research.

In the United States, I first and foremost thank my dissertation adviser Greg Urban and the other members of my dissertation committee, Sandra Barnes, Webb Keane, and Carol Muller, for their support, guidance, and helpful suggestions during the lengthy process of researching and writing the doctoral thesis upon which this work is based. I am also grateful to Randal Baier, Charles Capwell, Steve Ferzacca, the late Clifford Geertz, Ellen Koskoff, René T. A. Lysloff, Peter Manuel, Thomas Porcello, Guthrie Ramsey, Marina Roseman, Peggy Reeves Sanday, Anthony Seeger, Gary Tomlinson, Deena Weinstein, Sarah Weiss, Deborah Wong, and Philip Yampolsky for their intellectual inspiration and encouragement. I owe a special debt of thanks to R. Anderson Sutton for his support over the years, and for inviting me to submit a manuscript to the University of Wisconsin Press. I wish to thank as well my three undergraduate mentors: Richard Freedman, Wyatt MacGaffey, and Bill Hohenstein. A musicologist specializing in the French Renaissance, a British social anthropologist, and a maverick sociologist, these three scholars first set me on the path that led years later to the completion of this book.

I owe a debt of gratitude to David Harnish for his review of an earlier draft of chapter 1 and to David Novack for his detailed, insightful comments on an earlier version of chapter 4. I would also like to thank profusely Benedict R. O'G. Anderson, R. Anderson Sutton, Andrew Weintraub, and Sean Williams for their extensive feedback on earlier versions of the entire manuscript, and for their invaluable advice on translations and a wide range of Indonesian cultural, musical, and linguistic topics. Sharon Wallach patiently read every single word of this manuscript multiple times and, with her insightful and incisive comments and corrections, helped make this book far better than it otherwise would have been. Special thanks also go to Maxine Barry and Ken Jurek for their assistance with the music compact disc that accompanies this volume.

Research and travel funds were provided by the United States Indonesia Society and by the University of Pennsylvania Department of Anthropology. I am grateful for their assistance. During my years of graduate study, my fellow students at the University of Pennsylvania in the Department of Anthropology and the Department of Music provided me with intellectual stimulation and camaraderie, especially José Semblante Buenconsejo, Matthew Butterfield, Jacqueline Fewkes, Paul D. Greene, Deanna Kemler, Alexander "Lex" Rozin, Nastia Snider, Matthew Tomlinson, Elyse Carter Vosen, and especially Sarah Morelli. I will always be grateful for their friendship and for their thoughtful comments on my work, often requested at the last minute. Friends and colleagues from other departments and universities who kindly provided input, advice, and suggestions for this project include Harris M. Berger, Jennifer Connolly, Nicholas Crosson, Sara L. M. Davis, Kai Fikentscher, Peter Furia, Andrew Jewett, Eric A. Jones, Keith Kahn-Harris, Elisa von Joeden-Forgey, Richard Miller, Gabriel Morris, Norman Morrison, Sarah Moser, Jennifer Munger, Karl von Schriltz, Patricia Tang, Emily Vartanian, Michael Vartanian, Cynthia Po-man Wong, Juliet Wunsch, and the late Lise Waxer. Any shortcomings that remain in the text are entirely my fault.

At the Department of Popular Culture at Bowling Green State University I found a collegial and supportive environment in which to pursue this project. I thank all my past and present colleagues in Popular Culture and those in several other departments at BGSU as well, especially fellow ethnomusicologist and Indonesia specialist David Harnish in the College of Musical Arts, for their input and valued intellectual comradeship. I would also like to thank my hardworking graduate research assistants, Wei-Ping Lee, Michael Mooradian Lupro, and Adam Murdough, for scholarly and editorial assistance ably provided. Adam's work was so impressive that I asked him if he could prepare this book's index. He agreed, and did the job with his usual care and thoroughness. Finally, I would like to extend my thanks to all my students over the years, in particular the participants in my spring 2004 and 2006 graduate seminars on genre and authenticity in world popular music studies and the students in my spring 2005 graduate proseminar on popular music scholarship.

Portions of this work have been presented in various forums, including colloquia at the University of Wisconsin–Madison School of Music, the University of Pennsylvania Department of Anthropology, the Haverford College Center for Humanities, and the Bowling Green State University Department of Popular Culture. I am grateful for the feedback I received on those occasions. I am especially indebted to my fellow participants at the Royal Netherlands Institute Seventeenth Annual International Workshop on South-East Asian Studies, particularly organizers Bart Barendregt and Kees van Dijk, for their detailed comments on my research and ideas.

The publication of this work was made possible by subvention grants from the American Musicological Society, the Bowling Green State University Scholars Assistance Program, and the Center for Southeast Asian Studies, University of Wisconsin–Madison. I am most grateful for the support of these organizations. I would also like to convey my heartfelt thanks to Gwen Walker, Sheila Moermond, Barb Wojhoski, and the rest of the staff at the University of Wisconsin Press who worked on this volume for their patience and invaluable assistance bringing the project to fruition. Portions of the following work have been published in earlier forms. The material in chapter 3 first appeared in the journal *Indonesia* (volume 74, October 2002), and portions of chapter 4 were published in the edited collection *Wired for Sound* (Greene and Porcello 2005). I thank Cornell University Press and Wesleyan University Press for kindly granting permission to reprint parts of these articles.

I would like to thank my parents, Paula and Lawrence Wallach, my brothers Matthew, Ted, and Jordan, my sisters-in-law Cristina, Leah, and Diana, my grandmother Sara Shapiro, and the rest of my family for their support and for believing in me and cheering me on through many long years of study.

Finally, this book is dedicated to my wonderful son, Jonathan, who one day I hope will enjoy reading it.

MODERN NOISE, FLUID GENRES

Introduction

A BRIEF HISTORY
OF POPULAR MUSIC AND SOCIETY
IN INDONESIA

This book is an ethnographic investigation of Indonesian popular music genres and their producers and listeners during a period of dramatic political and cultural transformation. Through a ground-level examination of the production, consumption, and discursive representations of popular musics in Indonesia, I hope to shed light on complex cultural processes that play a vital role in contemporary young urban Indonesians' imaginings of the Indonesian nation, its place in the world, and its future. Furthermore, I intend to show how young Indonesian women and men from various social classes use popular musics to reconcile their disparate allegiances to and affinities for local, global, and national cultural entities.

The notion that cultural production and reception are linked to identity formation has become a commonplace in cultural studies, anthropology, ethnomusicology, and other human sciences. Such a premise suggests that the *actual encounters* of producers and consumers with particular artifacts—in situations both mundane and spectacular—should be taken seriously by scholars wishing to explore the construction of identity in particular times and places (see Porcello 1998). This ethnography, then, aims to highlight the social and experiential context of subjects' encounters with cultural objects, thus grounding its interpretations of those objects in the details of concrete settings and everyday experience. The interpretations of Indonesian popular musics contained in these pages are also informed by another key insight of cultural studies: due to the contested nature of its meanings and ownership, popular culture (especially popular music) is an important site of cultural struggle, and it can reveal a great deal about gender, class, and other social divisions characterized by unequal power relations operating in a society (see Frith 1981; Frith, Straw, and Street 2001; Middleton 1990; Ross and Rose 1994; and Walser 1993).

Inspired by recent work on the production, circulation, and reception of mass-produced cultural artifacts in modern societies (e.g., Anderson [1983] 1991, 1998; Appadurai 1996; Mahon 2004; Mazzarella 2003; F. Miller 2005), this study takes a "sonic materialist" approach to popular musics in Indonesia, examining the processes by which musical sounds—understood as forms of audiotactile material culture—are created, mediated, and disseminated, and the ways in which these sounds become meaningful in diverse everyday contexts.[1] Particularly valuable to this project is anthropologist Greg Urban's account of the production, discursive framing, and social circulation of cultural forms in modern complex societies (2001). Urban characterizes contemporary, mass-mediated societies as operating under a "metaculture of modernity" in which cultural forms (such as popular songs) are both *disseminated* as mass-produced artifacts (such as music recordings) and *replicated* through the creation of similar yet novel forms (for example, new songs in a familiar style). Urban argues that unlike societies that operate under a "metaculture of tradition," which value the precise reproduction of expressive forms (such as the recitations of myths), contemporary complex societies emphasize innovative elements when producing cultural objects, and the successful circulation of culture in such societies depends on these innovations and on how they are interpreted by audiences.

This ethnography aims to examine the processes of production, dissemination, replication, and interpretation of popular musics in Indonesia by tracing how these processes implicate and connect producers, performers, and listeners—all of whom play an active, creative role in the ongoing circulation of musical culture. To arrive at an understanding of these complex processes, this ethnography for the most part adopts a street-level perspective, engaging with the concrete details of the everyday lives of individuals in specific social settings. Thus the following investigation differs from the many anthropological studies of cultural processes under modernity that adopt a macro-level—often transglobal—analytical perspective. Instead, this book is composed of situated ethnographic narratives that illuminate the lives and concerns of actual people involved in the various stages of those cultural processes. As such, it seeks to reinsert human agency into our understandings of processes of cultural production and reception, which are too often reducible to a reified dialectic of commodification and resistance whose totalizing logic tends to discourage the sensitive, nuanced empirical inquiry that constitutes the ethnographer's greatest contribution to the study of modern national cultures.

In every context explored here, perceptions of *genre* connect sounds with particular meanings, and preoccupations with the maintenance or transgression of genre boundaries play a vital role in everyday understandings of popular music (Frith 1996, 75–95). Music scholar Richard Middleton writes, "A genre can be thought of as analogous to a discursive formation, in the sense that in such a formation there is regulation of vocabulary, types of syntactic unit, formal organization, characteristic themes, modes of address (who speaks to whom and after what fashion), and structures of feeling" (1999, 144–45). Music genres are discursively linked in complex ways to particular social categories, including class, gender, and ethnicity, and their reception among Indonesians from different walks of life can reveal a great deal about how they view themselves and others in their society. Unlike the majority of existing ethnographic studies of popular musics in non-Western countries (e.g., Atkins 2001; Meintjes 2003; Schade-Poulsen 1999; Stokes 1992; Waterman 1990; Waxer 2002; Yano 2002), this study does not focus on a single genre but rather investigates the relationships among different national and international genres relevant to the lives of urban Indonesians, particularly young people in the capital city.[2] Viewing the entire national popular "musicscape" as an arena of contestation, hybridization, and accommodation, I demonstrate the social and ideological significance of popular music genres in contemporary Indonesia and their intimate connections to competing, historically situated conceptions of nation and modernity.[3]

In doing so, this book joins a growing number of ethnographic and historical studies that examine the relationship between popular music and the formation of modern national identities (e.g., Greene 2001; Turino 2000; Yano 2002; Zuberi 2001). These works seek to understand the complex local-global relationships that constitute music genres perceived as somehow representing a nation-state and the values and aspirations of its people (see Turino 1999). In this study, I view national music and the nation as *mutually constitutive:* each is simultaneously a reification and a palpable presence that relies on the other to provide a legitimating framework. Thus "Indonesian" popular music appears to validate a particular sense of Indonesian-ness, just as the sense of Indonesian-ness generates a need for a recognizably Indonesian popular music.

Methods and Theories

There is nothing very precise, repeatable, predictable, verifiable, law-seeking, etc. about finding another person and talking with them [*sic*] about music.
Charles Keil (in Crafts et al. 1993)

It seems to me that our ethnographic and historical expertise in musics of the world must function as something more than raw data to be plugged into Western philosophical modes of understanding and conceptualization.
Monson 1999

As these quotes suggest, both methodology and theory have become epistemologically and ethically controversial subjects in contemporary ethnographic music research. Sherry Ortner has defined ethnography as "the attempt to understand another life world using the self—as much of it as possible—as the instrument of knowing" (1995, 173). In that spirit, the most important data source for the present study is classic ethnographic participant observation—interacting with Indonesians in a variety of contexts while paying close attention to verbal and expressive behaviors that shed light on the social meanings of popular musics in those settings. These data are supplemented by formal interviews with key figures in the Indonesian popular music industry, aspiring semiprofessional and amateur musicians, and ordinary fans from diverse backgrounds. Happily, I had little difficulty finding consultants for my research project as I traversed the various social networks of friends and collaborators that made up the relatively finite universe of Indonesian popular musicians. In fact, it was not unusual to encounter a musician or industry type who was well acquainted with several of my previous contacts, even if he or she was involved with a different music genre than they. These unexpected connections were an early indication of how barriers between music genres in Indonesia often were more apparent on the level of marketing discourse than on the level of social and musical praxis.

I first visited Indonesia in September 1997 to conduct what turned out to be a most rewarding dissertation pilot study. During my visit I was amazed by the level of musical creativity I observed in a range of popular genres and by the willingness of Indonesian musicians (including some of the country's most renowned recording artists) to take the time to speak with me about their music. I was also astonished by the large number of ordinary Indonesians who openly and bitterly spoke out against the then ruling Soeharto regime in their conversations with me. I returned to Indonesia to commence my dissertation fieldwork more than two years later, in October 1999. Between my two visits, Jakarta and other major cities were engulfed by catastrophic riots, and President Soeharto's New Order government (which had seemed to me so utterly entrenched and permanent during the fall of 1997) collapsed after thirty-two years in power. Indonesia then entered a tumultuous period of sociopolitical transition from which it has yet to fully emerge. Shortly after my second arrival in Jakarta, the People's Consultative Assembly selected progressive Muslim intellectual Abdurrahman Wahid (popularly known as Gus Dur) to replace B. J. Habibie, Soeharto's hastily chosen successor. Gus Dur thus became Indonesia's fourth president, an event that marked the start of a new democratic era in Indonesian history.[4]

From October 1999 to August 2000, I lived in a rooming house (*rumah kost*) in Kebayoran Baru, a South Jakarta neighborhood, and devoted my time to attending concerts, observing recording sessions, interviewing musicians (amateurs, professionals, and stars), and interacting with young people from different social classes in neighborhoods around the city. I engaged in similar research during frequent trips to the West Javanese provincial capital of Bandung (home of a remarkably disproportionate number of Indonesian popular musicians) and during visits to Yogyakarta, Surakarta, Surabaya, Madiun, Denpasar, and the Javanese towns of Pekalongan and Ngawi.

Ethnographic studies of complex societies cannot, of course, stop at the level of face-to-face interactions. Over the last two decades, anthropologists have increasingly recognized that in addition to everyday "forms of life" (Hannerz 1992) such societies possess public cultures mediated by texts and other circulating cultural objects, and that these have a transformative effect on everyday life and everyday experiences.[5] During the course of my fieldwork, I amassed a collection of over 250 commercially released cassettes and compact discs, to which I added my own field recordings of live performances and several compilations of unreleased or out-of-print songs kindly assembled for me by the artists and producers who originally recorded them. Thus the arguments I make in this study rely on both ethnographic and artifactual evidence, though I ultimately privilege the former as a necessary prerequisite for interpreting the latter.

In addition to analyzing music recordings, I examined a number of written sources to investigate the meanings of contemporary Indonesian popular musics. Indonesia enjoys a high literacy rate, particularly among urban youth, and newspapers and magazines play a vital role in conditioning the production and reception of music genres. In this book I also interpret what could be called "vernacular texts." These include T-shirt slogans, graffiti, stickers, posters, banners, decorations on vans and buses, and other forms of informal public print culture that often represent views different from those propagated by the elite-controlled official mass media (see Jones 2005). Such texts are often overlooked in studies of urban societies, yet they are an important semiotic resource, their ubiquity masking their significant influence on consciousness.

Last, the Internet has become an increasingly important resource for research into popular music in Indonesia. After I left the field, I attempted to keep abreast of developments in the Indonesian music world through a rapidly increasing number of Indonesian-language Web sites dealing with music and popular culture, as well as through regular e-mail correspondence with many of my research consultants. As a result of this research in cyberspace, by the middle of 2001 I concluded that the Indonesian popular music universe, while in many ways confirming predictions I had made in the field, had evolved into something different from what I had experienced during my time in Indonesia. As a result, mid-2001 marks the cutoff point for the period of time covered in this study.

Although I arrived in Indonesia with a list of familiar theoretical concerns absorbed in graduate school—globalization, identity, modernity, nationalism, youth culture—during my research I made an effort to listen to what Indonesians themselves considered significant about their music and not to impose a preset framework on what I encountered. The resulting work is a rather different study than the one I had originally proposed to carry out, particularly with regard to the importance I assign to socioeconomic class differences—perhaps the least developed area of inquiry in anthropological studies of Indonesia—relative to other types of social differentiation. Similarly, although I had anticipated that I would find a link between Indonesian popular music and the inculcation of an ideology of "modern individualism" among Indonesian youth, in fact I found music to function primarily as a tool of sociability, for collective enjoyment rather than private aesthetic experience. This ethic of sociality, about which much is written in the following pages, is ubiquitous in everyday Indonesian social life, and it extends even to activities of musical production in environments characterized in the West by creative isolation and carefully guarded privacy, such as recording studios.

The Backdrop: A Summary of Events in Indonesia, 1997–2001

Zaman Edan: kalo ngga' ikut edan, ngga' ngetrend!

[A Crazy Time: if you don't join the craziness, you're not trendy!]
T-shirt caption, Jakarta[6]

It used to be the New Order, now it's the Order of Renewal [*Orde Pembaruan*]!
Teris, a Tegalese migrant in South Jakarta

Democrazy
painted on the front windshield of a Jakartan *mikrolet*
(minibus used for public transportation)

In many ethnographies of Indonesia, especially those written during the seemingly quiescent years of the New Order (1966–98), current events are distant background noise if they are present at all. But during the years when my fieldwork was conducted, their impact was real and momentous. The following brief historical sketch is intended to contextualize the musical practices that this book investigates.

Indonesian popular music, like Indonesian society, was in a state of transition during the time period covered in this book. From the beginning of the Asian currency crisis (*krisis moneter* or *krismon*) in late 1997 to the political maneuverings and continued economic misery at the beginning of the new century, this transitional period for most Indonesians was characterized by occasional bouts of euphoria more than matched by feelings of disillusionment and despair (see Dijk 2001).[7] In 1998, after thirty-two years under President Soeharto's authoritarian, corrupt, developmentalist New Order (Orde Baru or Orba) regime, economic crisis and political turmoil overtook Indonesia, and the aging dictator was forced to heed widespread demands for his resignation.

T-shirt design, Jakarta. The caption reads: "Crazy Time: If you don't join in the craziness, you're not trendy!" See page 282, note 6, for a more complete explanation of this image.

Political graffiti on a wall encircling the Atma Jaya University campus, Semanggi, Central Jakarta. The slogans include: "Reject the military regime"; "Eject the Indonesian Armed Forces from Parliament"; and [General] *Wiranto + Habibie Go to Hell* (in English).

Amid violent student protests and rioting and mayhem in cities throughout the country—especially in Jakarta—Soeharto stepped down on May 21, 1998.[8] His successor, B. J. Habibie, faced a public eager for change and suffering greatly from conditions resulting from the monetary crisis that caused the Indonesian economy to shrink an appalling 13.5 percent in 1998 after decades of impressive growth.[9] After a turbulent year and a half in office, facing further student protests and the threat of national disintegration, a visibly relaxed, even jocular, Habibie publicly announced two days before the October 20, 1999, election that he would not seek another term.

The decision was greeted with cheers from reformers and activists, for during his short time in office Habibie had been the target of much criticism. Many claimed he was little more than a puppet of the former regime, and the ways in which Habibie appeared to be protecting Soeharto, his old boss, from prosecution enraged the activists who had forced Soeharto from power. But Habibie's administration also allowed freedom of the press, and for the first time in three decades Indonesians were offered a wide range of opinions and political orientations to choose from. Habibie's much-maligned term in office also saw the release of political prisoners, Indonesia's first free and open democratic elections since the early 1950s, and the resolution of the conflict over East Timor, when the former province's long-suffering population chose independence from Indonesia in a formal provincewide referendum. Nevertheless, Habibie failed to solve the country's economic woes, failed to bring corrupt officials to justice, and was unable to halt the escalating violence in Maluku, Aceh, and other troubled regions in the archipelago. Worst of all, Habibie did not prevent the horrific slaughter and destruction in East Timor carried out immediately after the referendum by the Indonesian armed forces and local pro-Indonesia militias as retribution for the East Timorese people's decision to secede.

Habibie has been all but forgotten. President Abdurrahman Wahid had slightly more success at fighting corruption and significantly reduced the military's role in politics, yet he did not make progress in strengthening Indonesia's devastated economy nor in stemming the rising tide of separatist movements in the outer provinces. Moreover, ex-president Soeharto was never brought to justice during Gus Dur's time in office either. A year after Abdurrahman Wahid's election by the People's Consultative Assembly, much of the euphoria of Reformasi ("reform" or "reformation," the rallying cry of those who supported the political transition) had evaporated, replaced by uncertainty and trepidation, and many ordinary Indonesians became bitterly disillusioned with national politics. In an example of the word games characteristic of Jakartan street corner society, a cigarette-stall worker told me sardonically that Reformasi really only stood for *repot-repot cari nasi* (much trouble to find rice), an allusion to the economic hardship that persisted in the country, seemingly heedless of who happened to be in power. As in the days of the New Order, many Indonesians regarded the *elit politik* (political elites) as a corrupt, self-serving clique absorbed in petty squabbles with little regard for the wishes or priorities of the so-called little people (*rakyat kecil*). After Gus Dur had served only eighteen months of his allotted four-year term, the People's Consultative Assembly impeached him and gave the presidency to Megawati Soekarnoputri, his former vice president.[10] A daughter of Indonesia's first president Sukarno, Megawati, known to her supporters as Bu Mega, once enjoyed tremendous popular support despite (or perhaps because of) her tendency to maintain an enigmatic silence in the face of political controversy. Unfortunately, Bu Mega's administration was no more successful than Wahid's in confronting Indonesia's myriad problems, which had become so serious that many Indonesian news commentators began to speak of a "multidimensional crisis" threatening the nation.

None of the national leaders mentioned thus far successfully addressed the most glaring social issue threatening Indonesia's stability: the widening gulf between the haves and the have-nots, the latter comprising the vast majority of Indonesians. Thus many Indonesians remained unconvinced that their leaders possessed a social and political vision for Indonesia that included not only the elite and middle classes but also the *rakyat kecil* (also known as the *wong cilik,* a loan phrase from Low Javanese), who make up most of the country's population and who had borne the brunt of the suffering created by the economic crisis. Indeed, the extreme class prejudice of New Order ideology, which viewed the poor as "backward" (*terbelakang*) and mired in obsolete ways of life, has persisted in Indonesian society and arguably still threatens the viability of Indonesia's fledgling democratic polity.

Slowdeath, a death metal band from Surabaya, East Java, describes the threat that the *social gap* represents to the Indonesian nation in their 1998 song "Crisis Prone Society," which alludes to the sporadic looting and violent unrest that characterized urban Indonesia at the time (original lyrics in English, reproduced exactly as printed in the cassette liner notes):[11]

> *Look at the exhausted and dejected poor*
> *Soon they'll lost* [sic] *their strength to endure*
> *So hard they work no difference they make*
> *Such grim fate must they take*
>
> *Crisis strikes hard with no warning*
> *The anger ends up in burning*
> *Primordialism becomes the key*
> *To solve this falling society*
>
> *This social fabric is being ruptured*
> *Overburdened and overload* [sic] *with prejudice*
>
> *This widening social gap is a perfect*
> *Breeding place*
> *For vehemence and hatred, burying the*
> *logical sense*
> *Crisis prone society*
>
> (From the album Learn through Pain [1998])

Turn-of-the-millennium Jakarta was indeed an unruly place. Frequent political demonstrations (*demo*), many orchestrated by politicians using paid demonstrators (cf. Ziv 2002, 32–33), worsened the city's already severe traffic problems. Street crime of all types increased exponentially, and with it, brutal, widely reported acts of retaliatory vigilantism. Yet life went on, and during the period of my fieldwork the city remained remarkably free of large-scale political unrest of the sort that had engulfed it in 1998. There are still those who remain hopeful that conditions will improve in the capital, even as others, mindful of the persistent social gap, await the next major cataclysm.

The Music Industry in the Era of Reformasi

The demise of the New Order occasioned a great deal of public debate and speculation among intellectuals, bureaucrats, composers, and journalists on the role that a new democratic and decentralized government might play in promoting traditional music and performing arts. Ultimately, however, market forces continued to dominate the Indonesian mass media, just as they had under Soeharto (Kartomi 2002, 141–42). After the fall of Soeharto, and especially during the period of optimism immediately after Gus Dur's election in October 1999, many companies in Indonesia's commercial music industry began a rebuilding phase. Despite skyrocketing prices resulting from the ongoing monetary crisis, they began purchasing new studio equipment from overseas and made plans to release new albums once more. An example of this new optimism is *NewsMusik,* a glossy Indonesian-language monthly music magazine modeled after *Rolling Stone,* which published its first issue in January 2000. The magazine covered both foreign and domestic popular musicians, privileging the latter, until it ceased publication in late 2002.

Though Indonesia's economic crisis continued, the country's music industry appeared to partially recover in 1999–2001, as evidenced by the number of successful new albums released in those years. By 2001, music sales had rebounded, though they had not risen back to precrisis levels. One notable development with regard to the music itself is that compared to the late New Order period, far fewer new recordings of protest songs were released by the mainstream music industry in the immediate post-Soeharto period (Kartomi 2002, 125). This decrease notwithstanding, the word *Reformasi*—well on its way to becoming an empty slogan—was frequently (sometimes cynically) employed to sell rereleased protest songs by Iwan Fals and other popular recording artists

(Barendregt and Zanten 2002, 72; Dijk 2003, 59; Sutton 2004). By contrast, Indonesian underground rock groups recorded a large number of highly political songs during this same period, including some in Indonesian rather than in English (Wallach 2003a). One reason for this was that these groups were freer to do so than during the New Order period, when writing protest songs against the government, especially in the national language, could land one in prison.

The existing literature on national popular musics in Indonesia consists primarily of article- or chapter-length historical/stylistic surveys and textual analyses (e.g., Barendregt and Zanten 2002; Bass 2000; Becker 1975; Frederick 1982; Hatch 1989; Kartomi 2002; Lockard 1998; Manuel 1988; Pioquinto 1998; Piper and Jabo 1987; Sutton 2004; Wong and Lysloff 1998; Yampolsky 1989, 1991). Although some valuable historical and sociological studies of popular music and its audiences have been written by Indonesian scholars (e.g., Kesumah 1995; Suseno 2005), most relevant works in Indonesian are standard popular biographies of major recording artists (e.g., Kartoyo and Sedjati 1997; Sumarsono 1998). A full-length, comprehensive history of postindependence popular music in Indonesia has yet to be written in either English or Indonesian, and it is beyond the scope of this study to attempt such a history here. However, although I focus on a recent historical moment in all its complexity, some additional information on the development of popular music in Indonesia is needed to situate what follows.

Unlike his nationalist predecessor Sukarno, who during his presidency (1949–66) crusaded against Western pop music, referring to it as a "social disease" and famously describing the rock and roll music of the era with the pejorative onomatopoeic phrase *ngak-ngik-ngek* (Sen and Hill 2000, 166), President Soeharto (1966–98) did not prevent international record labels from selling their wares to Indonesian consumers, nor did his government discourage Indonesian musicians who emulated international styles.[12] Also, beginning in the 1970s, the availability of inexpensive cassette players made recorded music artifacts accessible for the first time to a large percentage of Indonesia's population, part of a worldwide cassette revolution that dramatically transformed the popular music industries in developing nations (cf. Manuel 1988, 1993; Wong 1989/1990; F. Miller 2005). As in India, Thailand, Yemen, and other countries, the affordability of cassettes permitted the emergence and commercial viability of regional and working-class-oriented styles in the Indonesian market. Conversely, this new consumer technology allowed ordinary people easy access to the sounds and performance styles of globally circulating popular music—including the potentially populist, unruly noise of rock.

Under Soeharto's New Order, popular musicians constantly faced the threat of punishment or censorship by the government. This did not keep some of them, including Rhoma Irama, Harry Roesli, Iwan Fals, rockers Slank, and the *pop alternatif* group Dewa 19, from performing songs that could be construed as criticizing the Soeharto regime. Indeed, commentators who claimed that dissent was largely absent from late New Order society were clearly not paying attention to developments in popular music. Despite occasional harassment, censorship, and even imprisonment of the most brazen critics of the regime (for example, the late avant-garde composer and pop star Harry Roesli was imprisoned twice for criticizing the government), popular musicians for the most part enjoyed a degree of creative freedom that recording artists living under other totalitarian regimes would envy (Sen and Hill 2000, 184). During the same time, Indonesia also had an active musical avant-garde that specialized in combining international experimental music trends with indigenous aesthetic traditions (Kartomi 2002, 137–40). Thus neither social criticism expressed in song nor radical sounds were wholly absent during the New Order.

One major problem that has long plagued the Indonesian recording industry is rampant piracy (*pembajakan*), which severely limits the ability of record companies to generate revenue from their products. In postcrisis Indonesia, I was told by insiders in the music industry that the actual ratio of legitimate music cassettes sold to pirated copies sold was about 1:8; in the early 1990s, before the *krismon,* the ratio was closer to 1:6. As a result, despite a potential national market of roughly 225 million people, the music industry of the world's fourth most populous country was fairly small and decentralized (though still the largest in Southeast Asia by far [Sen and Hill 2000, 169]). No single record company dominated, and the major multinational music corporations (WEA, Sony, BMG, and Universal/Polygram, all relatively recent arrivals to Indonesia) had to compete with large, well-established national independent labels like Aquarius, Musica, Bulletin, and Virgo Ramayana, as well as with hundreds of smaller-scale, often quite specialized operations. Unlike the Indonesian film industry, a more capital-intensive enterprise that was virtually annihilated by the flood of Hollywood films and other foreign movies into the country (and by the meddling of the acquisitive Soeharto family), the various players in the Indonesian music industry have survived (and sometimes prospered) despite the conspicuous, well-publicized presence of foreign music in the Indonesian music market.

In 1995, MTV began to be featured on Indonesian national television (Sutton 2003, 324). This had a dramatic effect on the new generation of Indonesian recording artists, who, like young people throughout capitalist Asia in the 1990s (cf. Stocker 2002), were coming of age in an increasingly globalized mediascape. Slickly produced music videos broadcast on national television became a crucial means for promoting albums, and the influence of up-to-the-minute international musical trends intensified in Indonesia and other countries across the continent (see Chun, Rossiter, and Shoesmith 2004). Indeed, the political transformations of 1998–99 seem to have had less impact on Indonesian popular music than the introduction of MTV, though one reason for this is that Indonesian popular music was already highly cosmopolitan and often politicized long before the fall of Soeharto.

Music, Gender, and the State

Like most other aspects of public life, the realm of Indonesian popular music performance and production is dominated by men. Yet this patriarchal structure is nonetheless dependent on the talents and contributions of women not only in their roles as singers and dancers, but also as audience members and consumers. Popular music in Indonesia, as elsewhere, provides a site for both reinforcing and challenging gender ideologies through performance. Contested Indonesian notions of femininity and masculinity are constituted in musical performance, and such performances index the conflicts between indigenous and Western gender codes. Furthermore, genre ideologies and gender ideologies intersect in complex ways, and the limits of acceptable (and transgressive) behavior in performance vary greatly among the different genres of popular music.

A further clarification is in order here regarding the role of the Indonesian state in what follows. Much of the existing scholarship on Indonesian popular culture has focused on the intrusive role of the state and its attempts to construct its citizens (e.g., Mulder 2000; Murray 1991; Pemberton 1994b; Weintraub 2004; Widodo 1995; Yampolsky 1989, 1995). In these studies, the project of forging an Indonesian national culture tends to be regarded as sinister and hegemonic, and the rhetoric of culture is viewed as a tool of state domination (cf. Steedly 1999, 441–44). The present work differs in that I focus on a part of Indonesian popular culture characterized by a relative lack of state interference during a time when the ideological hegemony of the state was breaking down (at least in major cities), and I therefore take a more benign view of national cultural production. Indeed, far from encountering a timid generation brainwashed by years of New Order propaganda, I found Indonesian youth boldly experimenting with the myriad possibilities of identity in a postauthoritarian historical moment while at the same time maintaining a strong affective investment in the utopian nationalist project of Indonesia. Therefore, while the construction of national identity and belonging is of central concern to this study, neither the New Order government nor the more democratic administrations that succeeded it take center stage. Instead, I focus squarely on the voices of regular Indonesians involved with making and listening to music.

I readily acknowledge that the approach I have taken in this study has several limitations. First and foremost, the fact that my ethnographic research was largely confined to urban areas on the islands of Java and Bali, and mostly Jakarta and West Java province at that, obviously limits the applicability of my interpretations to the lives of Indonesians elsewhere in the country, although the products of the Jakarta-centered Indonesian national music industry do reach audiences all over the archipelago. A further shortcoming is the relatively short time frame of this inquiry—Indonesian popular music has a rich and inadequately documented history that is only alluded to in the following ethnography. My aim has been to provide a snapshot of a specific cultural moment in all its lived richness, and thus at times I have chosen to attenuate discussions of longer historical trajectories. Despite these shortcomings, I hope that the following study can raise productive new questions about popular music, national identity, and the cultural dynamics of contemporary complex societies in Southeast Asia and the world.

Outline of Chapters

This book is composed of two parts: "Sites" and "Genres in Performance." Part 1 explores a series of locations and describes the activities and interactions that take place there, the participants, and the particular musical forms that circulate within them. I discuss the meanings and social functions of these cultural forms and the behaviors associated with them within each particular context, connecting them to discourses on class, modernity, gender, and nation in contemporary Indonesia. Part 2 shifts the analytical focus from places to particular events unfolding in time, examining the specific and contested ways in which popular music genres are performed by musicians and received by audiences at live concerts.

The first chapter attempts to place the major Indonesian popular music genres in a broad historical and sociocultural context. Chapter 2, "In the City: Class, History, and Modernity's Failures," departs from strictly ethnomusicological concerns in order to provide a more detailed cultural account of this study's main field site: Jakarta, Indonesia's capital city and undisputed political and economic center. Through a cultural analysis of the diverse languages, spaces, and soundscapes of the Indonesian metropolis, I explore the role of socioeconomic class in fundamental urban processes of social differentiation (often based on a deceptive village/urban dichotomy) and the oft concealed but powerful role of class in the hegemonic discourses of modernity (*kemoderenan*) and development (*pembangunan*) so influential during the New Order. This chapter sets the stage for the ethnographic portraits that follow, which depict the many types of musical encounter that transpire in urban spaces.

Throughout the book I argue that musical phenomena must be comprehended through the social spaces they occupy and the varied material forms they take. Also, assessing music's meanings requires an understanding of the social activities and interactions involving musical forms that take place in particular social settings. Chapter 3, "Cassette Retail Outlets: Organization, Iconography, Consumer Behavior," focuses on the first of these settings. In this chapter I explore an obvious yet frequently overlooked site of musical encounter: stores that sell music recordings. The chapter describes the spatial organization, classification schemes, iconography, and behavior patterns that characterize these spaces and relates them to local understandings of musical genres. A wide range of retail outlets is included, from shops selling underground cassettes and accessories to enormous mall stores to stalls that sell pirated cassettes in *pasar tradisional* (traditional outdoor markets). I also discuss how the sale of music recordings conforms to the bifurcated cultural logic of Indonesian urban life detailed in chapter 2 and raise questions regarding imported and domestic music genres as markers of social distinction and status in contemporary Indonesia.

Chapter 4, "In the Studio: An Ethnography of Sound Production," further explores the relationships among music, genre, and cultural hierarchy by examining the interactional context of the recording studio, Indonesian popular music's primary site of artifactual production.

The chapter analyzes the creative and commercially motivated decisions made by participants in three different studio environments and examines how Indonesian music producers use sophisticated recording technologies to manipulate and juxtapose regional, national, and global sonic elements in the course of producing new musical commodities for the Indonesian market.

Music videos are essential promotional tools in the Indonesian music industry, and the imagery and settings used in them reveal much about the social meanings and (imagined) audiences of the musics they advertise. Chapter 5, "On Location: Shooting Music Video Clips," describes the making of two music videos, one for a dangdut song and the other for a rock song. Operating on different budgets and levels of technical sophistication, these two videos exhibit the play of local, national, and global signs in Indonesian popular musics and also betray certain cultural preoccupations with modernity and its moral consequences.

Chapter 6, "Offstage: Music in Informal Contexts," moves from the relatively sequestered environments of the recording studio and video location shoot to the streets of Jakarta, where music originally produced in studios is discussed, performed, and used by social agents to pursue personal and collective aims. In particular, I describe the milieu of "the side of the road" (*di pinggir jalan*) as a place where mostly male, mostly working-class Indonesians deploy musics and discourses to make performative assertions about community, poverty, gender, politics, and what it means to be an Indonesian in the contemporary world. The chapter proceeds to examine middle-class leisure spaces where musical performance takes place, including public areas on university campuses. In these different settings, musical performance plays a central role in a largely masculine culture of "hanging out" (*nongkrong*), which cuts across class lines. I reveal how "hanging out" is part of a particular orientation toward the presence of others, evident both in side-of-the-road interactions and on university campuses, which I call the "ethic of sociality." I conclude by demonstrating how this ethic of sociality exerts a strong influence on the ways in which global and Indonesian national music genres are used and interpreted by Indonesian youth.

The three ethnographic chapters in part 2 analyze particular concert events featuring the principal music genres explored in this study: dangdut, pop, and underground. To the previously introduced analytical issues of class, global/national/regional interactions, and sociality, the chapters that comprise part 2 sharpen the focus on the performance of gender—the various masculinities and femininities that emerge in the context of musical performances simultaneously coded by class distinctions and influenced by hybridized and multivalent cultural formations. Given the recent importance of gender analysis in much contemporary popular music and Southeast Asia scholarship, it may seem odd to wait until the second part of the book to focus on the performance of gender norms and ideologies in Indonesian popular musics.[13] I have chosen to proceed in this fashion in order to first highlight the equally salient role of the *performance of social class*, which has received comparatively little attention from researchers of music in Indonesia, and indeed from popular music scholars in general.

The first element of part 2 is chapter 7, "Onstage: The Live Musical Event," which examines a range of more formalized musical performances—that is, performances that involve a definite division between performers and audience and often, but not always, entail some form of payment for the performers. Live music can be encountered in a wide variety of contexts in Indonesia, and performances range from lone troubadours who play in buses and traffic intersections for spare change to elaborate stadium rock shows. Following a discussion interpreting the urban phenomenon of roving street musicians (*pengamen*), I examine more-organized performance events by analyzing the structure and logic of planned performance occasions (*acara*), using televised music award shows and a festival featuring pop, jazz, and ethnic fusion artists as case studies.

Chapter 8, "Dangdut Concerts: The Politics of Pleasure," examines two kinds of musical events in detail: live dangdut shows in Jakarta nightclubs, and outdoor dangdut performances held in the capital's working-class neighborhoods. I investigate the gendered symbolic and material exchanges that take place at dangdut performances and discuss their importance vis-à-vis dangdut as a "national" music genre. Chapter 9, "Rock and Pop Events: The Performance of Lifestyle," covers pop and rock music performances of Indonesian and Western songs in urban cafés as well as at concert events organized by committees of middle-class students, while chapter 10, "Underground Music: Imagining Alternative Community," focuses specifically on underground music events (which are also organized by committees of Indonesian youths) and explores the manner in which such occasions construct musical community through collective subcultural expression, raising additional questions about class, identity, and the cultural dynamics of global music movements. The chapter concludes with a general appraisal of the cultural role of music *acara* in modern Indonesia.

The conclusion summarizes the major findings of the study and draws on them to enter the now-familiar debate on the nature of cultural globalization. I argue that the conspicuous presence of Western and Westernized popular music in Indonesia has not obliterated a distinctive Indonesian national cultural sensibility but rather provides new means by which to resist, affirm, or reflect on what might constitute such a sensibility. Contemporary Indonesian youth identities would be unimaginable without popular music, which acts as an essential cultural referent for a range of social categories, the most important of which is class.

I close the book with two polemics. In the first, I raise the perennial question of what uses popular music has in modern societies and discuss how anthropologists have overlooked popular music's significance due to their conventional emphasis on tradition and continuity rather than cultural innovation and creativity. One of the most appealing aspects of popular music is precisely that it is "something new," and I argue that what Greg Urban (2001) has called the "metaculture of modernity" constitutes as proper a subject for anthropological inquiry as its rhetorical opposite, which he terms the "metaculture of tradition."

The second polemic challenges the still-common assumption that popular music is just another commodity for the ceaseless consumerist identity-shopping that seems to characterize contemporary life. Such a view, I suggest, overlooks music's essential social component, present even in its most mediated forms, and its remarkable ability to generate communal feeling and strengthen social bonds. Thus, in Indonesia, popular music, despite its capitalistic methods of production and distribution, is often used to defy the individualist, atomizing logic of the global economy and to encourage music makers and their audiences to form affective attachments not only to one another but also to an inclusive, democratic national vision that embraces diversity and cosmopolitanism.

Indonesians have their own approaches to popular music—to its populism, its artistic pretensions, its status as a sometimes profitable commodity, and its potential as an instrument for social and political change. Throughout this book, I attempt to portray the world of Indonesian popular music not as a unidirectional cultural flow from producer to consumer but as a set of continuously evolving discourses, practices, and performances that simultaneously implicate musicians, technicians, producers, listeners, critics, and other concerned parties. For this reason, the order of the chapters does not conform chronologically to the life cycle of a specific musical commodity. Instead, the topics they cover move back and forth between sites of production and reception, finally culminating in live performance, where these two processes occur simultaneously in the same locale. Yet an understanding of the lived reality of Indonesian popular music cannot be limited to the concert stage; all the types of musical encounter covered in the book are important, from the most reified and routinized (record-store shopping) to the most spectacular, immediate, and emergent (live performance). Each has its transformative possibilities as well as a role in the maintenance of cultural continuity and predictability in the Indonesian popular music universe.

PART ONE

Sites

1

Indonesian
Popular Music Genres
in the Global Sensorium

Saya suka semua jenis musik, dari jazz sampai . . . musik daerah!

[I like all kinds of music, from jazz to . . . regional music!]
taxicab driver, Jakarta

So what if we're a shitty metal band.
printed on a sticker for Puppen,
a veteran underground rock group
from Bandung, West Java

One result of Indonesian music's complex history, upon which the description in the introduction barely scratches the surface, is a wide array of music genres that coexist in the Indonesian music market and significantly shape the consciousness of Indonesian listeners. The following abbreviated list of genres is meant as an introduction. Certain national genres, especially dangdut, *pop Indonesia,* and *musik underground,* will reappear frequently in the following chapters, but all the genres discussed here are important, and examining the ways they interrelate is crucial for understanding Indonesian popular music as a whole. The list is based on categories Indonesians themselves use to discuss music, primarily in verbal interaction but also in the mass media, although their presentation here incorporates an etic viewpoint that synthesizes various data sources to create a branching taxonomy of genres. Descriptions of additional popular music genres of secondary importance to the present study appear in appendix B. The following discussion begins with Western imported music, moves to Western-sounding Indonesian pop music, and then considers two genres with prominent non-Western elements: dangdut and regional music. The final genre to be considered is underground rock music, which, while sharing many musical features with pop, is unique due to its grassroots mode of production and its specialized youth audience. As will be made clear, each of these categories carries with it expectations of musical form, assumptions about the composition of audiences, social prestige factors, and a distinct significance in the context of Indonesian national culture.

Pop Barat (Western Popular Music)

Published shortly before a general session of the People's Consultative Assembly, the cover of the August 9–15, 2000, issue of *Gamma* (an Indonesian news magazine akin to *Time* or *Newsweek*) depicts the principal political actors of the time (President Abdurrahman Wahid, Vice President Megawati Soekarnoputri, Golkar Party chairman Akbar Tanjung, and House Speaker Amien Rais) as members of the Beatles: their faces had been quite convincingly superimposed over a vintage photo of the Fab Four posing with their instruments. The caption underneath them reads (in English), *Don't Let Me Down*. In addition to being a clever way to send a message to Indonesia's perpetually squabbling leaders, this illustration on the cover of a respected Indonesian news magazine demonstrates both the familiarity and the cultural cachet of Western popular music in that country.

Imported popular music from Western Europe (primarily the United Kingdom), Australia, and the United States has long maintained a strong presence in Indonesia. The names of the most prominent international artists, from Elvis Presley to Britney Spears, are quite well known, despite the fact that most Indonesians understand very little of the English lyrics they sing (although I have been told that listening to Western pop songs is a common way for Indonesians to learn the English language). Despite its extensive promotion in Indonesia by marketing divisions of multinational conglomerates, music imported from the West constitutes a minority of the nonpirated cassettes sold in Indonesia. In the first ten months of 1999, domestically produced music outsold foreign music by 3 to 1 (Theodore 1999, 4). In 1996, before the economic crisis reduced the buying power of all but the most affluent

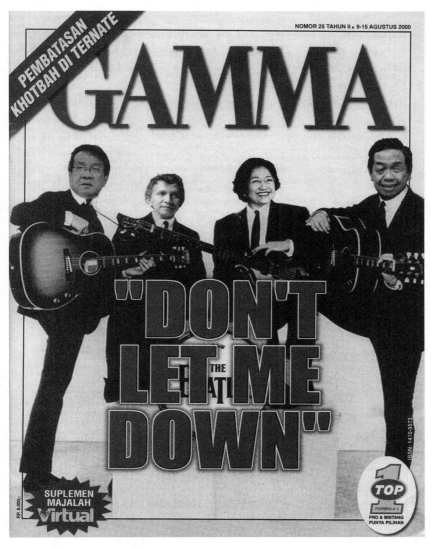

Magazine cover featuring major Indonesian politicians as the Fab Four.

(and most westernized) Indonesians, the ratio was 6.5 to 1 (ibid.). One reason for local music's dominance is undoubtedly the higher price of Western artists' cassettes relative to those by Indonesian artists (up to 40 percent higher); another is the persistent language barrier. Differing sociomusical aesthetics also play a role, however, and these will be discussed in subsequent chapters.

In general, Indonesian tastes in Western pop music tend toward two extremes: loud rock music at one end and treacly sentimental love songs at the other. Heavy metal and hard rock are among the most popular genres of Western popular music among both rural and urban youth, while the appeal of sentimental love songs is cross-generational and seems to be even greater than their appeal in the United States. Some large Indonesian record stores include an entire separately marked section for English-language love songs, many of which are produced exclusively for Asian markets and would be unfamiliar (and annoyingly, cloyingly sentimental) to Western listeners.

At the time of my fieldwork, other imported Western genres such as country, reggae, rhythm and blues, and folk maintained a more marginal status in the Indonesian market. Larger record stores occasionally devoted separate sections to them, but their audiences were limited. Western classical music (*musik klasik*) was frequently regarded as the most prestigious and refined of genres, but I found very few Indonesians who claimed they understood or enjoyed such music (a journalist told me that one had to be a "genius" just to appreciate it!). Instead, Western jazz (more precisely, the "smooth" jazz-pop fusion performed by instrumentalists such as Kenny G and Dave Koz and vocalists like Peabo Bryson) appeared to be the preferred music of the cultural and economic elite, representing a paragon of urbanity and modern sophistication.

Pop Indonesia

Pop Indonesia is the general term used to describe domestically produced, heavily Western-influenced popular music sung in Indonesian. Musically *pop Indonesia* closely resembles mainstream Anglo-American pop and rock, with the sounds of guitars, keyboards, bass guitar, and drums predominating, though the Indonesian language does lend itself to distinctive melodic contours generally not found in English-language pop songs. *Pop Indonesia* emerged as a recognized genre in the 1960s with artists such as the Beatlesque group Koes Plus and singers Eddy Silatonga and Emilia Contessa. *Pop Indonesia* rapidly supplanted the earlier national *hiburan* (entertainment) genre, which was based on Western popular music styles from before the rock and roll era, such as bossa nova and swing (cf. Lockard 1998, 83–87). Philip Yampolsky writes, "Hiburan was in all important respects a Western music, shallowly rooted in Indonesia. I suggest that Hiburan's importance to Indonesians lay more in its 'theater' than in its music: it demonstrated that

Indonesian performers and Indonesian languages could be incorporated into a clearly Western context. When Pop emerged, demonstrating the same thing with greater energy, and linking its audience to the dream-world of Western entertainment media, Hiburan dried up and blew away" (1987a, 14). Throughout its history, *pop Indonesia* artists have provided Indonesia's answer to the music of international stars such as Elvis Presley, the Beatles, Bob Dylan, and the Rolling Stones. Despite the prominent influence of Western hard rock, a style that tends to address both weightier and raunchier topics, *pop Indonesia's* primary lyrical themes are of romantic, sentimental love with some occasional light social criticism (Lockard 1998, 87–91).

Pop Indonesia is divided into several subcategories. In the period during which I conducted my research, *pop nostalgia* (also called *pop memori*) was the affectionate label given to *pop Indonesia* songs that were recorded in the 1960s, 1970s, and 1980s by such artists as Broery Maranthika, Frankie Silahatua, Leo Kristi, and Gombloh. *Pop kreatif* and *pop alternatif* were names given to newer styles that reflected contemporary global trends in rock and pop music and were usually ensemble rather than singer based. The most commercially successful bands in Indonesia in 1997–2001, including Cokelat, Dewa (formerly Dewa 19), Padi, Potret, Sheila on 7, and Wong, played this kind of pop, while top-selling solo artists like Titi DJ, Krisdayanti, Ruth Sahanaya, and Glenn Fredly sang what was sometimes called *pop kelas atas* (upper-class pop), an urbane, R & B-influenced pop style that emphasized smooth instrumental timbres, polished production, and vocal expressiveness.

Two other important *pop Indonesia* subgenres with specialized markets include *pop anak-anak* (children's pop music, usually sung by child performers—a much more significant genre in Indonesia than in the United States in terms of publicity and sales) and *pop Rohani* (pop music with Christian themes produced for Indonesia's Christian minority). Simple and catchy *pop anak-anak* tunes are the songs that initiate Indonesian listeners from different ethnic and social backgrounds into the world of national popular music. From there, the genres Indonesian young people choose to listen to depends to a large extent on their class position (see chapter 3).

Dangdut

Of all the genres of popular music in Indonesia, none has a larger nationwide audience than dangdut, a genre with a complicated and controversial history.[1] Dangdut resembles several other syncretic Asian musical styles—particularly in the Muslim world—with its nasal, ornamented vocal style, the proletarian character of its mass audience, and its association with sinful and otherwise disreputable activities (cf. Stokes 1992 on *arabesk* in Turkey and Schade-Poulsen 1999 on Algerian *raï*). Dangdut music evolved in part from popular Indian film songs rerecorded with Malay lyrics, but since its emergence in the late 1950s the style has developed along its own trajectory quite independent of the Indian film industry. In the late 1970s, as the cassette format was expanding and transforming Indonesia's music market, a singer and guitarist named Rhoma Irama "modernized" the music that had up to then been called *orkes Melayu* (Malay orchestra) by importing rock guitars (allegedly inspired by the British hard rock group Deep Purple) and sophisticated studio production techniques into the genre.[2]

The musical blueprint for dangdut created by Rhoma Irama's Soneta Group remains largely unchanged to this day when recording "original/ authentic dangdut" (*dangdut asli*), which still constitutes the majority of new dangdut releases. There is only one indigenous Indonesian instrument in a Soneta-style dangdut ensemble: the *suling*, a transverse bamboo flute from West Java (where it is known as a *bangsing*).[3] The other pieces in a typical ensemble include two electric guitars (rhythm and lead), two electronic keyboards (playing piano and string sounds, respectively), electric bass guitar, electrified mandolin, tambourine, Western trap kit, and the *gendang*, a pair of goatskin-covered hand drums modeled after the Indian tabla. *Gendang* and *suling*, the two main instruments of dangdut not found in pop or rock, are regarded as emblematic of the genre (not unlike the symbolic importance of fiddle and steel guitar to the sound and iconography of American country and western music). The basic dangdut lineup is sometimes augmented by saxophones, sitar, acoustic guitar, maracas, and other instruments, particularly on commercial recordings (see chapter 4).

Whether dangdut really is "Indonesian music" continues to be debated by critics and intellectuals who point to its foreign origins (e.g., Danu 2000). On the other hand, American ethnomusicologist Henry Spiller argues that despite dangdut's musical eclecticism, the music's meanings and functions are undeniably indigenous: "The driving 'dangdut' drum pattern that gives the genre its name is, of course, a simple ostinato that hearkens back to the earliest kinds of Southeast Asian music-making—despite this particular ostinato's distinctly Indian roots. The close connection between the dangdut rhythm and dance movements in the minds and bodies of dangdut fans is a manifestation of yet another long-standing Indonesian musical process—a connection between drumming and dance, and the ability of drum sounds to animate human bodies" (Spiller 2004, 268). Whatever the reasons for its mass appeal, dangdut remains *the* music of choice for Indonesia's nonaffluent Muslim majority, and its enormous popularity cuts across region, age, gender, and ethnicity. The middle class and the elite, on the other hand, have tended to be somewhat uncomfortable with dangdut, which they associate with backward village life and sexual permissiveness (cf. Browne 2000, 11–12; Pioquinto 1998). Non-Muslim Indonesians, such as Christian Bataks and Balinese, may also feel ambivalent toward it, though dangdut is not considered Islamic music per se, and in fact many strict Muslims consider dangdut to be sinful.[4]

Although it is considered the epitome of backwardness by its detractors, dangdut music has always been open to cosmopolitan sounds and technologies. Contemporary dangdut artists and producers have continued the genre's history of eclectically absorbing outside musical influences. Recent attempts to fuse dangdut songs with electronic dance music have yielded the subcategory *dangdut trendy,* which refers to dangdut recordings in which drum machines, samplers, and synthesizers replace the *gendang* and other conventional instruments of the genre (Wallach 2004, 2005). Examples of this subcategory include *dangdut disco, dangdut reggae, house dangdut, dangdut remix,* and many other variations. Oddly enough, many middle- and upper-class Indonesians consider these new hybrids to be even more low class and backward (*kampungan*) than the "pure" or "original" dangdut (*dangdut murni, dangdut asli*) that conforms to the style and instrumentation of dangdut recordings from the 1970s and early 1980s.

Musik Daerah (Regional Music)

> Middle-class people don't like this music.
> a Solonese traditional dance instructor,
> speaking about *campur sari* music, while a band
> played *campur sari* songs to an appreciative audience
> at a middle-class East Javanese wedding

In addition to the national popular musics mentioned above, every major ethnic group in Indonesia has its own regional music idioms, which are available on cassettes produced for specific ethnolinguistic markets.[5] Much of this music, known as *musik daerah* (regional music) or *lagu daerah* (regional song), is produced in provincial capitals rather than in Jakarta, though it is frequently sold in the capital city to urban migrant populations hailing from all over the archipelago. Although I occasionally encountered people who claimed to enjoy the regional music of other ethnic groups (Javanese fans of Sundanese pop, for example), most Indonesians were not interested in the regional music of ethnicities other than (perhaps) their own.[6] "Regional music" is a catchall category that includes every style of music sung in regional languages, from the most Westernized pop to the most stable indigenous performance traditions. These two examples exist on the ends of a continuum that contains a wide array of musical hybrids of local, regional, national, and global genres.

At one end of the *musik daerah* continuum are musical styles that appear to lack any Western influence. Their instrumentation, repertoire, and musical techniques all originate in indigenous court- or village-based musical traditions that have endured since long before the current era of McDonald's and megamalls. In Indonesia, regional traditional musics are recorded in multitrack recording studios and marketed in much the same way as regional popular music, and, with a few notable exceptions, their audiences are usually just as limited to a specific ethnic group or subgroup. At the same time, the long-standing and intense interest some Westerners have shown in studying Javanese, Balinese, Batak, Torajan, and other musical traditions is a source of pride to many members of those groups, and occasionally producers of traditional recordings will target the tourist market and markets overseas as well as local consumers. Last, regional traditional musics continue to be celebrated in numerous ethnomusicological monographs written by both Indonesians and foreigners.

Pop daerah is the label given to musics in regional languages or dialects that contain nontraditional elements. The extent to which local elements other than language are present varies considerably. At one extreme, a successful *pop Indonesia* song will be translated into a regional language and rerecorded without major changes in the music or the arrangement (Yampolsky 1989). But most *pop daerah* recordings draw from a separate, indigenous repertoire of old and new songs, and they often incorporate traditional instruments, rhythms, and melodic contours into their compositions. In addition to successful genres with wide audiences such as *pop Sunda*, *pop Batak*, and *pop Minang*, a multitude of smaller, more obscure *pop daerah* varieties, such as *pop Sumsel* (South Sumatran pop) also exist in more regionally circumscribed markets (Barendregt

2002, 415). *Pop Jawa* (Javanese pop) is the most successful and variegated *pop daerah* genre, which is not surprising given the numerical, political, and cultural dominance of the Javanese ethnolinguistic group in Indonesia.

Campur sari (literally "mixture of essences") is a recent style that evolved in the late 1990s in the Central Javanese cities of Solo and Yogyakarta. It combines *keroncong* (an older style of nationalized popular music played on Western and indigenous acoustic instruments), dangdut, and Javanese traditional music, and is sung exclusively in (usually "low," informal) Javanese. The popularity of *campur sari* rivals Indonesian-language dangdut in working-class Central and East Javanese communities, while many middle- and upper-class Javanese consider it *kampungan* (yet as the epigraph introducing this section demonstrates, many enjoy it nonetheless). *Campur sari* is not considered "pop," perhaps because its embrace of genres like dangdut and *keroncong* stands in opposition to the modernity pop supposedly represents.

Jaipong is another regional genre that complicates divisions between musical categories. *Jaipong* (also called *jaipongan*) is a rhythmically exciting popular music genre, supposedly inspired by Western rock music, that was developed in the 1970s by Gugum Gumbira Tirasonjaya, a visionary Sundanese composer, choreographer, and record producer (Yampolsky 1987b; Bass 2000). What sets *jaipong* apart from most other recorded nontraditional regional genres is that it uses no Western instruments or tunings; all the rhythms, instruments, and playing techniques of *jaipong* were derived from already existing Sundanese performance genres (Manuel and Baier 1986).

In the late 1970s and early 1980s, *jaipong* became part of a nationwide dance craze that transcended ethnic boundaries (Manuel and Baier 1986; Murray 1991, 104; Yampolsky 1987b). More recently, *jaipong* has become a major ingredient for new diatonically based hybrid genres, including *dangdut jaipong, house jaipong,* and even *ska-pong* (a fusion of *jaipong* and ska), that use mostly Western instruments combined with Sundanese percussion (often sampled). At the same time, unadulterated *jaipong* has declined in popularity, and in Jakarta it has been relegated once again to the *musik daerah* category.

Many of my consultants were surprised (and a little disappointed) when I told them that the only "Indonesian" music that could regularly be found in American music stores was Balinese or Javanese gamelan, with Indonesian pop and dangdut nowhere to be found. (Non-Javanese and non-Balinese were particularly nonplussed.) After all, *American* popular music was ubiquitous in Indonesian record stores! Far from being emblematic of the Indonesian nation, gamelan music for most Jakartans (including many ethnic Javanese and Balinese) was just another style of *musik tradisional*—a subset of *musik daerah* appealing only to the most traditionally minded members of a particular ethnic group—and thus was rather marginal to the multiethnic national project in which Jakartan youth were routinely taught to believe.

Musik Underground

The Modern Noise Makes Modern People
slogan printed on the cover
of a 1997 issue of *Morbid Noise*,
a Jakartan underground metal zine

When I scream I would tell the truth.
Fear Inside (Bandung underground band),
"Muted Scream" (1998)

Beginning in the early 1990s, the term *underground* has been used in Indonesia to describe a cluster of rock music subgenres as well as a method of producing and distributing cultural objects. By the end of the decade, nearly every major urban area in Indonesia was home to a local underground scene, the most prominent of which were based in Jakarta, Yogyakarta, Surabaya, Malang, Bandung, Medan, Banda Aceh, and Denpasar (cf. Barendregt and Zanten 2002, 81–83; Baulch 1996, 2002a, 2002b, 2003; Pickles 2000; Putranto and Sadrach 2002; Sen and Hill 2000, 177–81).

Musik underground is composed of several *aliran* (streams); among them are *punk, hardcore, death metal, grindcore, brutal death, hyperblast, black metal, grunge, indies, industrial,* and *gothic.* As this brief list suggests, all the *aliran* are imported genres; their names and stylistic features are derived from music from overseas. But while underground musicians' orientation (*kiblat*) is toward the work of foreign bands, the way in which the music is produced and distributed is resolutely local and grassroots based. Indonesian underground bands, like underground groups elsewhere, produce their own recordings or release them through small independent labels in limited quantities. Recording studio rental rates in Indonesia are astonishingly cheap, and the number of Indonesian underground cassettes on the market increased exponentially between 1995 and 2000 despite the economic crisis. In fact, the monetary crisis may have actually encouraged the development of local under-ground music, since overseas underground rock recordings, which had to be purchased by catalog at Western prices and in Western currencies, became prohibitively expensive.

During its brief history, there has also been a marked linguistic shift in the Indonesian underground scene from an early predominance of songs sung in English to a larger number of songs written in Indone-sian, which among other things helped expand the music's audience beyond middle-class students.[7] This shift was motivated by several aes-thetic, ideological, and political factors, prominent among them an in-creasing awareness of and pride in the sheer scale and productivity of the Indonesian underground music movement (Wallach 2003a).

In addition to recordings, members of the underground publish "zines" (homemade magazines, short for "fanzines") that cover the local underground scene and often address sociopolitical issues. Since the late 1990s, a significant number of electronic fanzines (or "webzines"), band Web sites, and Web sites representing particular local musical scenes have appeared on the Internet. The grassroots, small-scale na-ture of underground cultural production is discursively linked to an (im-ported) ideology of "do-it-yourself" independence that rejects "selling out" to major labels (which in Indonesia also includes the large inde-pendent record companies) and celebrates artistic autonomy, idealism, community, and resistance to commercial pressures.

As in underground scenes in the United States, a certain amount of ambiguity and overlap exists between definitions of "underground" as musical style and "underground" as independent production and distri-bution. Recurring debates on whether bands were "selling out" because they signed contracts with large commercial record companies became more heated in the underground with the rise of ska, an energetic guitar-and-horn-based style with Jamaican, British, and American roots.[8] During my first visit to Indonesia in late 1997, ska was just an-other underground *aliran*. By mid-1999, however, its status as an under-ground style had become controversial. There were several Indonesian ska groups on major labels, and the most successful—Jun Fan Gung Foo, Tipe-X, and Purpose—were selling hundreds of thousands of cas-settes across the archipelago (cf. Barendregt and Zanten 2002, 83). Also wildly popular were a number of ska band compilations with names like *Skamania* and *Ska Klinik*. Upper-class university students and street children alike knew the latest Indonesian ska tunes and the characteris-tic "running in place" dance steps with which to accompany them, while locally made ska T-shirts, stickers, patches, and posters featuring ska iconography's distinctive checkerboard graphics were on sale all over Jakarta in both upscale malls and outdoor markets. Ska had strayed far from its underground origins and had become, in the words of those who marketed the music, a "seasonal" (*musiman*), currently trendy (*lagi ngetrend*) music that appealed to a large cross-class youth audience.

Although other underground groups had managed to obtain major-label contracts, none had ever reached a level of commercial success commensurate with that of the new ska bands. This caused a negative reaction in the underground community, and in Jakarta the slogan *ska sucks* could be found spray-painted on walls and printed on stickers. Waiting Room, probably the first Indonesian ska band, which produced an independently released cassette in 1997, chose to abandon ska after its popularization, changing *aliran* on its second cassette (2000) to rap/funk/metal.[9] "*Ska is dead*," Lukman, the band's singer, told me, and many others in the underground scene agreed. Thus the ska boom stands as a case study of the instability of "underground" music as a category of music production versus a musical style.[10] Further consequences of the late '90s ska boom are explored in the next section.

The Formation of New Hybrids: Innovations and Juxtapositions

As will become clear in subsequent chapters, the genres listed above (and their audiences) do not exist in isolation from one another. Complex dynamics of influence, appropriation, and parody exist between them, such that dangdut rhythms sometimes appear on pop albums, dangdut bands at times play rock songs, *jaipong* groups sometimes play dangdut songs adapted to their instrumentation and tuning systems, and songs from the *jaipong* and *pop daerah* repertoires form the basis for many electronic dance music recordings. Among the more notable recent hybrids to appear on the Indonesian popular music scene are the following:

Dangdut remix (usually pronounced and sometimes spelled *dangdut remek*) is a term that denotes dance remixes of previously released dangdut songs. While dangdut remixes can be considered a subset of *dangdut trendy*, they stand out because the remix format allows producers to freely experiment with adding elements from traditional Indonesian musics, hip hop, *jaipong*, techno, and other genres to their compositions, usually through the medium of digital sampling (Wallach 2005, 142–46).

Hybrid genres *ska-dhut, ska-bon,* and *ska-pong* represented a new and unexpected phase of ska music's crossover from underground to mainstream genre. Unlike other briefly-in-vogue genres such as rap and R & B that were popular only with middle-class youth before declining and being replaced with trendier styles, ska's propulsive, danceable rhythms (which strongly resemble those used in *dangdut trendy* and *pop daerah*) have helped it to cross the social gap. The music's newfound popularity with the *orang kampung* (village/slum people) has encouraged the creation of new hybrids that combine the rhythms and sounds of ska with dangdut and *musik daerah.* The results of this innovation have met with mixed commercial success, but they certainly succeed in sheer inventiveness of a sort that can perhaps be found nowhere else in the world. One cassette released in 2000 titled *Ska Minang India* contains a song that appropriates the melody from "Kuch Kuch Hota Hai" (a popular Hindi film song), adds a programmed ska rhythm and brass arrangement, and is sung in *bahasa Minang,* a regional language spoken by the Minangkabau people of West Sumatra. The track even includes an ostinato part played with metal percussion samples resembling *talèmpong,* traditional West Sumatran tuned kettle gongs.

In the still-purist underground scene, at least two nationally known bands have experimented with combining death and black metal with Indonesian ethnic music. Kremush, a group from Purwokerto, Central Java, calls the resulting hybrid *brutal etnik,* while Eternal Madness, from Denpasar, Bali, prefers to call its music *lunatic ethnic grind death metal* (see chapter 4). These bands are extraordinary not only for their willingness to engage in cross-genre experimentation but also for the compelling nature of the results, which convincingly blend pentatonic traditional melodies and rhythmic accents with the instrumentation, vocal techniques, and musical conventions of underground metal.

"Ethnic Music" and the World Music Label

Whatever *aliran* or genre they play, Indonesian musicians tend to have some preoccupations in common. Few prominent musicians, with some notable exceptions, are immune to the desire to *go international*—an English expression, used frequently in the Indonesian mass media and in everyday conversations, which often really means making an impact in the U.S. market. An ironic twist to the desire of Indonesian pop musicians to reach an international market is that that market is more interested in Indonesian music that sounds "Indonesian" in some way than it is in thoroughly "modern" international pop music sung in an Indonesian approximation of English. The problem is that any popular music recording that draws on dangdut, *musik tradisional, jaipong,* or any other non-Western genre in order to sound distinctively "Indonesian" runs the risk of being considered *kampungan* by Indonesians themselves even as it conforms to international expectations for "world beat"-style music.

Indonesian pop and jazz musicians who have frequent contact with Westerners know that while the "world music/world beat" category may ghettoize them in the international pop music scene, this label provides their best chance for entering the prestigious and lucrative European-American market. As a result, some Indonesian musicians have experimented with adding "ethnic" elements to their compositions in an attempt to create a distinctively Indonesian brand of "world beat." The most successful of these experiments was carried out by the members of the Bandung-based jazz fusion group Krakatau (cf. Sutton 2002b, 23), who after many years of dedicated effort have received a considerable amount of international exposure for their uniquely hybridic music. This recognition was extremely hard-won, since in fact almost all of the market for Indonesian music is domestic, and the possibility of overseas promotion or distribution for the products of the Indonesian music industry is usually slim, owing to a combination of legal, economic, and ideological factors.

Dangdut Goes International

A final irony is that of all the genres of Indonesian popular music, dangdut has been by far the most successful in the international (albeit non-Western) market: Indonesian dangdut stars have found receptive audiences in several Asian countries, including Brunei Darussalam, Japan, Malaysia, the southern Philippines, Singapore, and Taiwan. In the late 1990s, a group of Japanese "world music" fans even formed their own dangdut group, O. M. Ranema, which, in the acronymic style of Indonesian dangdut group monikers, stands for *Orkes Melayu Rakyat Negara Matahari,* Indonesian for "Malay Orchestra of the People of the Sun Country." ("Sun Country" is of course a reference to Japan.) According to the group's Web site, which is available in Japanese and English but not Indonesian, the band has played several successful concerts in the Tokyo metropolitan area since the late 1990s. This kind of international recognition does not appear to have strongly influenced dangdut's domestic reception.[11]

Reacting to the chilly audience response to dangdut artist Iis Dahlia on a televised MTV Indonesia awards show we were watching, a young Javanese professional remarked, "Maybe dangdut has already *go international,* but it has yet to *go national!*" However, by 2001, a year after that conversation took place, dangdut music began to appear in slickly produced TV commercials for such global brands as McDonald's hamburgers (called "beef-burgers" in Indonesia in order not to mislead Muslims about their "guaranteed halal" status) and Sony electronics — a decision that was said to be based on solid market research (Kearney 2001; Kartomi 2002, 133). As dangdut slowly gains acceptance among urban middle-class Indonesians, it may be that dangdut's performers and producers will someday realize the wistful speculation of one Western ethnomusicologist: "Eventually perhaps *dangdut* may become as well known across the globe as Trinidad's *calypso* or Jamaica's *reggae*" (Kartomi 2002, 134). At any rate, dangdut will perhaps always enjoy the favor of one particular overseas audience: homesick middle-class Indonesian students studying abroad, many of whom never listen to the music at home.

2

In the City

CLASS, HISTORY, AND
MODERNITY'S FAILURES

Light reflects off my computer
monitor, not the glittering
rice paddy, not the sewing
machine's glittering
needle dipping like a cormorant into tomorrow's
Nike shoe and this is
the Culture at work.

Sun Yung Shin 2004

Jakarta is the least exotic locale in a country famous for being exotic. Although it has all the amenities one would expect from an ultramodern, globalized metropolis (for those who can afford them), foreigners and Indonesians alike tend to view the capital as an example of a failed, dystopian modernity—a blighted urban sprawl of traffic snarls, crime, poverty, open sewers, and pollution. Despite its political, economic, and cultural centrality, I spoke to very few residents of this massive city of approximately eleven million people who seemed to like living there very much. There is a saying in Jakarta: *Ibu tiri tak sekejam ibukota*—"A stepmother is not as cruel as the capital city [in Indonesian, literally 'mother city']." The perceived lack of communal ties between people and the difficult, competitive struggle to survive that confronts residents of the city are frequently given as examples of this "cruelty." Despite these misgivings, however, few residents would deny that Jakarta is the major center of production of Indonesian national culture, and has been so for the country's entire existence. In Clifford Geertz's memorable words, Jakarta is "where Indonesia is supposed to be summarized but perhaps is manufactured" (1995, 52).

The following overview of the cultural terrain of post–New Order Jakarta serves as a prelude to the ethnographic study of popular music that follows. Three themes emerge in a discussion of the spatial organization, speech styles, and social conditions that characterize everyday life in the capital city: first, a persistent dichotomization of rich and poor in everyday discourse, often based on an erstwhile urban/rural divide; second, the relationship between Indonesian historical memory and these class-based, discursive bifurcations; and third, the ongoing process of cultural innovation by social agents from all walks of life in response to the conditions of urban life. As the following discussion makes clear, this continual process of innovation and improvisation occurs against a backdrop of sensory unruliness created by the chaos of an overpopulated, divided, and indeed often cruel metropolis.

Jakarta as an Ethnographic Field Site

When I tell people in Jakarta that I'm from Surabaya, they say, "Oh, you're from Java!" As if Jakarta wasn't also on Java!

Samir, lead guitarist for Slowdeath

Jakarta is the main field site of this study, and in many ways, it is unique. Its size, level of commercial development, multiethnic population, and political centrality set it apart from Indonesia's other major cities, all of which are nonetheless influenced tremendously by developments in the capital. In this sense, Jakarta is an "exemplary center" for the rest of the nation, a site in which cultural power is consolidated and flows outward to the periphery (see Anderson 1990, 35–38; Guinness 2000), where it is both accommodated and resisted by local agents (Steedly 1999, 444). Indonesians often consider Indonesia's capital city a separate entity unto itself. Jakarta is located in the western portion of the island of Java, but the city is a Special Capital District (*Daerah Khusus Ibukota*) not included in the province of West Java. It is certainly not considered part of

"Java" (see Pemberton 1994b and the epigraph preceding this section), which as an unmarked term in Indonesia generally refers to the provinces of Central and/or East Java, where the majority of the population is ethnic Javanese (West Java, in contrast, is dominated by Sundanese).

To many Indonesians, Jakarta represents certain trends in contemporary Indonesian society taken to an extreme, including deepening class divisions, consumerism, westernization, and the replacement of reciprocity-based economic systems by economies based on discrete single-transaction exchanges. Each of these trends is present in most parts of Indonesia, including small towns and villages, but Jakarta is viewed as the exemplar for all of them, and many Indonesians in the provinces are wary of following its lead. Most people who live in Jakarta are migrants who often speak longingly of their home villages or cities elsewhere in the archipelago, but many admit that Jakarta is the only place where they can find real economic opportunity. For them, living in the capital is a necessary evil, and many in fact choose to leave their families behind in the village, where the cost of living is lower and family members can be insulated from the "corrupting" influences of the city. Even lifelong residents of Jakarta who can rely on extended networks of economic support may find those networks threatened by state-led development and the commodification of everyday life, leading to conditions of instability and unpredictable fortunes (Jellinek 1991; Murray 1991).

In short, Jakarta is the locus for a whole host of economic and social changes that have caused the "ethnographic ground" of Indonesia to shift "in ways unsettling to anthropology's culturalist sensibility" (Steedly 1999, 432). In this view, as the city and the lifestyles of its elites come to resemble those in other high-tech, newly industrialized Asian countries, the distinctiveness of Jakarta's Indonesian "culture" is eroded. The reality, however, despite the much-remarked-upon ubiquity of malls, cybercafés, McDonald's, cellular telephones, and Mercedes Benz vehicles in contemporary Jakarta, is more complex than a purely culturalist perspective might suggest, as is the city's relationship to the global modernity to which it aspires (see Guinness 2000). It is worth emphasizing that malls and American fast food have *not* taken over all of Jakarta; these new additions coexist with an extensive informal economy (Danesh 1999) that supports the majority of the city's inhabitants—a juxtaposition of economic and cultural logics that will be explored in more detail later in this chapter.

Jakarta: An Introductory Geography

Jakarta is so vast that during my fieldwork I was unable to find any maps of the city that covered its entire area. Jakarta's 255 square miles are divided into five municipalities (*kotamadya*): North, South, East, West, and Central (Forbes 2002, 410). Market-driven and state-led development over the last three decades has transformed most of what was essentially a loose, sprawling network of villages with a colonial-style town at the center into a congested metropolis of skyscrapers, malls, and teeming shantytowns (Grijns and Nas 2000). There are still places, especially on the outskirts of the city (which blend seamlessly into the surrounding areas of Bogor, Bekasi, and Tanggerang), where there are rice paddies and open fields.

The vast majority of Jakarta's inhabitants live in *kampung*, villagelike neighborhoods of single-family dwellings with varying population densities.[1] Middle- and upper-class Jakartans live in neighborhoods of large cement attached houses; many of the most fashionable of these are located in South Jakarta (Jakarta Selatan, or Jaksel), though East, West,

A garbage-choked canal under Sudirman Street, a main thoroughfare in Jakarta's central business district.

and North Jakarta have their own pockets of affluence surrounded by the *kampung* of ordinary residents. A small number of elite Jakartans have begun to move into high-rise apartment complexes located in the city center, which until very recently were inhabited mostly by members of Jakarta's large expatriate population.[2] These few escape the harrowing commutes undertaken daily by the numerous affluent city residents who work in Central Jakarta and who live in Pondok Indah, Kebayoran Baru, Bintaro, and other upscale neighborhoods of South Jakarta. The poor often commute even longer distances, by motorbike or on battered public buses and vans of various shapes and sizes.

Central Jakarta (Jakarta Pusat, or Jakpus) is the main hub for business and commerce, and its boulevards are lined with impressive steel and glass office towers and luxury hotels. The ground floors of these buildings house banks, restaurants, discos, upscale cinemas, and nightclubs and are nighttime destinations for Jakarta's elite. Beyond (and often beside) these narrow corridors of global capitalist cosmopolitanism is a vast and complex patchwork of neighborhoods, malls, mosques, monuments, universities, embassies, canals, government buildings, markets, and slums that together constitute a heterogeneous, chaotic metropolis — one that embodies everything that many Indonesians desire, dislike, and fear about the modern world.

Carnival and Dystopia: Jakarta, Modernity, and Traffic

> In recent years Indonesia has shed its exotic, fairy-tale image and emerged as a modern, enterprising nation.
>
> publisher's foreword,
> *Tuttle's Concise Indonesian Dictionary* (Kramer and Koen 1995)

> *You might be Indonesian if:* [. . .] *The first thing that comes to mind when hearing the word "Jakarta" is "macet"* [congested].
>
> excerpt from a humorous e-mail message that circulated widely
> in the late 1990s on Indonesian student list serves

As the metropolitan core of the Indonesian national project, Jakarta influences all corners of the archipelago, particularly with regard to the question of "how to be modern" (Yampolsky 1989, 9–10). To my surprise, a group of students at the Jakarta Art Institute (IKJ) hailing from various Indonesian provinces once described Jakarta to me as "*too* modern." At first this description surprised me, but in fact modernity, despite its considerable allure, also brings with it deep ambivalences, anxieties, and feelings of loss (Ivy 1995; Ferzacca 2001; Shannon 2006). Geertz has observed that in the developing world, "modernity turned out to be less a fixed destination than a vast and inconstant field of warring possibilities, possibilities neither simultaneously reachable nor systematically connected, neither well defined nor unequivocally attractive" (1995, 138). The ambivalence many Indonesians feel toward modernity and modernization is compounded by Indonesia's subaltern position in the neoliberal global order, which prevents most Indonesians from enjoying modernity's material and social benefits or, in the evolutionist parlance of the New Order, keeps most people in a "backward" (*terbelakang*) state.

The exacerbation of social inequality is one serious consequence of rapid and uneven economic development in Jakarta and in Indonesia more generally. Of even more concern to many Indonesians is the "individualism" (*individualisme*) that Jakarta represents: the possibility that the materialism and pressures of urban life combined with prolonged separation from solidary village communities will cause people to act selfishly, without regard for their families or communities.

Contemporary Jakarta can be viewed as a textbook example of what modernization theorists have called "overurbanization" (Sovani 1964). Gerald Breese writes, "This phenomenon [of overurbanization] has been noted with particular interest and concern because of the common observation, in newly developing countries, that with very few exceptions there appears to be much too large a population in urban areas to be supported by the employment, services, and facilities available" (1966, 134). Breese correctly notes that charges of overurbanization may be beside the point, since the overpopulation of cities in developing countries tends to result from the impoverishment of rural areas, which compels their inhabitants to migrate to cities in search of economic opportunity. This certainly has been the case on the overcrowded island of Java—the most densely populated island in the world—where many feel they have no choice but to seek work in Jakarta to support themselves and their families.

For many Jakartans, the abysmal situation on Jakarta's roadways, particularly its main thoroughfares, is a conspicuous example of the downside of modernity and "progress." Jakarta resembles most other capital cities in the developing world, where increasing numbers of motor vehicles, coupled with inefficient public transportation options, have created a seemingly insurmountable traffic problem. Jakarta's motor-vehicle traffic, particularly during rush hours, is legendary for its sluggishness. The word *macet* (clogged, stopped up) and the phrase *macet total* (totally clogged, i.e., gridlocked) are indispensable in everyday conversations—particularly when giving the reason for arriving at a meeting two hours late (cf. Ziv 2002, 86).

While some Jakartans blame *bajaj* (motorized trishaws) and public buses for causing Jakarta's hopeless traffic jams, in fact the congestion is a consequence of the rising affluence of some city residents. Around 86 percent of the cars on Jakarta's streets are privately owned vehicles (*Jakarta Post* 2000, 1), a much greater percentage than in the past, and several taxi drivers complained bitterly to me that some rich families in Jakarta owned cars for each member of their respective households, including one for each servant! Such overconsumption, they claimed, is why Jakarta's streets were so *macet*.

The individualist nature of private vehicle ownership, in addition to its role in creating tremendous traffic congestion, is offensive to working-class Indonesian sensibilities. Many privately owned vehicles in Jakarta have tinted windows that make their drivers invisible to those on the outside. Like the looming steel and glass skyscrapers along the main boulevards, the glinting opaque surfaces of tinted car windows speak to the arrogance (*kesombongan*) and power of those inside. This material expression of social distance exemplifies the *individualisme* (which in Indonesian has a meaning close to "selfishness") and lack of community that nearly everyone with whom I spoke, residents and nonresidents alike, associated with contemporary Jakarta. This arrogance receives its partial comeuppance through the very problem it creates. The city's traffic jams create a kind of transient cultural space that provides the opportunity for roving vendors, beggars, and street musicians to approach cars stopped in traffic or at intersections, hoping to catch the attention of stranded motorists. This leads to a "carnivalesque" atmosphere (see Bakhtin 1984; Stallybrass and White 1986), an ephemeral reversal of social status in which the city's mobile indigent come face-to-face with the elites trapped inside their air-conditioned capsules. Often beggars and street musicians are given loose change through cracked-open car windows more out of fear and annoyance than compassion, in the hope that these walking reminders of the *social gap* will leave the driver and passengers alone.

A new wrinkle in the controversies over Jakarta's *macet* problem is the return of pedal-powered trishaws (*becak*) to the streets of the city. These human-powered vehicles were banned by the New Order regime in the 1980s in a brutally repressive campaign to "modernize" Jakarta's streets (Murray 1991, 91–92). Since the demise of that regime, Jakarta's *becak* drivers have organized and held demonstrations seeking to regain their lost livelihoods. They have united behind the slogan *Biar Kami Ada* (Let Us [exclusive] Be), and a number of drivers have begun working on the backstreets of the city, in defiance of municipal ordinances. A number of people with whom I spoke opined that if the *becak*s were indeed permitted to return en masse to the capital, Jakarta's traffic would come to a complete standstill. Nevertheless, Jakarta's dystopian transportation problems have been caused not by the "backwardness" of nonpolluting, human-powered transport but by a *surplus* of "progress": the emulation of global standards of private affluence by an increasing number of prosperous residents. The impact of *macet total,* of course, does not affect only elites: ordinary Jakartans must also struggle to get from place to place, and while large, noisy crowds of people are regarded positively by Indonesians, roads choked with motorcycles, cars, *bajaj,* and buses are seen as just another example of the harshness and difficulty of city life.

The Dichotomized Cultural Logics of "Late" and Petty Capitalism

Jangan anda lupakan untuk berbelanja kepasar tradisional
Pasar tradisional murah meriah

[Don't you forget to shop at traditional markets
Traditional markets are cheap and cheerful]

a large sign in Pasar Santa, a "traditional" market area
in South Jakarta, located a short distance
from the megamalls of Blok M

As the preceding discussion suggests, Jakarta is really two cities, each based on a separate spatial, economic, and cultural logic (cf. Leggett 2005, 279). The first of these coexisting logics is based on reciprocity and loan-based petty capitalism, while the second is the product of high-technology consumer capitalism in its most recent "globalizing" phase (see Waters 1995). Thus humble food stalls cluster around multistoried malls, and one can purchase refill cards for cellular telephones either in spacious, air-conditioned stores or from street-side vendors, often for a slightly lower price.[3] Food, clothing, cassettes, even prostitutes (Hull, Sulistyaningsih, and Jones 1999, 15) are available in both the informal and the formalized economic sectors; Geertz (1963), in a study of the commercial life of Javanese towns, identifies the two types as "bazaar-based" and "firm-based" economies. This distinction is remarkably apt for describing the contemporary economic landscape in Jakarta as well.

The vast majority of Jakartans inhabit both economic worlds. Almost everyone eats at roadside food stalls; working-class *kampung* dwellers with formal-sector occupations have bank accounts and hang out in local Internet cafés (which represent an interesting intersection point of the two worlds, as I discuss later). Nearly everyone buys cigarettes from street-side cigarette kiosks (*warung rokok*) and purchases bottled water, cigarettes, and snacks from roving salespeople (*pedagang asongan*) at traffic intersections. This ethnography focuses primarily on those who are neither destitute nor rich and powerful members of the political and economic elite. Such people are generally comfortable in both economic spheres in their everyday lives.

The 2000 Jakarta Fair, held at the expansive Jakarta Fairgrounds in celebration of the city's 473rd anniversary (dated from the defeat of the Portuguese and the renaming of the city by Fatahillah), exemplified the coexistence of conglomerate- and bazaar-based economies in urban Indonesia. At the fairground entrance the visitor was confronted with rows of large, brightly lit tents showcasing commodities ranging from shiny new motorcycles to American junk food to cellular phones. In the darkened, blacktopped area behind these corporate-sponsored tents was a sprawling night market (*pasar malam*), complete with two freak shows, a *kuda lumping* ensemble (performers from East Java who execute amazing and dangerous feats while under trance), and rows of vendors selling plastic toys, pirated cassettes, street food, clothes, and other items from blankets spread out on the asphalt. Behind this night bazaar was a large stage that featured live dangdut music.

The coexistence of the two halves gives rise to a series of binary oppositions constitutive of a fundamental social distinction in Jakarta society that is far less about the difference between traditional and modern or rural and urban than about the difference between rich and poor.

Warung Capitalism

Indonesia's vast informal economy revolves around the *warung* (stall), which ranges in size from small cigarette kiosks to large tents accommodating a dozen or so customers, as well as a whole range of mobile and semimobile street vendors. Jakarta *warung* owners do not try to make their businesses stand out but rather strive to make them resemble the other *warung* in their category. They tend to choose humble, even self-effacing names like Warung Lumayan (Pretty Good *Warung*), Warung

Nasi Sederhana (Simple Rice *Warung*), or even Warung Tanpa Nama (*Warung* without a Name). Standing out is to be avoided in the informal economy; in contrast, the formal sector in Indonesia and elsewhere relies on brand-name recognition and attempts to convince consumers through advertising that a particular product is unique and superior.

Warung also tend to operate on the principle that twenty flower stalls situated in one place is preferable to each competitor operating in a different location—a strategy of concentration that keeps prices competitive but attracts many customers. *Warung* that serve specialized needs—those that sell upholstery, customized rubber stamps, banners, identification card photos, and so on—are usually found in a small number of highly concentrated locations in Jakarta. Music cassette stalls tend to follow a different strategy and are usually widely dispersed. Often there is only one *warung* that sells nonpirated music cassettes (usually along with other items) in a bazaar; temporary street markets may contain a scattered handful of vendors selling pirated cassettes at much lower prices. More common than either are pirated VCD (video compact disc) vendors who display their wares (which may include Hollywood movies, dangdut karaoke disks, and/or pornographic videos) in large clusters. In 1999–2000 they far outnumbered cassette stalls.

Most *warung* have regular customers (*langganan*) who often buy items on credit. In the competitive *warung* economy, continuing relationships with regular customers are necessary to ensure survival. And since participants in this economy strive for subsistence rather than accumulation, the inability of some customers to pay at certain times is acceptable as long as debts are eventually paid and a small amount of money does change hands.

More on the Discursive Bifurcation of Urban Life: Rich and Poor, Village and City

Katanya Jakarta ini kota, tapi buat saya, Jakarta kampung besar.

[They say Jakarta is a city, but to me, Jakarta is a big village.]
Titiek Nur, veteran dangdut singer

In the subtitled, partially censored version of the film *American Beauty* (1999) that played in Jakarta movie theaters during the period of my fieldwork, the line "I don't think there's anything worse than being ordinary," spoken by one of the teenage characters, was translated as "I don't think there's anything worse than being *kampungan* [low class, villagelike]." When afterward I asked two English-speaking, middle-class companions about this translation, they responded that under the New Order, being ordinary and not standing out was considered a virtue, but *no one* wanted to be considered low class and backward. Thus it would not make sense for a character in a movie to say she didn't want to be ordinary, but it would be understandable for her to say she would rather be anything but *kampungan*. This small example of cross-cultural translation illustrates how important the notion of *kampungan* is in Indonesian habits of self-definition. Although the root of the word (from *kampung*, "village") suggests a "village/city" dichotomous logic behind the epithet, in fact the axiomatic discursive opposition between *kampungan* and *kotaan* (citified) is more about cultural and economic capital than geographic location. Indeed, the fundamental structural opposition that shapes social perception in Jakarta is not *kampung* versus *kota* but have-not versus have. This paramount binary opposition is invoked in the following commonly heard distinctions:

1. *Mal* (mall) versus *pasar* ("traditional" market)
2. *Restoran* (restaurant) versus *warung makan* (food stall)
3. American cigarettes versus *kretek* (Indonesian clove cigarettes)
4. Dark, subdued colors versus bright (*ngejreng*) colors
5. Indonesian versus regional languages
6. English versus Indonesian
7. *Pop* versus dangdut

Very few commodities are not subject to category distinctions like those listed above. Even fruit, for example, is divided into expensive, often imported items like pineapples and strawberries, on the one hand, and "village" fruits (often sour or bitter) such as *gohok* and *salak,* on the other.[4] Just mentioning the latter fruits invariably provoked laughter among my research consultants. Likewise, in large Jakarta supermarkets, potato chips and other slickly packaged, Western-style snacks are often located in an aisle labeled "modern snacks," while shrimp cakes (*kerupuk*) and other locally produced foodstuffs that are sold in *warung* can be found in a separate supermarket aisle labeled simply "snacks."

Class, Nostalgia, and Modern Indonesian History: New Order versus Old

In the simplified binary logic of hegemonic national discourse, "traditional culture" is conflated with backwardness and poverty, and the modern becomes nearly synonymous with Western and westernized cultural elements. But examining the realities of everyday life in Jakarta reveals a more complex, nuanced range of cultural alternatives available to Indonesians. Lisa Rofel (1999), in her study of mainland Chinese factory workers, highlights how successive regimes in China have promoted divergent visions of national modernity. These "other modernities" are internalized by subjects and result in significant cultural and aspirational differences between successive generations of Chinese. In Indonesia, the New Order's developmentalist ideology generated a particular type of modernity that displaced the populist/nationalist version promulgated by Indonesia's first president, Sukarno.

The Sukarno era (1949–65) was a complicated, troubled period in Indonesian history, but it was also, particularly in the years immediately following independence, a heady time of seemingly endless possibilities. Despite the many problems and crises during Sukarno's rule, many ordinary Indonesians view the so-called Old Order (Orde Lama) with deep nostalgia as a time when they felt included in the national project.[5] In Jakarta's outdoor markets one can always find Sukarno calendars, stickers, and posters for sale, constituting a "second life" for the late president and an implicit critique of his successors (Labrousse 1994). Under the New Order (1966–98), many urban Indonesians enjoyed a dramatic increase in their standard of living as the Soeharto regime expanded the formal economy through its technocratic developmentalist policies, yet the regime seemed to ignore the aspirations of the "little people," the *rakyat kecil,* and appeared to exist for the benefit of a corrupt, exclusive caste of big businessmen, high-level bureaucrats, and military officers. Ruth McVey writes, "The New Order's triumph marked the consolidation of Indonesia's postrevolutionary elite, its achievement of self-consciousness, and its ability when threatened to reject the populism, political radicalism, and militant nationalism that had been part of its ideological baggage since the struggle for independence" (1982, 86). The rejection of populism in favor of elitism and of militant nationalism in favor of an openness to foreign investment and foreign products became central features of official culture under the New Order, particularly in its later years.

While the pursuit of material wealth, development, and modernity remains a powerful narrative for nation building in Indonesia as elsewhere, under the New Order these ideologies were deployed in a coercive fashion, and ordinary people were made to feel ashamed of their poverty and traditional village ways. Furthermore, many Indonesians were suspicious of Western-style consumerism and longed for the Sukarno years' rhetoric of self-sufficiency and national achievement. Many Indonesian Muslims also had deep reservations about idolizing the Christian West. These and other factors led to a certain amount of ambivalence toward the New Order regime's Western-oriented developmentalism, despite the allure that Western popular culture and consumer goods held for many Indonesians.

The differences between Sukarno's and Soeharto's Indonesia are still visible in the urban landscape; the crowded *warung* and outdoor bazaars in the park area surrounding Monas (Monumen Nasional, the National Monument in Central Jakarta, a structure meant to represent the newly independent Indonesian nation's greatness and the collective achievement of its people) contrast sharply with the sterile and exclusive air-conditioned megamalls in Jakarta's main shopping districts. In their own fashion, megamalls are also monuments—to the consumerism and increasing wealth of New Order Indonesia's middle and upper classes.

Modernity's Automatons: Old Order versus New

After ascending the marble stairs to the second floor of the National Monument, one enters a large atrium built around the central tower shaft. On the shaft is a tall, narrow pair of what look like elevator doors ornately decorated with green and gold woodcarvings.

Suddenly the doors crack open to the sound of an aged, worn recording of a Western-style choir and orchestra playing a patriotic Indonesian song. The portals slide apart to reveal an additional pair of inner wooden doors that open vertically. Behind this set of doors is a piece of paper under glass illuminated by a low-wattage bulb. The music stops, and the voice of Sukarno, Indonesia's first president, crackles through the speakers. It is a recording of the radio broadcast during which Sukarno read aloud the Proclamation of 1945, which declared Indonesia's independence from the Dutch. After Sukarno's speech concludes, the music begins again, and the two pairs of doors close creakily. The proclamation was a classic performative utterance (Austin 1975): with one verbal act, Sukarno constitutes an independent nation and a people (*rakyat*) where there was once only an archipelago that happened to be controlled by a single European colonial power (Siegel 1998, 22–27). The automated display at Monas attempts to re-create this foundational event in Indonesian history with a mechanical contrivance. But the overall effect is rather underwhelming, appearing almost to emphasize the quaint outdatedness of Sukarno's vision of an independent, prosperous nation beholden to no other.

It is instructive to compare the Proklamasi contraption inside Monas with another mechanical, moving display located inside Plaza Senayan, a multitiered, luxury megamall in Central Jakarta. Every hour, the large clock in the main gallery opens up to reveal six mechanical golden cherubs with generic European features. The cherubs play Western musical instruments to a soundtrack of rather eerie synthesized New Age music. The sound is pristine, and the expressionless automatons' gestures are fluid. Perhaps without intending it, the clock at Plaza Senayan is an ideal representation of New Order Indonesia—sleek, shiny, ostentatious, westernized, and possessing a disquieting unreality. While the National Monument is located in a large park open to everyone, the clock is the centerpiece of one of Jakarta's most exclusive and expensive shopping destinations, where most Jakartans—even some middle-class people—hesitate to enter. Thus two alternative visions of modernity, two "warring possibilities," to use Geertz's term, coexist in Jakarta's urban environment, one populist but perhaps outmoded, the other sophisticated and cosmopolitan but exclusivist.

A Shrine to Sukarno in Kebayoran Baru

An unusual architectural feature I encountered in a middle-class South Jakarta neighborhood illustrates the continuing attraction of the Sukarno period to some contemporary Indonesians. The feature in question was a privately owned and constructed monument to Sukarno located in the front yard of an unassuming private residence. The monument consisted of a larger-than-life white statue of the former leader surrounded by cement bas-reliefs of icons and slogans from the Sukarno era. These included *Bersatulah Bangsaku!* (Be As One, My Nation!), *Kita bukan Bangsa pengemis* (We are not a beggar Nation), *Digali diolah sendiri* ("Excavated and processed by ourselves," a reference to Sukarno's plan for self-sufficiency in the management of Indonesia's rich natural resources), and *Kita Taruhkan Kemerdekaan dengan Darah Patriot Bangsa* (We Stake Our Freedom with the Blood of the Nation's Patriots). An inscription on the base of Sukarno's statue read *Bung Karno lebih mentjintai rakjatnja dari pada dirinja* (Brother/Comrade Sukarno loved the people more than himself). It is highly unlikely that anyone would say the same about any current political leader in Indonesia.

Sukarno memorial shrine in the front yard of a private residence, Kebayoran Baru, South Jakarta.

The slogans were written in an old orthography of Indonesian that was superseded in 1972, during the New Order. Thus in the very spelling of the words, the inscriptions on the monument convey nostalgia for Sukarno's presidency and express opposition to the current state of affairs. While apparently the handiwork of a middle-class Jakartan, the nostalgia expressed by this vernacular monument for a lost historical moment is most keenly felt among the working and lower classes, for it was during the Sukarno period that they, as "the people" (*rakyat*), assumed the role of national heroes, became revolutionary patriots, and had a charismatic leader who claimed he spoke for them.

Social Bifurcation and the Jakarta Riots

Under the New Order, the Indonesian masses (*massa*) became associated not with national revolution but with antisocial chaos and criminality (Siegel 1998). The May 1998 riots that precipitated Soeharto's departure from the presidency were a prime example of this criminality—the disruptive potential of the *rakyat kecil* (little people) realized in a paroxysm of underclass rage against the gap between rich and poor. The so-called middle to upper classes (*kelas menengah ke atas*) fear the *rakyat kecil*, especially when they take the form of the *massa*, the "mass" capable of large-scale destruction of property and people. The lack of an effective police force and the ever-present threat of provocation make the *massa* especially dangerous. The mass shields its members from individual accountability, and it easily overwhelms all but the most deadly forces of law and order. Thus the mass represents the grotesque opposite of Jakarta's "individualism"—a de-individuated mob that acts single-mindedly.[6]

The gulf between the haves and the have-nots was thrown into stark relief by the violent events of May 1998. The following passage is from a published firsthand account of the riots written by Ita Sembiring, a young Batak woman active in Jakarta's entertainment industry.

Puji Tuhan sampai selepas mahgrib tidak ada kejadian berbahaya. Massa masih tetap bertahan di seputar Plaza yang belum "takluk" juga. Aku merasakan betapa tenangnya pada saat-saat begini jadi warga kampung saja. Lihat saja mereka, sangat berbahagia dan bebas menikmati udara segar. Sementara penghuni rumah komplseks mondar-mandir tidak karuan dengan penuh kecemasan dan ketakutan. Orang-orang yang selama ini tidak pernah aku lihat sekonyong-konyong bermunculan dan berjalan-jalan dengan tenang di seputar kompleks, Plaza, dan jalan raya. Laki-laki, perempuan, anak-anak, orang dewasa, orang tua semua sangat santai dan tenang sea-kan tidak terjadi apa-apa. Dan memang benar tidak terjadi apa-apa den-gan kelompok mereka. Betapa mereka menyadari saat seperti ini ternyata lebih enak punya kehidupan seperti yang mereka miliki. Tidak ada kekha-watiran akan kehilangan harta apalagi nyawa. Terlebih lagi mereka juga seakan sangat menikmati ketakutannya para orang "berada" itu sebagai ba-gian dari hiburan yang jarang-jarang bisa mereka nikmati. Sangat natural.

[Praise God, until well after sunset there were no dangerous incidents. The mass was still staying put around the plaza, which still had not "surrendered" (to the police). I thought, how relaxing, at moments like this, to just be a *kampung* resident. Just look at them, very happy and free to enjoy the fresh air while occupants of the housing complex paced back and forth aimlessly, full of anxiety and fear. People who until now I had never seen before suddenly emerged and strolled plac-idly around the complex, the plaza, and the main roads. Boys, girls, young children, adults, and old people were all very relaxed and calm as though nothing at all had occurred. And it was indeed true that noth-ing had happened to their group. How aware they were that at a mo-ment like this, it turned out to be better to have the life they themselves had. (For them,) there was no worry about losing their possessions, or what's more, their lives. Moreover, they also seemed to enjoy greatly (watching) the fear of the people "of means" (*berada*) as a sort of enter-tainment they could rarely enjoy. Very *natural.*] (Sembiring 1998, 51–52)

This striking passage portrays the social chaos and the breakdown of civility during the 1998 Jakarta riots as a rite of reversal. The formerly anonymous slum dwellers—the ubiquitous, mundane human backdrop to the Indonesian affluent urban lifestyle—"suddenly" emerged to taunt the members of the moneyed classes, whose conspicuous material wealth equally suddenly made them vulnerable and gave them good reason to be terrified by the encroaching angry mob.[7] For a short time until "order" was restored, the tables were turned, and two years later the Jakarta cityscape still bore the scars of the mob's actions. The broken windows, burnt-out malls (many rumored to contain hundreds of charred corpses), and gutted, blackened supermarkets that remained visible in commercial districts around the city in 1999–2000 indexed the collapse of the New Order's regime of social control over the masses, as well as the battered and economically crippled state of post–New Order Indonesia. Many Jakartans expected more massive riots to take place, though so far they have not. Instead, social violence in the city has taken the form of violent street crime, brutal vigilantism, and frequent gang wars (*tawuran*) between young men belonging to different schools and neighborhoods.

Soundscapes and Mediascapes: Crowded, Noisy, Fun

Locally grounded cultural meanings are influenced by a global sensorium of images, sounds, and movements, but this influence cannot be examined properly unless the *local* sensorium is also taken into account. The following section focuses primarily on Jakarta's sonic environment, which provides an aural backdrop for all the musical activities that take place there.

Jakarta is not a quiet city. The omnipresent roar of traffic, the cries of traveling street hawkers, the Islamic call to prayer emanating at regular intervals from loudspeakers over mosques, the high-pitched bleating of cellular phones, and the sounds of recorded popular music blaring from *warung* all create an atmosphere of noisy, boisterous humanity on Jakarta's streets and in its neighborhoods. In an article on the electronic soundscape of contemporary Java, R. Anderson Sutton (1996) describes how the availability of electronic amplification has helped to create a noisy aesthetic of overlapping sound sources that conforms to the positively evaluated Javanese (and Indonesian) concept of *rame* (crowded, noisy, fun), but that also perhaps embodies the chaos of the contemporary "crazy" existential condition of Javanese confronted with social transformation, new consumer technologies, and other trappings of modernity.[8] Thus, according to Sutton, the ubiquitous presence in Java of loud, often distorted, recorded sounds blaring out of loudspeakers in a variety of public spaces both extends indigenously derived sonic aesthetics and expresses the cultural and psychological dislocations resulting from the influx of new technologies, cultural influences, and life pressures.

An outdoor carnival (*pesta rakyat*, literally "the people's party") I attended in Lebak Bulus, South Jakarta, in early 2000 featured a variety of overlapping sound sources, including a loudspeaker system blasting pop, rock, and *dangdut disco* music and an overdriven megaphone set up in front of a rather lackluster *rumah hantu* (haunted house) emitting ghoulish screams, diabolical laughter, and other contextually appropriate canned sounds. By far the loudest sound source at the fair was the Roda-Roda Gila (Crazy Wheels)—also known as Tong Sten (short for Tong Setan, "Satan's Barrel")—an attraction for which one paid 1,000 rupiahs (at the time, US$0.16) to ascend a set of spiraling metal steps to a balcony around the top rim of a large wooden barrel, about fifteen feet high and ten feet in diameter. At the bottom of the barrel were two motorcycles. Once all the ticket holders were standing on the balcony, two young men entered, mounted the bikes, and gunned their engines. As they each ascended the inner walls of the barrel, riding nearly at right angles to the ground as they spiraled upward, the noise became deafening, and the air, trapped under a plastic tarpaulin covering the top of the barrel, filled with exhaust smoke. Soon the audience members began holding out 500 and 1,000 rupiah notes for the daredevil cyclists to grab as they passed. They would snatch the bills out of the onlookers' hands and let the money flutter to the ground, until by the end of their ride, as the two motorcycles spiraled downward, there were approximately 15,000 rupiahs lying on the ground below. This dramatic and raucous spectacle epitomized Jakartan working-class entertainment: crowded, noisy, fun, and dangerous, qualities summed up in local slang by the adjective *seru*—the literal meaning of which is "to shout"—which is sort of an extreme version of *rame* that is often also used to describe loud rock concerts.

The popularity of noisiness is not limited to working-class entertainments, however, as anyone who has ever watched an action or horror film in an upscale Jakarta movie theater (and heard the theater's deafening sound system) can attest. The high Indonesian threshold for loud sounds was apparent at an upscale audio-video product exposition held at the Jakarta Convention Center on February 12, 2000. The entire main hall of the convention center was filled with a raucous cacophony of action-film soundtracks, Western rock music, electronic dance tunes, and *pop Indonesia* karaoke videos. This was a high-end exhibition targeting Jakarta's adult middle class (thus dangdut was *not* among the genres represented); the electronics companies that took part originated from Japan, Korea, and the United States, including American audiophile companies Kenwood and Marantz. When I asked one of my companions why no Indonesian electronic firms were present, he replied that made-in-Indonesia electronic products were "no good" (*tidak bagus*). The high-prestige and high-priced wares on display in each booth competed for sonic space, such that even within the same company's booth different playback devices blasted different programs at the same time, creating a noisescape of overlapping envelopes of overdriven, full-spectrum sound. Such a soundscape contrasts sharply with the orderly use of recorded music in Western built environments, in which music is architecturally contained in clearly defined functional spaces (hallways, store interiors, restrooms, etc.) and in which sonic overlap, perceived as disorienting, is assiduously avoided (see Sterne 1997).

When I asked the same companion why the volume on everything was turned up so high, his reply was, "Because people want to hear what the stuff sounds like!" The middle-aged, well-dressed crowd making its way between the booths, which in addition to audio and video equipment offered everything from cellular phone plans to food processors, seemed unfazed by the high volume of sound enveloping them, even though the decibels generated by the hundreds of VCD players, stereo systems, and television sets playing at full blast approached rock-concert levels. While the exhibition visually resembled an orderly, clean, well-organized display of luxury commodities arranged to stimulate consumer desire, the aural dimension of the event was more akin to a *pasar malam* (outdoor night market), only louder.

Internet Cafés

One relatively new feature of the Jakarta landscape is the cybercafé, known locally as *warnet*, short for *warung internet*. Since the mid-1990s *warnets* have "mushroomed" (*menjamur*) all over Jakarta and other cities in Indonesia, especially those with high student or tourist populations (see Hill and Sen 1997; Sen and Hill 2000, 195–99).[9] In a magazine article about the *boom bisnis warnet*, Onno W. Purba, a local Internet expert, metaphorically connects the *warnet* concept to Jakarta's public transportation:

> *Kalau koneksi di rumah seperti naik mobil pribadi, sedangkan warnet itu seperti angkot (angkutan kota), kendaraan umum yang dipakai bareng-bareng. Ecerannya murah, jadi enteng buat masyarakat.*
>
> [If an (Internet) connection at home is like taking a private car, then the *warnet* is like the *angkot* (city transit), public transportation that people all use together. Each (rider's) share is cheap, so it's a light burden for society.] (quoted in Sujatmoko and Winarto 2000, 6–7)

Interestingly, the only time I have heard someone use the word *macet* to refer to something other than road traffic congestion was when the speaker was experiencing a slow Internet connection.

It is difficult to estimate the total number of Internet users in Indonesia. According to a 2000 news magazine article, in that year approximately one-half of 1 percent of the Indonesian population, or about one million people, were Internet users (Khudori and Winarto 2000, 16), compared with 50,000 to 100,000 users at the end of 1997 (Sen and Hill 2000, 194). The number of users continues to rise with the increasing availability of *warnet*s, which offer access at extremely low prices. The affordability of Internet cafés, which in 2000 could cost as little as Rp. 3,000 (at the time, less than US$0.25) per hour, made them wildly popular with university students and other young people.[10] An American expatriate working for one of the major Indonesian-language Web sites, astaga.com, told me that while his company had originally targeted affluent urban professionals, they soon discovered that the majority of their users were young people, approximately 45 percent of whom accessed the site through *warnet*s rather than from home or office. Since then the site's content has been modified to appeal more to the youth demographic, with features on music, fashion, and movies.

According to my observations of *warnet* behavior in Jakarta and other major cities, the two most popular activities in *warung internet* were searching for pornographic images (which are illegal in Indonesia but nevertheless easily accessible on the World Wide Web), a largely male activity, and online chatting, which involved both genders. An especially popular activity was flirtatious virtual chatting (*kencan*) with members of the opposite sex. The popularity of chatting and e-mail among Indonesian youth has given rise to a continually evolving written youth slang, with its own nonstandard spelling conventions. For example, in the early 2000s *lu* ("you" in Jakartanese) was rendered as *loe, elo, luh, lo,* or *elu; dia* (he/she) was sometimes spelled *doi;* and words containing the *au* diphthong were written with *o,* reflecting their pronunciation in colloquial speech. Adding unpronounced letters was also common, rendering, for example, the common emphasis particles *ya, sih,* and *nih* as *yach, sich,* and *nich.* Words were also elongated to show emphasis, for example, *asiiiiiiiiiiiiiiiiiiiiiikkkkkk* (cooool!). These colloquial spellings predate e-mail (cf. Siegel 1986, 204n), but this relatively new technology appears to have accelerated the rate of orthographic change, as different spellings move in and out of fashion. More recently, many young Indonesians have begun to omit vowels from common Indonesian and Jakartanese words to save space and time when sending wireless text messages. In a sense, Jakarta's *warnet* cyberculture, in which music, fashion, humor, and social interaction (via e-mail and chat programs) are paramount, constitutes a virtualized extension of the vibrant oral culture of urban youth.

Jakartan Multilingualism and Heteroglossia

Jakarta is a city of many languages, both foreign and indigenous. It is also a city dominated by one language, Indonesian, which functions as both the language of the street and that of the official mass media. Yet the Indonesian spoken between intimates at the local *warung*, the Indonesian heard in the latest hit song, and the Indonesian used by the announcer on a national newscast are not precisely the "same" language. In his 1934–35 essay "Discourse in the Novel," Russian literary scholar M. M. Bakhtin argues that

> [l]anguage—like the living concrete environment in which the consciousness of the verbal artist lives—is never unitary. It is unitary only as an abstract grammatical system of normative forms, taken in isolation from the concrete, ideological conceptualizations that fill it, and in isolation from the uninterrupted process of historical becoming that is a characteristic of all living language. Actual social life and historical becoming create within an abstractly unitary national language a multitude of concrete worlds, a multitude of bounded verbal-ideological and social belief systems; within these various systems (identical in the abstract) are elements of language filled with various semantic and axiological content and each with its own different sound. (1981, 288)

This argument gives rise to Bakhtin's influential concept of "heteroglossia"—the profusion of diverse forms of speech in contemporary complex societies. Adding to this notion, anthropologist Deborah Durham writes, "Heteroglossia is not . . . simply a condition of society at large. It is also a condition of individual consciousness; even 'inner thought' enters into discourse with different potential meanings" (1999, 391). Thus the multiple vocabularies and ways of speaking found in Jakarta index multiple identities and subject positions that reflect the city's complex social reality and resist attempts by the Indonesian state to create a "unitary," standardized language of the nation (Keane 2003). Jakarta's nonstandard speech variants of Indonesian include those known as *bahasa Prokem, bahasa Jakarta,* and *bahasa gaul* (see appendix C). This heteroglossia extends into the popular music sphere as well, in the collision of different sounds, genres, and sung languages encountered in the music performed, recorded, and listened to in the city.

The linguistic creativity of Jakartan residents in creating new ways of speaking, in juggling pronominal options, and in humorous wordplay is a response to the conditions of life in the metropolis.[11] Jakarta's reflexive heteroglossia originates from the need to create solidary speech communities across ethnic and linguistic boundaries, but also from the need to consolidate social cohesion within class-based groupings. For example, as soon as a trendy youth slang style originating among students (such as *bahasa Prokem*) spreads to the working classes, it is replaced by new slang styles. Thus speakers of university-based speech variants enact their difference from the masses in their linguistic choices. Using trendy vocabulary also marks one as *gaul* (cool and "with it") and distances oneself from the accusation of being behind the times and of being *kampungan*.

Divided Masculinities

A humorous e-mail circulated on February 10, 2001, over Philadelphia's Permias (short for Persatuan Mahasiswa Indonesia di Amerika Serikat, the Union of Indonesian Students in the United States) mailing list describes an interesting linguistically marked intragender bifurcation between "men," designated by the standard Indonesian word *pria,* and "guys," designated by the Jakartanese term *cowok.* The e-mail consists of an itemized list titled *Bedanya Pria dengan Cowok?* (The Difference between a Man and a "Guy"?). Three examples from the fifteen-item total are

> P [ria]: *Pakai dasi, kemeja, sepatu bertali*
> C [owok]: *(Masih) pakai kaos sekolahan yang sudah buluk*
>
> P: *Seimbang antara penghasilan dan pemasukan*
> C: *Seimbang antara hutang dan pembayaran minimum*
>
> P: *Punya akuntan, penjahit dan dokter langganan*
> C: *Punya salon, kafe dan bengkel langganan*
>
> [Man: Wears a tie, shirt, and shoes with laces
> Guy: (Still) wears school T-shirt that has gotten moldy
>
> Man: Balanced between income and expenses
> Guy: Balanced between debt and minimum payment
>
> Man: Has a regular [*langganan*] accountant, tailor, and doctor
> Guy: Has a regular salon, café, and mechanic]

As a circulating electronic text, this humorous piece is intended primarily for an audience of middle- and upper-class students—including, in this case, those studying abroad. As such, the *pria/cowok* dichotomy posited by the e-mail constitutes not a class division but rather a difference in cultural orientation, toward either the hedonistic, carefree life of an adolescent student or the responsibility-laden existence of a young professional. University students are confronted with both Western-style competitive individualism and a more relaxed, sociocentric philosophy of life consonant with the informal economy's practices of buying on credit and attempting not to stand out. The *cowok*'s insistence on wearing his old, moldy school uniform is perhaps a nostalgic gesture to a time when he could be a comfortable part of a larger whole. Thus he refuses to "advance," and like his working-class counterparts, whose lack of education denies them the opportunity to choose a professional career, the *cowok* leads a precarious economic existence in the pursuit of adventure and amusement. This humorous e-mail contains a resolution to the dilemma of choosing between being a "man" or a "guy": it validates both without privileging one over the other, while questioning whether it is really a choice at all. According to the introductory text accompanying the list,

> *Tidak semua pria dewasa menjadi "pria" ada juga yang masih begitu kekanakan setelah umurnya mencapai 40. Tenaaaang, jangan keburu marah dulu dengan kenyataan ini, mungkin memang sebagian orang dilahirkan untuk jadi "pria," tapi memang ada juga yang cukup menjadi "cowok" saja.*

> *Sekali lagi, jangan kawatir, terima saja diri Anda sebagai pria (P) atau sebagai cowok (C), toh semua punya nilai lebih dan kurang tersendiri. Dan yang tak kalah penting, percayalah kadang wanita tidak peduli.*

> [Not all grown men become "men"; there are also those who stay child-like after their age has reached forty. Relaaaax, don't immediately get angry with this state of affairs—maybe indeed a segment of people are born to become "men," but indeed there are also those for whom it is enough to just be a "guy."

> Once again, don't worry, just accept yourself as a man or as a guy; after all, both of them have their own plusses and minuses. And what's most important, believe me that sometimes women don't care (either way).]

The easygoing relativism expressed in this passage is common in Indonesian popular culture more generally, and it is apparent in many popular cultural forms that combine "modern" and "traditional" elements without appearing to choose one over the other. But the stance of easygoing tolerance can also serve to mask contradictions, instabilities, persistent inequalities, and the incompatibilities that exist between distinct ways of being in the world.

Likewise, the class contradictions of the city are both smoothed over and overemphasized in the service of particular ideological goals, while the reality of coexistence without integration persists and will likely do so for the foreseeable future. Perhaps one day resource-rich Indonesia will join the ranks of prosperous, industrialized Pacific Rim countries. But until that happens the discourses of modernity and modernization will be used as instruments of class struggle, as the dominant classes seek to delegitimate the lifeways of subaltern groups. Furthermore, the division between *pasar* (market) and mall indexes not only class divisions between people but, as demonstrated above, also divided subjectivities among Jakarta's diverse inhabitants.

Indonesian popular music plays a role in the class and cultural struggles described in this chapter. Music genres and the divisions and bridges between them are implicated in the tension between the longing for a solidary, egalitarian community, on the one hand, and for modernity, affluence, individuality, and a consumerist lifestyle, on the other. The energy exerted in the denunciation of dangdut music is a salient example of how some Jakartans aspire to modernity by denigrating a cultural form that is perceived as antithetical to this aspiration. Dangdut, the music of *warung*, villages, the "backward masses," is always on the losing end of the conceptual dichotomy between cosmopolitanism and provincialism, modern and traditional, rich and poor. Yet however much it is denigrated by elites, dangdut remains wildly popular. Furthermore, although the genre emerged during Soeharto's New Order, we shall see how dangdut music's inclusive, patriotic, and populist vision strongly resembles that associated with the Sukarno era.

The next chapter continues our exploration of urban spaces by examining an obvious but frequently overlooked site where music genres are displayed, contrasted, and categorized: the cassette store.

3

Cassette Retail Outlets

ORGANIZATION, ICONOGRAPHY, CONSUMER BEHAVIOR

Despite a growing interest in mass-mediated music among ethnomusicologists, ethnomusicological studies of record stores remain uncommon.[1] This is a bit odd, since record stores are crucial sites of musical encounter in the contemporary world (moreover, most ethnomusicologists I know spend a good deal of time in them!). These specialized spaces designed for the display and sale of musical commodities provide us with an ideal entry into the world of recorded popular music in Indonesia. Against the backdrop of current trends in the Indonesian music industry, this chapter investigates shelf categories, store layouts, decorations, employee and customer behavior, and ratios of imported to domestic product that characterize the various places where music is purchased in Jakarta. Several patterns emerge from this exploration. In particular, a survey of the different types of music retail outlets reveals signs of socioeconomic bifurcation of the sort outlined in the previous chapter. Also, the hierarchical presentation of musical genres found in nearly every Indonesian cassette retail outlet exemplifies how music genre is linked to class-inflected notions of prestige and value.

For my analysis I draw on Pierre Bourdieu's *Distinction: A Social Critique of the Judgment of Taste* (1984), a landmark study of class stratification and culture in France. Bourdieu argues against a direct correlation between socioeconomic status and cultural expression, instead asserting that certain embodied forms of knowledge become sources of "cultural capital," a separate entity from economic capital. Thus in Bourdieu's view cultural status and prestige do not follow directly from the relations of production but are negotiated in a cultural field of aesthetic alternatives in which some choices are more highly valued than others.

Genre as Metaculture

The interpretive construct of music genre shapes the form and meaning of recorded music artifacts for Indonesian music consumers. Anthropologist Greg Urban has emphasized the crucial role that discursive interpretations of cultural forms, which he terms "metaculture" (that is, culture about culture), play in the reception and circulation of those forms throughout a society: "Metaculture is significant in part, at least, because it imparts an accelerative force to culture. It aids culture in its motion through space and time. It gives a boost to the culture that it is about, helping to propel it on its journey. The interpretation of culture that is intrinsic to metaculture, immaterial as it is, focuses attention on the cultural thing, helps to make it an object of interest, and, hence, facilitates its circulation" (2001, 4). In other words, metaculture promotes the circulation of cultural forms (such as recorded music) by suggesting frames for interpreting their significance in the societies that produce them. Urban further argues that metacultural constructs play an important role in the creation of the objects themselves. "Construed in this way, metacultural interpretation is a force in the world of perceptible things, not just an arbitrary conscious representation of things construed as indifferent to their representation" (2001, 37). Thus, understandings of music genre are not employed solely to organize and classify existing music; they also encourage the fashioning of particular kinds of musical sound-objects that conform to these understandings.

The metacultural constructs of genre also point *outward* to the music's social contexts, indexing social spaces, specific communities, and types of music consumers. I would suggest that the complex whole of Indonesian popular music possesses sufficient coherence for it to be examined as a metacultural field of ideological and social oppositions manifested in particular genre ideologies.[2] What follows is an exploration of how these genre ideologies are expressed in items of material culture, the design of built environments, and the everyday spoken discourse of Indonesian listeners.

Genre and *Gengsi*: Indonesian versus Foreign Popular Music

Asking an Indonesian teenager why he or she likes a particular song, artist, or genre tends to elicit a shy smile and the response, *Ya, suka aja* (I just like it, that's all). But when one digs deeper, one discovers a complex moral economy in which music genres are ranked vis-à-vis one another based on a largely implicit system of class distinction (Bourdieu 1984), which in Jakartanese is summed up by the Hokkien Chinese-derived term *gengsi* (status consciousness, prestige). These relative rankings of social prestige and power in many cases determine which genres and artists Indonesians readily admit to liking, and which they do not.

When I taught a cultural anthropology course at Universitas Atma Jaya, a private university in Central Jakarta, I was advised to introduce my students to the term *xenosentrik* (xenocentric) in addition to *etnosentrik* (ethnocentric) on the first day of class. I knew it was customary for anthropology instructors in the United States to introduce beginning students to the concept (and hazards) of ethnocentricity, the belief that one's own culture is superior to all others, in order to contrast it to the relativistic approach of mainstream cultural anthropology toward cultural differences among human groups. Teaching students the concept of xenocentrism—the belief, common in postcolonial societies, that a foreign culture (such as that belonging to the former colonizer) is superior to all others, including one's own—was a new experience for me. Yet it soon became clear to me why such a term was necessary to teach the idea of cultural relativism to Indonesian undergraduates: "xenocentric" well described the attitudes many educated middle- and upper-class Indonesians held about a range of cultural phenomena, including business, government, religion, cinema, technology, and, not least, popular music.[3] In relation to this last item, my research findings strongly suggest that the strategies by which cassette stores displayed their wares tended to replicate and reinforce, if not create, a xenocentric status hierarchy that places Western (primarily British and American) music at the top, and ethnic and working-class Indonesian genres at the bottom of the *gengsi* scale.

Belief in the artistic superiority of Western music was not purely a function of socioeconomic class position, though there appeared to be a strong correlation between such attitudes and middle- or upper-class standing. I spoke with many working-class Indonesian music fans whose opinions of Indonesian popular music, especially dangdut, were as uncomplimentary as those held by middle-class fans, if not more so. For example, walking home from Atma Jaya University's campus one day, I was accosted by a middle-aged man hanging out on the corner of Jalan Sudirman and Jalan Teluk Betung in Central Jakarta. He seemed more than a little inebriated and was talking and joking with two women whom I had seen at local dangdut bars and whom a consultant had told me worked as prostitutes. Speaking in broken but understandable English peppered with American slang expressions, he asked me what I was doing in Indonesia. When I mentioned that I was interested in studying national popular music genres like dangdut and *jaipongan*, he became surprised and indignant. The following is a partial reconstruction of his remarks from my 1997 field notes:

> Oh, God! I can't believe you're studying *that*. Dangdut and *jaipong*—I don't know why the Indonesian people like this music. It is ah . . . [hesitation, as though searching for the right expression in English] . . . from the village. It is . . . [*"Kampungan?"* I asked him] . . . Yes! That's it. As for me, I like Grand Funk Railroad; Chicago; Deep Purple; Uriah Heep; [a name I could not identify]; Emerson, Lake, and Palmer; Jimi Hendrix; blues . . . [*"Flower Generation?"* I asked] . . . Yes, man! I'm forty—I was in that generation. When I was still in high school, twenty years ago, my friends and I were *proud* to have the posters: Janis Joplin; Emerson, Lake, and Palmer; the Beatles. But people in Indonesia—there is a problem with *apresiasi*—appreciation of good music. [. . .] Speaking for me—I don't think I'm *kebarat-baratan* [westernized], more Western than Western guys, but I appreciate Western music: blues, *klasik* [classical music], rock. That is what I think. It's interesting talking to you.

This man's comments reveal not only the easy contempt some urban dwellers hold for Indonesian national popular music genres but also the important connection between Western popular music, especially rock, and masculine generational identity. Knowledge of a particular Western musical canon, in this case rock music from the 1960s and 1970s, associated in Indonesia with the *Flower Generation*, was a source of cultural capital for the speaker. In contrast, he seemed embarrassed by the popularity of dangdut and *jaipongan*, which for him served as a reminder of the backwardness of his countrymen and their inability to appreciate "good music."

Some more-thoughtful music fans expressed ambivalence about the musical prestige hierarchy in Indonesia without denying the power it wields. The following is an excerpt from an e-mail I received from a Jakartan small businessman and former student activist in response to a query concerning his favorite kind of music.

Hallo Jeremy,

Langsung aja nich . . .

Kalau ditanya soal musik, aku paling bingung ngejawabnya. Aku memang suka musik. But what kind of music do I like? This is really confused me. Aku mau jujur aja. Sebenarnya aku ini snobist! Snobist yang sok tahu, biar nggak dibilang ketinggalan jaman, gitu. Tapi akhirnya, ya suka juga. Awalnya memang snob. Kata Harry Roesly, apresiator musik di Indonesia umumnya berawal dari snob. Banyak juga musisi negeri ini yang snobist duluan. Biar nggak dikatakan kampungan, lalu coba-coba musik barat, trus kebablasan jadi pemain. Itu biasa. Namanya juga anak muda. Coba tanya Pra, atau yang lainnya tentang latar belakang mereka bermain musik barat seperti fusion, rock, atau sekarang yang lagi trend di sini, ska. Selain itu, memainkan musik Barat tentu lebih praktis. Bayangkan, kalau main musik trad. yang instrumentnya seberat gajah sekarat, macam gong, saron [. . .] dll.

Lho, kok jadi ngelantur. Soal apa tadi? Oh . . . ya, soal musik yang aku suka. Jelas dong, yang kusuka kan jazz kuno, macam Louis Armstrong, Mile Davis, Herbie Hancock, Oscar Peterson dll. Yang jelas saya tidak membatasi diri hanya dengar aliran musik tertentu. Hanya lebih enjoy dengan yang saya sebut tadi. Itu saja. Masa' kalau lagi disco pake lagu gituan. Pokoknya lihat-lihat kesempatannya lah! [. . .]

[Hello Jeremy,

I'll get directly to the point.

If asked about music, I get very confused how to answer. I certainly like music. *But what kind of music do I like? This is (sic) really confused me.* I'll just be honest. Actually, I'm a snob (*snobist*)! A snob who's a know-it-all, just so it isn't said that he is behind the times, like that. But ultimately yeah, I like what I like. In the beginning, certainly a snob. Harry Roesli (a well-known composer, recording artist, and raconteur) says appreciators of music in Indonesia generally begin as snobs. There are also many musicians from this country who were snobs at first. So as not to be considered backward or low class (*kampungan*), they mess around amateurishly with Western music, then instantly think they've become players. That's what normally happens. You know, kids are like that. Try asking Pra (Budidharma, the bassist of ethnic jazz fusion group Krakatau) or others about their background playing Western music like fusion, rock, or the music currently in vogue here, ska. Aside from that, playing Western music is certainly more practical. Imagine, if you want to play traditional music, the instruments are as heavy as an elephant in its death throes, like *gong, saron* (. . .) etc.

Hmmm . . . I'm digressing here. What was I talking about just now? Oh . . . yeah, the matter of music I like. It's clear of course, what I like is old jazz, like Louis Armstrong, Mile(s) Davis, Herbie Hancock, Oscar Peterson, etc. Clearly, though, I don't limit myself by only listening to a particular stream of music. I only *enjoy* more the music I just mentioned. That's all. It would be impossible if I'm disco dancing to use songs like that (old jazz)! The main thing is to look around at the situation *lah!*]

After expressing discomfort with the apparent elitism of his musical taste, the writer admits he likes one of the most prestigious categories of music, Western jazz. Moreover, he prefers *jazz kuno* (old-time, literally "ancient," jazz), not the watered-down jazz-rock-pop fusion that dominates the Indonesian and international jazz market. By writing that musicians play Western music so as not to be considered *kampungan,* the writer implies that non-Western music in Indonesia, including traditional music with its impractical, heavy instruments, is backward and low class. Yet to subscribe to this view is to be a *snob,* that is, to care too much about *gengsi.* So finally the writer disavows his elitism with the quite plausible claim that he listens to all kinds of music depending on the situation and that he just happens to enjoy traditional jazz best. This easygoing relativist stance is reminiscent of the conclusion to the humorous "man" versus "guy" e-mail discussed in the previous chapter.

As an intellectual familiar with post-structuralism and postcolonial theory, the writer is uncomfortable with the argument that Western music truly is superior to indigenous Indonesian music. He even cites (somewhat unconvincingly) logistical problems with moving heavy instruments as a reason why musicians choose to play Western instead of traditional music, as though practicality were of greater concern to them than artistic value. (Performing Western music, after all, also requires heavy and expensive equipment, from amplifiers to drum kits to mixing consoles.) Nevertheless, Indonesians from a variety of social and class backgrounds share the view he describes but does not quite endorse, according to which standards of musical excellence emanate from a Western "elsewhere" (Baulch 2003). This elsewhere is spatially and sometimes temporally distant, as in the case of 1950s American jazz or 1970s British hard rock. It is not difficult to associate such an attitude with the "brainwashing" effects of globalized Western popular culture. I would argue, however, that in Indonesia such a view is also part of a *local* strategy for distinguishing oneself from "low-class" and rural Indonesians through a self-conscious display of cultural capital. Evidence for this interpretation can be found in the conspicuous class-based differences in musical consumption in Indonesia.

Genre, Class, and Status:
A View of the Indonesian Music Industry

All the music retail outlets discussed in this chapter operated in the social and economic context of the Indonesian music industry, which in 1997–2001 was in the midst of a historic transition from a highly class-segmented to a more unified music market. Indonesia's class differences were obvious and frankly acknowledged, and they permeated social life. Music industry workers therefore tended to view the Indonesian popular music market not as an undifferentiated mass of consumers but as a social ladder of different socioeconomic classes. According to the marketing director of the Indonesian Repertoire and Promotions Division of a major transnational record company with extensive operations in Indonesia, these class levels were labeled A to F. She stated that A- and B-class consumers in large cities (Jakarta, Bandung, Surabaya, Medan) preferred Western music, while their counterparts in smaller cities preferred upscale *pop Indonesia*. C and D consumers preferred sentimental, melodramatic pop (*pop melankolis*, also known pejoratively as *pop cengeng*, "weepy pop"; see Yampolsky 1989) and, of course, dangdut. She added that the crowded E and F socioeconomic levels are composed of people too poor to buy music and therefore do not factor into the industry's marketing strategies.

Although most consumers do not employ these music-industry labels, they tend to explicitly associate particular musical genres with either *menengah ke atas*, "middle to upper," or *menengah ke bawah*, "middle to below," consumers. Only children's pop (*pop anak-anak*), which appeals to children of all classes, and underground music, which attracts a cross-class youth subcultural audience, constitute partial exceptions to this rule. For example, "middle-to-upper"-oriented *pop Indonesia*, often termed *pop kelas atas* (upper-class pop), is readily distinguishable from more working-class-oriented pop music by its slicker, American R & B-influenced production, jazzy arrangements, and upbeat lyrics, as well as significant differences in promotional strategy and artists' image.

The class-inflected status hierarchy of musical genres is reflected in the range of retail prices for different types of cassette. Legitimate cassette prices in Indonesia are generally *pas* (fixed, exact; not subject to bargaining) and thus are remarkably consistent regardless of the location of purchase, though at smaller stalls one is more likely to receive a slight discount when buying several cassettes at once. The following is a list of cassette prices by genre in Jakarta in late June 2000:[4]

Western Imports: Rp. 20,000 (approximately US$2.50 at the time)
Pop Indonesia: Rp. 16,000 to Rp. 18,000 (US$2.00 to $2.25)
Dangdut: Rp. 12,000 to Rp. 14,000 (US$1.50 to $1.75)
Indian Film Music: Rp. 10,000 to Rp. 11,000 (US$1.25 to $1.38)
Regional Music (*Musik Daerah*): Rp. 10,000 to Rp. 13,000 (US$1.25 to $1.63)
Underground (independently produced and distributed): Rp. 10,000 to Rp. 17,000 (US$1.25 to $2.13)

Although the price of imported Western music cassettes was rather high for most Indonesians (and was twice as much as the cost of some *musik daerah* cassettes), it was nevertheless much lower than the retail price of Western music products in the West. This was made possible by manufacturing the cassettes domestically under license from multinational media corporations. Western compact discs were also locally manufactured, but their prices were much higher than those of cassettes, which were still by far the best-selling recorded music format in Indonesia in 1999–2000.[5] In June 2000, locally produced Western compact discs could cost as much as Rp. 80,000 (at the time, approximately US$10.00), while compact discs by Indonesian artists cost approximately Rp. 50,000 (US$6.25). Since these prices were far higher than those of cassettes, compact discs were considered a format designated for A and B consumers. Very few dangdut recordings were released on compact disc; a dangdut producer told me such items would not sell well and would only be used as ideal masters for the production of pirated cassettes. Among new releases, only *pop Indonesia* albums that had already been commercially successful as cassettes were released on compact disc.

For much of the 1980s and 1990s, the sheer number of consumers in the so-called C and D markets compensated for their relatively weak

Table 3.1 Recorded music sales data for Indonesia (units sold), 1996-99

Type	1996	1997	1998	1999 (October)
Indonesian cassettes	65,396,589	49,794,676	27,635,739	30,100,077
Foreign cassettes	11,374,089	14,005,340	9,637,200	11,395,590
Indonesian CDs	265,475	778,370	315,910	532,900
Foreign CDs	474,980	2,053,840	2,732,410	2,086,290
Karaoke VCDs	19,500	701,870	1,335,390	4,196,590
Karaoke LDs	21,375	21,975	2,205	1,050
Total	77,552,008	67,356,071	41,658,854	48,312,497

Source: Theodore 1999, 10

individual purchasing power, and in fact genres such as dangdut that targeted this audience, while low on the *gengsi* scale, were quite profitable for record companies. In the early and mid-1990s it was not unusual for a dangdut cassette containing a hit song to sell more than a million legitimate copies—an unheard-of amount for *pop* records at the time. This situation changed drastically in the aftermath of the 1997-98 economic catastrophe.[6] A comparison of music sales in the years before and after Indonesia's economic collapse provides insight into the relative ability of Indonesians from different social classes to weather the crisis. Table 3.1 is sorted by foreign and local music and by consumer format. Almost all music sold in Indonesia during the period covered in the table was in the form of prerecorded cassettes, but music was also available on compact disc, video compact disc (VCD), and laser disc (LD). The latter two formats, obscure in the West, contain images as well as sounds and were often used to accompany karaoke performance. They contain primarily Indonesian music.

These figures reveal a story of the relative power to withstand economic turmoil at various levels of the Indonesian class structure. The upper and middle classes, with their high rates of personal savings, suffered far less than the poor, who had little or no savings and could not cope with the steeply rising prices of consumer goods. A striking statistic from this table is that sales of the highest-priced commodity, foreign compact discs, actually *increased* 33 percent between 1997 and 1998, during the height of the economic crisis. It is tempting to posit a perverse kind of *gengsi* logic behind this increase, and behind the fact that the number of foreign compact discs sold in Indonesia decreased the following year. According to this logic, conspicuous consumption in the form of purchasing Western compact discs during the height of an economic crisis would powerfully demonstrate one's elite status and separation from the immiserated poor, many of whom were now unable to buy even the cheapest local cassettes.

In October 1999, the sale of cassettes by Indonesian artists over the previous eight months amounted to less than half the total figure for 1996. Due to competition from the rapidly growing VCD medium (which is even more dominated by piracy than cassettes), it is unlikely that Indonesian cassette sales will ever rebound completely, even after the economic outlook of the country improves. This situation led some recently arrived multinational recording companies to conclude that the "middle to lower" market segment was no longer profitable, a result of its decreased spending power and habit of buying readily available pirated albums.

In postcrisis Indonesia, many of the most successful new recordings have been by *pop alternatif* and ska groups like Sheila on 7 and Jun Fan Gung Foo (both artists on the Sony Music Indonesia record label) that have crossed over to an economically diverse audience. This success has often occurred against the expectations of record-label personnel, who did not anticipate such high sales (Sheila on 7's eponymous first album, for example, sold over one million legitimate copies). That *pop alternatif* artists associated with urban middle-class youth have become accepted in lower social strata is evident in a claim I heard from several people in the Indonesian music industry: the current youth market in Indonesia is far more uniform across class boundaries than in previous generations, a situation attributed to the influence of MTV and other recently introduced outlets showcasing global popular culture. Such a claim, however, does not diminish the phenomenon of widening social inequality in Indonesia in the face of both economic globalization and economic crisis. Indeed, the New Order's aggressive economic development policies may well have resulted in a more unified popular culture coupled with a more polarized society.

Music Consumption at the Ground Level: A Taxonomy of Jakarta's Music Retail Outlets

If we confine ourselves to the legitimate music market and ignore for the moment pirated products, we find that the prices of products for sale in different kinds of retail outlets do not differ markedly. The manner in which recordings are displayed is also quite similar, but the *experience* of shopping for cassettes can differ widely between a large mall music store and a small cassette stall. In the former, one usually finds that well over half of the music for sale is imported, whereas in cassette stalls that operate in the informal, "bazaar" economy, Western music cassettes usually account for less than 25 percent of total shelf space. The precise ratio of imported to Indonesian cassettes varies depending on the economic circumstances of the surrounding neighborhood. For instance, the cassette stalls I visited in Kampung Muara, a poor area in North Jakarta, offered very few Western cassettes for sale but featured a wide selection of dangdut cassettes, while the stall I frequented in middle-class Kebayoran Baru, South Jakarta, had many more imported and *pop Indonesia* cassettes on offer and significantly fewer dangdut titles.

Warung Kaset

Warung kaset (cassette stalls) distinguish themselves sonically from the other stalls in a traditional bazaar by the loud recorded music they emit outward to passersby. The type of music played depends on the sales-clerk, though sentimental pop ballads, often in English, are a frequent choice. These establishments are decorated spartanly, relying on the sound of the music and the colorful cassette packages on display to attract customers. Most sell a range of other nonperishable items in addition to cassettes: plastic toys, batteries, headphones, and the like. Cassettes for sale in the stall are not displayed alphabetically but are usually separated into unlabeled categories. The most common of these implicit classifications, to judge from the different artists represented in each section, are Western pop, Indonesian pop, dangdut, Javanese, Sundanese, Islamic, and children's music. The classification scheme does not separate regional pop and traditional music recordings from the same region. In these *warung*, Western music cassettes are usually placed on the highest shelves behind the counter, while Indonesian music is displayed on lower shelves and inside the counter. This practice appears to elevate foreign music to a higher status, but it may simply result from the desire to protect the stall's most expensive items from damage or theft. Nevertheless, after visiting innumerable Indonesian cassette stalls, I concluded that the spatial separation between Indonesian and foreign music was carefully maintained in a manner suggesting that more than security concerns may be at stake.

In nearly all *warung kaset,* the customer has the option of trying out a recording on the stall's sound system before purchase, to test it for defects (which are rare, in my experience) and to determine if he or she likes the music. Usually the salesclerk opens the cassette's shrink-wrap with a small knife blade (if it had not yet been opened) and then uses a small motorized device to fast-forward the tape a little to get past the leader (the blank space at the start of a tape). In Indonesia, leaders are rather lengthy—up to 20 seconds or so—as a result of the local method of duplicating cassettes. The clerk then places the cassette in the stall's tape deck and plays a segment of the first song at a volume sufficient to fill the entire space of the stall. The cassette continues to play until the customer asks to hear another song or tells the salesclerk he or she has heard enough. The salesclerk will then immediately resume playing the cassette that had been playing previously, until another customer makes a request. In this way, the musical background of the stall is never interrupted by long silences.

Jakarta *warung kaset* proprietors buy their cassettes in small amounts wholesale from distributors located mostly in the Glodok area of North Jakarta. They make choices regarding which cassettes to stock based on previous sales, and in most cases they do not buy more than one or two copies of a single title. As a result, customers wishing to purchase a popular title are often cheerfully told that that cassette has sold out. The music selection at cassette stalls, where the majority of Indonesians purchase their music, is generally comprised of about 20 percent foreign and 80 percent Indonesian titles. Stall proprietors stock only titles they believe will sell to a broad public; thus albums by more avant-garde Indonesian recording artists such as Krakatau, Harry Roesli, or Djaduk Ferianto are generally found only in large music stores (see the discussion later in this chapter), if they are available at all.

Mall Stores

Jakarta's gigantic air-conditioned malls offered a cosmopolitan alternative to shopping in traditional markets with their mud and squalor. They were places for the fashionable to see and be seen and to experience a taste of global consumer culture. Like malls in the United States, until recently, no Indonesian mall was complete without at least one store selling recorded music artifacts.[7] Targeted at middle-class and elite consumers, upscale mall music stores were typically decorated with an eclectic, bewildering assortment of images from Western culture.

A cassette store in a South Jakarta mall.

The wall decorations in a music store located in Plaza Senayan (see chapter 2) included a portrait of Beethoven, a blown-up photograph of Kurt Cobain (the late singer of the American band Nirvana), a depiction of the Mona Lisa smoking a large marijuana cigarette, a poster of a Norwegian black metal band, and a reproduction of a Bob Marley album cover. Another mall store, Tower Music, located in the fashionable Menteng shopping district, had a display of small flags on one of its shelves. The countries represented were Indonesia, the United States, Ireland, Japan, Germany, and Britain. There was no flag representing Malaysia, Singapore, or any other neighboring Southeast Asian country, suggestive of a cosmopolitan musicscape based more on cultural power than on geography. Even the name of the store evoked Tower Records, a transnational music retailer that at the time had yet to reach Jakarta.

While all record stores I visited in Indonesia sold some Indonesian recordings, music boutiques in upscale malls tended to carry mostly Western music. In my explorations of the most upscale stores, those located in Plaza Indonesia, Plaza Senayan, Pondok Indah Mall, and Taman Anggrek, I also found that compact discs actually outnumbered cassettes. Dangdut albums, if present at all, accounted for less than 5 percent of shelf space; regional (*daerah*) genres were largely absent. Mall stores usually sorted recordings alphabetically in labeled shelf categories.

These categories usually included standard Western genres (jazz, R & B, country, etc.), while locally produced recordings (predominantly *pop kelas atas*, upper-class pop) were frequently relegated to shelves labeled "Indonesia" that took up as little as 10 percent of total shelf space. Although upscale mall stores always played music in the background, there were no facilities for testing recordings one wished to buy. Clerks were not permitted to open the shrink-wrap of cassettes and compact discs for customers.

Mall music stores present themselves as portals to an imaginary realm of global consumer culture. Signs of local specificity that would place the store in an Indonesian context, including use of the Indonesian language on posters and signs, are minimized or eliminated. Indonesian music is marginalized as a marked category, while Western music and culture are represented in a spectacular fashion.

Large Music Stores

A third music retail alternative to cassette stalls and mall boutiques is the handful of large music stores located in major cities. These establishments, which stock a wide variety of indigenous and foreign musics, are located in department stores such as Sarinah or the Pasaraya at Blok M or are housed in stand-alone structures like Aquarius, a record-store chain owned by one of Indonesia's largest national record companies. The rest of this section investigates in detail the ways in which the Jakarta Aquarius store displays its wares, which run the full gamut from Western art music to traditional regional genres.

The Aquarius music store located in the Bulungan area of Blok M in South Jakarta consisted of two rooms in 1999–2000. The larger room held both Indonesian and Western compact discs (mostly the latter), Indonesian children's pop, and a large selection of Western cassettes, while a smaller one contained mostly Indonesian cassettes. Interestingly, in the center of the "Indonesian" room there was an arrangement of tape players with headphones, with which customers could test cassettes. No such array existed in the large room.[8] These tape machines resembled those found in *warung kaset*, though the experience of listening was somewhat privatized. I say "somewhat" because I often observed two or more customers trying to listen to a song through the same pair of headphones at the same time. The presence of this listening equipment appeared to be a concession to shoppers accustomed to the cassette-stall buying experience.

Table 3.2 Inventory of cassette categories at Aquarius Musik, main room

Shelf label	Contents	Shelf units
Classic	Western classical and light classical music	1.0
Instrumental	Western New Age and instrumental pop	1.0
Soundtrack	Recent Hollywood film soundtracks	1.0
Compilation	Collections of pop hits, mostly love songs	2.0
Jazz	Jazz-pop fusion, some traditional jazz	2.0
Alternative/ Modern Rock	Western rock bands sharing a nonmainstream, punk-influenced aesthetic	2.0
Rhytm + Blues [*sic*]	American R & B and hip hop	2.0
Dance	Various Western electronic dance genres such as house and techno	1.0
Rock + Pop	Western rock and pop artists	17.0
New Releases	Recent titles, both Indonesian and Western	1.5
Top 40	Ranked best-selling albums, from both Indonesia and the West	2.0
Children	Indonesian *pop anak-anak* (children's pop)	1.0

The Western music available in cassette format at Aquarius was divided into several specific subcategories, not all of which corresponded completely with conventional Western classifications. The shelf categories are listed in table 3.2. The number in the far right column indicates the number of shelf units dedicated to each named category; each shelf unit held about fifty different cassettes, depending on how they were arranged.

Indonesian children's pop was the only indigenous musical category present in the large room. I suspect that the storeowners were concerned that middle- and upper-class consumers preoccupied with social prestige (*gengsi*) would not even want to enter the Indonesian music room. Such consumers often buy children's pop cassettes for their offspring; this practice is not a threat to *gengsi* because small children are not expected to have developed cultivated musical tastes or to understand English lyrics. It may also be the case that Indonesian children's pop benefits from the fact that it lacks a real equivalent in Western pop.

The rest of the Indonesian music cassettes sold by Aquarius were located in a room to the far left of the store's front entrance. Its total inventory was a fraction of that in the large room (10 versus 33.5 shelf units), and the five categories that appeared on shelf labels did not reflect the same level of genre specificity, as table 3.3 illustrates.

Table 3.3 Inventory of cassette categories at Aquarius Musik, Indonesian room

Shelf label	Contents	Shelf units
Compilation	Various artists, mostly *pop nostalgia*	0.5
Indonesia	Indonesian pop, Indonesian rock, alternative, R & B, metal, and so on	5.0
Dangdut	Dangdut, *dangdut trendy, orkes Melayu* (dangdut's historical precursor)	1.0
Etnic [sic]	Primarily *pop daerah* (regional pop) from different parts of the archipelago, including Java, Sunda, Maluku, Sumatra (Malay, Batak, and Minangkabau), North Sulawesi (Manado), Irian Jaya, even East Timor. Also some Javanese and Sundanese traditional music	1.0
Unlabeled	Indonesian jazz, jazz-pop fusion, and ethnic fusion jazz; patriotic songs; *keroncong*; Indonesian house music; *nostalgia* collections	1.0
Rohani	Western and Indonesian pop music with Christian religious themes	1.0
Unlabeled subsection	Indonesian Islamic pop	0.5

In the large room near the entrance to the small one, two shelf units were devoted to displaying the forty top-selling cassettes of the week, both Indonesian and Western. This was one of the few sections of the store where imported and domestic music shared shelf space and seemed to compete with each other on equal footing. Table 3.4 is a list of the top forty best-selling albums for the week of January 22, 2000, as compiled by the Aquarius store.

This list is fairly representative: the ratio of Indonesian to foreign entries is 2:3 (16 to 24; in other weeks the balance was tipped more favorably toward the former), and it is dominated by musical genres associated with the middle class: Western pop, sophisticated "upper-class" Indonesian pop, and Western hard rock music. I never saw a dangdut cassette included in the Aquarius Top Forty. While in table 3.4 Western recording artists occupy the top three slots, in other weeks Indonesian recordings held those positions. The list also indicates the preference among many Indonesian consumers for "greatest hits" compilations (eleven in total, seventeen if one counts albums containing "live" recordings or new studio arrangements of familiar songs) over albums of new, unfamiliar material, a preference that appeared to be shared by Indonesians from all walks of life.

Table 3.4 Top forty best-selling albums at Aquarius Musik, week of January 22, 2000

No.	Artist	Album title	Description
1	The Corrs	*MTV Unplugged*	Western, quasi-Celtic pop
2	Celine Dion	*All the Way: A Decade of Song*	Western sentimental pop ballads
3	Westlife	Self-titled	Irish "boy band"
4*	Rossa	*Tegar* [Resolute]	*Pop kelas atas* (upper-class pop)
5*	Chrissye	*Badai Pasti Berlalu* [The Storm Will Surely Pass]	Newly arranged songs from a classic 1970s pop album
6*	Various	*Hard Rock FM Indonesia Klasik*	Compilation of Indonesian rock bands
7*	Padi	*Lain Dunia* [Another World]	*Pop alternatif*
8*	Dewa 19	*Best of Dewa 19*	*Pop alternatif*
9	Boyzone	*By Request*	Irish "boy band"
10*	Melly	Self-titled	*Pop alternatif*
11	Bryan Adams	*The Best of Me*	Western mainstream rock
12	Various	*Everlasting Love Songs 2*	Western sentimental pop ballads
13*	Sheila on 7	Self-titled	*Pop alternatif*
14	Metallica	*S & M 2*	Western hard rock/metal backed by a symphony orchestra
15*	Bunglon	*Biru* [Blue]	Smooth jazz–influenced pop
16	Sheila Majid	*Kumohon* [I Beseech]	Malaysian jazz–influenced pop
17	Alanis Morissette	*Unplugged*	Western alternative rock
18	Richard Clayderman	*Chinese Garden*	Western pop-classical crossover
19	Korn	*Issues*	Western "hip metal" (hip hop + metal)
20	Various	*'99: The Hits*	Western Top 40 compilation
21	Rage Against the Machine	*The Battle of Los Angeles*	Western "new school" hardcore/hip metal
22*	Sherina	*Andai Aku Besar Nanti* [When I Grow Up]	Children's pop (*pop anak-anak*)
23	Various	*Forever*	Western sentimental pop ballads
24*	Dian Pramana Poetra	*Terbaik* [Best]	*Pop kelas atas*
25*	Syaharani	*Tersiksa Lagi* [Tortured Again]	Vocal jazz
26	Savage Garden	*Affirmation*	Western mainstream pop
27	George Michael	*Songs from the Last Century*	Western mainstream pop
28	Metallica	*S & M 1*	Western hard rock/metal
29	Santana	*Supernatural*	Western Latin-crossover pop rock
30*	Rita-Sita-Dewi	*Satu* [One]	*Pop kelas atas*
31*	Romeo	Self-titled	*Pop kelas atas*
32*	Ruth Sahanaya	*Kasih* [Love]	*Pop kelas atas*
33	Various	*L Is for Love*	Western sentimental love ballads
34	Foo Fighters	*There Is Nothing Left to Lose*	Western alternative rock
35	Eric Clapton	*Chronicles*	Western mainstream rock
36*	Purpose	*Tiger Clan*	Ska
37	Various	*The End Of Days*	Hollywood movie soundtrack
38	Guns 'n' Roses	*Live Era '87–93*	Western hard rock
39	Various	*American Pie*	Hollywood movie soundtrack
40*	Noin Bullet	*Bebas* [Free]	Ska

Note: * = Indonesian title

Mobile Cassette Vendors

A final type of commercial music retailer is worth mentioning. Along with a veritable army of other mobile salesmen who traveled through my neighborhood in South Jakarta selling everything from brooms to ice cream novelties, a mobile cassette vendor would make his way through the streets pushing a wooden cart in which a car stereo system was installed. The cassettes he sold—all legitimate copies, not pirated—were intended to appeal to the servants and *warung* proprietors of the neighborhood, not its more affluent residents. Thus the selection of recordings was dominated by dangdut and regional music from Sunda and Java, including cassettes of village folk genres (such as Sundanese *kliningan*) that were difficult to find in Jakarta cassette stores.

In addition to cassettes, the "circling-around dangdut" (*dangdut keliling-keliling*) vendor sold toys, brushes, and other household items from his cart. His approach was signaled by the dangdut music blaring out of the cart's speakers as he rolled it down the street. The tape deck installed in the cart was also used by potential customers to try out cassettes in the manner of a *warung kaset*. Although Western music was

Dangdut keliling: mobile vendor's cart with built-in speakers selling cassettes, toiletries, sandals, and other items.

not wholly absent from his stock, the circling-around dangdut seller managed to circumvent—that is, circle around—Jakarta's prestige hierarchy of genres by targeting rural migrants, not city people, as his primary customers.

Sources for Underground Music

In an interview with an Indonesian fanzine, Robin Malau, the guitarist of Puppen, comments:

> *Kebanyakan cara indie jualan, sampe-sampe ngga berasa bahwa mereka itu sedang melakukan transaksi dagang . . . antar teman, promosi mulut ke mulut . . . seperti untuk kalangan sendiri gitu . . . bagus lho . . . positifnya, itu juga salah satu cara approach yang lebih akrab kepada pasar, lagian mo begimana lagi?*

> [For the most part the *indie* way of selling is such that it is not felt that they are making a commercial transaction . . . between friends, word-of-mouth promotion . . . like for their own social circle, y'know? . . . it's nice . . . the positive thing is that it's also one way to *approach* the market that is friendlier—why would you want anything more?] (Interview posted on Puppen's now-defunct Web site, www.not-a-pup.com/multi .htm, ellipses in original)

In keeping with this point of view, underground cassettes are, as a rule, not found in mall stores, cassette stalls, vendors' carts, or any other conventional retail outlet. It is in fact technically illegal to sell them, as the Indonesian government does not collect any taxes on the transaction.[9] Legitimate (nonpirated) commercially released cassettes in Indonesia usually come with a small strip of paper indicating that the manufacturer has prepaid a percentage of the cassettes' value to the government. To purchase underground music cassettes, which lack these strips of paper, one must know someone in the underground scene, attend a concert event, or visit one of a small number of urban specialty shops that sell underground music and accessories.

Every underground concert event I attended during my fieldwork included itinerant vendors who set up shop on blankets either inside or on the grounds outside the concert venue. Their merchandise included T-shirts, stickers, cassettes, compact discs, photocopied fanzines, and sew-on patches. Here imported and indigenously produced recordings were generally sold side by side; the peddlers' wares were usually not separated by their country of origin but rather mixed together, arranged alphabetically or in no particular order at all. Thus only an insider to the music scene could distinguish foreign groups' cassettes from Indonesians', since most Indonesian underground band names were in English and their album graphics made use of iconography similar to that of Western albums. Of course, the sharp difference in cassette prices persisted, though stickers with Western band logos were usually pirated and did not cost more than those with Indonesian band logos, which were sometimes also unauthorized copies.

Reverse Outfits

The oldest standing retail establishment in Indonesia for the sale of underground music and accessories was located not in Jakarta but in a quiet residential neighborhood in the West Javanese city of Bandung. Since the early 1990s, Reverse Outfits had sold both imported and Indonesian underground music; in the years after the onset of the economic crisis, the store placed increasingly greater emphasis on the latter.

Reverse Outfits was located on the property of Richard Mutter, an *Indo* (part native, part European) who was in his late twenties during the time of my fieldwork. Richard is the former drummer of Pas (Precise), an alternative rock group that originated in the Bandung underground scene and released a cassette on a small independent label in 1994, but has since released six albums for the large national recording company Aquarius Musikindo and has met with significant commercial success. The store was part of a complex that included a rehearsal/ recording studio for Richard's record label, 40.1.24 (named after the neighborhood's postal code), and facilities for creating posters and graphics. Originally a source primarily for imported underground music, which the store purchased via mail order, the inventory of Reverse Outfits shifted dramatically between 1997 and 2000 as a result of two factors.

First, the economic crisis and the devaluation of the rupiah made imported cassettes and compact discs prohibitively expensive, as the store not only had to pay full price for each item in U.S. dollars, but also had to pay substantial shipping and handling costs. Thus the amount of imported music on sale at Reverse Outfits declined considerably after 1998. The lost inventory was replaced by way of a second development: the exponential increase of independently produced Indonesian underground music recordings during the same period.

Like the Aquarius store, Reverse Outfits was divided into two rooms. At the time of my first visit to the store in the fall of 1997, the inner room was used to display recordings from overseas, while the outer room contained a glass display counter, similar to those found in *warung kaset,* filled with domestically produced underground music. Neither room made use of shelf categories.

While imported underground music was usually sold in the form of compact discs, Indonesian underground music was sold on cassette. As of September 2000, only one underground label had ever released a compact disc: a band compilation produced by 40.1.24 Records in 1997 that could still be purchased at Reverse Outfits three years later. The economic crisis prevented any subsequent compact disc releases, but the number of new cassettes continued to grow. By the time of my return to Indonesia in 1999, Reverse Outfits had combined its musical inventory. Its few remaining imported compact discs were placed on the top two shelves in the front room's glass display case, while a substantial number of Indonesian underground cassettes were displayed in no particular order on the bottom shelf. Thus even in this context the hierarchical separation between foreign and indigenous music was maintained.

In addition to Reverse Outfits, by 2000 a small but growing number of underground boutiques (*toko underground*) had opened in Jakarta, Bandung, Surabaya, Denpasar, and other cities. These establishments were often owned and operated by veteran underground scene members (often those who had graduated from or dropped out of universities and were in need of a means of earning their livelihoods) and sometimes included rehearsal and recording studios. Some stores, such as Ish-Kabible Sick Freak Outfits Shop in Jakarta, produced their own T-shirts and stickers.[10] Studio Inferno, located in Surabaya, even had its own Internet café. These outlets, like Reverse Outfits, sold both foreign and Indonesian shirts, stickers, hats, and recordings and were focal points and important hangout spots (*tempat nongkrong*) for members of the scene.

Underground boutiques existed in a gray area between the formal and the informal economies, and while they depended on impersonal, commercial transactions for survival, they adhered to the underground's ethic of do-it-yourself authenticity. Although Reverse Outfits did stock Pas's Aquarius cassette releases, all the other titles it sold were released by small independent labels. The other boutiques I visited did not sell "major label" Indonesian cassettes at all, even those released by groups that were formerly part of underground scenes.

Cassette Piracy and Vendors
of Illegally Copied Cassettes

No inventory of the sites of music commerce in Indonesia would be complete without some remarks on cassette piracy. Given that most legitimate Indonesian cassettes cost over Rp. 12,000 each during the period of my fieldwork, it was hardly surprising that the vendors of illegally copied versions priced at Rp. 6,000 or less attracted many buyers. The quality of these pirated versions varied, but they were often not markedly inferior to the originals. Color copiers enabled pirates to accurately reproduce the original graphics of legitimate releases, and high-quality cassette duplication machines could approximate the original's sound quality. In addition to selling illegal copies of complete albums, pirated-cassette vendors sold unauthorized compilations of current hit songs. These were usually either dangdut or pop compilations, and their graphics, usually a collage of miniaturized cassette covers representing the different songs, varied widely in sophistication. One advantage the pirated compilations had over legitimate hits collections was that they could combine songs released by different recording companies, since they were not bound by copyright restrictions. Thus, pirated hits compilations were not only cheaper but also more likely to contain every hit song popular at a particular time.

Surprisingly, not all Indonesian musicians whom I interviewed vehemently opposed piracy. After all, if one's work is pirated, it indicates that one's music has achieved a measure of mass acceptance. During an interview in 1997, Harry Roesli, one of Indonesia's foremost composers/musicians/social critics, proudly showed me a pirated hits compilation featuring his controversial song "Si Cantik" ("Ms. Beautiful," a song about a grandchild of Soeharto who was suspected of dealing the popular drug Ecstasy) as the first track. He considered the cassette to be evidence that the subversive political messages in his music were successfully reaching the masses. Many members of the underground scene claimed that the mainstream acceptance of underground music was proven by the fact that some death metal bands' cassettes (usually those released by major labels) had been pirated and were being sold in outdoor markets alongside the customary rock, pop, and dangdut offerings.

Buyers of pirated cassettes were categorically assumed to be members of the working class by my consultants. Members of the middle class were purportedly too concerned with status (*gengsi*) to consider purchasing such items, which were thought to be of inferior quality.

The poor, on the other hand, were said to have the attitude of *asal denger aja* (as long as you can hear [it]) and to have no qualms about the uneven quality of illegally copied cassettes. Pirated cassettes thus occupied the lowest prestige level among recorded musical artifacts. They were sources of popular pleasure, but unlike underground and legitimate commercial cassettes, they could not act as expressions of cultural or subcultural capital (Thornton 1996), even if they happen to be illegal copies of otherwise prestigious Western music.

Conclusions: Recorded Music, Display, and Musical Value

Cassette stores in Indonesia display hegemonic and xenocentric understandings of music genres that ghettoize indigenously produced musics, subordinate them to international music products, and maintain segregated, unequal relationships between them. The two partial exceptions to this rule, Christian (*Rohani*) music and underground music, are notable for their connection to subcultures reliant on cultural texts and forms produced outside Indonesia as well as within. The presentational logic that places musically similar Indonesian and Western recordings in separate areas of the store preserves the myth that they are incomparable despite their sonic similarities. While perhaps preserving a sense of Indonesian cultural uniqueness, this metacultural separation can also present Indonesian popular music as second-class and less worthy of serious attention. In the larger stores dominated by Western imports, such presentational logic deceptively suggests that Indonesian-produced popular music is a minority taste in Indonesia, despite sales figures that consistently demonstrate otherwise.

In addition to the lack of differentiation between Indonesian pop genres in most Indonesian music stores, "regional" (or "ethnic") music is also a catchall category in which the most traditional and the most contemporary styles are displayed side by side. The "regional" category is thus even less differentiated than Indonesian national music, which is always at the very least divided between pop and dangdut categories.

Dangdut, the most popular style in Indonesia, is usually marginalized in store displays. Conversely, Western music, a minority taste, is highlighted and carefully categorized by subgenre. An alternate display strategy of placing Western *and* Indonesian rock, for example, in one shelf category sorted alphabetically by artist with no regard to country of origin still seems unthinkable in mainstream outlets and even in many underground music stores. One reason for this is that Western and Indonesian music are perceived as existing on different ontological as well as economic planes. The incommensurable categorical differences between Indonesian and Western music are summed up by the term *gengsi*, status consciousness. Indonesian popular music, no matter how westernized, is considered to be of inherently lesser status than international Anglo-American music. Indonesian music is believed to require less cultivation (*apresiasi*) to enjoy and is therefore more accessible to nonelites. According to the widespread xenocentric view of musical value in Indonesia, the music of the village is *kampungan*, backward and low-class, and even higher-status Indonesian pop still cannot aspire to the greatness of international pop and moreover is forever subject to the withering accusation that such music simply imitates the sounds of Western originals.

Despite the apparent investment made by music retailers in keeping Indonesian and foreign music separate and unequal, it is important to emphasize that the categorical and presentational logics of Indonesian record stores discussed in this chapter contrast sharply with those of most Indonesian consumers. In general, Indonesians do not strictly segregate their record collections into Western and Indonesian categories, and they use more differentiated genre labels to describe Indonesian popular music than appear on record-store shelves: rock, underground, rap, ska, metal, R & B, and so on. Nevertheless, I found that the discursive divide between "Indonesian" and "foreign" was very much present in statements Indonesians made about the value of different types of popular music, as was the suspicion that Indonesian versions of Western genres were derivative and inferior. Thus the Indonesian music fan is suspended between doubts about the authenticity of westernized pop music and misgivings about the village backwardness of music regarded as authentically Indonesian. But as we shall see in the following chapters, this state of ambivalent suspension leads to many creative attempts at resolution, rewarding in their own right, as the quest for an authentically Indonesian, modern music continues undaunted.

4

In the Studio

AN ETHNOGRAPHY

OF SOUND PRODUCTION

The sources of Indonesian popular music are extraordinarily diverse. Middle Eastern pop, American hip hop, Ambonese church hymns, Sundanese *degung*, British heavy metal, European house music, Indian film song, Chinese folk music, and Javanese *gendhing* are but a fraction of the influences one might detect on a single cassette. Despite this complexity, however, the question of where the music on an Indonesian popular music cassette "came from" generally has one simple, straightforward answer: it was produced in a multitrack recording studio most likely located in Jakarta.

The multitrack recording studio—by which I mean a facility enabling the recording of several musical parts, successively or simultaneously, that can then be processed, edited, and combined (mixed) to create a final musical product in which the presence of each part in the overall sound is carefully calibrated to achieve maximum aesthetic impact—has unquestionably become the most important musical "instrument" in the world over the last fifty years. The particular ways in which users of multitrack studios have manipulated sounds have transformed definitions of music itself and given rise to new, competing discourses of sonic aesthetics, musical authenticity, and creativity (Théberge 1997, 191, 215–22; see also Doyle 2005; Greene 2001; Greene and Porcello 2005; Katz 2004; Meintjes 2003; Porcello 1998; Wallach 2003b; Zak 2001). Indeed, the myriad creative practices enabled by studio technology around the world have in many places fundamentally reshaped musical sounds, concepts, and behaviors, to use Alan Merriam's well-known triadic scheme for the anthropological study of music (1964).

In this chapter I present accounts of three different Indonesian recording studios. The first, 601 Studio Lab, was a large professional studio complex with high-quality equipment used for recording dangdut and *pop Indonesia;* the second, Paradi Studio, was a smaller, state-of-the-art facility used to record Indonesian pop, jazz, and R & B artists. Both of these studios were located in residential areas in East Jakarta. The third studio, Underdog State, was a more modestly equipped facility in Denpasar, Bali, that specialized in the recording of underground rock music. In the following pages I describe the participants, situations, discourses, and "sound engineering" (Greene 1999) practices that characterized everyday life in these three recording studios. Throughout the discussion, three themes are emphasized: metacultural understandings of genre as they are applied to music production, the use of sound technology as a tool for cultural innovation involving the hybridization of existing genres, and the social dynamics among the participants. These dynamics differ markedly from those generally found in Western recording studios, and they fundamentally shape how popular music recordings are produced in all three sites discussed in this chapter.

601 Studio Lab: Mainstream Dangdut and Pop Production in a Professional Studio

601 Studio Lab is a multipurpose commercial recording complex used to record a variety of popular musics. The facility is located in an upscale housing development in Cakung, a newly developed area on the far outskirts of East Jakarta. It occupies a two-story house that had been converted into a sophisticated recording complex—though until 1999 one had to enter the vocal booth through the kitchen. Edy Singh, the music producer in charge of running the studio, explained to me that it was located so far from the center of Jakarta to discourage musicians and their entourages from spending all their leisure time there. Such people have a tendency to *nongkrong,* "hang out," in recording studios at all hours, even and especially when there is no recording to be done.

The studio offers a very impressive array of music recording technologies. At the time of my initial visit in 1997, the first floor housed a twenty-four-track analog studio used for recording dangdut, rock, and pop music, while upstairs was a thirty-two-track digital studio (with over one hundred virtual tracks) used for producing electronic dance music and creating dance remixes of dangdut songs. The studio also owned samplers, synthesizers, amplifiers, and racks full of state-of-the-art electronic effects. In another upstairs room a few powerful computers were set up; these were used for mastering, sequencing tracks, and creating cassette cover designs.

The fact that most of this technology originated in the so-called developed world was not without consequence. Raymond, the head engineer of the second-floor digital studio at the time of my first visit, told me he had struggled to learn English so that he could understand the technical manuals for the studio's equipment. He proudly reported that, after spending countless hours with an English-Indonesian dictionary, he now understood about 40 percent of the vocabulary in these manuals, and our conversations (in Indonesian) contained an abundance of English technical terms: *frequency response, gain, panpot, distortion,* and so on.

The spatialized division of labor between analog and digital recording technologies suggests that the producers at 601 Studio Lab had adopted the natural/synthetic and "dirty"/"clean" sonic distinctions often employed by popular music producers and consumers in the West (cf. Théberge 1997, 207–8). I was told that dangdut, like rock and roll, had to have a warm, rough, and unpolished sound. To record it digitally would be unthinkable, "not dangdut." Furthermore, everyone I spoke with at the studio agreed that the *gendang* drum—dangdut's central percussion instrument—sounds too thin and "clicky" if recorded digitally.[1]

Producing Dangdut

601 Studio Lab, according to Edy, was "the house that dangdut built." Indeed, the well-appointed studio owed its existence to dangdut music, more specifically to the wealth generated by hit dangdut songs released by Edy's father, Pak Paku (aka Lo Siang Fa), a successful dangdut cassette producer whose company, Maheswara Musik (a subsidiary of national independent label Musica), owned and operated the studio.

Pak Cecep, the Sundanese chief engineer of the ground-floor analog studio and a former rock musician, described for me the steps involved in producing a contemporary dangdut song. These are significant because they indicate that the worldwide spread of multitrack sound-recording technologies has not completely standardized the process of recording popular music in all parts of the world. Actual sound-engineering practices serve local needs and agendas, and they are

Pak Cecep at work in 601 Studio Lab, Cakung, East Jakarta.

shaped by preexisting aesthetic concerns. According to Pak Cecep, 601 studio personnel learned their craft by *praktek langsung, tanpa pendidikan* (direct practical knowledge, without education). Echoing New Order developmentalist discourse, Pak Cecep described dangdut as "left behind" (*ketinggalan*); for instance, while Indonesian pop producers had been using MIDI sequencers for over a decade (i.e., since the late 1980s), dangdut producers had only begun using them three years earlier (in 1994).

Pak Cecep spoke of two basic methods for recording dangdut. Some operators prefer to record all the vocals first, but he prefers to start with the instrumental accompaniment. He usually begins with rough vocals and the "piano" part of the song, which are later erased and rerecorded. With the piano and vocal tracks acting as a guide, the *gendang* (which Pak Cecep called the *tak-dhut*) is recorded over an electronic metronome, with the *tak* of the smaller, higher-pitched drum and the *dhut* of the lower drum on separate tracks. Next, the *tak* sound is reinforced by the sound of another *gendang* or by a muted electric-guitar string—a *tung*. In dangdut it is vitally important that the *gendang* be recorded and mixed properly, lest it sound too soft (*terlalu lembek*) in the final product. The instrument ideally should have an intense presence in the mix, an effect created by close miking of the drums and the use of reverberation and delay effects for the *tak*. Engineers at 601 used a special microphone designed for recording Western kick (bass) drums to record the *dhut*, so that its sonic presence (particularly its low-frequency response) was comparable to the visceral kick-drum sounds on contemporary rock and pop recordings. The audible result of these particular engineering practices is a powerful-sounding instrument that takes up the same sonic "space" as the kick, snare, and tom of a Western drum kit in contemporary pop and rock recordings. The sound of this technologically mediated *gendang* is quite distinct from the usual (also mediated) sound of tabla—the *gendang*'s organological source—in globally circulating recordings of Indian classical music, wherein the paired drums tend to sound more "natural" and less in the forefront of a mix. (An appropriate analogy would be the difference between the sounds of the drum kit on a rock versus a jazz record.)

After the *gendang* is recorded, usually by one of the top three Indonesian *gendang* virtuosos, Hussain, Madi, or Dada, an electric bass guitar is added.[2] Dangdut bass is difficult to play, requiring agility and a strong rhythmic sense, as it involves wide intervallic leaps and rapid, forceful motion resembling that found in salsa bass-playing. (The precise origin of this resemblance is something of a mystery, but in fact Latin American dance music and dangdut share many musical affinities, which could stem from Indonesians' knowledge of the former, from simple convergence, or, most likely, from both of these factors.) The recording of the bass-guitar part is followed by the laying down of rhythm section tracks consisting of a piano and a "clean" (nondistorted) electric guitar playing the chords of the song. The "piano" is always electronic—acoustic pianos in playable condition are exceedingly rare in Indonesia and are not usually found in recording studios. As in the case of the heavy bronze instruments of the gamelan, it is far easier to approximate the sound of a piano with a sampler or a synthesizer than to find room for such a massive apparatus. Pak Cecep explained that the clean electric guitar (*gitar klin*) is always recorded "dry" (*kering*) in dangdut; that is, without artificial reverberation or other effects added. This is one of the trademark features of the genre; further, the guitar's thin, percussive sound allows it to slice through the thick wall of midrange sound generated by the other instruments.

The fifth step, after recording *gendang*, bass, rhythm guitar, and piano, is the addition of a keyboard *pad* (often a "church organ" sound) that provides harmonic/chordal accompaniment to the song.[3] The *pad* (also called the *blok* or *rendaman*) fills out the overall sound and, as its name suggests, is supposed to lie beneath the other instruments, tending to be nearly inaudible in final mixes. Two separate keyboard "string" tracks are added next. To my knowledge, actual string ensembles are never used to play these parts on dangdut recordings; they are always played by synthesizers. The strings are divided into higher and lower octaves and are used to play "fill-ins," melodic phrases that fill the spaces between vocal passages. Pak Cecep remarked that the musical phrases played by the strings resemble those found in Indian film music (*mirip-mirip India*), in which string ensembles, both actual and electronic, have historically played a prominent melodic role.

The next step in Pak Cecep's method is to add percussion instruments, which are generally sampled and sequenced unless the producer is older and inexperienced with the new technology. Every dangdut song must include a tambourine track, the function of which is analogous to that of the high-hat and ride cymbal in pop and rock. Maracas are also frequently used in addition to the tambourine. Other percussion instruments are used primarily for fill-ins and are often incorporated into introductory or transitional instrumental passages. These instruments may include sampled congas, tympanis, gongs, and trap drums.

While actual drum kits are almost always part of a live dangdut ensemble (where they fill an auxiliary role in a percussion section dominated by *gendang* and tambourine), they are very rarely used in the studio. Like those of pianos, string ensembles, and other unwieldy, difficult-to-record sound sources, the sounds of the drum kit on most dangdut recordings are created through digital means. This practice is not only more cost-effective but also significantly influences the listener's expectations, such that if a dangdut song were ever recorded with actual drums, pianos, and strings, the result would likely sound strange and nonidiomatic to dangdut fans.

After the percussion is layered atop the original *tak-dhut* rhythm, Pak Cecep records the remaining instruments, all of which are used for melodic fill-ins. Since vocals are usually present in just over half of a dangdut song's total length, there is ample room for contributions from several different fill-in instruments. Required instruments include distorted lead guitar and two *suling* (bamboo flutes), one large and one small, tuned to the same scale an octave apart. Electrified mandolins (another import from Indian film music) were once standard in dangdut ensembles, but they have become somewhat less common in both recordings and live performance. Other instruments that play fill-ins in dangdut recordings include nylon-stringed "Spanish guitars" (for flamenco-like flourishes), saxophone, sitar, trumpet, oboe, keyboards (playing accordion, organ, piano, or analog synthesizer sounds), and the occasional traditional metallophone (usually *bonang* or *saron*). Fill-in instruments play alone or sometimes in unison with other instruments; for instance, in dangdut arrangements the mandolin often doubles the *suling* melody. In late 1999 and 2000, a popular fill-in instrument on dangdut recordings was the violin (*biola*), thanks to the contributions of a versatile young Indonesian violinist named Hendri Lamiri, who also played on numerous *pop Indonesia* albums released at that time. Lamiri was often asked to contribute violin parts to the most heavily promoted first and second songs on a dangdut cassette.

Interestingly, many of the "ethnic" instrumental sounds occasionally used for fill-ins on dangdut recordings are actually digital samples imported from the West. Dangdut producers make frequent use of the controversial Proteus "World" digital sample module and other "world music" sound libraries to add convincing sitars, gamelan instruments, and other "ethnic accents" (*logat etnis*) to their recordings. Critics in the West have decried these sound libraries as cultural imperialism in a box, serving up decontextualized sounds from the world's musical traditions as exotic raw material for Western music producers (e.g., Théberge 1997, 201–3). In this view, the predatory sonic appropriation made possible by this technology is a predictable extension of the musically and economically exploitative practices of First World "world music" or "world beat" artists (Feld 1988, 1996, 2000; T. Taylor 1997). This critique, while certainly powerful, does not address the possibility of *non*-Western producers, such as those at work at 601 Studio Lab, using these sonic tools for their own sound-engineering projects (see Davis 2005).

Below is a schematic summary of Pak Cecep's preferred method for recording the instruments of a dangdut song:

1. Guide tracks (metronome, sync tone [for MIDI sequences], rough piano, and vocals)
2. *Gendang* (*tak* and *dhut*)
3. Electric bass guitar
4. Electric rhythm guitar and electronic piano
5. "Pad" keyboard
6. Keyboard string sounds (high and low)
7. Percussion (tambourine, maracas, etc.)

8. All instrumental "fill-ins"
9. Vocals and backing vocals (see the discussion later in this chapter).

Clearly there are a large number of instruments to manage in a typical dangdut recording. Of course, one plausible (though rather deterministic) explanation for why dangdut songs have such crowded arrangements is that multitrack studio technology makes them possible. There is, however, another, more important reason for the sonic density of dangdut song arrangements that relates to dangdut's genre ideology of sonic inclusiveness: rather than producing music that stands in dialectical opposition to rock, pop, disco, traditional music, or any other musical style, dangdut producers, one could argue, attempt to absorb aspects of them all. But while dangdut recordings tend to use far more instruments than are usually part of a live dangdut ensemble, nonidiomatic instruments tend to be employed sparingly, usually as "fill-ins."

Whereas some *pop Indonesia* arrangers use Western musical notation to write out parts for each instrument in an arrangement, this practice is rare in dangdut. Most dangdut musicians do not read Western musical notes (known as *toge,* "bean sprouts," among Indonesian arrangers). The only notation they utilize occasionally is a handwritten chord chart similar to those used in jazz. For melodic instruments, most musicians play by "feeling" (*filing*)—using their own intuition and knowledge of dangdut style to generate their contributions. Again, a small number of virtuosos generally play on cassettes (Pak Cecep named just five *suling* players who at the time played on almost every dangdut song recorded in Jakarta); these experienced performers have little trouble choosing appropriate fill-in parts for songs.

After Pak Cecep records all the instruments in an arrangement, he records vocals on the remaining tracks. The time spent on recording vocals varies depending on the ability of the singer and the importance of the song being recorded. Vocals on a "champion" (*jago;* Betawi, *gaco*) song—usually the first song on a cassette and the one that is promoted through video clips and radio—may take three times as long to record as the other songs on a cassette. While instrumentalists are free to improvise their fill-ins, vocalists must precisely follow the melodic line—every melismatic twist and turn—of the composition, as previously recorded on a demo tape. Vocals are usually recorded sequentially, line by line, with the performer and the studio crew stopping and redoing all mistakes and proceeding in this fashion until the entire song has been completed. This can be a long and arduous process, sometimes taking over fifteen hours of studio time to complete one six-minute-long *jago* song's vocals.

Hierarchies of Musical Value in Dangdut Production

The scheme outlined above suggests that in dangdut music, the vocals play a more central, structuring role than in rock and pop music. I found further corroboration for this hypothesis when an amateur *gendang* player advised me to study the instrument by purchasing dangdut karaoke cassettes (which separate the vocals and the instruments into separate audio channels, allowing one to add one's own amplified voice over the accompaniment) and suggested that I play along with the track containing the *vocals* and nothing else. An experienced *gendang* player is thus able to reconstruct the entire rhythm of a song with only the vocals for a guide; often when other people heard me practicing rhythms on the *gendang,* they asked me what song I was playing, when in my mind I had only been playing abstracted rhythmic patterns and accents. Another clue is that although dangdut songs usually contain extended instrumental passages between sung verses and refrains, I have never encountered an entirely instrumental dangdut recording. Such a recording would violate genre conventions, because all the melodic, rhythmic, and sonic features of a dangdut song ideally derive from a vocal melody that constitutes its most essential component.[4]

Ranking second in dangdut's hierarchy of musical value is the beat. The *gendang* is the only instrument in the mix that rivals the vocals in volume, and the search for the perfectly recorded *gendang* preoccupies many Indonesian sound engineers. Until recently a dangdut recording without a "live" *gendang* was unimaginable, but with the advent in the 1990s of *dangdut disco* and other new hybrids, along with the development of digital sampling and looping technology, this is no longer the case. Nonetheless, the most controversial aspect of *dangdut trendy* recordings, according to many fans, was that they do not contain a real *gendang.* In early 2000, a successful *pop dangdut* hit recorded by Evie Tamala, "Aku Rindu Padamu" (I Long for You), lacked the *gendang* entirely, which may have made it more accessible to a middle-class audience. According to the album's liner notes, the song was an example of something called *unpluged* [*sic*] *dangdut*; instead of being played on the standard electrified dangdut instruments, its arrangement was dominated by violin (played by Hendri Lamiri) and acoustic guitars. This particular hybrid was engineered to attract an audience that was usually turned off by the dangdut beat, while retaining the interest of the core dangdut audience by virtue of its characteristically melancholy vocal melody and simple, plaintive lyrics.[5]

Another noteworthy feature of dangdut recordings is the prevalence of unequal, alternating pairs of instruments, a characteristic also found in gamelan and other indigenous Indonesian ensembles. The *gendang* consists of a large and a small drum; songs are recorded with both a smaller, higher-pitched *suling* and a larger, lower-pitched one; and even the string synthesizer parts are divided into lower and higher voices. A similar pairing could even be said to exist between the mandolin and the lead-guitar parts in a dangdut song. All these paired instruments are not played simultaneously but rather alternate in the course of the song. Is there an underlying musical/cultural logic at work behind these pairings? Ethnomusicologist Marina Roseman (1987, 1991) describes how the Temiar of peninsular Malaysia ascribe complementary gender meanings to the unequal pair of bamboo stampers they use in musical performances, with the smaller (and higher-pitched) tube representing woman and the larger, lower-pitched stamper signifying man. These stampers are played in alternation. Although I cannot claim the same ideological significance for the unequal instrumental pairs found in dangdut music, there does seem to be a connection between Indonesian ideas of complementarity (in which the presence of one entity implies the presence of the other) and the pairing of different-sized musical instruments in a range of ensembles. Furthermore, this notion of implicative copresence and complementarity seems to operate in the sphere of gender relations as well. Later chapters develop this idea further.

High-Tech but "Close to the People"

Dangdut's producers and fans often use the Indonesian verbs *merakyat*, "to be close to the people," and *memasyarakat*, "to be close to society," to describe dangdut music (see Weintraub 2006). Populist rhetoric aside, however, dangdut cassette production is highly centralized, high-tech, and capital-intensive, not unlike commercial country music production in Nashville. As in Nashville, a mere handful of well-paid session musicians play on almost all commercial releases, and to my surprise I discovered that the parts not played by these highly skilled professionals are often played by a computer: on dangdut recordings produced by younger arrangers, all keyboards and percussion parts other than the *gendang* (tambourines, maracas, trap drums, etc.) are programmed and played by a MIDI sequencer. While unquestionably depriving many studio session musicians of work, these technological advances have not dramatically changed the sound of the music and do not detract from the overall "liveness" of the final mix.[6] Although the sound quality on dangdut recordings has improved and the performances they contain have become technically flawless, the "pure" dangdut sound has remained fairly unchanged for the past two decades. Further, given the music's extraordinary cross-generational popularity, it seems unlikely that the genre will lose its stylistic conservatism. In dangdut, then, new technology is used to create familiar sounds in a more cost-effective manner, not to create new stylistic innovations.

Low-Tech Origins

The origins of dangdut songs contrast sharply with the capital-intensive process by which they are recorded. Hopeful composers usually submit songs to dangdut producers in the form of cassettes and handwritten lyric sheets. On such tapes (which are often old dangdut cassettes that have been recorded over), the songwriter usually sings the composition accompanied only by an acoustic guitar. In other instances, the only accompanying "instrument" on the recording is an empty pack of cigarettes striking a table. This is not viewed as a problem, however; as explained earlier, the vocal melody is the most important musical component of a dangdut song, with everything else left up to the arranger, should the song be chosen for recording. Rough song demos are often recorded by members of dangdut's primary audience — working-class and unemployed men — and this point of contact between producers and their market appears to be important. Pak Paku, the owner of 601 Studio Lab, was always willing to listen to the work of unknown songwriters who submitted cassettes, rather than relying exclusively on professional songwriters with a proven ability to produce hits. Some of his greatest successes, such as the male singer Asep Irama, first came to him as penniless hopefuls bearing cheaply recorded demo cassettes. Asep Irama (who received permission from Rhoma Irama to use "Irama" in his stage name) was reportedly so destitute that he made the entire journey to Pak Paku's North Jakarta office on foot.

Singers are also frequently recruited from the ranks of local performers from humble backgrounds. Pak Hassanudin, 601's dangdut vocal coach and producer, explained to me that there is no formal training necessary for singing dangdut; one either loves the genre and learns everything by listening to cassettes, or one cannot perform it. Even successful pop singers cannot sing dangdut well, he remarked, although dangdut singers usually have no trouble singing pop!

Dangdut vocal producer Pak Hassanudin during a recording session with artist Murni Cahnia, Cakung.

Unlike Indian film music, in which a very small number of "playback singers" have dominated recordings (Manuel 1988, 1993), dangdut vocalists are expected to have their own distinctive styles that set each of them apart from all the others. A frequent criticism of younger singers made by dangdut fans is that their vocal styles are too derivative of those of established stars. For example, some newer male singers are said to sound too much like Meggi Z or Rhoma Irama. Newer female singers, on the other hand, are more likely to be accused of having no singing ability at all and relying entirely on their looks, and almost all are compared unfavorably to the stars of the past, particularly the still-active queen of dangdut, Elvy Sukaesih.

One reason why dangdut vocals take so long to record, I was told by several producers and engineers, is that many singers are chosen for their faces (*muka*), not their voices, and their vocals therefore have to be painstakingly recorded and then processed electronically in order to be "acceptable." Three months before my first visit, 601 Studio Lab had acquired an Intonator, an electronic pitch-shifting device used to correct off-key singing, for the purpose of improving vocal quality in recordings and compensating for singers' limitations. Thus even the most low-tech of dangdut instruments, the voice, may be altered and enhanced by the mediating apparatus of the multitrack studio. Yet, as Pak Cecep pointed out, in vocal tracks "the important thing is the soul" (*yang penting jiwanya*) of the performance, not its pitch accuracy.

Sound and Language: Recording *Pop Alternatif*

601 Studio Lab was truly a multimediated place, and Edy's house, located a few blocks away in the same housing complex and where I stayed over often during the course of my research, was an extension of the studio. On a typical afternoon the house was filled with an aural collage of simultaneous, overlapping sounds: digitized gunshots and explosions emanating from a computer game, obscenity-filled American English dialogue from a DVD or satellite television channel, drum and keyboard patterns being played back on the sampler equipment in an upstairs bedroom, and occasionally the idle strumming of an acoustic guitar by one of the resident musicians. Often ideas for *pop Indonesia* songs or parts of them were generated by the informal music-making activities taking place in the house. One night Edo, one of Edy's chief producer/arrangers, demonstrated to me how he could produce an entire pop song in his room in under four hours with a sampler, an electric guitar, a digital keyboard synthesizer, and an extensive library of compact discs, including both commercially released recordings and specialized audio discs containing all manner of sounds and short musical passages expressly intended as raw material for sampling and looping.

Edy began branching into *pop Indonesia* when dangdut remixes, with which he had found his first commercial success, decreased in popularity. (He claimed he was not yet ready to try producing conventional dangdut albums.) In late 1999, Edy and his producer/arranger Edo started directing their energy toward producing an album by a young Sundanese singer-songwriter, who they hoped would produce a major hit for them. Patty (whose name appeared as "Fetty" on the recording studio schedule, reflecting an Indonesian pronunciation of her name) was a university student in her early twenties and a veteran of the Bandung underground rock scene. She had played in two bands previously (bass, guitar, and vocals), had some recordings to her credit, and now wished to become a solo artist. Originally Patty was to record three songs for an album to be titled *Tiga Warna* (Three Colors) featuring songs by three different women artists representing three genres: pop, R & B, and (Patty's contribution) *pop alternatif.* But when problems arose in the search for suitable pop and R & B artists, the strength of

Patty's original material encouraged Edy to scrap the Three Colors project in favor of a full-length album by Patty, which was to contain nine songs she wrote or cowrote and one cover song. The latter was the sentimental "Perjalanan" (Journey), written and originally recorded by Franky Sahilatua, a popular Indonesian folk-rock performer and songwriter of the 1980s whose music is now usually classified as *pop nostalgia*. Edy said he chose this song in order to provide the listener with a familiar guidepost on an album of new songs. Most of Patty's album, which was produced, arranged, and partially performed by Edo, fits well under the category of *pop alternatif*: catchy, guitar-based songs played over sampled rhythm loops. One slightly unusual song became known as the *ska-dhut* track because it featured a (sampled and looped) *gendang* track and a fast, upbeat-stressed rhythm.

I observed several recording sessions during which Patty sang vocals over Edo's previously recorded instrumental accompaniment. I found these sessions remarkable for their seriousness and intensity balanced by humor and an easygoing flexibility. Many people tend to be present at an Indonesian recording session, some of them not directly involved with the recording. Typically in attendance at Patty's *take vokal* (vocal recording sessions) were Edo the producer; Wandi the tape operator; Patty's friend Ira, who had come from Bandung to attend the sessions and provide moral support; Sonny from Asli Group (one of Maheswara Musik's most successful pop bands), who was there to help come up with harmony vocal lines and just to hang out; and myself, the ethnographer. At various points, Edy came into the studio to listen to what had been recorded and to give advice to Patty. He often suggested to her that she try to sound more *genit*, "flirtatious," and *keanak-anakan*, "childlike," without overdoing it and losing her own distinctive voice.[7] The main problem, Edo and Edy agreed, was that the "soul was still empty" (*jiwanya masih kosong*) in Patty's vocals. They sounded too "sad" (*sedih*) and lacked *filing*.

Despite these frustrations, the mood in the control room remained cheerful and easygoing, punctuated by moments of intense seriousness, but never impatience or annoyance. I was surprised that when the tape operator accidentally erased part of the vocal track (which had contained an unusually inspired take) due to a careless error, no one expressed anger or irritation. During a smoke break in the middle of an especially intense session, Edo walked out of the studio into the hallway and began to dance comically to the dangdut music emanating from a radio by the front entrance, using the music to "relieve stress" while

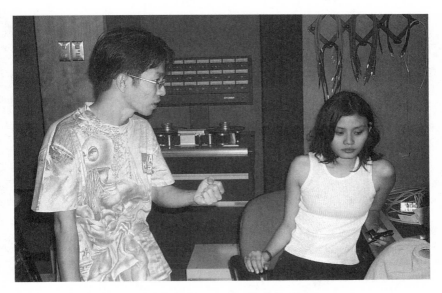

Edy Singh discusses a song with Patty in 601 Studio Lab, Cakung.

lightening the overall mood of the recording session participants (see chapter 8).

References to other musical genres and other places abounded during the session. Dangdut and Michael Jackson were brought up in discussions of sounds and techniques that Patty should avoid, although the conversation about the first of these seemed to partially contradict Edy's advice that Patty, in effect, sing more like a dangdut singer. At one point, Sonny sang a pentatonic harmony vocal line from one of Patty's songs "Javanese"-style (i.e., with a strong Javanese accent and traditional Javanese vocal timbre) for the amusement of the others. In another instance, Edo admonished Patty for swallowing syllables in her vocals and therefore sounding "Malaysian." "We're in Indonesia!" (*Kita ini di Indonesia!*), he insisted. Although at the time this seemed a rather insignificant moment in the continuous flow of conversation in the studio, I would suggest that what it means to be "in Indonesia" musically is hardly a self-evident statement. This sense of placement is constituted through cultural work such as that which was taking place in the studio at that very moment: the creation of a song in the national vernacular accompanied by a spectrum of technologically mediated sounds, providing one possible answer to the question of what it was to be a young, modern "Indonesian" in the year 2000 (cf. Yampolsky 1989, 9–10).

Recording and Loneliness

One Thursday night, considered a night of heightened supernatural activity by many Indonesians, Patty refused to finish a vocal recording shift because she was afraid. There was at least one reported *hantu* (ghost) in 601 Studio Lab — a spectral, silent young woman who was sighted in the kitchen next to the vocal booth by a few members of the staff, including Edo and Pak Cecep, the chief recording engineer. Even though Patty could see the others in the control room easily through the double glass panes, she felt isolated and vulnerable in the vocal booth. Although some may regard this incident as just an example of superstition in an otherwise modern, high-tech environment, in my view it illustrates perfectly the ethic of sociality I explore throughout this ethnography, in which the noisy presence of others is not only tolerated but valued, and its absence is considered threatening, a cause of loneliness and susceptibility to supernatural harm.

Critics of multitrack recording claim that the practice of overdubbing, of recording each part separately at separate moments in time, isolates musicians and eliminates the spontaneity of live performance. In 601 Studio Lab, the isolation of the vocal booth was sometimes construed as problematic, but not for these reasons. The separation of the performer in the sound booth from the producer, the engineer, and the hangers-on in the studio control room was considered necessary for recording vocals, and sometimes for recording instruments, but it did appear to be a cause of discomfort that studio workers attempted to overcome. A common practice for dangdut producers like Pak Hassanudin was to plug in a microphone to communicate with the person in the sound booth and leave it on, rather than using the built-in talkback system that required pressing a button to open a channel every time one wished to speak to the person on the other side of the glass. Although leaving a communication channel open could possibly interfere with the recording process, causing feedback or bleed-through, it allowed for easier and more direct communication with the singer and made it possible to put him or her more at ease, despite his or her physical isolation.

Lilis Karlina and Ethnic Techno-Hybrids

Lilis Karlina, who in 1999–2000 was one of Indonesia's most successful young dangdut singers, also records at 601 Studio Lab. Lilis's philosophy regarding musical innovation was similar to Edy's. In an interview she told me she paid close attention to international trends such as (in

1999) Latin crossover pop but also enthusiastically drew on "ethnic" elements, her trademark, when seeking new material to record. "I *am* Sundanese, after all," she explained. Many of Lilis's biggest hits have been dangdut-ethnic hybrids. Her song "Goyang Karawang" (Dance of Karawang) mixed dangdut and *jaipongan,* a combination to which the lyrics explicitly referred (cf. Spiller 2001). Her most recent hit, "Cinta Terisolasi" (which can mean both "Isolated Love" and "Love Stuck Like Cellophane Tape," the latter perhaps more characteristic of dangdut songs in its use of a prosaic simile to describe the tenacity of romantic love), contained a melancholy, "Mandarin"-style violin part (played by the ubiquitous Hendri Lamiri) reminiscent of the Chinese *er-hu* and a *jaipong*-like rhythm that Edy identified as actually originating in Banyuwangi, a region on the eastern tip of Java. Despite the difficulty of playing this nonstandard rhythm, the demand for this song encouraged many local dangdut ensembles to devise ways to perform it using the standard instrumental lineup, and in a short time it became a staple at live dangdut concerts. More recently, Lilis recorded a duet with Malaysian dangdut star Iwan that contained conspicuous Latin and disco elements, one of a handful of recordings released around the same time that experimented with combining dangdut and Latin sounds, among them Rhoma Irama's *Euphoria 2000* album.

One of Lilis Karlina's new songs was arranged by Cahyo, a talented pop arranger on Edy's production staff (Edy told me with a smile that all his staff *had* to work on dangdut songs, whether they wanted to or not). The rough mix I heard was extraordinary, incorporating Turkish, Indian, and hip hop rhythms. It included no fewer than six drum tracks employing three different types of drums—an ordinary *gendang dangdut,* a *dholak* (South Asian two-headed folk drum), and a set of *jaipongan*-style Sundanese barrel drums—all played by percussion virtuoso Hussain. Cahyo described the track as *musik gado-gado*—literally "music that resembles a mixed peanut salad." Music makers and listeners often use this expression to describe music that incorporates numerous different styles. Unfortunately, Lilis, who loved the song, discovered that the recording's key was beneath her vocal range, so the track needed to be either transposed by an electronic pitch-shifter or rerecorded (I'm not sure what she chose to do, or if the song was ever released).

Edy then told me something that surprised me. Another song Lilis would be recording for her new cassette was written by none other than *pop alternatif* songstress Patty. Apparently, one day Patty and Edo were jamming at Edy's house with guitar and sampler, and Patty decided to write a "Malay"-style song. The resulting demo recording, which includes voice, acoustic guitar, and a sped-up sampled *gendang* loop, resembles a fast-tempo, rather aggressive dangdut song with these words in the refrain:

> *You kawin lagi!*
> *Lebih baik bunuh diri*
> *Tapi aku takut mati.*
>
> [*You* married again!
> Better to kill myself . . .
> But I'm afraid of death.]

The defiant way in which Patty sings these lines makes the song humorous and angry, both characteristics that are a little unusual in a dangdut song about heartbreak, yet it accurately expresses the predicament of many Indonesian women whose husbands take another wife (polygyny is legal in Indonesia, as Islamic religious law allows one man to marry up to four wives). The use of the English *you* instead of the usual *kau*, *engkau*, or *kamu* (usually the first of these when anger is being expressed) is highly unusual in dangdut or in any other genre, but it is sometimes used in coarse everyday speech. Despite these oddities, when Edy played the song for Lilis, she instantly liked it and wanted to record it. It was difficult for me to interpret how Patty felt about Lilis's request, but mostly she seemed ambivalent about the honor of being perhaps the first female *pop alternatif* artist to write a song for a dangdut star. The song itself, as performed by Patty, owes more to the "woman-scorned" angst of global pop artists like Alanis Morissette (who had played an enormously successful concert in Jakarta a few years earlier) than to the dangdut song canon (the song is neither despairing nor flirtatious), yet it seemed to fit Lilis's progressive, cosmopolitan outlook and assertive image.[8]

The Anxieties of Global English

A final ethnographic anecdote about 601 Studio Lab suggests some of the limits to the atmosphere of creative collaboration and experimentation encouraged by Edy. I was listening to another of Patty's demos, a slow, heartbreak-inspired song titled "Mungkin Terlalu Lama" (Maybe Too Long [a Time]). Toward the end of the song, after the final chorus, Patty begins singing *oh baby I love you* repeatedly over the song's chord progression. This sudden shift from Indonesian to English, which sounded like a spontaneous outburst, appeared to be the emotional climax of the song, reminding me of the many Indonesian musicians who had told me that emotional directness was easier with English lyrics (cf. Wallach 2003a, 67–68). But when I commented to Edy and Edo about that part of the song, they laughed and assured me that all the *I love you*'s would be eliminated in the final version because they were inappropriate. Although Patty and many other young Indonesian songwriters frequently sang, wrote, and even thought in English phrases when practicing their craft, these phrases were considered out of place in mainstream commercial *pop Indonesia*. One of the songs on Patty's album actually does contain some English, but only in a short introductory section. Patty sings, *Goodbye, far-e-well to you, it's time to say goodbye . . . but I wish you well* in an electronically processed voice that seems to float in the ether over a detuned, almost unrecognizable drum-loop sample. This would seem to be an appropriate use of English, part of a "weird" (*aneh*) introductory section framing the song and analogous to the English-language samples used in Indonesian electronic dance music (Wallach 2005, 143), but not part of the song itself, and certainly not representing its emotional high point.

Thus the conventions of *pop Indonesia*, as enforced by cultural gatekeepers like Edy, limit artistic expression. In this case, Patty's use of English *I love you*'s on the demo tape undermined the ideological mission of *pop Indonesia* by pointing to a seeming deficiency in Standard (poetic/confessional) Indonesian's capacity to express authentic emotions. By switching to English, Patty revealed Indonesian to be expressively lacking compared to a foreign language that the majority of the pop audience, especially those listeners who live outside large cities, viewed with ambivalence and incomprehension. Furthermore, Patty's apparent need to resort to singing in English calls into question the supposition that Western-style pop music can be fully Indonesianized. Such a supposition legitimates *pop Indonesia* as a patriotic, unifying force for the nation instead of an antinational example of (post)colonial mimesis.

Paradi Studio: Cosmopolitanism and Computer-Assisted Composition

Located in a quiet, affluent neighborhood in Pancoran, East Jakarta, is the showroom for Paradi, the main supplier of high-end recording and sound equipment for companies and individuals in the Indonesian music industry. During my visits in 1999–2000, Paradi's expansive, state-of-the-art equipment showroom was also a working studio, though this fact was not widely publicized. Surrounded by high-powered computers, sound modules, keyboards, effects racks, and mixing equipment, Andy "Atis" Manuhutu, an Ambonese record producer, arranger, performer, and songwriter, pursued his mission to bring a new sound to the Indonesian music market. Before arriving in Jakarta after the fall of Soeharto, Andy worked for many years in Los Angeles for Michael Sembello, a respected producer and film soundtrack composer best known for his work on two 1980s Hollywood motion pictures, *Flashdance* and *Gremlins*. Sembello also produced an album of pop ethnic fusion songs for Andy that was released in Indonesia in 1993 but has since gone out of print.

Andy's music was unusual in the Indonesian context in two main ways. First, its rhythmic sensibility, chord voicings, and arrangements were far closer to those employed in American R & B than the music of any other Indonesian producer/arranger, a result of Andy's long apprenticeship in California. Second, although the majority of Andy's compositions were in one language or the other, some combined Indonesian and English, often with one language used for the verses and the other for the chorus. Although other recording artists occasionally inserted an English phrase into an Indonesian-language song for humorous effect, I had not encountered any other who lyrically placed the languages on equal footing. The reader will recall the previous anecdote about Patty's demo tape, in which Edy deemed the English lyrics sung at the end of the song inappropriate for a commercial release in Indonesia, as well as the practice discussed in chapter 3 of keeping Western and Indonesian music spatially separate in Indonesian record stores.

Certainly Andy's decision to record songs that alternate between English and Indonesian (and, in one Latin-tinged song, Indonesian and Spanish) constituted an artistic risk of sorts.[9] But Andy was interested primarily in middle-class and elite consumers (in contrast to Edy, whose background in dangdut made him more of a populist), and in our conversations he argued that the tremendous influence of Western popular music has created a hybrid subjectivity in Indonesia, especially among youth, which embraces and identifies with global pop artists. He explained that young, affluent listeners are therefore not invested in maintaining the artificial separation between "Indonesian" and "non-Indonesian" music demanded by old-fashioned nationalist rhetoric; rather, they long for indigenous pop music that acknowledges their affective attachment to global popular culture and to English. In the course of my research among young, educated members of the multi-ethnic, urban middle-to-upper class, I found much evidence to support

Andy's argument. However, his claims seem to apply most of all to Chinese Indonesians and to Christians like himself, people who do not feel the persistent ambivalence and anxieties about Western culture felt by those Indonesians who identify themselves as members of the Islamic world.

Andy's desire to create a more globally oriented national pop music meant that he did not seek to water down his compositions to make them palatable to a mass audience. In his songs he employed the seventh and ninth chords used in American R & B rather than the standard triadic chord progressions found in *pop Indonesia* (including pop songs with hip hop rhythmic influences), and he favored a more syncopated, complex rhythmic feel on his recordings. He claimed that the sophisticated young consumer of popular music in Indonesia prefers more *"authentic-sounding"* R & B.

In addition to bringing a new approach to Indonesian pop, following his arrival in Jakarta Andy tried to introduce the American music industry's ethic of professionalism into the day-to-day workings of his production company, which he co-owned with Paradi's owner. This was not always easy. The singers with whom he worked complained that he was a harsh critic—*"His number one favorite thing to do is intimidate people!"* said one, half-jokingly—and many employees had trouble understanding why he could be stern and serious during work hours and then become relaxed and friendly after work ended. Andy also encouraged his artists to negotiate contracts carefully and to seek legal representation, both rather unusual practices in a music business where informal patron-client relationships between producers and artists were the rule.

Two singers who worked with Andy were Amanda and Anggie, sisters who came from a family of female performers. Their maternal grandmother was a *keroncong* singer; their mother sang *pop Indonesia*. The sisters chose American R & B, which they sang with skill and savvy, and they mentioned Aretha Franklin as a primary role model. Their mother used to read them the *Jakarta Post* regularly in order to teach them English, and both sisters spoke the language fluently, though during the period of my fieldwork their studio banter with Andy was dominated by colloquial Jakartanese Indonesian.

Amanda and Anggie helped write the melodies and lyrics for their songs, as Andy encouraged his artists to be involved in the writing process. Their songs were often obliquely about Christian themes, though the lyrics were always ambiguous, and the compositions could be interpreted as love songs. This was exemplified in song titles like "B My

Savior" and "Satu Bersamamu" (One with You). The sisters, who were raised in a Javanese Muslim household, had converted to Protestant Christianity (to their mother's dismay), as had many of the singers who worked with Andy.

Like many contemporary music producers around the world, Andy was able to play back an entire song from his studio computer. On the afternoon of February 14, 2000, during one of my visits, he was working on an as-yet-untitled song for which twenty tracks had already been sequenced, all of them using the electronically generated sounds stored in the memory banks of the keyboards and sound modules in the studio. The instruments that these sounds were designed to resemble, to judge from their names on the computer screen and their actual timbre, included a Rhodes electric piano, an electric bass, a grand piano, a wood block, a shaker, a tambourine, two snare drums, a kick drum, cymbals, a sitar, a string section (on two separate tracks), and an ethereal synthesizer sound called "InTheAir."

The techniques Andy used for inputting each sound varied. Often he physically played instrumental parts into the sequencer without much editing, in order to preserve a "*human feel.*" String parts, by contrast, were entered using a computer mouse to place notes on a musical staff on the screen, in order to produce the more open chord voicings characteristic of real string ensembles but difficult and counterintuitive to play on a keyboard. Bass and drums, the foundation of the song, were inputted by triggering the sounds in real time from a synthesizer keyboard. Andy then edited these parts extensively—his sequencing software allowing him to do so with great precision—until the exact rhythmic feel he intended could be realized. Using a computer keyboard, Andy could input numerical values that controlled how far ahead of or behind the electronic metronomic pulse an instrument was sounded. Andy told me he always set the kick (bass) drum at zero, exactly "*on the beat.*" The snare drum was moved slightly behind the beat, while the attack of the bass-guitar notes was usually moved considerably behind the beat, about twenty-four milliseconds, in order to produce the right "*groove*" (see Keil and Feld 1994).

Unlike the drums, whose time intervals were consistent throughout the entire song, the bass part was more flexible, and parts of the bass line that "*sounded cool*" in the original performance were kept as they were. The rest of the track could also be computer edited: discordant or extraneous notes could be deleted, specific sounds could be changed (from an acoustic to an electric piano, for example), and new sections could be created by cutting, copying, and pasting musical material in the same way that text is manipulated on a word processor.

Partway through my visit, Amanda and Anggie arrived. After a short interval of friendly small talk, Andy asked Amanda to sing her vocal line on top of the electronic playback. While she sang, Andy coached her, and Anggie occasionally inserted backing harmony vocals. The singing techniques favored in Indonesian traditional music (and in dangdut) differ from the less nasal, more diaphragmatic technique used in Western music, including R & B. During Amanda's performance, Andy shouted out reminders in English: "*Don't get lazy!*" "*Don't fade out on me!*" "*Same power!*" to encourage her to project from her diaphragm through an entire stanza, so that the final syllables of a phrase would not trail off. Since Amanda was not using a microphone, it was harder to conceal when she ran out of air while singing. She was also advised, "*Don't slide the note—hit the note!*" when she sang with excessive portamento.

Although Andy called the habits of trailing off at the end of vocal phrases and sliding up to notes "laziness," these habits are in fact quite common in dangdut and *pop Indonesia,* so much so that they are really more like techniques than habits. Indeed, descending, melismatic vocal lines that slide languidly down to the tonic are an important element in dangdut's expression of musical sensuality (R. Anderson Sutton, personal communication, August 2000). These techniques are difficult to unlearn, even for those whose primary orientation is toward Western pop, and few Indonesian singers are told to do so.

After Amanda sang the song a few times, Andy returned to adding more tracks to the instrumental accompaniment. Although very "American" in his working methods in some ways, he also had the very Indonesian capacity to perform delicate tasks in a room full of noisy distractions. Somehow while the others in the room were laughing, joking, and loudly talking on their cell phones, Andy managed to use the keyboard to play a sampled tabla part that enhanced the overall impact of the song. "*Notice I wasn't playing the tabla ethnically,*" remarked Andy proudly afterward, saying that the part instead had a "*black groove,*" "*the way an American would play it.*" In fact, Andy's choice to add a tabla to the song was influenced by "Desert Rose," the 1999 international hit song by Sting and Algerian *raï* star Cheb Mami, which contains some North African percussion. (A video for the song had appeared earlier that day on a television tuned to MTV kept above Andy's mixing desk.) The fact that tabla sounds figure prominently in dangdut recordings was most certainly not a consideration. Andy copied and pasted the tabla part so that it recurred throughout the song. He then asked Amanda to sing once more over the playback. "*Swing with the tabla now,*" he instructed.

The activities that took place in Andy Atis's studio exemplify a cosmopolitan impulse in Indonesian popular music production; they also provide a glimpse of how religious difference can be encoded into music recordings. Using sophisticated technology that allowed a single musician to create an entire multitrack soundscape, Andy brought global sounds into the Indonesian context, his mission to create world-class music entailing the avoidance of all things "ethnic," including vocal technique.

Andy's music was intended to compete directly with the imported products it resembled, yet the segregationist practices of music retail outlets prevented a relationship of equal footing between Western and Indonesian R & B; the former was considered a specific, separate genre with its own conventions that was meant to be less *easy listening* (accessible and pleasant sounding) than pop, while the latter was grouped with the other *pop Indonesia* styles, inviting inappropriate comparisons and expectations.[10] As with the other music producers discussed in this chapter, Andy Manuhutu used the recording studio as an agent of cultural change by harnessing its ability to facilitate the creation of innovative musical fusions. The final studio discussed in this chapter represents a similar strategy of techno-hybridization that is employed in the service of some strikingly dissimilar social and artistic goals.

Techno-Hybridity in the Underground: Eternal Madness and Underdog State

Our third studio offers a different perspective from those provided by 601 Studio Lab and Paradi. The Underdog State recording facility is located in a middle-class residential neighborhood in Denpasar, Bali. It is quite low-tech and low-budget compared to the recording studios discussed previously in this chapter—much of its recorded output is produced on a Tascam 424 four-track cassette recorder—yet the engineering strategies of its owner, Sabdo Mulyo ("Moel"), are equally ambitious. Moel is the bassist, vocalist, and main songwriter of Eternal Madness, a Denpasar-based metal band that holds the distinction of being one of the few Indonesian groups attempting to combine traditional (in this case, Balinese) music with the modern noise of underground metal.

Moel at Underdog State, Denpasar, Bali.

Like similar facilities in other cities, Underdog State is a favorite hangout spot. In addition to a recording studio, it contains a rehearsal space, a silk-screening workshop (for creating band T-shirts, stickers, and cassette covers), and a billiards table. The house occupied by Underdog State acts as a base camp for many members of Bali's sizable underground music scene, which is known for its strong punk, black-metal, and hardcore contingents. Eternal Madness plays death metal, a style that is more popular in the Jakarta and Surabaya underground scenes than in Bali—and plays it with a definite twist. The group, which at the time of my visit in mid-2000 consisted of Moel on bass and vocals, Putu Pradnya Pramana Astawa (Didot) on guitar, and a drum machine, has created a new subgenre for its music: *lunatic ethnic death grind metal.* In an undated Indonesian press release, the band claims its 2000 cassette *Bongkar Batas* (Break Down Boundaries) "is a work of art that responds to the blindness and deafness of Indonesian musicians toward exploiting their own identities in the concept and style of metal music." This extraordinary album, most of which was recorded at Underdog State, contains some definite "Balinese" elements: pentatonic melodies, a Balinese funerary chant, and abrupt rhythmic transitions strongly reminiscent of *gamelan gong kebyar,* the flashiest and most aggressive Balinese gamelan style (see Tenzer 2000).

Eternal Madness uses no traditional instruments, and the distorted, metallic onslaught of its music, complete with the raspy, growling vocals characteristic of the death metal subgenre, often seems to overwhelm the other elements in the music. Yet even in the most conventional passages on *Bongkar Batas* there is an audible difference that, while subtle, seems foreign to the conventions of death metal music. This sonic difference is located in the unusual rhythmic relationships between the drum machine, the guitar, and the bass, which resemble those existing between instruments in a traditional Balinese ensemble. Balinese traditional music is organized around points of rhythmic convergence at the ends of phrase units. Until those points are reached, however, the different metallophones in an ensemble are rarely struck at the same time. Instead of playing together in unison, each musician's instrument occupies a distinct place in the measure, filling up the sonic space with an interlocking, overlapping web of sound, "a dynamic intertwining of rhythms and tones" (Herbst 1997, 112). Moel revealed that this effect of "playing against" (*main kontra*) was achieved in Eternal Madness's music through the unique way in which the songs on the album were recorded.

Moel explained that when recording a song, he starts with a rhythm guitar part that plays the basic riffs (in gamelan terminology, the "nuclear melody") of the piece. Next, lead-guitar parts are added over the riffs; these parts resemble the decorative melodic phrases that ornament the nuclear melody in Balinese gamelan music. The original guitar track is then erased. Only then are the programmed drums added. Rather than the guitar following the beat of the drums, then, the drums play *around* the guitar, playing accents, filling in empty space, and marking transitions the way the *kendang* (traditional Balinese barrel drum, different from the *gendang* used in dangdut) player would in a gamelan performance.

Although Moel uses only samples of a standard Western trap-drum kit, he intentionally programs the drum machine to evoke Balinese drumming styles. He told me that he often uses the machine's sampled China-crash cymbal to play the part of the *kecrek*, loud crashing cymbals played in traditional Balinese ensembles that punctuate the core melody. Many of the drum parts Moel programs would be extremely difficult or impossible for an actual drummer to play; so far Eternal Madness has not found a human drummer capable of replacing their drum machine.

After the drums are programmed and recorded, Moel adds the bass guitar. He claimed that the bass is like the large gong in a gamelan ensemble. To my ears, the bass lines in Eternal Madness songs more often play the role of the *bonang* (tuned rows of kettle gongs). Like the *bonang,* Moel's bass plays countermelodies "underneath" the nuclear melody, while the gong marks the end of musical phrases. Moel's growled, death-metal-style vocals are recorded last.

The method for recording Eternal Madness songs (first guitar, then drums, then bass, then vocals) is quite unlike the standard technique for recording rock music employed by both Indonesian and Western producers: drum tracks first; then bass; then guitars, keyboards, and so on; then vocals. The latter method guarantees that all the instruments will follow the same rhythm (dictated by the drums) with minimal deviation. In contrast, Eternal Madness creates hybrid music through an unorthodox use of music technology that reflects Balinese aesthetics more than those of rock, allowing a greater degree of rhythmic independence for each instrument.

From the Village to the World

Studio-based sound-engineering practices tend to facilitate a certain level of reflexivity. The nature of the recording process lends itself to a particular kind of critical engagement with the work that is taking shape through it, which encourages thoughts about the music's origins, meanings, and potential audiences (Porcello 1998; Meintjes 2003). Moel has many such thoughts regarding his music. Eternal Madness's two albums, *Offerings to Rangda* (1996, now out of print) and *Bongkar Batas* (2000), both released on small, independent record labels, target an Indonesian underground audience, but again with a twist. Moel does not believe that death metal fans in Jakarta and other large cities like his music very much; they consider it too "ethnic" and therefore low-class and backward (*kampungan*), akin to the way middle-class urban Indonesians regard dangdut and *pop daerah.*[11] But Moel believes that an international audience would find his music interesting and unique. Eternal Madness received positive responses to its music during a visit to Australia, and Moel hopes his music will one day reach an international underground audience, perhaps even a world music/world beat audience, even though the latter is often comprised of "grown-ups" too old for loud youth music like metal (cf. T. Taylor 1997, 6).

Moel claims that he does not want to be an American, but rather that his goal is "to be a Balinese who plays death metal music" (*jadi orang Bali yang main musik death metal*). He doesn't want to copy an

American sound, and if that is not good enough for the America-obsessed kids in Jakarta, so be it. Instead of focusing exclusively on the urban centers of the underground music movement in Indonesia, Moel has taken his music directly to rural areas all over Java and Bali, riding ferries, buses, trains, and motorcycles to smaller villages and hamlets. Moel claims that this promotional strategy has allowed him to sell fifteen thousand copies of *Bongkar Batas,* which is more than many major-label Indonesian rock cassettes sell unless they score a big hit. He criticizes members of large urban underground scenes like Jakarta and Bandung for having what he calls a "racial" (*rasial*) view of rural listeners, that is, a prejudice bordering on racism. Moel, on the other hand, finds that this rural audience appreciates the traditional elements in the music of Eternal Madness as well as the band's occult and mythological imagery, which resembles those found in the most popular underground genre in rural areas: black metal. Thus, the music of Eternal Madness appeals to rural audiences by joining together local folklore, village music traditions, and a generation-specific musical style with both national and global dimensions. This combination seems to have had less impact on urban areas. Although city-based underground scene members with whom I spoke seemed to respect Eternal Madness's music, they were generally not interested in following the group's lead and creating their own ethnic hybrids. Indeed, EM's undertaking appeared rather tangential to the central aspirations of the Indonesian underground scene.

Moel has not lost sight of the international market; he told me he planned to rerecord four songs from *Bongkar Batas* with an actual Balinese gamelan, part of an EP intended "for export." He was collaborating on this project with Yudena, an avant-garde Balinese composer, who planned to use computer software to adjust the tuning of the gamelan ensemble to make its contribution compatible with the preexisting instruments on the recording. This project, then, is a sort of "remix," and like the addition of Sundanese and Javanese musical elements in dangdut songs, it represents a kind of "retraditionalization" of popular sounds. In this case, the objective appears to be making the "ethnic" component in Eternal Madness's music more intelligible to an international underground/world beat audience.

While the sonic juxtapositions found in dangdut could be said to be symptomatic of a characteristically Indonesian mode of coping with the heterogeneity and fragmentation of modern life, the techno-hybrid grooves of Eternal Madness, like those of Krakatau and other progressive ethnic groups, suggest fusion more than juxtaposition. Rather than evoking coexistence without synthesis, Eternal Madness uses multitrack technology to create recordings that meld together ethnic and underground sounds, such that it is often quite difficult to detect where one begins and the other leaves off. This, of course, appears to be the point. The powerful music of Eternal Madness expresses the triumph of the individual over the pitfalls of the postcolonial condition, in which modernity, on the one hand, and pride in one's traditional cultural heritage, on the other, are often viewed as mutually exclusive alternatives. Eternal Madness "breaks down boundaries" between these two poles—which might otherwise prevent postcolonial subjects from achieving a unified subjectivity—with "*a wild sonic attack of twisted rhythms and howling vocals*" (Eternal Madness official Web site).

Conclusions: Technology, Hybridity, Sociality

This chapter has visited three recording-studio environments and analyzed the musical and cultural dynamics that take place in them. We have seen how processes of musical production and innovation are realized through technological means and how they are framed by particular notions of genre and subgenre. Greg Urban (2001, 55–56) suggests that anthropologists investigate "sites of replication" in contemporary complex societies, where cultural forms are primarily circulated by dissemination (rather than replication, that is, reperformance), in order to understand the specialized knowledge and skills necessary to produce new culture. An examination of recording studios in Indonesia does indeed provide important insights into how and why recorded artifacts are produced.

First, understandings of the musical genre are paramount in determining how a song is recorded and promoted; in turn, the production decisions of producers, arrangers, and other specialized personnel can transform or reconfigure these understandings. For example, the notion that dangdut should be recorded "live" with analog equipment instead of with state-of-the-art technology was once widely shared, but now the idea that dangdut music benefits from high production values, MIDI programming, and sophisticated mixing equipment has become accepted among producers and sound engineers. Developments like these reconfigure the genre expectations of performers, producers, and listeners (though sometimes they also generate a longing for older, now-obsolete sounds, a phenomenon Tim Taylor calls "technostalgia"

[2001]). On the other hand, genre expectations have a strong "inertial" component (Urban 2001), and many attempts to create novel musical forms do not succeed commercially, thus severely limiting their cultural impact. Music producers gamble on the acceptance of the new hybrid genres they invent, and if the gamble is successful, as it was in the case of Lilis Karlina's Sundanese/Chinese/Banyuwangi/dangdut hybrid "Cinta Terisolasi," the commercial rewards can be well worth the risk.

Second, it is worth repeating that despite the potential of multitrack recording and electronic music technology to isolate performers, mechanize music production, and attenuate musical interactions, studio production in Indonesia remains an exuberantly social process, and most musical decisions are made collectively. The tendency in the West to treat the recording studio as a sterile musical laboratory off-limits to nonparticipants appears not to have traveled with the technology. One reason for this, aside from the generally more sociable quality of life in Indonesia, is the lack of formally trained recording engineers who take themselves and their technical mastery seriously enough to attempt to impose a technocratic disciplinary regime on the performers who enter their domain (for counterexamples see Meintjes 2003; Moehn 2005). A second reason relates to the remarkable ability of Indonesian musicians and producers to concentrate on the performance of complex tasks in the studio while surrounded by crowds of people noisily sharing the same space. Despite all its potential distractions, participants seem to prefer the jocular unruliness of the typical Indonesian recording-studio environment to the loneliness they might feel working by themselves.

5

On Location

SHOOTING MUSIC VIDEO CLIPS

As is the case with recording studios, a discussion of Indonesian music videos must take into account the interactional dimension of cultural production: the negotiation of meaning and the concretization of metacultural abstractions that take place "on location," in this case, at taping sessions for Indonesian video clips. In the following discussion I also wish to extend my arguments regarding social class in Indonesia. While the ascendancy of mass-mediated popular culture coincided with (and arguably anticipated) the elision of class stratification and the rise of the middle class in Western countries, in Indonesia and elsewhere in the developing world the national popular cultures that have emerged in the last half century have had to respond to perseverant class distinctions—most conspicuously, the continuing presence of a poor and uneducated majority that nonetheless possesses some purchasing power. We have seen how in the Indonesian national popular music industry there arose a two-tiered hierarchy that distinguished between westernized, cosmopolitan national music and non-Western— but still national—music genres. Keeping this normative market segmentation in mind, I now turn to a discussion of Indonesian music videos and how they embody and develop assumptions about the social constitution of their audience and index class-inflected differences vis-à-vis cultural debates on modernity, cosmopolitanism, and Indonesian national identity.

Recorded Sound and Televisual Image

I view both static and moving images as contextualizing supplements to sound in popular music. My approach is therefore the opposite of the one assumed by cinema studies and generally prevalent in Western thought, which tends to elevate sight as the most "truthful" of the senses (Feld [1982] 1990). I am thus sympathetic to Andrew Goodwin's (1993) critique of studies that focus on music video's fragmented, "postmodern" character (e.g., Kaplan 1987). These analyses draw on film theory to elucidate the often disconnected, pastichelike visuals of music videos while largely ignoring their sonic dimension. Goodwin argues that it is precisely the soundtrack of music videos that provides them with coherence and affective unity, for music videos are intended to be not miniature films but rather imaginative visualizations of particular songs, and they follow a musical rather than a cinematic logic.

In general, the visual marketing of popular music tends to erect boundaries around its audience, while musical sound allows for greater ambiguity and social polysemy. This property may be intrinsic to the aural medium itself, which crosses physical boundaries with ease. Cultural critic Rey Chow writes: "While the image marks the body, in music one has to invent a different language of conceptualizing the body, that is, of perceiving its existence without marking and objectifying it as such" (1993, 392). In other words, musical sound is a felt presence that transgresses the boundaries of self and other that are traced by visual images. It is only through specific framing devices—both discursive and visual—that the embodied, affective intensity of musical encounters can be channeled efficiently into identity projects, lifestyles, and social narratives. In their attempt to promote the consumption of a specific musical artifact, music video producers make a series of explicit, if often contradictory, claims about the identities of artists and listeners by deploying a rhetoric of moving images that locates powerfully ambiguous sounds in visible bodies and in imaginary but recognizable social spaces. On a more fundamental level, exploring the tension between the polysemy of sound and the markedness of image can provide insight into a paradoxical feature of popular music everywhere: the fact that a medium that contains such powerful associations with particular social categories so easily transcends those categories in its reception.

Music Video in Indonesia

When I arrived in Jakarta in October 1999 to begin my dissertation fieldwork, the city's attention was focused on a Special Session (Sidang Istimewa) of the recently elected People's Consultative Assembly. Fears of a repeat of the massive rioting that had engulfed Jakarta in May 1998 caused the normally congested thoroughfares of the city to be eerily quiet. No one could predict what the outcome of the session would be or whether it would lead to an eruption of violence. I, too, followed the session's proceedings on television, watching the representatives of competing political parties debate and deliberate over which candidate should become Indonesia's fourth president. To my surprise, the sober-minded television coverage was periodically interrupted by Indonesian pop, rap, and rock music videos, which appeared alongside the somewhat more predictable commercials for national brands of tea, vitamins, and milk. From my perspective, this was roughly akin to an American network broadcasting a Metallica video in its entirety in the middle of coverage of the Republican National Convention. One of the newscasters on the station I was watching (SCTV) commented that the music could "calm" viewers during this time of tension and uncertainty. In fact, music videos are ubiquitous on Indonesian television, and they frequently appear as filler between regular programs in addition to appearing in programs devoted to music. Apparently, this was the case even during news coverage of a momentous occasion in Indonesian history.

Making music video clips is an essential promotional activity for the Indonesian music industry. Without an accompanying *klip* broadcast on Indonesian television (which usually involves giving some form of payola to each television network), a newly released single in a commercial genre has little hope of finding an audience. The production methods for creating clips vary according to genre and budget, and although it is beyond the scope of this ethnography to fully analyze filming techniques employed in Indonesian videos, it is possible to make a primary distinction between dangdut song clips and pop/rock clips. Dangdut clips tend to feature the leisurely paced, often narrativized visuals found in karaoke videos and are often shot on location (although one might expect them to resemble the musical sequences in Indian films, this does not appear to be the case). Pop/rock clips are usually shot in television studios and tend to feature the faster edits and stylish, striking visuals of Western music videos broadcast on MTV and other global music channels. Often *dangdut trendy* videos are of this type as well, but not always; they sometimes appear to combine both approaches. In 1999–2000, production budgets tended to be significantly higher for pop/rock videos than for dangdut clips.

Images of Tradition and Opulence: Shooting a Dangdut Clip

On November 6, 1999, I attended the shooting (*syuting*) of a dangdut video clip that took place over the course of a long seventeen-hour day in various Jakarta locales.[1] The featured artist was singer Iyeth Bustami, and the clip was for her soon-to-be-released song titled "Cinta Hanya Sekali" (Love [Happens] Only Once). Iyeth, an ethnic Malay from Riau province, had made a name for herself previously as a singer of Malay pop (*pop Melayu*), a regional (*daerah*) genre with an audience concentrated in Riau, coastal Sumatra, and Kalimantan (Indonesian Borneo). This was her first foray into a national style, and the concept behind the single was to bring together Malay pop's sentimentality with dangdut arrangements and rhythm. Maheswara Musik, the record label co-owned by Pak Paku (the father of Edy Singh, the record producer mentioned in the previous chapter), was releasing Iyeth's album, which, like most dangdut cassettes, was named after its first song—in this case, "Cinta Hanya Sekali." The shooting schedule was as follows:

9:00 a.m. to 1:00 p.m. (approximately): Shooting on location in Cijantung Mall, East Jakarta.

2:00 p.m. to 4:30 p.m.: Exterior shots of dancers and singer in the "Riau" section of "Beautiful Indonesia in Miniature" (Taman Mini Indonesia Indah), a Disneyland-like theme park located in East Jakarta that contains replicas of traditional buildings and artifacts from all of Indonesia's provinces, including now-independent East Timor.[2] Set-up for interior shots inside one of the Riau dwelling replicas.

5:00 p.m. to 9:00 p.m.: Shooting at an affluent private residence on the far eastern outskirts of Jakarta.

9:30 p.m. to 2:00 a.m.: Interior shots at Taman Mini and exterior nighttime shots on the steps of a traditional Malay wooden house (*atap limas*) replica.

This was not a high-budget production: the crew had only one camera, and their video equipment was comparable to that used for

Dancers in traditional costume perform for the camera during the making of the video clip for Iyeth Bustami's "Cinta Hanya Sekali," Taman Mini Indonesia Indah (Riau Exhibit), East Jakarta.

videotaping wedding receptions (in fact this was one of the services offered by the production company hired to make the clip). Nor was shooting on location particularly expensive: in Indonesia, outdoor filming does not take place on a "closed set"; the presence of people, cars, animals, and so on in the surrounding environment is tolerated, and there is no army of security guards to keep people out. Often shooting takes place without formal permission from the local authorities, though they are usually notified. At the theme park, Iyeth, the camera crew, and the other performers attracted an audience of park visitors who gathered around and watched them. Another music video clip was being shot simultaneously in the same exhibit area in front of a different Riau Malay structure, this one for a Muslim children's pop song. A choir of preadolescent girls wearing brightly colored Islamic headscarves gestured in unison and pretended to sing for the camera, momentarily catching the attention of passersby.

Because Iyeth was from Riau and her ethnicity was part of her musical persona, the Riau exhibit at the "Beautiful Indonesia in Miniature" theme park was chosen as a backdrop for the clip's dance sequences, which featured three male and three female dancers in traditional

Malay dress. During the editing process, these sequences would be interspersed with scenes of Iyeth wearing traditional Malay garb lip-synching the song. The interior shots in the theme park depicted Iyeth and the male actor who played her love interest dressed as bride and groom according to Malay custom (*adat*), part of a dream sequence in which Iyeth forlornly imagines her inattentive boyfriend finally marrying her in a lavish traditional ceremony.

In contrast, the scenes shot in the mall and the private residence (the house of a well-to-do public prosecutor, a friend of one of the crew members) depicted Iyeth and her onscreen boyfriend in stylish contemporary clothes. At the house, they were filmed sitting in a garden, riding in a shiny red sports car rented for the occasion, and interacting in the house's well-furnished living room. There were also scenes of Iyeth sitting alone in a bedroom, pining after her lover and lip-synching the song with tears in her eyes. (*Air mata palsu!* [Fake tears!], scoffed a crewmember.) The shooting was laborious, with frequent delays caused by equipment malfunctions, and many members of the rather large crew often had little to do other than smoke and chat. Iyeth endured the waits and the repeated takes without losing her composure, sneaking an occasional cigarette between shots. When I inquired, she vehemently denied growing weary of hearing a recording of her song played back over and over for each filmed sequence.

Unlike the nonnarrative pastiche of images found in many Western rock and pop videos, this particular clip was based on a rudimentary story. Narratives based on a song's lyrics are common in dangdut videos, and producers whom I interviewed claimed that their audience preferred stories that narrativized the lyrics of dangdut songs. In this particular clip, a young woman (Iyeth) and her handsome but neglectful boyfriend (a light-skinned young actor who appeared to be of partial European or Arab descent) are drifting apart because he is too busy to pay attention to her. In the clip, whenever the two lovers are together they are interrupted by the ringing of the boyfriend's cellular phone; he then answers the phone, begins talking, and abruptly walks off, leaving his girlfriend. Like the song itself, the clip concludes not with a happy ending or any other resolution of the narrative, but instead with the young woman continuing to tearfully lament her fate as the song's repeating refrain fades into silence.

The two main locales depicted in Iyeth's video are "traditional" "Riau" and "modern," stylish Jakarta. In a sense, the artificial traditional setting of Taman Mini's "Riau" exhibit constitutes a visual parallel to the aural representations of traditional Indonesian music in dangdut and *pop daerah*. Like the digital sampling of regional ethnic instruments, the dwelling replicas in Taman Mini are decontextualized approximations of cultural objects. The physical forms of these replicas (sonic, visual, or tactile) signify particular cultural traditions. But despite (or perhaps because of) the nontraditional methods of their creation, these cultural simulacra are powerful signs of "local culture" in the Indonesian mediascape, which, like mediated cultures elsewhere, has a tendency to reduce local cultures to a series of decontextualized, replicable artifacts that can be *re*contextualized as objects of value in a national (or international) cultural economy. Such objects derive their meaning and value not from their primary context of use but from public debates and negotiations over their significance for the nation and the market.

In the same vein, the visual juxtaposition of "traditional" settings and expressive culture with affluent, modern locales and objects (malls, middle-class homes, cellular phones, sports cars) in Iyeth's music clip resembles the layering of "ethnic Indonesian" and "modern Western" sounds in a single dangdut or *pop daerah* recording, suggesting that one can be both "Indonesian" (a national identity that for most Indonesians also includes belonging to a subnational, regional ethnicity) and "modern" at the same time. This, then, constitutes an important type of cultural work performed by videos and recordings, as they capture the fantasies and aspirations of an audience with multiple allegiances, conflicting desires, and dreams of unattainable wealth and comfort.

There is another possible interpretation of this particular video. Perhaps Iyeth's boyfriend neglects her because he has an unhealthy infatuation with modern technologies and comforts (symbolized by his cellular phone and sports car), and his abandonment of her is constitutive of his abandonment of "traditional culture," to which Iyeth, in her fantasies of a traditional village wedding, still clings. If one subscribes to this reading (which no one I spoke to on the set seemed to endorse), the video contains a critique of modern consumer culture and its erosion of traditional values. Yet the images of glamorous affluence in the mall and living room scenes nonetheless remain seductive, and Iyeth's fashionable attire in those scenes demonstrates that she is a fully modern individual despite her ties to the village. Also, the scenes in her large, private bedroom suggest that her character comes from a middle-class background. Perhaps the message the clip conveys is that one should avoid becoming *excessively* modern and leaving village customs behind completely, for this can only lead to heartbreak.

Shooting a close-up of Iyeth, Taman Mini.

Another component of the cultural work performed by music video's rhetorical manipulation of images is the visual embodiment of the music. Iyeth's facial expressions, the tears in her eyes, the traditional costumes and refined movements of the dancers, the silky blue nightgown that Iyeth wears in the bedroom scenes (which she put on over her clothes while fully dressed) all convey information to the viewer about how to move to the music and what types of desiring and desirable bodies are moved by it.[3] The clip's combination of recognizable (albeit unreal) social settings and displayed human bodies — recognizable by their costumes, movements, and emotional expressions — situates the song in an idealized social context. This purposeful "translation" of musical sound into televisual image endeavors to focus audience desires on the musical artifact as a metonym for the urban opulence, female beauty, and folkloric authenticity portrayed in the clip.

Thus successful video clips are not those that portray a plausible social world for the song to inhabit, but those that through compelling sound and spectacle suspend viewers' disbelief. Anthropologist Edward Bruner writes, "The function and the promise of national myths is to

Iyeth performing for the camera, Taman Mini.

resolve contradictions, if not in life, then in narrative and performance" (2001, 900). National popular cultures can also perform this function through their projection of persuasive fictions of identity that elide the contradictions inherent in stratified societies.

Ultimately, sales of Iyeth's album proved disappointing, even though the clip did receive some television airplay and the song was nominated for a Dangdut Award.[4] Edy Singh attributed the cassette's lack of commercial success to Iyeth's singing technique. Because her roots were in *pop Melayu,* not in dangdut, he explained, she sang with too much Western-style vibrato, which was inappropriate for singing the vocal ornaments (*cengkok*) of dangdut-style vocals. Thus dangdut fans reacted negatively. Several fans with whom I spoke did say they thought "Cinta Hanya Sekali" was too weepy (*cengeng*) to be good dangdut. Dangdut songs can, of course, be sad (and often are), but their vocals usually do not make use of the sung histrionics of sentimental pop: vibrato, strong vocal projection, staccato phrasing, and wide intervallic leaps.

Iyeth's single thus represents an unsuccessful experiment in musical hybridization; to employ Greg Urban's terminology, its novel combination of sentimental *pop Melayu* and dangdut failed to carve out new social pathways for its dissemination that could combine the audiences of different genres (2001). The album might have enjoyed greater success had it been marketed solely to a Riau audience, but problems with distribution and piracy, and the limited size of the Riau market, necessitated finding a large national, multiethnic audience for the album in order to achieve Paku's commercial goals for it. Edy blamed the album's failure to achieve those goals on a failed sound-engineering experiment that produced a musical hybrid that lacked vigor, so to speak, in the marketplace.

Shooting a Rock Clip: Netral's "Cahaya Bulan"

While Iyeth's dangdut video evoked both traditional village life in Riau and the metropolitan affluence of Jakarta, many Indonesian pop and rock videos take place in a fantastic, surreal universe that has no obvious connection to actual places in Indonesia. What follows is an account of a very different sort of video shoot: the making of a rock video for a song by Netral (Neutral), a Jakarta-based band that had four albums to its credit. Netral emerged in the early 1990s as one of the first commercially successful Indonesian alternative rock bands. Its music is heavily influenced by Nirvana, the Sex Pistols, and Metallica, and the band was once known as the "Indonesian Nirvana."[5] Netral's video for "Nurani," a song released in 1999, was one of the clips SCTV played during the broadcast coverage of the Special Session of the People's Consultative Assembly.[6]

The video shoot described next was for a video clip intended to accompany a newly recorded song titled "Cahaya Bulan" (Moonlight), one of two new songs included on Netral's upcoming "greatest hits" compilation. Because I was personally involved, in a minor fashion, in the production of this clip, at times I switch to a more autobiographical mode of narration.

The song's few lyrics are simple but poetic:

> *Cahaya bulan menemani aku* [repeat]
> *Mencumbu mesra singgasana malam*
> *Bersenda gurau hibur bintang–bintang*
>
> [Refrain:]
> *Walaupun sedih dan senang melanda hati*
> *Kau tetap cahaya bulanku.*

[The moonlight keeps me company
Fondly caresses the night's throne
Joking around, entertaining the stars

(Refrain:)
Although sadness and joy overwhelm the heart,
You are always my moonlight.][7]

In spite of the meditative tone of the text, the song is a loud, punk-influenced rock anthem with soaring electric-guitar solos and pounding drums. The words are sung with triumphant bravado by Netral's lead vocalist, Bagus Dhanar Dhana, and multitracked backing vocals, performed by versatile *pop Indonesia* and *pop Rohani* singer Dessy Fitri, echo the song's pivotal verse, "The moonlight keeps me company." After attending a portion of the recording of "Cahaya Bulan" in a West Jakarta studio complex two months earlier, I was invited to the shooting of the song's video clip, which was expected to be the primary vehicle for promoting both the song and the "greatest hits" cassette on which it was to be included. The experience of observing and participating in the production of this video clip revealed a visual logic of global-national-local hybridity distinct from that of Iyeth Bustami's video. Both clips, however, manipulate widely circulating images of social spaces, bodies, and embodied motion to create a narrative context for a particular musical encounter. Each of these manipulations, in its own way, expresses something significant about the contemporary existential condition of the videos' assumed audiences.

June 6, 2000

I arrive at Mega Sport, an expansive outdoor sports complex located in Senayan, Central Jakarta. At 9:30 p.m. on an oppressively humid Tuesday night, the complex is still filled with young people playing soccer, beach volleyball, and basketball. Walking past the crowds, I notice that the beach-volleyball sandbox farthest from the entrance is closed off from view by a tall black curtain. On the other side of the curtain a surrealistic sight greets the visitor: a long string of glowing light bulbs bunched together lies half-submerged in the sand in front of a fifteen-foot-tall cage made of chain-link fencing and wooden poles painted black, roughly 12′ x 12′ square. Inside the cage a drum kit and two guitar amplifiers are set up (the latter are unplugged, of course—there would be no actual playing of instruments during the shoot, just miming the gestures of playing). In the middle of the

Between takes on the set of the "Cahaya Bulan" video clip, Senayan, Central Jakarta.

sandlot, facing the cage and the light bulbs, an enormous, hulking camera crane stands surrounded by glowing video equipment. The whole scene is eerily lit by blue and yellow simulated moonlight, apparently inspired by the song's theme.

Around the giant sandbox are the three musicians (two band members and one additional guitarist), various technicians, makeup people, hangers-on, girlfriends, and a group of friends/extras for a planned sequence involving the cage (dubbed the *kandang ayam* [chicken coop] by those present), in which a mob of Netral fans surround and attack the structure while the band mimes playing the song. The motif of a band playing inside a steel cage while crazed audience members thrash around the cage has a long history in heavy metal music videos. Both the director and the band members, ardent fans of Western 1980s metal, were well aware that videos produced in that decade by Scorpions ("Rock You Like a Hurricane," 1983) and Megadeth ("Wake Up Dead," 1987), among others, utilized such a visual device. The use of the steel cage and the crazed fans in the "Cahaya Bulan" clip is a clear homage to those videos and an example of how televisual conventions can circulate globally.

Also present on the set are two young child actors, twin girls, made up to look like diminutive vampires. They are the "models" for the clip. In Indonesian popular music videos, the *model* is a nonmusician who plays a central character in the clip—a protagonist in a story, an enigmatic object of desire, an audience member, or just a friend hanging out with the band members. There is even a *Best Model* award category at the MTV Indonesia Video Music Awards.

One might ask what child vampires are doing in a rock video for a loud song about moonlight. James Siegel analyzes the figure of "Draculla" (who is almost always female, though usually not a child) in the popular comedic theater of 1980s Central Java, arguing that the character's "popularity depends on her foreignness" (1986, 92). In his view, Draculla represents the limits of the Javanese language to make sense of the world; she is thus "a way to accommodate the heterogeneous, given the failure of Javanese mythology to do so during the New Order" (303). Although of foreign origin, according to Jakartans with whom I spoke the Draculla (also called *vampir*) acts very much like the malevolent spirits in local mythologies (see Geertz 1960, 16–29, for an extensive inventory of Javanese village spirits). Some university students explained to me that Draculla was the "American" version of a *pocongan*, *gendruwo*, or other Indonesian spirit, disregarding the fact that few Americans actually believe in vampires, whereas malevolent ghosts and spirits are very much a part of everyday life for many Indonesians.

The final image of Netral's video is the three musicians sprawled unconscious in the sand with fang marks on their necks, while the vampire twins stand over them and lip-synch the song's backing vocal part. The triumph of the vampires over the band members suggests that the latter may have been too weak to resist the influence of evil spirits (Geertz 1960, 29), and it also highlights the danger of making oneself susceptible to those spirits through certain behaviors, such as letting one's mind wander or being alone at night. Thus the vampire girls are not simply characters appropriated from globally circulating horror films; they also play a particular culturally specific role in the narrative of the music video that, as I will demonstrate, relates directly to the themes of the song.

Another performer's image was later edited into the final version of the clip: a shirtless man breathing fire. Fire-eaters are a familiar sideshow attraction at Indonesian carnivals; they are usually members of traveling *kuda lumping* (Javanese trance dancer) troupes. Although fire-eaters could be considered as generic and "placeless" as Hollywood vampires, this particular decontextualized image seems to signify an unspecified Indonesian locality. Similarly, blurred shots of Netral's

drummer dancing to the music, with arm movements suggesting Javanese dance, were also spliced into the final edit. Like the images of the
fire-eater, these enigmatic images appear toward the beginning of the
clip and seem to obliquely reference the Indonesian national context
without fully invoking the discourses of traditional culture.

Having a *bule* (white person) at a video shoot in Indonesia is
something of a novelty, so I am not surprised when Puput, Netral's
manager, asks me to participate in the crowd scene. I agree and when
the time comes, I join a group of about twenty-five enthusiastic young
men standing on the cage's perimeter, waiting for the director's signal.
As a tape of the song begins booming over the loudspeakers, the crowd
becomes frenzied, attacking the chain-link fence with all its strength.
The entire structure begins rocking violently around the band
members playing inside the cage, who seem not the least bit concerned
when the fence comes within inches of their heads.

During the melee I realize with dismay that the "chicken coop" had
obviously not been built with safety in mind. Before long the chain
links begin to break, exposing sharp metal points, and the wooden
supports start to buckle under the onslaught. This causes the shooting
to stop twice in order to prevent the structure from collapsing entirely;
I notice that the imminent threat of the chicken coop's collapse fails to
lessen the ferocity of the attacks on it. By the time the first two takes
(together lasting about seven minutes) are finished, I am gasping for
breath, my hands are bleeding (gashes from a broken chain link), and
my shoes are filled with damp sand. The director then calls for another
take, followed by several more.

Afterward, I join the crowd around a small monitor screen to watch
the playback (Indonesian music video producers cannot afford film
stock; they use video cameras almost exclusively). I am disappointed to
find that the video footage does not quite capture the violence of the
actual event, and some of our gestures even appear halfhearted and
staged. I try to pick myself out in the chaotic scene, deciding that a bit
of self-consciousness is justified considering the very real possibility
that millions of Indonesians would soon be viewing my image on their
television screens. Then the director decides to film a close-up of the
drummer playing alone in the cage surrounded by the mob. I am quite
relieved when the final take for this sequence fails to bring the entire
structure down on our heads.

Violence and Sociality

At Iyeth Bustami's video shoot, I had certainly become familiar with the boredom caused by repeated takes and long waits between shots, but I had failed to grasp how truly exhausting performing for the camera could be, especially in the humid, stagnant Jakarta air. As a result of my experience at the Netral video shoot, I came to better appreciate the hard work Indonesian recording artists put into making videos. More importantly, I learned something about collective effort and the awareness of self and other in Jakarta. Surprisingly, aside from my hand injury and one particularly zealous participant who collapsed of heat exhaustion and dehydration (and quickly recovered), no one was hurt during the filming of the sequence. This was clearly not due solely to good fortune. Despite the violence of the proceedings, no one collided with or accidentally struck another participant, and I heard no one complain about the behavior of any other participant. I also realized that the steel cage was torn apart so quickly because, rather than thrashing about separately, all the other participants were working in concert, moving together in a manner that inflicted major damage in a very short period of time. I wondered if American youths would have been so efficient.

A bit more ominously, the behavior of the crowd also reminded me of other common forms of young men's collective action in Jakarta, including riots, gang fights, and *gebukin maling,* the beating of suspected thieves (often to death) by an angry mob, which occurred at least once a week in Greater Jakarta during the period of my fieldwork (the *Jakarta Post* called it being "mobbed to death"). In all these examples, violent, destructive acts are carried out with deadly efficiency by a group of young males, and the responsibility for those actions is diffused among them, so that as a result no one is ever prosecuted. Although all we did was perform for a rock video, I noticed certain undeniable behavioral parallels. Was it easier for the mob to continue destroying the cage because of the knowledge that no single individual would be blamed for its destruction and for any injuries that might result? This, perhaps, was the dark side of Indonesian social life, in which individual responsibility dissipates and allows groups to act with stunning violence against external targets.

Whether or not such comparisons between art and life are appropriate, paying attention to basic habits of sociality and to fundamental orientations toward physical space, the presence of others, and the burden of responsibility is part of an ethnographic perspective that is frequently missing from studies of popular music and other kinds of global media culture. Had I not joined the video mini-riot of Netral fans, I, too, might have overlooked these phenomena.

After the riot scenes, what remained of the steel cage is quickly disassembled and preparations are made for more individual close-ups of band members performing in front of a different backdrop. By this point it is well after four in the morning. I do not stay quite until the end; I have to teach an early morning class at Atma Jaya, so I gratefully accept a free ride home from a group of people leaving the set. We leave just after 5:00 a.m., when only the last of Eno the drummer's close-up scenes remain to be shot. "*Kasihan buat Si Eno* [Poor Eno!]," **says Bagus as we leave Eno behind, driving away into the sultry predawn darkness.**

Netral's video clip, with its visual references to Surrealism, horror movies, and Western heavy metal videos, aspires to be part of global culture. Nearly all the cultural references it contains would be intelligible to consumers of popular culture around the world. Unlike Iyeth's video, there are neither images of "traditional" Indonesian life (with the possible exception of the fire-eater and the blurry "Javanese" dancer) nor any recognizable Indonesian locales. Although the video was shot on location in an outdoor urban sports complex, the set had been transformed into a strange, fantastic landscape bearing no relationship to the settings of daily life. Yet the fact that the song in the video is sung in Indonesian and performed by visibly Indonesian musicians influences the responses of Indonesian viewers, for whom the clip's global images are recontextualized by their appropriation by an Indonesian rock band.

Moreover, an analysis of the specific images in the video reveals their connection not only to the song's lyrics but also to the general cultural themes of loneliness, fear, and the threat of the supernatural. The band plays a song about solitary contemplation of the night sky while standing inside a steel cage surrounded by crazed fans attempting to break through the metal fencing. The fans are unsuccessful, and in the end, the band falls victim to two young vampires. Are these disconnected, unrelated images, or can they be assembled into a larger narrative? Solitude is hazardous in Indonesian thought not only because it causes loneliness (*kesepian*), but also because it leaves one vulnerable to attacks by spirits. It is only fitting that a rock band that "shuts out" its fans and

Netral performing for the camera inside the "chicken coop."

compatriots (through arrogance, perhaps), preferring to be kept company by the moon alone, would be victimized by vampires—dangerous supernatural entities that, like Indonesian rock music itself, have been indigenized from a foreign source. Thus in the video clip the price the band members pay for repelling those around them is an unpleasant encounter with Draculla. But the video of "Cahaya Bulan" also tells a slightly different story: that of the fans who aggressively move to the music and form a collective body. The powerful musical sounds unite them in shared *keramaian* (crowded noisiness) and protect them from the fate suffered by the band members themselves. Although the distant moon and stars cannot protect one from Draculla, loud music and the company of others can.

Cultural Production and the Ethic of Sociality

Interactions between social agents at sites of commercial cultural production are part of larger patterns in Indonesian society that shape how people respond to music and to one another. A striking characteristic of cultural production in Indonesia is that it is nearly always an intensely social process. Solitary creation is not highly valued, though it is admitted as a possibility. But even then, creative inspiration is often derived from the surrounding social environment. The complex relationship between the hybrid, multiply positioned subjectivities of contemporary Indonesian youth and the ethic of sociality—the idea that one's well-being depends on the conspicuous presence of others—shapes everyday lives and interactions. Popular music, as meaningful cultural form and social practice, provides us with an ideal vantage point for observing how this relationship works.

6

Offstage

MUSIC IN INFORMAL CONTEXTS

What happens to the musical artifacts created in recording studios? After recordings are mixed, mastered, duplicated, packaged, distributed, promoted through video clips, and displayed in retail outlets, their fate becomes more uncertain. Some recordings become hits, others do not, depending on the number of consumers who choose to buy them. Whatever the reasons for their success, hit recordings and the songs contained on them circulate widely and become a recognized part of Indonesian public culture, available to serve diverse agendas. As a result of the limited commercial shelf life of Indonesian cassettes, a hit song often outlives its original commodity form and becomes a free-floating entity reanimated through formal and informal performances, until, if it is popular enough, it is rerecorded or the original recording of the song is rereleased on a compilation cassette.

Local, informal performances of mass-mediated music—the music created in recording studios like 601 Studio Lab—are prevalent in Indonesia, where they are part of a vibrant oral culture of informal socializing in which musical performance plays an important role. As an accessory to informal male social gatherings in particular, a guitar is nearly as indispensable as cigarettes. Indeed, one seldom sees a group of young men hanging out in Jakarta without at least one of them strumming a battered acoustic guitar. Although informal performers cannot re-create exactly the recorded artifacts that inspire them (much less the fantasy environments of music video clips), they do replicate aspects of the sounds contained in the recordings and thereby contribute to the circulation and popularity of some songs. More importantly, by exploring how songs produced in recording studios and promoted via video clips take on a life of their own in specific social settings, we can begin to address a question that preoccupies both music producers and ethnomusicologists: why do listeners choose to consume popular music?

Popular music's role in the informal leisure activities of Jakarta's youth constitutes a source of meaning and value that social actors draw on in their daily struggles with the stress and atomizing forces of urban life. Among working-class men, playing popular songs on the guitar and other instruments is considered a valued skill and an important source of entertainment for those who lack the funds for other leisure activities. It is *murah meriah* (literally "cheap and cheerful") and provides an opportunity for self-expression, collective enjoyment, and occasional reflection on the conditions of life in the capital city. For middle-class and elite youth, singing and performing popular songs can also relieve stress and create bonds of solidarity between people. In fact, the practice of creating and strengthening social bonds through informal performance does not vary much across class lines, even if the music chosen as the vehicle for such sociability often differs. In all cases, though, Indonesian popular songs provide a shared expressive resource for participants in informal socializing regardless of their class or ethnic background.

By the Side of the Road:
The Art of *Nongkrong* (Hanging Out)

Apa artinya malam Minggu
Bagi orang yang tidak mampu?
Mau ke pesta tak beruang
Akhirnya nongkrong di pinggir jalan.

[What is the meaning of Saturday night
For those who can't afford anything?
Want to go to a party, don't have money
In the end (just) hang out by the side of the road.
Rhoma Irama, "Begadang II"[1]

In urban Indonesia, the side of the road (*di pinggir jalan*) is a site of possibility, of adventure, and of longing for the sensual pleasures of city life that always seem just beyond reach. Jakarta has an exceedingly active street life, and musical performance is an important component of the largely masculine culture of *nongkrong* (hanging out), which pervades all aspects of street-side social activity. *Nongkrong* means literally "to squat," but in popular usage it means to socialize in groups, usually in public or quasi-public spaces. Although I have observed groups of young men on a side street squatting in a circle, talking and smoking, most *anak tongkrongan* (kids who hang out) in Jakarta do not actually squat on the ground but prefer to sit on benches in front of food stalls (*warung*), neighborhood-watch security posts, or other roadside locations. Those unable to obtain work *nongkrong* all day long, but the prime time for hanging out is from the end of *magrib* (sundown prayers), to the *subuh* prayers at daybreak. From evening on into the night, almost every cigarette kiosk located by a main thoroughfare is host to several young, working-class men sitting in a group, talking, laughing, gambling, smoking, drinking bottled tea, playing battered old guitars, and singing, their voices barely audible over the continuous roar of Jakarta traffic.

Friends and acquaintances in Jakarta frequently warned me not to associate with the young men who hung out at *warung*. I was told that they were dangerous, possibly criminals, and that they would attempt to take advantage of me as a naive foreigner. Despite these warnings, I would frequently visit with groups of guitar-playing men at food and cigarette stalls, and for the most part I found them welcoming and flattered by my attention to their performances. What follows is a description of three hangout spots, all located a short distance from my boardinghouse in Kebayoran Baru, a middle-class residential area in South Jakarta. Each site is different, but at each of them musical performance plays a vital role in social interaction.

The Warung Gaul

A small, nondescript kiosk located on Wolter Monginsidi Street, a congested main thoroughfare in Kebayoran Baru, the Warung Gaul was the designated evening hangout spot for a group of men in their late teens and early twenties when I first arrived in Jakarta. It was the type of establishment usually called a *warung rokok,* "cigarette stall," although it also sold snacks, drinks, dried instant noodles, and some minor household items.

Some of the Warung Gaul's regulars worked as security guards in nearby banks and office buildings, while others worked as waiters, assistant mechanics, or laborers. They came from a variety of ethnic and linguistic backgrounds, including Javanese, Sundanese, Betawi, and Minang. There was even a young, friendly Acehnese snack vendor who occasionally dropped by. One regular, a short, muscular man named Ucok, was born and raised in Lampung, a province on the southern tip of Sumatra. His parents both came from the West Javanese town of Tasikmalaya, and he spoke Sundanese, Javanese, and Indonesian, though he did not know *bahasa Lampung,* the Malay dialect spoken in his province of origin. All the regulars were unmarried, Muslim, and under thirty.

Gaul is an important and multifaceted word in Jakarta youth culture. In common usage it can mean sociable, cool, or trendy. *Bergaul* means to converse informally and intimately; its meaning is close to the American Yiddish expression "to schmooze." A commonly used variation is *pergaulan,* "social intercourse," while *kurang gaul,* literally "insufficiently sociable," means to be out of touch or unhip, and in Jakarta slang the word *kuper,* short for *kurang pergaulan* (insufficient schmoozing), means "uninformed" or "unaware." The Warung Gaul was located a few blocks from a hair salon that billed itself as "Jakarta's Salon *Gaul,*" and the regulars at the *warung* called the Jakartanese Indonesian they spoke with one another *bahasa gaul* (cool/social language), the language spoken between friends.[2] This language, rather than Low Javanese or any other *bahasa daerah* (regional language), was the medium of communication and sociability at the Warung Gaul.

The first Warung Gaul proprietor I met was Ridwan, a twenty-three-year-old migrant from Tegal, Central Java.[3] Ridwan, who called himself the "chairperson" (*ketua*) of the *warung* and was probably the one who gave the *warung* its nickname, was well liked by the other regulars. He lived in a nearby boardinghouse (*rumah kost*) located behind an Internet café and worked long shifts at the *warung,* from around eight in the morning to eleven-thirty at night, every day except Sunday. After dark, as cars, trucks, *bajaj,* and buses streamed by less than ten feet from the wooden benches, the group of young men gathered at the *warung* to sing, talk, tell jokes, play cards, or just lean against one another and stare into space.

At night one could often hear squealing and rustling sounds from three enormous rats who lived behind the stall. Ridwan would laugh at my discomfort when they approached us; "*mouse my friend,*" he would say in his broken English. Other characters in this nocturnal scene included traveling vendors of fried rice and *siomay* (fish dumpling), various passersby, and even the occasional customer in search of cigarettes. Early in the evening, the roar of rush-hour traffic often drowned out the music, which usually consisted of one of the *warung* regulars strumming softly on a guitar, singing in a tentative voice. As the night wore on, these solitary performances would give way to loud collective efforts when the whole group joined in the singing.

Often it seemed as though conversation at the Warung Gaul consisted of little more than reciprocal accusations of craziness. "He's crazy!" the regulars would say, pointing at a friend, or else they simply placed an index finger diagonally across their foreheads—a sign for *miring kepala*, literally "slanted head," an expression meaning a defective or lobotomized brain—and gestured toward the recipient of the joke. Humor was an important aspect of Warung Gaul interactions, and certain jokes and puns were uttered repeatedly. A favorite was to say one worked as a *pengacara* (lawyer), which turned out really to be a shortened form of *penganggur banyak acara* (unemployed [but] with lots of engagements). Another was the multilingual saying *no money, nodong; no cewek, nongkrong* (*no money,* rob [someone]; *no* woman, hang out). This was an apt statement on the culture of *nongkrong:* first, it acknowledged that resorting to crime to obtain what one could not have was always at least a rhetorical possibility for nonaffluent young men in Jakarta, when the sense of relative deprivation created by the surrounding opulence became too difficult to bear. Second, the expression indicated that while hanging out was enjoyable, it was also a consolation of sorts. The regulars at the Warung Gaul readily acknowledged that if they had money or girlfriends, they would not be spending all their time hanging out by the side of the road. It was common knowledge that most of them suffered from *kanker* (literally "cancer" but in *bahasa gaul* short for kan*tong* ker*ing*—"dry pocket," i.e., broke) most of the time. Much of the longing expressed through Warung Gaul regulars' performances of sad, sentimental songs of heartbreak and disappointment could be considered a response to this condition. Indeed, evenings in the Warung Gaul seemed to be characterized by the contrast between equal measures of the warmth of companionship and the coldness of unrequited longing.

Ridwan used to tell me that after I would leave, the rest of the *anak* (kids) would stay up all night and sometimes go hang out at Blok M, the nearby fashionable shopping district. I learned later that actually the group usually dissolved around midnight, each member returning to his boardinghouse to sleep until morning. Ridwan also boasted frequently of his many girlfriends back in Tegal and in Jakarta, about whose existence I grew increasingly skeptical. By that point I had realized the truth: that playing music and hanging out at the Warung Gaul every night was the sole source of amusement for most of the regulars.

The young men at the Warung Gaul did not spend all their time on musical performance. Gambling was another common pastime, one they were quite passionate about. (Ridwan was a notorious gambler, often losing more than a week's pay in a single evening.) But it was clear that *dangdutan* (informal dangdut performance) was central to the culture of *nongkrong,* as was the performance of slow and sentimental vintage pop compositions known as "nostalgia songs" (*lagu nostalgia*). Significantly, while a single musician accompanying himself on guitar could play *lagu nostalgia,* proper *dangdutan* usually required some sort of percussion instrument in addition to the guitar and thus was a more social activity. Vocal imitations of melodic "fill-in" instruments in dangdut songs—lead guitar, flute, mandolin, and so on—were also part of *dangdutan* performances. These were often sung with an exaggerated nasal voice imitating the instrument's timbre, sometimes after shouting out the name of the instrument on the original recording: "*suling!*" "*melodi!*" "*mandolin!*" ("bamboo flute!" "lead guitar!" "mandolin!").

Thus there seemed to be a subtle distinction made at the Warung Gaul between *lagu nostalgia* and dangdut song performance, in which the former was considered an expression of individual longing and the latter a more collective and celebratory affair. Often a solitary performer of *nostalgia* songs sang quietly to himself, ignored by the others around him, while dangdut songs usually caught the attention of the entire group.

Partway through my fieldwork, Ridwan became ill and returned to his home village (*pulang kampung*) in Tegal. His younger brother Rizal, a talented guitarist who commanded a large repertoire of Indonesian pop and dangdut songs, replaced him. Rizal's role was central in strengthening the Warung Gaul's collective identity; shortly after arriving he decorated the inside of the *warung* with drawings and photographs framed with bits of wood and plastic drinking straws. He also wrote the names and phone numbers of the regulars (including those of the ethnographer) on the wooden floor of the stall and pasted one-hundred-rupiah coins to the front panel of the *warung* guitar to simulate the volume and tone knobs of an electric guitar.

Rizal's most ambitious plan was to acquire an inexpensive *gendang* for the *warung's* nightly *dangdutan* by pooling the regulars' financial resources. Unfortunately the regulars were unable to find a *gendang* they could afford. After three or four Sundays spent looking, the cheapest one they had found cost Rp. 60,000—too expensive, despite my own modest contribution to the fund. In fact, because 60,000 rupiahs at the time was only slightly more than eight dollars, I was tempted to simply pay for the *gendang* myself. I decided, however, that such an act would imperil the egalitarian relationship of reciprocity I enjoyed with the *warung* regulars and would lead to social discomfort. Besides, no one had asked me to contribute more than I already had.

Reciprocity and Its Hazards

It was unclear to me how the Warung Gaul made any money at all. Every time I offered to pay for my Coca-Colas and Teh Botols at the end of the night, Rizal refused. There were usually very few paying customers after dark, and some of these had to be turned away due to a lack of change. According to Rizal, most of the customers of the *warung* bought items on credit (*berhutang*). Although not an ideal business practice in some ways, the refusal of immediate payment succeeds in establishing a more lasting social relationship in which one party has an obligation toward the other. As mentioned in chapter 2, most *warung* in Jakarta have regular customers (*langganan*) who are permitted to buy on credit in return for their continued patronage.

Maintaining reciprocal relationships was paramount at the Warung Gaul. Rizal once harshly criticized one of the regulars for being a *peminta*, a "moocher," saying he was *kurang gaul* (uncool). I did not learn the exact circumstances that led to this accusation, but it was clear that excessively taking advantage of the buying-on-credit system imperiled the relationship of equality and reciprocity that formed the foundation of *pergaulan*, just as being too quick to pay could threaten it.

Though he often told me he liked Jakarta and wanted to stay there, after four months Rizal also returned to his family's home in Central Java and was replaced by Agung, who was a nonrelative and a stakeholder in the *warung*'s business. Agung was less willing than Ridwan and Rizal to let the *warung* regulars buy snacks and cigarettes on credit. His resulting unpopularity among the regulars led some to choose to move their evening hangout to another *warung rokok* located across the street. Other former regulars started hanging out after hours in the *warung internet* near where Ridwan used to live, taking turns playing Sony PlayStation games while listening to dangdut on a stereo that during business hours was set to a pop radio station. By the time my fieldwork was near its end, Agung had started closing his stall early in the evening for lack of business. The Warung Gaul was defunct, a consequence of a breakdown of reciprocity between proprietor and regular customers.

American Dreams

A recurring theme in the discourse and performances of the Warung Gaul was that of longing. Although this is hardly surprising given the subordinate social position of the regulars and the high level of material affluence that surrounded them, I was surprised to find how much of that longing was focused on the country I call home. While the knowledge of English among the Warung Gaul regulars ranged from a little to virtually nonexistent, almost everyone expressed a desire to learn the language, which they associated with the excitement of America, with its wealth and "free sex." Rizal complained that his parents had not been able to afford to send him to high school, and thus he had never had the opportunity to learn English, a complaint I heard from many working-class Indonesians. Other Warung Gaul regulars who had studied English complained that even after many years of study their grasp of the language was insufficient. They frequently asked me to translate a variety of English phrases of the sort that were ubiquitous in the Jakarta landscape. Among them:

1. Lucky Strikes (American cigarette brand).
2. "Taste the Freedom" (slogan for "Kansas" cigarettes, a so-called American brand not found, to my knowledge, in the United States).
3. Hollywood movie titles, for example, *Pretty Woman, Basic Instinct, Fatal Vision, Double Impact, Trained to Kill.*
4. Money Changer (a sign that could be found all over Jakarta but that the Warung Gaul regulars did not comprehend).
5. "Winds of Change" (a ten-year-old song by the German heavy metal band Scorpions that was still wildly popular in Indonesia).
6. Hand Body Cream (many cosmetic products in Indonesia have English names).
7. Creambath (a term commonly used in salon advertisements; at the time I had to admit that I had no idea what it meant).[4]

These examples illustrate how English was associated with popular entertainment and commodities in the experience of the young men at the Warung Gaul. Aside from wanting to learn English, the young

men who hung out at the Warung Gaul (and countless other young,
working-class Indonesian men with whom I spoke) were frank about
their adoration of *Amrik,* the Jakarta youth slang term for the United
States, and their fervent desire to go there. Ridwan even told me that he
someday wanted to go on a hajj to America, using the same word he
would use to describe a pilgrimage to Mecca.

A major component of the regulars' fascination with America appeared to be their oft-expressed desire for *cewek bule* (white chicks),
whom they saw as both more beautiful and more sexually available than
Indonesian women, although their only real contact with them was
mediated by filmic and televisual images. I frequently found myself
explaining to them that I had no sisters nor was I acquainted with any
foreign women in Jakarta (both true, as it so happened), and I often
became exasperated by the regulars' persistent fixation on *bule* women.[5]
Once when Ridwan was enthusiastically discussing his plans to attract a
cewek bule I asked him how exactly he intended to flirt with a foreign
woman when he could not speak English. His solution, after some
thought, was that I would do the *"dubbing"* for him, substituting English for Indonesian, so that his intentions would be made clear to the
object of his affection.[6] Reflecting on this response helped me to realize
that to young Indonesians the United States was not a distant, foreign
land but rather an intimately familiar realm of fantasy and dreams. The
Indonesian practice of subtitling American television shows and films,
which familiarized Indonesians with the sounds of English and rendered their meanings seemingly transparent, created the illusion of a
lack of cultural and geographical distance. Similarly, the flood of American and quasi-American commodities promoted and advertised in
idiomatic Indonesian could easily be mistaken as "signs of recognition" (Keane 1997) from American cultural producers, rather than the
product of locally managed branches of remote, giant multinational
corporations.

Even educated, middle-class Indonesians were often surprised
when I told them it took me over thirty hours to travel from New York
to Jakarta. It was hard for them to grasp that places like New York City,
Los Angeles, and the bucolic American suburbia depicted in Hollywood movies were so physically distant when the global media made
them so phenomenologically near. Nevertheless, while the young men
of the Warung Gaul may have overestimated their significance in the
eyes of America, they also suspected that their relationship with the

phantasmagoric *Amrik* of their dreams was ultimately one-way, a dialogue only in their imagination. Indeed, a recurrent theme throughout Indonesian popular culture was a kind of yearning for a reciprocal, affirming gesture from the country that set the standard for popular culture, despite the lingering ambivalence many Indonesians felt toward the world's sole superpower. Such reciprocity remained elusive, but the yearning continued.

One night at the *warung* one of the regulars, a Betawi security guard named Mahmud, gave me a list of Indonesian expressions he wanted me to translate into English. The first few were standard conversational phrases, but to my surprise they were followed by a list of phrases I recognized as dangdut song titles. I was uncertain as to the purpose of translating Indonesian song titles, but Mahmud seemed particularly insistent, and he showed great satisfaction when I translated them for him. Perhaps he enjoyed imagining his favorite dangdut songs as global, English-language pop enjoyed by people all over the world and respected by the elites in his own country. Perhaps he also saw the small symbolic act of translating a quintessentially Indonesian musical idiom into English as a form of talking back to the globally dominant American cultural industry. My ability to translate dangdut song titles was "proof" that the unequal producer-consumer relationship between American/global culture and Indonesian culture was potentially a two-way street. It was as though if only the former would be more receptive and less arrogant, a relationship of egalitarian reciprocity could replace the current hegemonic/subaltern relationship between the two countries.

The awareness of a lack of parity between America and Indonesia, and by extension between myself and the other regulars, led to some friction at the Warung Gaul. Some of the regulars occasionally spoke to me in a nonstandard, rough (*kasar*) variant of Javanese or Sundanese instead of Indonesian, even though they were well aware that I would have difficulty understanding them. This always generated laughter among the group. I interpreted this as their "revenge" on me for my ability to speak a language *they* did not understand, as much as they wanted to learn it, and for somehow learning their language, too.

I suspect that the language barrier was a primary reason why Western pop songs were not part of the Warung Gaul's repertoire, though this was not the only cause. The only English-language song I heard occasionally at the *warung* was "Why Do You Love Me," a song recorded decades ago by the Beatlesesque Indonesian pop group Koes Plus. Most singers did not know much of this song beyond the first line, but because the song had been recorded by an Indonesian band, they seemed to feel more comfortable with it than with English-language songs recorded by Western groups.

The Warung under the Tree

A few blocks away from the Warung Gaul, on the corner of two secondary roads and surrounded by affluent Kebayoran Baru residences, was the Warung di Bawah Pohon, "The Warung under the Tree." At least this was what the regulars called it in my conversations with them; it is possible that prior to my arrival this particular hangout spot did not have a name at all, and it was my occasional presence that led to a reflexive search for a name. (In contrast, the Warung Gaul appeared to already have had a corporate identity of sorts before my arrival.) At night a dozen or so young men, many of them servants or night watchmen for the surrounding households, regularly congregated and played music on a more elaborate level than the performances at the Warung Gaul.

On a good night, depending on who was around, the Warung under the Tree had a full ensemble of musicians who frequently switched instruments during the course of the evening. The ensemble included two well-worn acoustic guitars, one used for playing chords and the other for playing bass lines transposed to a higher octave, as well as a plastic *gendang* that was actually an office water-cooler bottle. In skillful hands the hard, unforgiving plastic skin of this instrument could approximate the different sounds made by a real *gendang* or a Western trap kit, depending on the song. One of the *warung* regulars was particularly adept at playing this *galon* (from the word for "gallon"); the others told me he was a *jago*—a "champion" or virtuoso—on the makeshift instrument. The final core component in the ensemble was a *gicik,* an idiophone made from three rows of punctured and flattened bottle caps nailed into a stick of wood about nine inches long—a kind of homemade tambourine. The *gicik* is a quintessential Jakartan street instrument, often played by child beggars to accompany their singing as they try to catch the attention of motorists sitting in traffic. Its role in the *warung*'s ensemble was to play tambourine parts in dangdut songs and cymbal parts in pop songs. The sound of the group was occasionally augmented by handclaps and empty bottles struck with metal spoons or banged together like large glass claves. Played together, these humble instruments created a surprisingly full sound.

As I watched the regulars at the Warung under the Tree perform, I was struck by the amount of laughing and smiling I saw and by the seeming lack of macho posturing, teasing, and aggression that Americans tend to expect from gatherings of young males. No one quarreled over who could play what instrument next or ridiculed someone else's playing mistakes. Anyone who was interested could join in the performance by singing or playing improvised percussion. On one occasion a quiet, awkward young man, occasionally described as "crazy" by the others, carefully placed some bottle caps in an empty cassette case and tried to shake it in time with the music. After a few attempts to follow the rhythm, he gave up. Although no one made fun of him, he seemed to become shy and embarrassed (*malu*), which kept him from continuing.

One night while the band was playing a dangdut song, a luxury car pulled up to the side of the road and two men wearing well-pressed slacks and neckties emerged. They each bought a bottle of tea, which they drank impassively while standing next to the seated *warung* regulars, who at the time were deeply engrossed in their performance. The two customers completely ignored the spirited playing surrounding them, avoiding eye contact with the musicians. Finally the thinner of the two men returned the now-empty bottles to the *warung's* proprietor and blithely handed him a twenty-thousand-rupiah bill—a rather large denomination with which to pay for two beverages priced at Rp. 1,000 each. The *warung* proprietor managed to find enough change to give back to his customer, and then the two men returned to their car and unceremoniously drove off, safe once again behind the tinted window glass. The musicians, for their part, did not pay much attention to the customers either. They were most likely accustomed to similar demonstrations of Jakarta's social gap, the yawning gulf between the young men hanging out on the side of the road and the people they often referred to as the *kaum berdasi* (necktie-wearing caste). This incident illustrates the limits of the affective community created by *dangdutan*. One of *dangdutan's* most important functions for men hanging out by the side of the road is to create a sense of group belonging, but the music cannot compel those who refuse to join in.

Pondok Cinta: The Watchman's Post

Begadang jangan begadang
Kalau tiada artinya
Begadang boleh saja
Kalau ada perlunya.

[Stay up all night, don't stay up all night
If there is no reason (for it)
Stay up all night, just go ahead
If there is a need.]

Rhoma Irama, "Begadang"

Pondok Cinta, literally "love shack," was the nickname the regulars gave to an elevated security post on the corner of two other secondary roads in Kebayoran Baru. It did not seem to be a very effective post, since the bamboo blinds on its three walls blocked most views of the street. The job of the night watchmen was to *begadang*, "stay up all night," and thereby (supposedly) to contribute to the safety of the neighborhood. For their efforts the official night watchmen were paid Rp. 200,000 a month (at the time around US$35), hardly a princely sum even by Indonesian standards.

The regulars at the Pondok Cinta were older than those at the two *warung*, ranging in age from late twenties to midforties; some were married, others were aging bachelors. Most were unemployed or semi-employed in the informal sector, but they were not impoverished; in fact, at least three of the men owned cellular phones. The regulars came

A performance at the *Pondok Cinta*, Kebayoran Baru, South Jakarta.

from different ethnic backgrounds: there were Sundanese, Javanese, Betawi, and one Batak, who was the recipient of a certain amount of ethnically motivated ribbing from the others. Those who dropped by occasionally ranged from an illiterate vegetable peddler from Bogor to a portly middle-aged physician who lived in a house nearby. In the course of a long night of hanging out, the regulars smoked, played cards, drank hot tea, and occasionally ordered Indomie (Indonesian instant ramen noodles) from the open-all-night *warung* across the street. In addition to performing music, the men also enjoyed sharing their knowledge of Indonesian vernacular wordplay, particularly by creating humorous abbreviations and acronyms (*singkatan*) as well as puns (*plesetan*). One typical (though rather offensive) example of the made-up acronyms I heard at the Pondok Cinta is this list of names of Indonesian ethnicities:

Betawi = beta*h di* wi*layah* (enjoys being in the area [of Jakarta])
Sunda = su*ka da*ndan (likes makeup, personal adornment; a reference to
   the reputation of Sundanese men and women for glamour and vanity)
Batak = ba*nyak* tak*tik* (many tactics; a reference to supposed Batak
   treachery and deceitfulness)

Such wordplay was a form of idle amusement to fill a long night, but it also functioned to create solidarity in the group. Like musical performance, verbal games created shared references among group members, and the (often obscene) humor they contained could lead to reflections on ethnicity, sexuality, language, and other facets of the group's everyday experience.

Of the three street-side locations discussed in this chapter, the regulars at the Pondok Cinta took music the most seriously. They used a real *gendang*, occasionally a real tambourine, and a guitar that could stay in tune. Sometimes one of the regulars even brought a portable electronic keyboard, on which he played "piano" accompaniments and "string" melodies for dangdut songs. A book filled with handwritten song lyrics was kept at the post. A few of the regulars, including the *gendang* player, occasionally played semiprofessionally at weddings and other performance occasions.

The Pondok Cinta repertoire consisted primarily of dangdut compositions. The regulars performed many of the same songs as local dangdut bands, but their repertoire was weighted toward those originally recorded by male singers. When one of the men did sing a song originally sung by a woman singer (sometimes singing an octave lower, sometimes in falsetto), he would not alter the lyrics to reflect a male perspective. At the Pondok Cinta, I was asked to translate dangdut lyrics into English and sing them, something the regulars seemed to enjoy hearing. I suspect the reason for this was the same as that for the positive response I received when I provided translations of dangdut song titles at the Warung Gaul.

The regulars at Pondok Cinta would often play without interruption from around eleven at night until the next morning. As soon as they heard the call of the muezzin from a nearby mosque loudspeaker, all music immediately ceased "out of respect." Shortly thereafter, the group dispersed, riding away on motorcycles or leaving on foot.

The Ethic of Sociality and the Culture of Hanging Out

Musical performance in these varied street-side settings conformed to a larger ethic of sociality prevalent in Indonesia. Music making in such settings was intended primarily not for impressing others but for creating an atmosphere of camaraderie and relaxation. In fact, performances by the side of the road were essential expressions of this ethic, manifested in the relationships between different participants and often in the sung texts themselves.

Many dangdut songs, like "Begadang II," the Rhoma Irama composition quoted earlier, make explicit references to street-corner life. At the Warung Gaul, the line *akhirnya nongkrong di pinggir jalan* (in the end hang out by the side of the road) was sometimes replaced by the enthusiastically sung, *"akhirnya nongkrong di Warung Gaul"* (in the end hang out at the Warung Gaul). On one occasion, Ucok, one of the regulars, began singing a long, improvised variation on a pivotal line in the song: *"mau ke pesta tak beruang"* (want to go to a party, don't have money). While strumming a repeating open chord progression on the *warung*'s guitar, he chanted:

> *Mau jalan tidak punya . . . uang*
> *Mau makan tidak punya . . . uang*
> *Mau pesta tidak punya . . . uang.*
> (etc.)

> [Want to go places, don't have . . . money
> Want to eat, don't have . . . money
> Want to party, don't have . . . money.
> (etc.)]

As he sang, he encouraged the others to join in on the last word, "money," creating a kind of call-and-response pattern. The undercurrent of menace beneath the humorous veneer of his performance was apparent. His musical complaint, with its insistent repetition, expressed the unceasing frustration of life by the side of the road and dissatisfaction with never possessing the means to participate in the phantasmagoric realm of leisure and consumption depicted in advertisements and television programs and represented by the mansions, bars, malls, and restaurants of affluent South Jakarta.

In addition to being a lament of sorts, and perhaps a commentary on my presence at the hangout session, Ucok's song, I suspect, was also a protest directed at the government, the wealthy, and anyone perceived as having the power to change the situation of ordinary Indonesians and yet choosing not to do so. Later that night, during a long, animated conversation about Indonesian politics, Ucok stated that Indonesia was rich in natural resources, but that the nation's wealth was not utilized (*mengolah*) wisely and in a way that benefited the many. The others agreed; the perception that Indonesia would be a prosperous country if the *koruptor*s at the top would just share their wealth fairly was widespread among working-class people in Jakarta. Indeed, much working-class support for the movement to bring Soeharto to justice was predicated on the rather unlikely possibility that the Indonesian government would be able to confiscate the billions of dollars the former dictator had siphoned off from the people and use the money to pay off debts and alleviate poverty in the country. To nonaffluent young men in Jakarta surrounded by glaring evidence of tremendous wealth illegitimately gained and conspicuously flaunted, facing a life of limited means was thus a reason for vociferous protest, rather than for fatalism and acquiescence.

In a sense, Ucok's performance can be contrasted with the usual dangdut and *nostalgia* repertoires at the Warung Gaul; although the songs in those repertoires often express resignation, give aesthetic form to a shared sentiment of longing, and invite listeners to commiserate, in most cases the cause for the misery is ostensibly heartbreak, not class oppression. It is quite possible that my presence as an outsider encouraged Ucok's musical outburst, though I will never know for sure, but regardless his vehemence definitely seemed to make the other regulars uncomfortable.

In addition to "Begadang" and its musical sequel "Begadang II," both quoted earlier, numerous other Rhoma Irama compositions were performed at the Warung Gaul. The *warung* performers enjoyed singing Rhoma's songs not necessarily because the men endorsed the didactic messages those songs contained, but because the lyrics addressed the circumstances of their lives. Rhoma Irama has recorded songs about gambling ("Judi"), bachelorhood ("Bujangan"), staying up all night ("Begadang"), drug use ("Narkoba"), stress ("Stres"), and other commonplaces in the lives of young, nonaffluent Indonesian men. The song "Bujangan" (Bachelorhood) is exemplary in this respect:

> *Katanya enak menjadi bujangan*
> *Ke mana-mana tak ada yang larang*
> *Hidup terasa ringan tanpa beban*
> *Uang belanja tak jadi pikiran.*

> [They say it's nice to be a bachelor
> Going here and there, there's nothing off-limits
> Life feels light, free of burdens
> Spending money is not given a thought.]

A later verse is

> *Tapi susahnya menjadi bujangan*
> *Kalau malam tidur sendirian*
> *Hanya bantal guling sebagai teman*
> *Mata melotot pikiran melayang.*
> *O bujangan.*

> [But the hard thing about being a bachelor
> Is every night sleeping alone
> Only a long pillow to keep you company,
> Your eyes wide open, your thoughts drifting.
> Oh, bachelorhood.]

In the informal performances I observed, the eventual moral of the song, that it is better to marry and settle down than to risk having too much fun as a bachelor, was beside the point, and most performers and listeners preferred to hear the tune as a humorously ironic celebration of the life of a working-class bachelor. Often the didactic messages of Rhoma Irama songs became targets of *warung* humor. For instance, the *anak Warung Gaul* often sang "Begadang," the song admonishing listeners for staying up all night for no reason, right after someone declared his intention to do so.

The Threat of Arrogance

Despite the strong element of inclusiveness in *nongkrong* sociability, inclusiveness and acceptance did have their limits. An important term in *nongkrong* discourse, and in Jakartan speech in general, was the Jakartanese word *belagu* (proud, arrogant), roughly equivalent to the Standard Indonesian *sombong*. Someone who was considered *belagu* was often, quite simply, one who refused to *bergaul*, to socialize with others. *Belagu* behavior violated the ethic of sociality that structured interactions between equals, and it placed this equality in question. If one did not hang out with others, it was taken as a sign that one felt superior to them. Often acquaintances who walked by the Warung Gaul without stopping to sit and chat (often because they were on the job) were called *belagu* in a semi-joking way by the men hanging out. Moreover, in the discourse of the street corner, this term's meaning was extended beyond the interpersonal realm of *nongkrong*. The proindependence Acehnese and the newly independent East Timorese were deemed *belagu*, as were Chinese Indonesians, who were criticized for not "mixing" with *pribumi* (native, non-Chinese) Indonesians (cf. Siegel 2000). Media celebrities who cut themselves off from ordinary people were also labeled *belagu* (I was to find out later that celebrities in Indonesia try hard to avoid creating this impression among their fans), as were women who were not open to amorous male advances. *Belagu* celebrities were said to "forget themselves" (*lupa diri*) as a result of their fame. This was also said of people who had moved up in social status and displayed arrogance when interacting with their old friends.

As a foreigner, an American whom everyone assumed was wealthy, I was constantly at risk of being considered arrogant, of being *belagu*. If I had not stopped by for a while or if I didn't stop and chat every time I passed, I was especially vulnerable to that accusation. Such accusations can be dangerous. Too much arrogance invites a violent reaction—as mentioned above, many Jakartans told me that they perceived Chinese, East Timorese, and Acehnese to be *belagu* or *sombong* and implied that the arrogance of these groups justified their victimization at the hands of the Indonesian majority. Those who warned me against associating with the *anak tongkrongan*—"guys hanging out"—also framed their warning in terms of arrogance: having a white foreigner associate with them would go to the men's heads, and they would be more brazen in their behavior toward others, particularly women passersby, and feel superior to other roadside groups. (I did not observe this among the *anak tongkrongan* I knew.)

One Night in Kebayoran Baru

To give the reader a sense of the goings-on of a typical night, following is a description based on field notes from the night of February 16, 2000, a Wednesday. On this night, after having to cancel a trip to Bandung due to a lingering stomach illness, I decided to visit some of the local neighborhood hangouts. This night also marked the first time I stopped at the Pondok Cinta security post.

1. The Warung Gaul, approximately 8:20–10:50 p.m. When I arrive only Rizal, the proprietor, and his friend Andie are there, sitting on a bench and strumming a guitar. Agus, Mahmud, and another young man are inside the office building of Agus's employers, watching dangdut video clips on television. On the screen I catch a glimpse of Iyeth Bustami's video for "Cinta Hanya Sekali," the shooting of which I attended [see previous chapter]. I decide not to mention this fact to those present. When I ask why they are not hanging out outside at the *warung*, they reply that outside it is too *sepi* (lonely, deserted), even though they in effect are causing the "loneliness" by choosing to remain inside. Within an hour or so other young men begin to arrive, and the three watching television go outside to join them. I remark to the group that I have not been feeling well (*kurang enak badan*, literally

Dangdutan at the Warung Gaul, using the body of the guitar as a percussion instrument, Kebayoran Baru.

"body is less than pleasant"), which results in my becoming the recipient of two unsolicited and rather rough shoulder massages.

Over the next two hours, an uninterrupted soundtrack of dangdut and *nostalgia* songs accompanies the talking and joking of the *warung* regulars. The songs are played with voice, guitar, and various improvised idiophones, including bottles, a key chain, and a wooden bench, as well as the body of the acoustic guitar itself, which one performer beats rhythmically, *gendang* style, while another strums.[7] The participants pay varying levels of attention to the music, depending on who is playing what. At times the whole group sings together when they know the words to a particular line of a song. Toward the end of my stay, Ucok monopolizes the guitar once again, playing the same open chord progression (C–G–F) over and over and singing semi-improvised lyrics. Those surrounding him, for the most part, seem to ignore his performance. I finally excuse myself shortly before eleven, one of the first to leave.

2. The Warung under the Tree, 11:00 p.m.–12:20 a.m. After a short conversation with the workers at the open-all-night *warung seafood* down the road from the Warung Gaul, I head in the direction of the Warung di Bawah Pohon. On this night, there is only one guitar; it is accompanied by the *gicik* (homemade tambourine-like instrument) and the *galon* (plastic water-cooler bottle). I am asked to play a song on the guitar, and I try to oblige by playing "Ball and Chain," a 1990 song by the California punk band Social Distortion. Although the seven participants are unfamiliar with the song, they follow along enthusiastically, trying to approximate the sounds of the English lyrics. They are more successful in following the song's melodic contours, which by the second chorus they have mastered. They then demand I sing the song translated into Indonesian, which I do, rather awkwardly. While I play, Yusuf adds a dangdut rhythm to the song on the *galon*, which further amuses the group.

It is getting late and we are running out of songs, so I suggest an Indonesian children's song conventionally sung at the end of gatherings and performances. The song's refrain, which can be subject to an unlimited number of repetitions, is

> *Pulang, marilah pulang*
> *Marilah pulang*
> *Bersama-sama.*

[Go home, let's go home
Let's go home
All together.]

Our version of the farewell song lasts over six minutes and undergoes several rhythm changes. After it ends, we all say good night and go our separate ways, walking out of the gaslit area around the *warung* into the surrounding warm, quiet darkness.

3. The Pondok Cinta, 12:22 a.m.–3:10 a.m. Weary from illness and a night of performing and socializing, I walk back to my rooming house. I am less than a minute away when I hear some acoustic dangdut music emanating from an elevated bamboo platform on a street corner, with its back facing the street. Moving closer to investigate, I see three men seated on the platform, one singing and playing a guitar, another playing a small *gendang*, and the third sitting behind him listening. I approach and they acknowledge me silently and continue playing. The guitarist is about twenty-five, younger than the other two men, and his instrument is in better condition and in better tune than those played by most roadside musicians. After a few classic dangdut songs, the two musicians switch to playing a socially conscious Indonesian rap song titled "Putauw" (Heroin), by Neo, a popular hip hop group, and then return to the dangdut repertoire. I am impressed by the *gendang* player's ability to mimic hip hop beats on his drums.

　　The three men are soon joined by a heavyset man who accompanies the music with an ingeniously constructed idiophone consisting of a pair of metal spoons and a metal knife. He uses this improvised instrument to create high-pitched, metallic sounds resembling those of a tambourine. I am impressed by the skill of all the musicians, especially the *gendang* player, who manages to produce pleasing sounds using an undersized drum with a torn skin *tak* head and a cheap plastic *dhut* head. The guitarist is no less skilled—in addition to dangdut and *pop Indonesia*, he flawlessly plays the guitar parts to Eric Clapton, Eagles, and Metallica songs, though he does not sing them.

　　More people, all men in their late twenties to early forties, begin arriving, despite the late hour. Some of them take turns singing with the musicians. Among the later arrivals is a local physician as well as an intense, fortysomething man named Ismail who was once an aspiring dangdut singer. Pak Ismail tells me that aside from Latin music, he dislikes all *lagu Barat* (Western songs) and only listens to dangdut, which he studied intently from audiocassettes for over three years when he was trying to build a singing career. After someone tells him that I am visiting Indonesia to learn more about dangdut music, he spends over two hours talking to me between songs about dangdut's early history (mentioning Mashabi and several other *orkes Melayu* stars), the complicated melodic ornamentations (*cengkok*) that a good singer must master, and how Meggi Z's vocal style is superior to Rhoma Irama's because it is "purer" and less rock influenced. Ismail expresses skepticism about current trends in youth music, saying that the musical preferences of the "young kids" (*anak muda*) are "not yet settled" (*belum stabil*, a phrase often used at the time to describe the Indonesian polity). I finally excuse myself around 3:10 in the morning, saying politely that I need to go home because I do not want to forget anything Ismail has told me. In truth, I am also exhausted; I have stayed out far later than I had planned.

According to Ismail, eventually all the Indonesian kids rushing to follow the latest pop music trend will settle down and embrace their true music: dangdut. This notion that dangdut, in contrast to pop, is somehow immune from changing fashions and represents musical maturity was shared by many working-class men who spoke to me about Indonesian music. It is worth noting that while the younger regulars at the Warung Gaul and the Warung under the Tree expressed enthusiasm for contemporary rock and pop songs, their actual performing repertoire consisted of older pop songs that had withstood the test of time and dangdut compositions. Thus it is conceivable that by following musical trends these young people were simply enlarging their musical vocabularies without abandoning their parents' music for their own. In addition, dangdut and *pop nostalgia* were recognized as contextually appropriate for hanging-out activities. They were, in effect, the requisite soundtrack to life by the side of the road, whether they were one's favorite style of music or not.

Gendered Spaces

In the course of her research with street children in the Javanese city of Yogyakarta, Harriot Beazley reports encountering among her consultants explicit statements regarding behavioral norms for women, especially concerning nighttime behavior.

For example, when I talked to boys and girls on the street, they often mentioned how girls were "supposed" to behave. I was intrigued by this rhetoric and asked them to tell me exactly what was expected of young women by Indonesian society. The children (both boys and girls) answered that women in Indonesia cannot go out after 9:30 in the evening, they cannot go where they please, they cannot drink alcohol, they cannot smoke, they cannot have sex before marriage, they cannot wear "sexy" clothes, and they cannot leave the house without permission. They must be good, nice, kind and helpful, and stay at home to do domestic chores and to look after their children or younger siblings. These answers from the children are a clear example of how gender roles are internalized at an early age. (Beazley 2002, 1669)

While Jakarta is often considered more cosmopolitan and permissive than smaller, more "traditional" cities like Yogyakarta, the statements Beazley relates sum up rather well the attitudes I encountered among Jakarta's working-class youth. Nighttime hangouts were clearly male-oriented, largely homosocial spaces. One night a friend of Rizal's visited the Warung Gaul. He arrived on a motorcycle, his girlfriend riding behind him. While her boyfriend joked around for about fifteen minutes with the young men at the *warung*, she sat silently on the motorcycle, looking more than a bit uncomfortable. She waited there with averted eyes until her boyfriend returned to the motorcycle and they drove away. Similarly, when I asked Jono Z, one of the Pondok Cinta regulars, why his wife did not hang out with him at the security post, he said it was because he wanted to keep her away from the "naughty mosquitoes" (*nyamuk nakal*), by which he meant disreputable men hanging out at night, much as he was. Despite these sentiments (which I heard voiced many times by working-class Indonesian men), two other regulars' wives frequently showed up at the Pondok Cinta with their husbands, and they often joined in the singing.

I concluded that women had to be a little brave to hang out at night, but that women who opted to do so were not excluded. Women who chose to hang out at night were usually older and married; I was told that young girls were either at home protecting their virtue or, alternately, out in search of males with a bit more money than those who hung out all night by the side of the road. The situation was quite different among Jakartan university students, where women, while usually a minority, would hang out and socialize with young men without risking censure. This difference in gender norms is inseparable from class distinctions and the ways in which such distinctions index differing attitudes toward Western secular values regarding social interactions between unmarried men and women. The next section explores the culture of *nongkrong* in Indonesian university life, where popular music fills a role similar to the one it plays at *warung*, that of facilitator of social intercourse and group solidarity.

On Campus: Middle-Class Hangouts

Even during the New Order, many Indonesian students saw their campuses as safe havens. In late 1997, when Soeharto's grip on power still seemed unbreakable, students at the Institut Kesenian Jakarta (IKJ) told me that they were free to do what they wished on their campus, including smoke marijuana and sing about politics, without the military and the police harassing them. In post–New Order Jakarta, I found that college campuses had not changed much, aside from the prevalence of posters and banners sporting brazen political slogans. Groups of students still hung out together on campus, often with guitars, and unlike their counterparts by the side of the road, often in mixed gender groups. University campuses were considered *rame* (crowded, noisy, sociable, fun) places. At the private university where I taught classes one semester, Western and Indonesian pop music blared out of the office of the student music activity group at all hours of the day, loud enough to be heard in many classrooms. Often one also heard someone trying to play along with the music on a worn old drum kit kept in the office; this show of musical prowess could be quite distracting to class instructors.

The everyday existence of most of the Jakarta university students I knew differed little from that of the Warung Gaul regulars: they did not have much money, they lived in cheap boardinghouses (*rumah kost*) or with their families, ate at inexpensive *warung*, and spent much of their time hanging out with their friends. They had also begun hanging out at *warnet*s (Internet cafés) chatting and surfing the World Wide Web, as had an increasing number of nonstudent youth in Jakarta. The main difference between the students and the Warung Gaul regulars was the students' potential for social mobility, of someday having enough money to participate in a middle-class world of consumerism and individualism (see the discussion at the end of chapter 2). Thus the similarities between students and nonstudents were temporary and are counterbalanced by significant differences in both everyday behavior and prospects for the future.

I attended a particularly memorable campus *nongkrong* session that took place at Universitas Prof. Dr. Moestopo, a private university in Senayan, Central Jakarta. I had gone to Moestopo's campus to interview Wendi Putranto, the editor in chief of *Brainwashed*, one of Jakarta's oldest and longest-running underground zines.[8] A senior in Moestopo's Faculty of Communications, he had also recently begun working for an Indonesian-language, student-oriented Web site, bisik.com (*bisik* = whisper), writing music reviews and editing the portion of the site dedicated to underground music.

I met Wendi at the entrance to campus, and we walked a short distance to the Faculty of Communications student senate office, a small, partially air-conditioned room decorated with political posters and flyers. One wall of the office was adorned with two battered and vandalized plastic riot police shields and a gas mask, "spoils of war" from the clashes between Indonesian soldiers and student demonstrators in 1998–99. On one of the shields, the slogan *aparat keparat*, which paired the Indonesian word for "troops," *aparat*, with *keparat*, an obscenity meaning "bastard" (yielding "barracks bastards"?), was etched in large block letters on the clear plastic. A large poster on another wall depicted former president B. J. Habibie standing over a map of Indonesia and sporting a Gorbachev-like birthmark on his bald head. Over his head was written *Bapak Disintegrasi*, "Father of Disintegration," alluding to a similarity between the violent movements for independence that troubled Habibie's brief presidency and the breakup of the Soviet Union under Gorbachev. The office also included a library/bookstore consisting of old and new books on Indonesian politics and culture, among them a battered hardcover copy of Sukarno's *Di Bawah Bendera Revolusi* (Beneath the Banner of Revolution), a weighty tome that was banned during the New Order and had yet to be reprinted. Wendi explained to me proudly that existing copies of the book were quite valuable.

In addition to acting as the home base for the *Brainwashed* zine (which had acquired a fairly large staff in its five years of operation) and a preferred hangout for South Jakarta's punks, the Faculty of Communications was also home to a cottage industry that manufactured T-shirts with politically subversive slogans. Wendi was wearing an example, a black shirt featuring the text *"Fuck Capitalism!"* Many local punk and hardcore bands also produced their merchandise at this facility.

I asked Wendi if he often stayed up all night hanging out in the senate office. Not as much as before, he replied. During the months of student demonstrations preceding Gus Dur's election, the office became a kind of headquarters, and he frequently spent the night there with other campus activists. At the time, the office had a computer with Internet access, which the students used to communicate and record their experiences. Unfortunately the computer was stolen; Wendi suspects "provocateurs" were behind the theft.

Wendi introduced me to the Mohawk-wearing guitarist of a punk band named Error Crew, whom he joked was a *punk intelek*, meaning both an intellectual punk and a punk "in *telek* [Javanese for 'shit']." Several other members of punk and hardcore bands also came by, as well as some politicos. Soon a hanging-out session, complete with guitar sing-alongs, was in full swing, and would last until early in the morning.

In addition to performing their favorite rock and underground songs, the students had much to say on the topic of Indonesian popular music, no doubt due in part to the presence of a curious American music researcher. They debated whether dangdut was "hegemonic," but at the same time they decried the hypocrisy of MTV Indonesia for introducing a dangdut video show but refusing to include dangdut artists in its annual video music award contest. (As it happened, a few months later, MTV introduced a *Best Dangdut* category at its 2000 awards show.) Although for the most part they viewed dangdut as "mass culture" music in the purest Adornonian sense, some of the students spoke admiringly of a punk band from Yogyakarta named Soekarmadjoe (the name means "difficult to advance/progress"), which had switched to playing dangdut music after deciding that dangdut, not punk, was the true "*working class*" music of Indonesia. (According to the members of Soekarmadjoe, whom I later met, this story is not entirely accurate. See chapter 10 for more on this group.)

The subject of *pop Indonesia* brought out other controversies. A campus activist criticized *pop alternatif* bands like Potret and Dewa 19 as being purely derivative of Western groups. He also expressed skepticism regarding underground music as an effective force for political and social change. Other students defended the underground, as long as it maintained its ideological purity. Wendi told me to ask some of the punks what they would say if their bands were offered a major-label contract. Their emphatic response: No! One added that he would actually accept but then just steal the money and run.

The students were divided on the issue of language choice in song lyrics. While Error Crew's guitarist said that in the future there could be Indonesian punk bands that sang convincingly in Indonesian, other punks opined that English was more "international" and more appropriate for underground music. "Indonesian is good for dangdut," said one disparagingly. Punks are the most ideologically driven subsection of the underground, the only group for whom "lifestyle" tends to matter more than the music. Thus it is not surprising that they have clung most stubbornly to singing in English, no matter how ungrammatical and incoherent. I had assumed that this choice meant that punk music really was sellout-proof in the Indonesian-language-dominated mainstream music market. As it turned out, I was mistaken; later that month in a mall record store I encountered a cassette of punk songs sung in fractured English by a group called Rage Generation Brothers (*Our Lifestyle,* 2000) released on a large, commercial record label.

We debated, well into the night, the works of the Frankfurt School, postmodernism (*posmo*), methods of qualitative communications research, Anthony Giddens's concept of the Third Way (one of the most influential ideas among Indonesian intellectuals at the time), Noam Chomsky's *Manufacturing Consent,* and the writings of Karl Marx and Antonio Gramsci. At various points, nearly two dozen people crammed into the office to participate in the discussion or just to listen. While the students were sympathetic to leftist and social democratic thinkers from the West, they also were critical of Western ethnocentrism and hypocrisy. For example, they were especially opposed to international intellectual property law, which they perceived as limiting free trade (and thus contradicting the neoliberalism that is otherwise hegemonic in the West), and which they critiqued for putting developing countries at a disadvantage, since patents and copyrights tend to be owned by entities based in the developed world.[9]

I was consistently impressed with the level of knowledge I encountered; the experience was certainly at odds with the accounts I had read by both Indonesian and foreign scholars of the alleged laziness and mediocrity of Indonesian students and intellectuals (cf. Mulder 2000, 232–33). These students were knowledgeable and socially aware, and through hanging out, listening to and creating music, and debating ideas, they forged a collective but nonexclusive identity for themselves. Unlike the regulars at the Warung Gaul and their more apathetic classmates, these students approached American and Indonesian popular culture not with longing but with a critically engaged stance, aware of both the injustices and the emancipatory possibilities of the contemporary world.[10] What was striking was the importance of underground music in developing this critically engaged stance: if Chomsky's words provided a guideline for oppositional thought, then the music of the American group Rage Against the Machine, or of the numerous Indonesian rock groups that band influenced, gave a sense of what being oppositional *felt* like. Moreover, interest in that band often preceded interest in the progressive author. Wendi himself credited Rage Against the Machine for first teaching him about "ideology and oppressed people" (*ideologi dan orang tertindas*), its music providing an impetus for his political activism.

Sociality, Solidarity, and Musical Meaning

Other contexts of informal musical performances and conversations about music in Jakarta include karaoke sessions in all manner of public and private spaces as well as performance and listening activities in living rooms, dorm rooms, bedrooms, and servants' quarters. In each of these contexts, popular music is a shared reference point for people from diverse ethnic backgrounds. Like the Indonesian language itself, especially its colloquial variants and verbal art genres, music promotes social harmony (*rukun*) across ethnic, regional, and other social boundaries by creating a participatory space for collective enjoyment, and occasionally by providing an impetus for reflexive interpretation of one's social position.

It is perhaps unfashionable to claim that shared values and meanings exist across socioeconomic boundaries, as though different groups in a society share a "deeper" underlying culture that somehow transcends radical differences in life experience and opportunities for social advancement. Nevertheless, I found that certain similarities exist, to the point that working-class urban Indonesians resemble university-educated middle-class Indonesians in their social interactions far more than might be expected in such a polarized society. This resemblance does not, of course, erase the wide gulf that exists between haves and have-nots in Indonesian cities, but it points to a cross-class affinity that might some day have sociopolitical ramifications.

Indonesian nationalism arguably succeeds not only due to the ethnic neutrality of the Indonesian language and Indonesian popular culture, but also Indonesians' longstanding ethic of tolerance for various forms of social difference. The culture of *nongkrong* exemplifies this ethic of tolerance and informality, as well as the value of achieving social harmony without erasing the differences that exist among individuals. Even as a non-Muslim American, I became accepted at the Warung Gaul as long as I participated and showed up consistently over weeks and weeks—though it remains true that such acceptance would probably be more difficult for a Chinese Indonesian to gain.[11] *Nongkrong* sociality is predicated on an ethic of reciprocity in which the obligations are equal for both parties, and the nonhierarchical, open, and accepting nature of hanging-out culture makes the refusal to *bergaul* seem offensive and indicative of *kesombongan,* of an attitude of arrogant superiority, on the part of the refuser.

Finally, *nongkrong* sociality illustrates one of the central points of this ethnography: that in Indonesia music making is irreducibly social. Moreover, I want to suggest that it is possible to view almost all music-related activities in Indonesia, from recording to performing to listening, as shaped and informed by an interactive sensibility derived from *nongkrong* sociality. From this perspective, the cultural work of hanging out is anything but trivial.

PART TWO

Genres in Performance

7

Onstage

THE LIVE MUSICAL EVENT

We now move from the informal performances of everyday urban settings to more-structured performance events where, unlike at local hangout spots, a perceptible division exists between performers and audience. These sites include public places where humble street musicians perform with hopes of monetary gain and social recognition as much as the elaborate stages of stadiums and television studios. At all levels of formal performance, issues of sponsorship, sociality, and the collective negotiation of multifaceted identities shape the form and meaning of the music being performed.

Lebak Bulus Stadium, Jakarta, March 9, 2000
   The rock band onstage launches into its signature tune, garnering an immediate, enthusiastic response from the audience. Soon it seems as though the entire stadium of normally restrained and laconic young students are dancing, smiling, and singing the words of the song together. A few dozen dancers form a growing "conga line" of connected bodies that jubilantly snakes it way through the crowd. The song is "Radja" (King), in which the song's protagonist dreams of being king. The refrain is

> *Tapi aku bukan Radja,*
> *Ku hanya orang biasa*
> *Yang selalu dijadikan alas kaki pada Sang Radja.*

Aku hanya bisa menahan dan melihat
membayangkan dan memimpikan tuk menjadi seorang radja.

[But I'm not a king
I'm just an ordinary person
Who is always made to be the sole of the king's foot
I can only endure and watch
Imagining and dreaming about being a king.]

After the guitar solo and third repetition of the refrain comes the high point of the song, in which the lyrics of the whole song are summarized and accompanied by easy-to-follow melodic vocables.

Na na na na hei ya
Na na na na hei ya
Na na na na hei ya
Na na na na
Ku bukan seorang radja!

Hei ya na na na na hei ya
Na na na na hei ya
Na na na na
Ku hanya orang biasa!

[Hei ya . . .
I'm not a king!

Hei ya . . .
I'm just an ordinary person!]

For the brief duration of the song, nervous questions of national identity, Western culture, socioeconomic class, and cultural difference dissolve into an ecstatic communitas of shared musical experience, and the audience exults vicariously in the predicament of the ordinary (Indonesian?) person portrayed in the song. Caught up in the spirit of the moment, I decide that the performance exemplifies one of the great things about popular music—the celebration of ordinariness over the drive for wealth and status (which otherwise preoccupies the middle-class Jakartan youth in the audience), accompanied by a thinly disguised critique of power.[1]

The by-now-familiar themes of genre, social class, gender, sociality, and hybridity are important in an examination of the many forms of onstage live musical performance in Indonesia. For the present purposes, I define "onstage performance" as any performance situation in which there is a socially recognized division between performer(s) and audience and some form of payment is offered to or expected by the performer(s) from the audience and/or from a third-party sponsor. To gather material for this chapter and the three chapters that follow it, I attended a total of eighty-three concert events in venues on the island of Java in 1997 and 1999–2000. I also observed and recorded numerous other less-structured performance occasions in malls, buses, train cars, clubs, and other public spaces. From these varied experiences I have developed a tentative, general account of the live musical event in Java.

Performances, Audiences, and Inclusiveness

The "performance event," a phrase that has become increasingly important in ethnomusicological and anthropological research, is regarded as a privileged locus for the examination of locally situated musical and cultural meanings, where sound and behavior can be analyzed together as constitutive of a larger whole (Stone 1982). Developments in the other human sciences have encouraged this focus. The foundational texts of what has become known as the "performance approach" were written by folklorists and linguistic anthropologists interested primarily in performed speech genres. In one such work, Bauman ([1977] 1984) describes performance as involving (1) some type of *framing device* (see Goffman 1974) that sets it off from the normal flow of events; (2) an acceptance of responsibility on the part of the performer; and (3) an "emergent" quality, which holds the potential for unexpected outcomes. Bauman and Briggs (1990) suggest further that performance events can be viewed as occasions for critical reflection on social life. Ethnomusicologist Regula Qureshi writes, "A performance becomes a locus in which old meanings are tested and new ones are negotiated; where rules are enforced, broken, and rewritten; and where musical meanings are interpreted and felt anew, as memories are fashioned into icons relating to the present moment" (2000, 827). Musical performances in Indonesia, through demystifying aspects of social existence (such as class and gender categories), evoking memories, and offering affectively compelling experiences, generate reflection and even transformations in consciousness. We will see how the emergent meanings of the onstage performance event are subject to the varied and often conflicting agendas of participants, and how meanings are negotiated in response to multi-sensory experiences of musical sound and spectacle.

Popular music performance events in Indonesia, like performances everywhere, ultimately resist any single agenda, and both complicity and resistance to hegemonic forces, from consumer capitalism to Indo-nesian official nationalism, may be present at the same moment. In the following discussion, however, I am less interested in the cultural poli-tics of live musical events than in the importance of musical perform-ance in the formation of subjectivities on both the individual and the collective levels. We have seen how characteristic processes of creative innovation and hybridization in Indonesian popular music production have uncertain and multiple social effects. The immediacy and emer-gent quality of live musical performance intensifies this unpredictabil-ity, as audiences actively coparticipate in establishing the meanings of an event. The process of ongoing interpretation involves all the partici-pants in a performance situation and primarily operates via the realm of affective experience, simultaneously personal and shared. On the social and individual dimensions of musical performance Qureshi writes: "The physical sensation of sound not only activates feeling, it also activates links with others who feel. In an instant, the sound of music can create bonds of shared responses that are as deep and intimate as they are broad and universal. The ephemeral bond of a sonic event does not commit to physical contact—though it may elicit it. Experiencing music together leaves the personal, individual, and interior domain unviolated. At the same time, the experience becomes public, shared, and exterior" (Qureshi 2000, 810).

The ability of particular musical events to create social bonds with-out necessarily dissolving self/other boundaries has been commented on by psychoanalysts (e.g., Nass 1971), and the creation of collective sen-timent and social solidarity through musical performance has been dis-cussed by music researchers in a wide variety of cultural settings, from rain forests to raves (e.g., Feld [1982] 1990; Seeger 1987; Thornton 1996). Researchers in European-American popular music in particular have asserted the existence of a close link between self-conscious, individual identity formation and the generation of collective sentiment in the flow of performance (e.g., Berger 1999; Fikentscher 2000; Nelson 1999; Shank 1994). Indeed, if one accepts the notion that identity and subjectivity are constructed through dialogue with others (C. Taylor 1991), musical performance events constitute an important, emotionally heightened arena where such interactions take place.

Popular music performances in Indonesia, as in the United States and elsewhere, have significant implications for questions of identity and affect, but they also follow particular cultural logics of hybridity and sociality peculiar to Indonesian representational practice. In particular, musical performance events in Indonesia enact an ethic of *inclusiveness*, within which musical differences indexing social differences between people and their divergent allegiances are rhetorically transcended. Through the juxtaposing, parodying, and blending of musical genres, performers and audience collaborate in the creation of a hybridic, self-aware, ephemeral community in which unassimilated differences coexist as a dizzying array of alternatives—Indonesian, modern, traditional, trendy, American, global, populist, elitist, Muslim, ethnic, and so on— that not only do not line up easily into simple binary oppositions but also cannot be placed easily into a single coherent framework. This performed multiplicity nevertheless conforms to an ethic of radical inclusiveness and the promotion of social solidarity, both of which are key components of a vernacular Indonesian nationalism that is perhaps expressed more eloquently in popular music than in any other Indonesian mass medium.

Benedict Anderson elucidates the grassroots appeal of Indonesian nationalism among Javanese in the following passage: "The urge to oneness, so central to Javanese political attitudes, helps to explain the deep psychological power of the idea of nationalism in Java. Far more than a political credo, nationalism expresses a fundamental drive to solidarity and unity in the face of the disintegration of traditional society under colonial capitalism, and other powerful external forces, from the late nineteenth century on. Nationalism of this type is something far stronger than patriotism; it is an attempt to reconquer a primordial oneness" (Anderson 1990, 37). While Anderson is speaking specifically of Javanese, I found that the achievement, through performance, of a national "primordial oneness" underlying surface social and musical diversity was a recurrent theme in live musical performances in multiethnic urban contexts. But this sense of underlying unity differs from that of the integrated, well-ordered hierarchical universe that Anderson describes as the idealized Javanese "traditional society." James Siegel (1986) has argued that the boundaries of the latter ideal society are coterminous with the High Javanese speech community, and that linguistic heterogeneity, translation, and the failure of linguistic communication itself threaten its coherence. I would argue that the "oneness" of modern Indonesian nationalism, by contrast, is polyvocal, multilingual, heteroglossic, cosmopolitan, and inclusive, and its boundaries are inherently porous.

This discussion thus builds on the insights contained in chapter 6 regarding Indonesian "sociality" and the polyphonic unity and solidarity achieved through "hanging out" and other collaborative, participatory endeavors. At Indonesian popular music events, genres become virtual participants in an interactive, intersubjective space in which identities are forged, questioned, reinforced, pried open, and reconfigured in a spirit of play and experimentation. Despite these events' seeming frivolity and shallow eclecticism, and the undeniable pleasures they provide, this is a serious game that has high stakes as it confronts and interrogates *non*virtual social categories based on class, gender, religion, and ethnicity that impact people's lives in concrete ways.

Taking all these issues into account, we turn first to the variety of onstage performance events that one encounters in Jakarta.

"Live Music" in the Capital: From Streets to Stadiums

Terms for live performance vary in Indonesian: the English phrase *live music* is frequently used, as is *musik langsung* (literally "direct music") and *musik hidup* (live music). Performing musicians are everywhere in urban Java: at train stations, aboard trains, in mall food courts, at *warung,* in city buses, and of course at nightclubs, cafés, outdoor stages, and other specialized performance venues. In Jakarta, almost all the music performed in these various settings is popular music, mostly national Indonesian or Western genres. The few exceptions include occasional Western classical music concerts sponsored by European cultural institutes and the live gamelan music found in five-star-hotel lobbies and at lavish ethnic Javanese weddings.

Live performance is not heavily mythologized in the Indonesian popular music scene. There is little sense that concerts are somehow prior to or more authentic than recordings; this is not surprising given that recordings generally determine the sound of live performances and that popular music fans generally emphasize recorded songs over artists. Live performance is simply one of many modalities through which music is experienced, though it is certainly one of the more intense and pleasurable. In urban Java there is a robust demand for live music. Successful Indonesian recording artists, particularly dangdut singers, can earn sizable incomes from live appearances. Often this income far exceeds what they earn in royalties from album sales (mostly due to disadvantageous arrangements with recording companies and the ever-present problem of cassette piracy). In Jakarta, established artists regularly perform in stadiums, at five-star hotels, at prestigious nightclubs, and in television studios for live or prerecorded music broadcasts.

Yet media stars participate in only a small percentage of the live performance events taking place on any given night in the capital city. Jakarta stages are mostly inhabited by amateur, semiprofessional, and undiscovered artists, and these performers are the focus of most of the discussion that follows. My account of live music in Jakarta commences at the far opposite end of the performer spectrum from the high-paid stars, with performers whose "stage" is the city streets or the interiors of buses, trains, and food stalls: humble street musicians slinging battered, colorfully decorated guitars, who roam through the city in search of spare change. The work of these performers, known as *pengamen*, constitutes the most abundant (if banal) source of live music in Jakarta, and for this reason they deserve more than passing mention.

Pengamen (Street Musicians): Contested Performance

Jangan kau nyanyikan lagu sumbang itu
Sebab,
Aku dengar petik gitar semalam
Yang kau bawa di keramaian kota.

Kau yang tegar dalam sebuah
perjalanan
Kapan kita nyanyikan, akhir sebuah
lagu malam.
Tanpa suasana kita terus bernyanyi
Berdendang teriknya penghidupan.

["Do not sing that indecent song
Because,
I hear the strumming of your guitar all night long
That you carry around in the hustle and bustle of the city."

You who stubbornly continue on your
journey
When will we sing to the end a
song of night?

Without warmth or openness, we sing on and on,
Singing of the stifling deadness of our lives.]
"Tembang Bagi Pengamen"
(A Song for Traveling Street Musicians),
in Badjuridoellahjoestro 1994 [2]

Not everyone I met while in Indonesia shared this poet's sympathy toward street musicians. *Pengamen,* traveling performers/mendicants in Indonesian cities, were often criticized as little more than beggars who were unwilling to work (*malas kerja; ngga' mau usaha*). Taxicab drivers were particularly vociferous in their criticism, weary of being approached at intersections by armies of young men carrying out-of-tune guitars and singing off-key *pop nostalgia* songs.

While the majority of *pengamen* play battered acoustic guitars, some also play ukuleles, violins, hand drums, empty plastic water bottles, and tambourines. More accomplished street musicians often play in mobile ensembles of these instruments. Other *pengamen,* usually older, play traditional instruments such as the Javanese *celempung* (zither) or *kendang* (barrel drum); in Jakarta those musicians are less common than in other Javanese cities. Another category of *pengamen* consists of sight-impaired men who carry portable sound systems from bus to bus and sing along to dangdut karaoke cassettes through inexpensive, distorted microphones. *Waria* (ladyboys; transgendered cross-dressers) also sometimes work as *pengamen,* with karaoke equipment or without.

Many of the more skilled amateur musicians I met who played informally by the side of the road (see chapter 6) worked as *pengamen* (verb form: *ngamen*) from time to time to make some extra money, sometimes even traveling to other cities to do so. But since the most common donation given to most *pengamen* (and beggars) in Jakarta was a one-hundred-rupiah coin, and the cheapest meal with rice at the time was around Rp. 3,000, the possibility of having significant earnings left at the end of the day was slight for most street performers. A trio of *pengamen* who played on buses told that me on a good day they could make Rp. 10,000, still barely enough to pay for meals. Nevertheless, they told me that they enjoyed performing, and that playing music was better than a life of crime and better than working a regular job.

Some famous Indonesian singers began their careers as *pengamen,* most notably rock legend Iwan Fals (considered by many to be Indonesia's answer to Bob Dylan and Bruce Springsteen), who was a sort of patron saint revered by legions of street musicians. Inspired by "Bang" (Older Brother) Iwan, some *pengamen* wrote their own songs with topical, politically satirical lyrics; traveling street poets also recited verses on political issues, including resistance to anti-Chinese racism and military violence. The *pengamen* I met could play several Iwan Fals songs, though they usually played more crowd-pleasing tunes—current pop hits and *pop nostalgia*—when seeking donations. I found that the skill and enthusiasm with which these *pengamen* played Iwan Fals compositions when requested to do so often contrasted sharply with the lower quality of their renditions of songs by other artists.

Anak Jalanan

In Jakarta I encountered groups of children, often siblings or cousins, who roamed the streets of busy areas like Blok M until late at night, approaching pedestrians and motorists in a quest for rupiahs. They sang schoolchildren's patriotic songs or performed their own compositions about life singing on the streets, accompanying themselves on ukuleles and *gicik*. Some of these children help support their families instead of attending school, the fees for which many families cannot afford. In Indonesian popular culture the "street kid" (*anak jalanan*) is a tragic but hopeful figure, representing the failure of the Indonesian government to provide for all its citizens but also the creativity and enterprise of Indonesian youth. The *anak jalanan* who sings for his or her sustenance is an especially enduring social stereotype in Indonesia, but the reality street children face is one of marginalization and harassment (Beazley 2000, 2002). Experienced child singers command a sizable memorized repertoire that includes pop and dangdut songs.

Adult *pengamen* are almost always male and appear to represent a particular Indonesian male ideal—that of the free traveler who gets by through his wits rather than through employment. Yiska, a seventeen-year-old *pengamen* in the city of Bandung, told me that she made more money than most because it was so unusual for people to see a female street performer, and that since she had already been singing in the street for four years she was accustomed to the heat and exhaust fumes from the local buses. She added that during those years she did not attend school. Privately, a male friend of Yiska's told me that her career of singing and playing guitar on buses was far better than "selling herself" (*jual diri*), in other words, better than following many other teenage girls from poor families into prostitution.

The guitar-slinging young men who loiter at traffic intersections and play in front of windows of halted cars (briefly mentioned in chapter 2)

Anak jalanan (street children) singing for money, Lebak Bulus, South Jakarta. The child on the right is holding a *gicik*.

often neither sing nor play very well. They typically endeavor to make enough noise to cause motorists to crack open their window and hand them some rupiah coins just to be rid of the nuisance. These *pengamen* immediately cease performing once they are paid and move on to the next stopped vehicle (cf. Siegel 1986, 119, and the poem quoted above). Street musicians on buses and trains tend to be more skilled and less co-ercive. Performances on buses often begin with a short speech by a solo musician or one member of an ensemble, addressing the "audience" and expressing hope that the passengers will enjoy their humble musical of-ferings. After one or two songs, a member of the group or a companion passes around a used plastic candy bag, the top edge neatly folded over, to collect monetary contributions. Usually no more than a handful of commuters throw coins in the bag, an action for which they are politely thanked. The *pengamen* then jump off the next time the bus stops and move on in search of other audiences.

Street musicians occupy the lowest level of public musical perform-ance, and the "breakthrough" into performance (Hymes 1975) they at-tempt is contested by the others present. By withholding contributions and by ignoring the musicians, members of the captive "audiences" of *pengamen* attempt to deny the existence of a performance frame. If what is taking place is in fact not a performance but something more mundane, such as a request for alms, onlookers are not obligated to reciprocate or even pay attention. Indeed, the word *pengamen* is often translated simply as "beggar" (though in Jakarta mendicants who do not sing or play instruments are usually called *pengemis*, not *pengamen*).

Pengamen and Musical Replication

Whether their audience regards them as public nuisances or as welcome entertainment during a long, exhausting commute, *pengamen* are important agents of musical replication who operate outside the official mass media. They respond, of course, to market forces and musical trends but, like the amateur musicians by the side of the road, also reclaim commercially recorded songs as grassroots music of "the Indonesian people," reanimating high-tech recorded performances through low-tech live renditions. In mid-2000, it was common to hear the hit song "Jika" (If), a duet by *pop alternatif* stars Melly Goeslaw and Ari Lasso, played by street musicians throughout Jakarta. The song was sometimes hard to recognize when performed solo with an acoustic guitar, without the complex, multilayered electronic accompaniment on the recording, but listeners seemed to enjoy hearing these renditions, which were the closest most of them would ever come to hearing the "real" song (that is, the version on the recording) performed live.

If one refrains from treating national identity as a given, the role of *pengamen* in domesticating the products of the Jakarta-based national culture industry deserves consideration. If *pengamen* are living icons of "the folk" (*rakyat*), as so many of them claim, then the music played by *pengamen* is ipso facto folk music, representing ordinary Indonesians and constituting a musical heritage shared by all citizens, from the humblest to the most affluent. The street musician's command of the Indonesian popular music repertoire can be said to prove that Indonesian songs are for everyone, that even the most destitute are included in the national community the songs presuppose but, to paraphrase Clifford Geertz, in fact help to manufacture. *Pengamen* act as living radios, playing the songs the people want to hear in a performance economy that includes Indonesians from all levels of society, including those who are too poor to afford radios or cassettes of their own and do not figure into the marketing calculations of record companies. However, the fact that *pengamen* lack the patronage of a record company or other source of power and wealth makes them fraudulent performers in the eyes of many Indonesians. The modest contributions *pengamen* gain in the course of a day can be regarded as alms, not sponsorship, and their lack of institutional support, while constituting the source of their grassroots credibility, also becomes a reason to dismiss them.

The Social Organization, Structure, and Functions of *Acara*

A more formalized, less contested type of musical performance is known as the *acara* (event), a term that generally refers to any organized occasion featuring an audience and a performance of some type. While the presentations of *pengamen* take place on contested terrain and are not always accepted by the audience as actual performances, *acara* are considered legitimate contexts for live music, not least because, unlike street performances, they enjoy the material support of sponsors.

The *acara* is an important category in urban Indonesia, and the term denotes a more culturally salient phenomenon than "concert" (*konser*). *Acara* are not necessarily music related; they can be symposia, for example, or presentations, but they usually involve live music of some sort. They can be held to raise money for a charitable cause (*malam peduli*), to honor a university or high school graduating class, to celebrate a national holiday, to advertise a new consumer product, to launch a new Web site, or for a variety of other reasons. All *acara* have a sponsor or sponsors and are usually organized by a committee (*panitia*). Event organizers are respected professionals in Jakarta; they are frequently hired by committees to help find sponsors, hire security and soundmen, and assist with various other arrangements.

The most indispensable player in the *acara*, regardless of the type of entertainment featured, is the master of ceremonies. Emcees are usually paid much more than musicians, and their role in keeping the crowd happy is crucial to the event's success. According to a semiretired dangdut emcee living in a village in Central Java, a good emcee must be able to "look at the situation" (*lihat situasi*) and comprehend what the crowd wants without letting things get out of control. He told me that faster songs (*dangdut hot*) should be played at the beginning of the evening, whereas balladlike dangdut songs (*dangdut slow*) should be played toward the end, to calm the crowd. A sensitive emcee knows the precise moment at which to instruct a band to switch from one style to the other in order to avoid unrest and dissatisfaction.

Strong parallels exist between different kinds of *acara*. Dangdut shows always have an emcee, as do most underground concert events. Often the emcee at larger events is an entertainment personality—an actor, a model, or a comedian—while at smaller-scale events the role may be filled by a particularly charismatic member of the organizing committee. The emcee at dangdut shows is always male, and he usually sings a few songs in the course of the evening in addition to performing the important tasks of welcoming guests, introducing performers, and acknowledging sponsors. At *acara* featuring other types of music (e.g., pop, rock, and underground), women emcees are as common as men, and emcees of both sexes commonly work in pairs or groups. These emcees also address the crowd and introduce musicians, but rarely sing with them. A central task for emcees at pop and rock events is to promote the corporate sponsors' products through door prizes, audience contests, and frequent "plugs" inserted into their customary banter.

The Cultural Work of Performance

Acara serve many purposes, but among the most significant is providing an opportunity for reflection on the conditions of contemporary Indonesian cultural life. The use of performance occasions to confront cultural contradictions and social changes has been well documented in Indonesia; an early example is James Peacock's study of *ludrug* in Surabaya (1968), which describes performances of this proletarian theatrical genre as "rites of modernization," in which distinctions between what is modern versus what is old (*kuno*) in then newly independent Java/Indonesia were central to the narrative, displacing conventional Javanese cultural themes of refined (Javanese, *alus*) versus coarse (*kasar*). Similarly, the popular music performances I attended in Indonesia in 1997–2000 also addressed the existential conditions of their audiences.

One of the most striking aspects of *acara* is their innovative juxtapositions of local, national, and global cultural forms. These hybrid constructions can be provocative, reassuring, humorous, or some combination thereof to audiences preoccupied with questions of identity and allegiance in a rapidly changing society.

Geertz (1995, 145–51) describes a curious performance event in an East Javanese village staged by the graduating members of an English class at a *madrasah*, a Javanese Islamic school. He first notes the eclectic sounds and images on display at the event, including blaring recorded popular music and the decorations onstage. "Even before it started, the event—[decorative] coconut fronds, folding chairs, Muslim dress, 'The

Protocol' [a strange English-language reference to the two female emcees], rock-and-roll, the religious high holiday, and an imperfect, urban-type banner—had a definitely contestatory, multicultural feel about it. Homemade post-modernism, designed to unsettle" (1995, 146).

In Geertz's account, a climactic segment of what was an increasingly bizarre series of skits and performances involved a group of clowns singing a strange song with English lyrics, after pantomiming a street brawl. "They sang this ditty over and over again in a series of over-the-top parodies of popular song styles: the Indonesian ones called *dangdut* and *kroncong*, Bob Dylan, hard rock, country, what may have been Elvis, and a number of others I didn't certainly recognize" (1995, 148). This serial montage of musical genres resonates with much that took place at the urban musical *acara* that I attended. Due to its rural, religious Muslim setting, this particular performance elicited, according to Geertz, a feeling of extreme unease in the audience, which was composed of parents and elders. Such a spectacle would likely earn a more positive reaction from an urban youth audience. Geertz attended this unusual *acara* in 1986. Had it occurred in the year 2000, ska, punk, and black metal may well have been included among the genres parodied by the students, as the town of Pare where the *acara* took place (and the site of Geertz's original fieldwork in the 1950s) was by then home to an active local underground scene and a regional fanzine called *Dysphonic Newsletter*.

Geertz concludes: "The evening was a stream of moralities, mockeries, ambivalences, ironies, outrages, and contradictions, almost all of them centering in one way or another around language and the speaking (half-speaking, non-speaking) of language. Uncrossable lines were crossed in play, irrationalities were displayed in heavy quotation marks, codes were mixed, rhetorics were opposed, and the whole project to which the school was dedicated, extending the impact of Islam, perhaps the most linguistically self-conscious of the great religions, on the world through the learning of a world language [English], was put into question" (1995, 151). Geertz then adds that this was the only *acara* he attended in four decades of contact with this particular village that was conducted entirely in Indonesian and English, with no Javanese at all spoken onstage. In fact, the *acara* he describes seems to resemble, in both language and content, less the usual events in a Javanese village than those *acara* I observed in Jakarta, Bandung, and Yogyakarta. Much like the urban *acara* I attended, it drew from national and international sources more than from the local performance traditions one might expect to see in a village.

Although Geertz highlights the use of language and code switching in the event he describes, he also mentions other dimensions—sartorial, aural, iconographic, musical—as contributing to the overall "contestatory" feeling of the proceedings. The following discussion of musical *acara* in Bandung and Jakarta, which are more secular and less conflicted about Western popular culture than rural East Java, deals as well with the themes of parody, mimesis, and juxtaposition of local, national, and global cultural forms. These themes are detectable at many levels of the event, musical and nonmusical, including the spatial layout of the stage itself. Below is a description of the stage at a particularly elaborate music *acara* held in Bandung in 1999 and sponsored by the cigarette brand Bentoel Mild. The event was titled "Mildcoustic" and was based loosely on the "unplugged" concept invented by MTV, in which televised musicians play miked acoustic rather than electronic instruments onstage in order to generate a sense of liveness and immediacy (cf. Auslander 1999, 94-111). The event showcased an unusual combination of Indonesian rock, Indonesian jazz, and ethnic fusion ensembles. The music of the headlining group, the Bandung-based Krakatau, in fact combined these three genres, and several others, into a unique musical blend.[3]

December 7, 1999

The stage is enormous, and its decor appears to have been influenced by the studio sets used in "MTV Unplugged" concert videos. On either side of the stage are traditional Sundanese instruments: gongs, kettle gongs, barrel drums, and the like. In the center section traditional metallophones share space with four Western trap drum kits, instrument amplifiers, and, most impressive of all, a Yamaha acoustic grand piano on its own riser to the right of center stage. Krakatau bassist Pra Budidharma's electric fretless bass guitar stands proudly near the rear of the stage in its upright stand during the entire show, as though surveying the scene.

Audience members arriving early can watch continuously playing television ads for Bentoel Mild clove cigarettes, with their accompanying slogan *jangan anggap enteng* ("don't consider [them to be] lightweight," a play on the Indonesian word *enteng*, which also means "mild"), projected on three large video screens, one on each side of the stage and one looming behind it. During the actual performances, the three screens show closed-circuit video images of the bands performing; these images are alternated with canned footage of Balinese dancers, photographs of ancient Hindu-Javanese statues, an image of a human eye opening and closing, and colorful computer animation sequences incorporating the bands' monikers. The Bentoel ads are also replayed (without sound) during the performances, as are some distractingly gory animation sequences culled from *The Wall*, a surrealistic 1979 film created by the British progressive rock band Pink Floyd.

Like many other aspects of this *acara*, the material projected on the video screens presented global, national, and local cultural objects juxtaposed through technological means. Images of Indonesian jazz and rock bands, traditional dancing, and fragments of a canonical rock film jostled against one another, forming an electronic backdrop to live performances that themselves creatively combined elements from each cultural source. In this case, the reduction of culture to electronic images allowed for the placing of elements from different cultures on equal footing, as part of a repetitive series. And as in other examples of techno-hybridity in Indonesian popular culture, the "traditional," "ethnic" elements were arguably the most decontextualized and distorted by this process, which tends to serve the modern capitalist interests that give life to *acara*.

More on the Logic of *Acara*: Televised Award Shows

Award shows featuring mediated and live entertainment are a common and popular event on Indonesian television, and the features of such events—emcee banter, videos projected on large screens, and the distribution of awards—have been adopted by other, nontelevised *acara*. Award shows celebrate the people and products of the Indonesian entertainment industry, and they are popular enough that the names of accomplished directors and music producer/arrangers are almost as familiar to the Indonesian public as those of actors and musicians. The music for these *acara* is usually recorded in advance and played back as musicians mime their performance. Usually the singer adds live vocals on top of the prerecorded accompaniment, but he or she may choose to lip-synch as well.

Indonesian award shows are both national and transnational in character. The events themselves are modeled after globally circulating shows like the Academy Awards (which is broadcast every year on Indonesian television) and proceed along globally familiar lines: national celebrities, usually in pairs, introduce award categories, name the nominees, open a sealed envelope, and announce the winner. The audience then responds with applause. This repeated sequence of events is interspersed with comedy skits, musical performances, and commercial breaks (during which the live audience in the studio is entertained by the improvised antics of professional comedians). Western popular music is largely absent from awards *acara*, since these events are intended to celebrate the creativity and excellence of the Indonesian culture industry—thus, they participate in the comfortable but untenable fiction that the national entertainment business is the main provider of popular culture in Indonesia. In reality on a typical broadcast day local television productions share air time with American sitcoms, Indian film musicals, Hong Kong kung fu epics, Latin American and Middle Eastern telenovelas, Hollywood movies, and other imported programs, and radio airwaves, movie theaters, and record stores are similarly multinational in their offerings.[4]

Although the form of the award *acara* is ostensibly global, nationalistic themes and representations of the lives of ordinary Indonesians abound at these events, particularly in the prerecorded video segments spliced into the broadcast and projected on large screens for the live audience. At the 2000 MTV Indonesia Video Music Awards held on June 3, 2000 (and broadcast eight nights later), each category was announced in a short film featuring an Indonesian celebrity playing the role of a working-class Indonesian: a *tukang jamu* (traditional herbal-tonic seller), a *becak* driver, a snack peddler, and so forth. At the end of each segment (usually around thirty seconds long), the celebrity would address the audience and give the name of the next award. Award categories were always in English, so the incongruity of seeing a famous comedian in the role of a *sate* vendor or a street-side monkey trainer, or seeing a beautiful singer in the guise of a harried, overworked office assistant was matched by the incongruous words they spoke—each segment ended with the character suddenly breaking the dramatic frame by abruptly facing the camera and announcing the next category (*Best Director,* etc.). These introductory segments for each award were among the most creative and entertaining portions of the event, a humorous reminder of the particular national context of this replica of a global institution.

And yet much of the award show sought to distance its subject matter and its audience from ordinary Indonesians. "*MTV is about music, entertainment, and lifestyle,*" said one smiling presenter, a well-known radio personality, before launching into an Indonesian speech about the contributions of costume designers to music video. His English-language statement was met with applause — the young, affluent audience celebrating perhaps the cosmopolitan sophistication of both the speaker and itself. The speaker's mention of "lifestyle" is highly salient. In Indonesian, this English loanword is consistently associated with middle-class popular culture, youth, and consumerism. No one would ever state that dangdut was "about lifestyle."

The many English phrases used in the MTV awards show were left untranslated. In contrast, at a dangdut awards *acara* I attended, which was televised on the privately owned TPI (Televisi Pendidikan Indonesia, "Indonesian Educational Television") network, all three times the winners in categories for *Cover Song Terbaik* (Best Cover Song) were introduced, the announcers first took pains to explain what a *cover song* was: a song made popular by an earlier artist that had been rerecorded by another.[5] Unlike other award *acara* I had viewed or attended, all of which used English words, this dangdut award show did not presuppose any knowledge of English on the part of its audience. Apart from the use of the phrase "cover song," even the award categories were in formal Indonesian (i.e., *Lagu Terbaik* instead of "Best Song"). The event also lacked the spirit of humor and play with Indonesian working-class stereotypes that characterized the MTV award video segments. Such ordinary Indonesians were instead assumed to comprise the primary audience of the dangdut award show. Nonetheless, the evening was not without references to global culture: one example, a highlight of the event, was a dangdut version of the Three Tenors. Instead of international opera superstars Luciano Pavarotti, Plácido Domingo, and José Carreras, veteran dangdut singers and songwriters Meggi Z, Mansur S, and Basoefi Soedirman came onstage in tuxedos and took turns singing a classic dangdut tune.[6]

In all the *acara* discussed here, technological virtuality sets the stage for a particular sort of cultural collision in which the "Indonesian" is performatively constituted through the appropriation of sounds, images, objects, and languages into a national project in dialogue with Western modernity. The national is the meeting ground for both the local and the global, where allegiances constantly shift and collide. It is not sufficient therefore to assert that Indonesian national culture is "a" hybrid. More precise is the statement that Indonesian national culture is performed as an interactive field of hybridic possibilities that at times engage with each other but more often just coexist, like the disparate images on the "Mildcoustic" video screens. Thus what distinguishes Indonesian popular culture is not dialogue or synthesis but polyvocality and simultaneity. As these examples have shown, this simultaneity is exploited and presented as spectacle by commercial interests. But these interests must in turn respond to consumer demand, a complex, multifaceted entity created by the amalgamated desires, aspirations, identity projects, and affective investments of the Indonesian audience, or some segment of it.

Taking the preceding discussion into account, in the three chapters that follow we turn to an examination of the main genre categories covered in this book and their multiple realizations in performance. In keeping with our focus on inclusiveness, however, we will pay special attention to the noisy, disruptive presence of other genres at performances ostensibly dedicated to a single kind of music, whether it is dangdut, pop, or underground. Also important to the interpretations offered in the following chapters is the performance of gender, class, and national identity within the metacultural performance frame of a particular genre. Each genre's performance conventions reveal distinct strategies of incorporation, exclusion, and hybridization in performance contexts vis-à-vis the various sorts of social and musical differences that present themselves in the performance frame. These strategies reveal the complex and divergent responses of popular music audiences to the ethical and cultural challenges of life in a multiethnic, modern capitalist nation stratified along lines of gender and class.

8

Dangdut Concerts

THE POLITICS OF PLEASURE

Whether the event took place in a smoky, darkened nightclub, at a wedding celebration in a cramped *kampung* backyard, or among thousands of revelers at a large outdoor festival, I found that the structure and personnel of dangdut *acara* were remarkably consistent. The key performers were a master of ceremonies, several singers of both genders, and an instrumental ensemble consisting of *gendang, suling,* two electric guitars, electric bass guitar, two electronic keyboards, tambourine, trap drum set (often played by the same musician who played the *gendang*), and, in some cases, electrified mandolin and/or a brass section. Singers generally operated independently of instrumental groups and sang with several different local ensembles.

Instrumentalists were nearly always male. Kendedes Group, named for Ken Dhedhes, the legendary queen of the thirteenth-century Javanese kingdom of Singasari, was formed in 1976 by singer/*gendang* player Titiek Nur and was the only all-female dangdut ensemble active in Jakarta in 1999–2000. Although I have witnessed Titiek sing and play *gendang* at the same time, this mode of performance was highly unusual. In every other dangdut performance I attended, male and female dangdut performers sang and danced but did not play instruments onstage, and their backing bands were composed entirely of men.

Usually the band began with an all-instrumental introductory song to get the audience's attention. This lasted for three to five minutes and was followed by a lengthy speech (often two minutes long or longer) by the master of ceremonies welcoming the crowd, commenting on the

Dangdut recording artist Titiek Nur playing the *gendang* while singing at the author's farewell party, Cinere, South Jakarta.

occasion, and finally introducing the first singer of the evening. After the speech, the band "called" the first vocalist by playing a *selingan*, a short musical interlude that lasted one or two minutes, during which the first performer would take center stage and prepare to face the audience. *Selingan* were often instrumental versions of dangdut songs but did not have to be: some groups played *pop Indonesia* or *keroncong* compositions; even instrumental renditions of Western pop songs (including "The Cup of Life," the 1998 World Cup theme song performed by Puerto Rican pop star Ricky Martin, and "The Final Countdown," a 1986 hit by the Swedish hard rock group Europe) were sometimes played.

The band would end the *selingan* as the first singer, who was always a woman, picked up the microphone to address the crowd. After the customary Islamic greeting, *Wassalamulaikum warakhmatullahi wabarakatuh* (Arabic, "Peace be with you and may God be merciful and bless you"), to which the audience would reply *Walaikum salam!* (Arabic, "Unto you, peace!"), she would deliver a short speech in formal Indonesian welcoming the audience and acknowledging the sponsors of the event, then introduce her first song.

Usually singers only sang two songs each while the backing band's personnel remained constant throughout the performance. After the first singer's second song ended, the master of ceremonies would speak again, the next singer (usually also female) would be introduced, the band would play another instrumental interlude, and the whole cycle would repeat itself. It is worth noting that while singing two songs might not seem difficult, the average dangdut song is twice as long as most pop tunes, and the band could decide to lengthen a song depending on the crowd's reaction. A well-received performer could repeat a song's refrain three or four times more compared to the recorded version. On the rare occasion when a singer did not garner a positive reaction from the audience or was obviously unprepared, the band would cut the first song short, and the next singer in line was called to take his or her place. Although songs were never repeated in the course of a single event, they were mostly taken from a rather limited repertoire of old chestnuts and new hits, so different dangdut shows would have similar set lists. Dangdut performance events usually lasted several hours, often from 9:00 p.m. until after 2:00 a.m. Daytime performances in urban neighborhoods from roughly 10:00 a.m. to 4:00 p.m. were also common. The performance would end with a final instrumental *selingan* by the band, often the children's tune "Marilah Pulang" ("Let's Go Home"—the same final song that was played by the Warung under the Tree band in chapter 6), which was performed as the exhausted audience slowly filed out and the emcee bid the audience farewell. The entire structure of dangdut *acara* was meant to be orderly and predictable and was intended to contain the unruly forces unleashed by the sensual performance of dangdut music and the presence of crowds of young working-class men.

Woman dangdut singers' outfits were markedly different from everyday Indonesian clothes. They fell into two main categories: long evening gowns and high heels or skimpy outfits usually involving miniskirts, black leather, and knee-high boots (cf. Browne 2000, 25). Male singers and male instrumentalists often wore brightly colored, matching jackets and ties, also unusual dress in Indonesia, particularly in poor and working-class communities, where the urban elite was contemptuously referred to as the *kaum berdasi*, "necktie-wearing caste." Such extravagant costumes indexed wealth, prestige, and Western-style urbanity— village clothing styles were rare in the performance of a music forever tainted by the association with backward village life. On the other hand, the cheap fabrics and bright (*ngejreng*) colors of dangdut costumes and the "scandalous" outfits worn by some female dangdut singers indicated a distinctly working-class sensibility, and dangdut fashion differed not only from the traditional costumes of "regional music" performers but also from the MTV-inspired sartorial choices of Indonesian pop and rock artists. Thus, like dangdut music itself, dangdut costumes were not considered "traditional" yet were not quite "modern" either (cf. Sutton 2003, 329–30).

Dancing Behavior at Dangdut Concerts

The dangdut concerts I attended were highly participatory events. During a successful performance the audience was not expected to listen passively but rather to dance enthusiastically to the music. The characteristic dangdut dancing activity was known as the *joget* or *joged*. *Joget dangdut* styles varied considerably from one individual to another: movements ranged from complicated arm gestures reminiscent of Javanese and Sundanese traditional choreography to barely moving at all. The dance itself was simple in its most elemental form: to *joget* one takes two steps forward, then two steps back, or the other way around. *Joget*ting was almost always done in pairs, which could be male-male, female-male, or female-female; the first combination was the most common.[1] Partners faced each other and coordinated their moves: one stepped back when the other stepped forward. While executing these steps the arms were frequently held up, with the hands in fists tucked close to the front of the chest, thumbs pointing upward. As one stepped back and forth, the fists moved up and down in a circular motion, as if they were slowly pedaling a bicycle. There was no intentional physical contact between partners, and dancers usually avoided making eye contact with each other. Dancers *joget*ted with either a neutral facial expression or a wide grin and often appeared to be oblivious to those around them. *Joget*ting was considered a pleasurable activity in itself, apart from the quality of the music, and it was believed to have the ability to "relieve stress" (*hilangi stres*). Writing about audiences at dangdut concerts, Philip Yampolsky comments, "Indeed, the aim of their dancing is apparently to be transported to a state where they are unaware of their surroundings, free of self-consciousness and inhibition" (1991, 1).

The origins of the dangdut *joget* are unclear. It does not strongly resemble the dance moves of Indian film music—the probable origin of the dangdut rhythm—nor any traditional Indonesian dances. One dangdut fan told me that the *joget* came from the cha-cha, a claim that is entirely plausible. Beyond the basic *joget* steps, dancers could execute slow turns (*pusing*) and add hip and arm movements, but these embellishments were not necessary. *Joget*ting was not supposed to require special skill, and nearly everyone, from very young children to the elderly, could *joget*, though in public spaces the dance was most often associated with young adult men. There were no consistent gender differences in *joget* style, though women were more likely to incorporate hip movements and other gestures typical of dangdut singers, whose dance was of a different sort.

In contrast to the audience, woman dangdut performers were expected to *goyang*, a word that literally means "to sway." This movement required more skill than the *joget*, and singers were expected to perform it while singing. The *goyang* involved a slow, circular, undulating motion centered on the hips that could progress up and down the body or stay in one place. This dance move was responsible for much of live dangdut's reputation for sensuality and eroticism (*erotis*). Particularly skilled female performers were said to possess a *goyang yang aduhai* (an astounding undulation), a phrase that recurred in emcees' spoken introductions. Male dangdut performers sometimes gestured and danced onstage, but they were evaluated based on their vocal rather than their dancing skills. Women performers, on the other hand, were evaluated based on their singing ability, dance movements, and physical appearance. Often strength in one category could offset criticism in another. Titiek Nur once remarked to me that the only reason dangdut performers performed suggestive and sensual dance movements onstage was to draw attention away from their deficiencies as singers.[2]

Dangdut and Gender Ideology

The scholarly encounter between gender studies and the anthropology of Indonesia has been extraordinarily fruitful (Steedly 1999, 437-40). The valuable insights contained in studies and edited volumes on the subject (e.g., Brenner 1998; Cooper 2000; Ong and Peletz 1995; Sears 1996; Tsing 1993; Williams 2001) derive in part from the ability of their authors to reflect productively on the contrast between the two competing gender ideologies, one broadly Western, the other broadly Southeast Asian, that inhabit such studies. To simplify a bit, the first views men and women as two often hostile groups locked in an unending and unequal struggle for power, a struggle in which women's bodies are objectified and made to serve a patriarchal order. The second concept of gender difference is more prevalent in traditional Southeast Asian societies and regards men and women as making up two halves of a complementary whole. Ideally, in this view both groups struggle to preserve harmony between the genders through their respective spheres of influence. According to anthropologist Nancy Cooper, in Java, "[a]lthough the scales of gender balance tilt in favor of men, misogyny is rare; harmony is usually maintained, and (noninstitutionalized) violence kept in check" (2000, 610). Contemporary urban Indonesia is influenced by both views. Patriarchal capitalism and the commodification of female sexuality coexist uneasily with older (equally patriarchal) discourses of complementarity and respect for women's power (see Cooper 2000, 608-9; Brenner 1998). In Jakarta, the resulting tension is partially resolved through the figure of the *janda,* the widow or divorcée.

"Most women in dangdut clubs," a married, middle-aged Betawi man once told me with obvious distaste, "are women who do not have husbands [*yang tidak punya suami*]." *Janda,* the women who did not have husbands but were once married, were seen as vulnerable and sexually available, and in everyday male parlance they were contrasted with "virgins" (*perawan*) or "maidens" (*gadis*), never-married women whose virtue must be respected and guarded. Young *janda* without children were called "flower divorcées/widows" (*janda kembang*) and were considered desirable but of questionable morality. Thus it was regarded as permissible to exploit those women who defied normative expectations;

the women who were neither still "virgins" nor half of a married couple were fair game for objectification and sexual commodification, while women who were married or not-yet-married were "kept safe" by a patriarchal code that supposedly "respected" (menghormati) women's power but in fact most valued female subservience to men.

The majority of the professional dangdut singers whom I interviewed were *janda* with children. Unlike the traditional singer-dancers described by Cooper, these dangdut singers did not have a respected Javanese or other ethnic "tradition" they could use to legitimate their vocation, and in the face of dominant cultural values they could only cite economic motivations resulting from a condition of poverty and want to explain why they sang (cf. Pioquinto 1995). "I only sing to get money [*cari duit*]," one club singer told me matter-of-factly. The husband of this particular singer had taken a second wife, leaving her essentially to her own devices to support herself and her young daughter. Often she had to leave her child at home alone when she was out at night singing at the clubs; on those occasions she gave the neighborhood watchman some "pocket money" (*uang saku*) to check on her daughter periodically during her absence.

But while the economic motivations for singing dangdut were painfully real, they could not account for the pride with which one singer told me she knew over one hundred songs, nor for the fact that the singer quoted in the preceding paragraph enjoyed singing dangdut at informal gatherings of musicians and had taught her daughter (who was in fact quite talented) to sing dangdut as well. While women rarely danced to dangdut music in public for their own enjoyment, dangdut producers told me that married women (*ibu rumah tangga*) constituted the majority of those who bought dangdut cassettes, and indeed the thematic material contained in most popular dangdut songs portrayed the typical agonies and heartbreaks of working-class Indonesian women's lives: husbands remarrying, husbands' infidelity, and abandonment by deceitful lovers. It is therefore entirely plausible that some dangdut singers sing about their own feelings and experiences and perform for their own enjoyment as well as for the purpose of entertaining a crowd. Thus, although dangdut concert stages can easily be viewed as places that objectify and exploit women, dangdut *songs* appeal to both genders, though perhaps for different reasons: while the music's danceability appeals to men, the lyrics appeal to women, and listening to and performing dangdut songs may in fact provide one way for Indonesian women to "relieve stress" in their own lives.

Audience Participation: The Wages of Sin?

The most common interaction between performers and audience was known as *saweran,* the public offering of monetary gifts. To *nyawer* meant to hand one or more rupiah bills to the singer while he or she was singing onstage. A single *saweran* ranged from the equivalent of US$0.08 to US$8.00 or more. Audience members would give an assortment of bill denominations that usually added up to small amounts at outdoor concerts and large sums at indoor nightclubs. Unlike the street musicians discussed in the previous chapter, dangdut singers never solicited monetary contributions. Offering them rupiah bills was a "sign of recognition" (Keane 1997) not only that a performance was taking place but also that it was a particularly effective performance. After graciously but wordlessly accepting the money, the singer, singing all the while, would casually toss it onto the floor near the back of the stage. The total amount of *saweran* was later split among the singers and musicians at the end of the night. At dangdut concerts audience members also sometimes climbed up to the stage and danced with the singer. Most were not brazen enough to actually try to *joget* with the singer, but rather ascended the stage in pairs and *joget*ted on either side of him or

Singer and fan holding *saweran* (monetary offerings), Cikanjur.

her. During their dance, one or both audience members would present *saweran* to the singer before finally descending from the stage.

Male dangdut singers also received money from the audience, but with female singers in particular the presentation of money by male audience members appeared to bring a release of built-up tension between the singer, the audience member, and the onlookers. In her study of "seduction scenarios" in rural Java, Cooper discusses how performances by women singer-dancers called *waranggana* (a more polite term for the more widely used *talèdhèk*) provide the opportunity for men to express their "potency" by their remaining "impassive in the face of temptation" (2000, 618). She writes, "In these seduction scenarios, men are publicly exposed to situations involving women who test their personal control and thus their ability to avoid a commotion and preserve the general harmony" (620). Although urban dangdut differs in numerous important respects from Javanese village performance traditions, the presentation of money to dangdut singers by male patrons also exhibits men's self-control and power, and for the audience it is a cathartic event, since it signifies the giver's intention to refrain from embracing or otherwise initiating improper physical contact with the singer, in spite of her charms as a "temptress."

The monetary offering thus has value not just as a display of personal wealth but as an index of personal restraint: the patron rewards the singer and the musicians for providing an opportunity to test his resolve in the face of sensual temptation. The greater the temptation, the higher the reward. *Saweran* is thus an example of gendered role playing in dangdut that illustrates the tensions in Indonesian working-class life between village-based conceptions of female and male power, on the one hand, and urban culture's tendency to commodify (and thus remove agency from) female sexuality, on the other. In a sense, then, dangdut singers and their male audiences live out the uneasy coexistence between different constructions of gender and agency by engaging in cultural practices such as *saweran* that, arguably, both respect and objectify the female performer whose performance is simultaneously a commodity and a channeler of powerful cultural forces.

Dangdut Clubs: Gender, Sexuality, and Relieving Stress

Dangdut concerts in Jakarta take place in a variety of performance settings, but they can be divided into two basic categories: those that take place in indoor nightclubs and those that take place on outdoor stages (*panggung*). The latter are sponsored events that are open to the public or charge a small admission fee, while the former are more expensive and cater to a well-heeled, mostly male clientele. Large and small live dangdut concerts of the second type are regular occurrences in poor urban neighborhoods, and they constitute one of the primary forms of popular entertainment for working-class city dwellers (cf. Murray 1991, 83; Browne 2000).[3]

Dangdut nightclubs were largely a Jakarta phenomenon. These establishments catered to working-class men with a modicum of disposable income, of whom there were many in Jakarta. ("Even a *tukang becak* [pedicab driver] can afford to come here!" claimed one nightclub patron. When I asked him to clarify how such an individual could possibly afford the nightclub's high prices, he added that it would have to be a "*tukang becak* who's just sold some land!") Dangdut clubs tended to be dark, loud, stuffy, and un-air-conditioned. (Many working-class Jakartans I met did not like air-conditioning, complaining that it made them too cold and caused susceptibility to illness.) They were considered places of ill repute by many Jakartans, and indeed, paid female companionship, outright prostitution, and the imbibing of alcoholic beverages (forbidden in Islam) were ubiquitous in, if not essential to, these establishments.

The dozen or so dangdut clubs I visited during the period of my fieldwork ranged from small, cramped rooms in outlying areas of Jakarta featuring small-time local performers to the lavish subterranean club Bintang-Bintang (Stars) located in an underground parking garage near the Blok M Bus Terminal, which attracted nationally known dangdut recording artists, including Iis Dahlia, Murni Cahnia, and Iyeth Bustami. The vast majority of dangdut singers, even at the upscale venues, were *kelas cere* (Betawi, "minnow class") performers who had little chance of becoming recording artists and who spent their careers performing songs from cassettes recorded by more successful entertainers.

The music at dangdut nightclubs was provided by an all-male house band and a rotating group of singers, usually five or six women and two or three men. The patrons were almost all men; women at dangdut clubs typically fell into three main categories: hostesses employed by the club, "freelancers," and singers. In many establishments, official hostesses (known in polite Indonesian as *pramuria*) wore uniforms or had identification cards clipped to their clothes to distinguish them from freelancers.[4] Women who engaged in *freelancing* (the English term was used) were sometimes prostitutes, sometimes simply young women looking for kicks. They were not employed by the club, but their presence was

Flyer for a March 2000 concert featuring recording artist Iis Dahlia at Bintang-Bintang, Blok M's most luxurious dangdut nightclub.

usually tolerated, since in the course of an evening they would order numerous expensive (but nonalcoholic) drinks at the bar for which their male companions were expected to pay, thus providing a source of additional revenue for the club.

Unlike most other places I visited in Jakarta, dangdut nightclubs were sites of significant alcohol consumption, despite the high prices of drinks at these venues. A middle-aged male dangdut fan and amateur singer told me that if one drinks alcohol while *joget*ting, one becomes not drunk, sick, and dizzy (*mabuk*) but just more relaxed, and the dance becomes more pleasing (*enak*). Alcohol also appeared to be a factor in determining the amount of *saweran* presented to performers by patrons. Visibly intoxicated men were often the most generous patrons, perhaps because the alcohol lessened their tendency toward frugality, but also because the temptation to lose one's self-control, which they were paying off, so to speak, with their gift of cash, was that much greater as a result of their compromised state. I occasionally observed visibly intoxicated patrons who did in fact initiate intimate physical contact with women on the dance floor, but this complete surrender to desire was unusual and certainly not valued by the other patrons. Such behavior was never directed toward a singer while she was performing.

One reason many men gave for liking dangdut is that it was "good to move to" (*enak bergoyang*) or "good to *joget* to" (*enak dijogetin*). It is worth noting that in my observation the majority of male patrons at dangdut clubs were content to dance with each other rather than with hostesses or freelancers. (This practice also meant a less expensive night out.) In fact, despite their unsavory reputation Jakarta's dangdut clubs were not considered major hubs for prostitution. Men who were mainly in search of sexual encounters tended to go elsewhere, to brothels or to the city's abundant discos, massage parlors, hotel coffee shops, and karaoke bars that specialize in sexual services (Hull, Sulistyaningsih, and Jones 1999, 57–62).

The "free," unchoreographed dancing at dangdut clubs relieves stress and is a tremendous source of pleasure for Indonesian men, especially when accompanied by a pulsating rhythm and a sensuous female voice (Spiller 2001). Dancers at dangdut clubs often wear an expression of unself-conscious bliss, eyes closed, mouth in a broad smile. This expression contrasts sharply with the neutral, deadpan face most adult male Jakartans tend to wear in public places and formal portraits. Dangdut performance, then, is more than musical entertainment. Live dangdut music at clubs creates a gendered social space where public displays

Dangdut singer Oppie Sendewi performing at Club Jali-Jali, Parung.

of euphoric emotions by men, generally uncommon in Indonesian society, are permissible.

More on Dangdut and "Stress"

"Getting rid of stress" (*hilangi stres*) was the most commonly voiced justification for male behavior in dangdut bars. Activities like dancing to dangdut music, watching attractive singers, and consuming alcohol were deemed necessary for relieving stress, which many men viewed as caused less by one's problems than by constantly worrying about them. Stress, according to one young Betawi dangdut enthusiast in his late twenties, results from "too much thinking about something" (*terlalu banyak mikirin*) and can be cured by "refreshing" (*represing*) activities such as *joget*ting, traveling to the countryside, and going to dangdut bars. But, as his father (also a longtime dangdut fan) commented, too much "refreshing" can also anger one's wife. I asked him what married women (as opposed to the unmarried women who frequent dangdut bars) do when they feel stressed. "They keep it stopped up inside [*membuntu*]!" was the lighthearted reply, and he held his breath and puffed up his cheeks to demonstrate.

Brenner (1998, 149–57) argues that in Solo, Central Java, men are expected to engage in "naughty" (*nakal*) activities and spend money irresponsibly in order to satisfy their "desires" (*nafsu;* Javanese, *nepsu*), while women, considered the anchors of the domestic sphere, are expected to repress their passions for the sake of the household. The difference in Jakarta is that the Western-influenced concept of "stress" is invoked to explain or excuse male behavior—an example of the heterogeneity of discourses surrounding Jakartan dangdut performance. Every aspect of the dangdut nightclub experience is designed to both relieve stress and extract money from patrons: the paid female companionship; the expensive, potent alcoholic beverages; the physical beauty and lavish dress of the singers; and of course the amplified sound of dangdut music performed live. Of course, spending all one's money at a dangdut club might in the end increase one's stress level, but this possibility did not seem to concern the male patrons with whom I spoke.

"Stage Dangdut": People's Music in the Urban Village

At Jakarta's dangdut clubs, the nightly dangdut performances were routinized and through repetition lost some of their "eventful" character. In

The author videotaping a neighborhood dangdut concert featuring the Betawi ensemble OMEGA Group, Lebak Bulus, South Jakarta. Photograph by Donny Suryady.

contrast, open-air concerts were relatively infrequent, special events. These outdoor performances in urban neighborhoods were the occasions where dangdut was closest to the people, the music at its most inclusive and participatory. Professional and semiprofessional dangdut bands played at festivals, at weddings, and at other sponsored affairs that were usually open to the general public free of charge or cost a nominal admission fee. They took place in open fields and backyards and could draw thousands of spectators from the surrounding *kampung* and beyond.

Many of those in the audience were young men who would *joget* in the crowded area in front of the stage, but children, older men, and married women, who usually stood around the dancing area in a large semicircle, were also present in large numbers. Young women were less common, particularly at nighttime events; those who did attend these performances, especially without boyfriends or husbands, were said to be "brash" or "brave" (*berani*).

For the most part, outdoor dangdut shows were intended for local young men, most of whom could not afford to frequent nightclubs, and at a successful show they would *joget* enthusiastically into the night, ogle the female performers, and shower them with money. According to

Susan Browne, "in a society where the poor have no economic, social, or political power, for male audiences at *dangdut kampungan* [*sic*] performances, singer-dancers represent an escape from their lack of power into a classless world of gendered power" (2000, 34). This "classless" world is dominated by glamorous spectacle, musical pleasure, and the dissolving of boundaries between participants, even as the complex dynamic of gendered exchange described above continues to operate between female performers and male audience members.

As mentioned earlier, the pleasure of *joget*ting is very much tied to the genre ideology of dangdut as a music that gets rid of stress. The following description is from an unusual *acara* at a wedding in a Betawi *kampung* on the far southern outskirts of Jakarta that began not with dangdut music but with music from a related genre that has a vastly different metacultural ideology attached to it.

Cirendeu, Saturday night, July 15, 2000
The taxicab drops us off at the soccer field, the site of the evening's concert. It is a familiar scene: vendors' carts selling snacks and drinks line the path to the entrance and the perimeter of the concert site, the dim light from their kerosene lamps our only guide in the darkness. Mud and lack of visibility make the path treacherous as crowds of spectators make their way to the *acara*. Up ahead a brightly lit stage approximately eight feet high comes into view. Onstage are nine performing musicians in matching red uniforms playing music that sounds like dangdut. What strikes me as unfamiliar is the gaping, empty semicircular space in front of the stage, an area usually filled with swaying and shouting male audience members. A solitary figure gyrates eccentrically to the music; no one else seems to pay him any attention. He dances alone in the semicircle, seemingly in a trance, swaying back and forth without lifting his feet. He is occasionally joined by a few small boys between the ages of seven and ten who squat down in the mud and watch the show for a while before rejoining the large crowd gathered around the semicircle. Everyone else is holding back.

I ask why almost no one is dancing. An audience member tells me that the music playing isn't dangdut but *qasidah* or *gambus* (he says he isn't sure which one, though it is almost certainly the former)—syncretic, Islam-identified genres sung in Indonesian and Arabic. The instrumentation is identical to that used in dangdut, save for the addition of a green electric violin, which is played by an older man who also acts as the event's master of ceremonies. The sound is very similar to dangdut, but the vocals are less sensual and more florid. The young woman singers are all wearing colorful evening gowns and brightly colored Muslim headscarves; the latter appear to have the effect of restraining the large young, male audience from interacting with them. During the emcee's lengthy orations between songs, members of the audience impatiently shout, "Dang-DHUT!" Their hoarse demands are ignored, but finally the last of the *qasidah* songs is played, the singers suddenly lose their headscarves, and less than a minute into the first new song the semicircle in front of the stage is packed with dancing young men. Older men, women, and children remain in the crowd surrounding the de facto dance floor. The same singers sing as before, with the help of a middle-aged, offstage singer who doubles their vocals. Now the singers in front of the stage have to contend with the more brazen members of the crowd below them grabbing their dresses and reaching out their hands when they draw near. The singers are now also occasionally joined onstage by a series of male dancers from the audience who ascend in pairs and present small-denomination rupiah bills to the singers as they dance on either side of them. In other words, the event has been speedily transformed into a typical dangdut concert in every respect.

Although musical performance's ability to create a feeling of social solidarity among participants is taken as a given by many music scholars, how this actually occurs is a murky issue. The example described above underscores the ways such claims should be qualified. Dangdut concerts bring people together in part through sonic characteristics deemed attractive by listeners, such as danceable rhythms, attractive melodies, and the comfortable familiarity of a standard song repertoire. Beyond this, the essential ingredient is a metacultural understanding of the dangdut genre that defines the music as quintessentially Indonesian (*ciri khas Indonesia*), intensely pleasurable (*asyik*), and belonging to everyone (*musik kita-kita*, "the music of all of us"). Thus while the *qasidah* played by the band at the *acara* described above was musically not very distinct from dangdut, its metacultural definition as an "Arab" music of Muslim piety and seriousness discouraged dancing and euphoric feelings among all but the most oblivious members of the audience, children and madmen. Once music recognized as "dangdut" started, a feeling of *communitas* appeared to arise among the now actively engaged audience members as they danced together in front of the stage.

Audience at an outdoor dangdut concert in Cikanjur.

Of course, genre ideology is by itself not sufficient to create *communitas,* that state of undifferentiated oneness with the assembled collective that Victor Turner (1967) identifies as a central goal of ritual. To be efficacious the performance must be good according to established aesthetic criteria. The evaluative dimensions I heard most often from fans included the quality of the sound system, the skill of the *gendang* player, the singer's voice, and the appearance and dancing ability of female performers. Dangdut performances that excelled in these criteria were sure to create a feeling of unity in the audience, and the local reputations of the band and the singer would benefit accordingly.

Dangdut Hybridity

The drive for inclusiveness, itself an outgrowth of everyday Indonesian sociality, characterized dangdut performances. In addition to the musically eclectic *selingan,* the instrumental interludes that connected the different singers' turns at the microphone, other musical genres regularly emerged at dangdut concerts and could take surprising forms. In dangdut nightclubs, the band often took a break during which *house dangdut, jaipong, house jaipong, dangdut disco,* and Western house music cassettes were played and the dance floor filled with patrons attempting to dance to these alternative rhythms. In one nightclub I visited, the band itself played a long instrumental *jaipongan* piece, cleverly using the electric dangdut instruments in ways that convincingly mimicked the sounds of the Sundanese gamelan instruments that usually performed this genre. According to a singer at the club, music played in this fashion was called *pong-dhut* (*jaipong* and dangdut).[5]

Outdoor concerts may represent dangdut in its quintessential state—a people's music available even to those who cannot afford to buy cassettes—but even at these events dangdut often coexisted with other genres. In the spring of 2000, the popular Indian film song "Kuch Kuch Hota Hai" (Hindi, "Something, Something Generally Happens") was often performed at dangdut concerts. Two popular Indonesian ska songs, one a *ska Cirebon* composition sung in a Cirebonese dialect of Javanese, the other a more conventional ska song performed in Indonesian by Tipe-X, entered the "stage dangdut" (*dangdut panggung*) repertoire. Oppie Sendewi, a popular local dangdut singer, described these ska songs as "*ska-dut*" since they were played with dangdut instrumentation (which in fact was not that different from that of a traditional ska group). The young male audience responded enthusiastically to these

Oppie Sendewi and fans at an outdoor concert, Serpong.

songs, shifting from *joget*ting to the more aggressive "running in place" dancing style associated with ska. At one concert, young men formed ska dance circles with their arms around one another. Thus the inclusive universe of dangdut continues to expand outward, embracing (nationalized) global musical trends as source material for populist national entertainments.

The inclusion of non-dangdut genres in dangdut performance events as "breaks" is matched by dangdut's shadowy presence at pop and underground concerts. But rather than constituting only an embellishment and a gesture toward inclusiveness in the performance frame, dangdut's incursions into concerts featuring these more westernized genres are more likely to resemble a return of the repressed.

9

Rock and Pop Events

THE PERFORMANCE OF LIFESTYLE

Chapter 7 investigated the *acara* as a culturally meaningful unit, and the preceding chapter applied those insights specifically to the world of dangdut performance. We learned how musical performance could break down social boundaries and explored the central role of genre and gender ideologies in conditioning concert-related behaviors. This chapter extends the analysis to include two middle-class-oriented rock and pop events: bands performing at upscale cafés, and student-organized concert festivals. We will see how traces of dangdut and other excluded genres appear in these settings, often in unexpected ways, and also how these types of *acara* contribute to national cultural debates over class, gender, and Indonesian identity in the contemporary world.

Café Music: *Top Forty* Cover Bands

Most young, upwardly mobile Jakartans with whom I spoke (including those in the dangdut recording business) expressed fear of and disgust toward dangdut nightclubs and could never imagine setting foot in one. For them, nightlife in the city consisted of an assortment of trendy cafés and bars featuring Western-style rock/pop bands playing the latest imported and Indonesian hits plus some old chestnuts. I found that the instrumentation of these bands (generally known as *Top Forty* groups) was almost as standardized as that of live dangdut ensembles. The typical *Top Forty* lineup consisted of three singers—one male, two female, usually wearing tight black clothing—backed by an all-male band composed of an electric guitarist, a keyboardist, an electric bassist, a trap drummer, and a percussionist. The latter played congas, bongos, timbales, cymbals, and the like—all foreign imports—rather than any indigenous percussion instruments. Generally, the male vocalist also acted as the emcee at the band's performances, addressing the audience and soliciting song requests. Groups of this sort played regularly in café districts like Kemang; in fashionable Central Jakarta clubs like Bengkel Night Park, Hard Rock Café, and Planet Hollywood; in upscale mall food courts (such as the one in Plaza Indonesia); and other urban venues frequented by Indonesian elites and expatriates from North America, Asia, Europe, and Australia.

During my stay in Indonesia, the repertoire of these *Top Forty* groups was remarkably uniform at any given time and consisted of about 75 percent foreign and 25 percent domestic songs. One male vocalist told me that Western hits tended to remain popular longer than *pop Indonesia* songs did, and therefore learning to play the former was a better time investment. When I asked *Top Forty* performers if they preferred Indonesian or Western pop, they invariably answered that it depended on the particular song. A male singer added that Western pop was more difficult for men to sing because it required a higher vocal range, whereas *pop Indonesia*, with a few exceptions like Dewa 19, was usually sung in a lower, more comfortable part of the male vocal range. He added that women's vocals were just as difficult in both categories, an observation with which his female colleague agreed.

In addition to Indonesian- and English-language pop (the latter including hits by artists ranging from Elvis Presley to 'N Sync), *Top Forty* bands played regional *pop Batak* and *pop Menado* songs when they were requested, and, as I discovered, most *Top Forty* groups knew how to play at least two dangdut songs. These songs inevitably included "Terlena" (Swept Away); popularized by singer Ikke Nurjanah, and "Kopi Dangdut" (Dangdut Coffee), a highly danceable song recorded by Fahmy Shahab and based on a melody pilfered from the international Latin hit "Moliendo Café."[1] It was not entirely clear why these two songs in particular were popular among middle-class audiences; it is perhaps significant that the lyrics of both songs describe being "swept away": the refrain of the former contains the pivotal line *Ku terlena asmara* (I've been swept away by romantic passion), while the verses of the latter repeats the lines

Dan jantungku seakan ikut irama
Karena terlena
Oleh pesona
Alunan Kopi Dangdut!

[And it's as if my heart follows the beat
Because I've been carried away
By the bewitching spell
Of the Dangdut Coffee Rhythm!]

If dangdut constitutes an irresistible intervention in social space, these lyrics could be interpreted as celebrating the blissful surrender of the listener to the seductions of that music. This theme seems rather appropriate for dangdut songs appealing to middle-class Indonesians who feel the sensuous pull of dangdut music in spite of themselves, and who must appear to surrender a portion of their self-control in order to enjoy it. Whatever the reasons for their popularity, "Terlena" and "Kopi Dangdut" were part of the nightly sets of many *Top Forty* bands, and if one requested a dangdut song from the group (as I did on several occasions, to the utter astonishment of the performers), one usually heard one of those two compositions.

As in many other contexts where dangdut music was introduced, the moment at which a *Top Forty* band launched into a dangdut composition after a series of pop songs produced a transformative effect on the café setting, even though the dangdut songs were performed without the trademark *gendang* and *suling* instruments. The band members onstage frequently lost their usual serious demeanor, which conveyed concentration and professionalism, and smiled openly at one another and at the audience. Some musicians would even start to *joget* onstage as they played their instruments. Interestingly, these gestures and facial expressions were markedly different from the stone-faced, sober expressions usually worn by "real" dangdut instrumentalists performing in clubs, on outdoor stages, and on television (cf. Browne 2000, 24); instead they resembled the blissful behavior of dangdut *fans*. The performers in a sense became their own audience: they were entertained by the music they themselves were playing, and their onstage comportment enacted the "relieving stress" effects of dangdut for the vicarious enjoyment of the spectators. Significantly, in addition to fulfilling certain genre-based expectations of dangdut's euphoria-inducing properties, the performers' stance also distanced them somewhat from the composition that they were playing, as if both they and the audience were coconspirators in a game of simultaneous enjoyment and disavowal.

Often the audience was unwilling to actually dance when café bands played dangdut songs but was nonetheless quite appreciative — deciding, perhaps, that an upscale café was a safe place to enjoy the occasional dangdut song without being considered *kampungan*. In 1999–2000, in addition to songs by the likes of Santana, Whitney Houston, Backstreet Boys, *pop alternatif* group Sheila on 7, and Indonesian singer/songwriter Melly Goeslaw (particularly "Jika," her hit duet with former Dewa 19 vocalist Ari Lasso), *Top Forty* bands often played "Terlena" and "Kopi Dangdut" toward the end of their set, and these two songs often received the most enthusiastic responses of the night. Many middle-class urban Indonesians admitted to me that although they disliked most dangdut songs, they really enjoyed "Terlena" and "Kopi Dangdut" — the reason they gave for this was that these songs could be heard in the nightspots they frequented. These two songs, which were also well known and popular among members of dangdut's core audience (among my field recordings is an impassioned male falsetto version of "Terlena" performed at the Pondok Cinta; see chapter 6), provided the opportunity for café musicians and audiences to indulge in dangdut's guilty pleasures. The popularity of these compositions lends evidence to the oft-voiced argument that urban middle-class Indonesians secretly enjoy dangdut but for reasons of status and prestige (*gengsi*) pretend that they do not.

Though they inhabit very different social and musical worlds, in some respects Indonesian *Top Forty* bands resemble *pengamen*, the roving urban street musicians discussed in chapter 7. Performers in both categories attempt to please an audience and make a living by embodying through performance a particular musicscape, and both try to maintain a repertoire of currently popular songs. On the other hand, café musicians are conduits for global sounds, and their polished renditions of pop hits bring an aura of cosmopolitan leisure and sophistication to the spaces they inhabit. Street musicians do not have access to these channels of cultural and material power and instead, with the limited means at their disposal, reproduce familiar songs that gesture not to the phantasmagoric, glamorous world outside Indonesia, but to everyday life with all its hardships. *Pengamen* are considered a nuisance because their humble, impoverished presentations are devoid of escapism — they embody the grim realities of life that deflate the pop fantasies of the songs they sing. In contrast, *Top Forty* bands' performances, like malls, invite members of Indonesia's affluent minority to pretend they are in an imaginary, postnational elsewhere removed from the squalor and want of Jakarta's streets.

Student-Organized Musical Events

Unlike the entertainment at awards shows discussed in chapter 7, the repertoires of *Top Forty* groups index the transnational character of the contemporary popular musicscape in Indonesia, though they also show a marked tendency toward xenocentrism. To appreciate the full range of musical options that exist for urban Indonesian youth, we must turn to the less self-consciously urbane, more grassroots-based types of performance events organized by and for young Indonesians themselves.

A common type of popular music event in Jakarta and other large Indonesian cities at the turn of the millennium was the daylong music festival organized by university or middle-class high school students. Such events could last over twelve hours, with forty or more amateur, semiprofessional, and professional performing ensembles participating. The most elaborate of these festivals were held in soccer stadiums, attracting thousands of spectators—mostly fashionable, cell phone-toting middle-class youth. These young people were able to afford the price of admission, which in 1999–2000 ranged from 11,000 to 15,000 rupiahs (at the time, less than US$2.00), a substantial sum for working-class Indonesians. As mentioned in chapter 7, the two key components of student-organized *acara* were a committee (*panitia*) composed of peers, which coordinated the affair and a sponsor or sponsors, usually corporations that covered the costs of mounting the event in exchange for the opportunity to advertise their products at the site. These *acara* were advertised through colorful flyers that listed the sponsors, headlining bands, and the time and location of the event, and were posted on university campuses and other locations where middle-class youths congregate.

Because most *acara* in Jakarta obtained sponsorships from major corporations, they tended to be larger and more elaborate affairs than student-organized events in the United States. Standard provisions included an enormous stage with professional-quality sound and lighting, a wide assortment of instrument amplifiers, two large video-projection screens on either side of the stage, and (invariably) a fog machine. The most humble student rock group participating in the event had the

Kresikars 2000, a student-organized *acara* in Kuningan Stadium.

opportunity to play on the same stage and through the same sound equipment as the headlining artists. Also, committees could often afford to invite the most popular recording artists of the day to perform at their events. These headliners, who played short sets of five or six songs, commonly took the stage at ten or eleven at night, more than twelve hours after the official start of the event. At first I was surprised to find successful recording artists like Gigi, Melly Goeslaw, Netral, Padi, and /rif good-humoredly tolerating extremely Spartan backstage accommodations—often little more than a cramped, windowless dressing room with no indoor plumbing and a thin curtain for a door—in order to play at these events. The reward for tolerating these conditions was the opportunity to play before a large, enthusiastic audience of young music fans—though many in the audience, after having spent an entire day under the hot sun watching less-established groups perform, would be quite exhausted by the time the headlining acts took the stage.

As one might expect in such a self-conscious cultural arena, references to local, national, and global musical genres, both present and absent, abounded at student-organized *acara*. Dangdut was a frequent subject of attempts at humor; the very presence of (prerecorded) dangdut music at such events often sufficed to provoke embarrassed and riotous laughter from the audience. At one event, when the stage was momentarily lit by yellow lights, an emcee commented that it was "like a dangdut concert" (Indonesians with whom I spoke considered yellow to be an especially low-class color). At another, clowns and cross-dressers indulged in lascivious dances when a dangdut song played on the prerecorded soundtrack; this received an uproarious response from the middle-class student audience.

Most bands that performed at student-organized *acara* were relatively inexperienced and played other bands' songs. In Jakarta and Bandung, they seemed to cover English-language songs exclusively, while at concert events in Yogyakarta I witnessed bands performing songs by Indonesian rock bands Gigi, Pas, and /rif. Bands that played at *acara* were divided into three categories: *band seleksi* were amateur bands that paid a fee to audition and were selected by the organizing committee, *band dukungan* (supporting bands) were more experienced and accomplished student groups invited to perform at the event, and *bintang tamu* (guest stars) were often full-time professional musicians and included nationally recognized recording artists.

"Guest star" bands were paid for their appearance; they included bands that performed skillful covers of Western groups and those that played their own compositions. Most artists in the latter category, which included established underground groups as well as bands signed to large commercial record labels, had recorded their own albums, while those in the former group had not. Each of the *bintang tamu* cover bands specialized in one Western style or artist; for example, Tor, one of the more creative Jakarta-based performing groups, specialized in covering the songs of 1960s rock legend Jimi Hendrix. Similarly, a Jakartan group called Rastafari played Bob Marley songs and other examples of 1970s reggae, the popular cover band T-Five was known for its versions of 1990s hip hop and R & B songs, and a dozen or so groups specialized in replicating the sounds of "hip metal" artists such as Korn and Limp Bizkit. These groups often endeavored to reproduce not only the sounds of the bands they covered but also their costumes and stage moves, which they learned through studying live concert videos. In general, the guest-star cover bands' repertoires differed little from those of the younger groups that preceded them. At a single event it was not unusual to hear the same Rage Against the Machine or Korn song performed five or six times by different bands possessing vastly different skill levels.

Not all cover bands aimed to create exact replicas of preexisting songs. Tor, the band mentioned earlier, was unique among the cover

Hendrik, Tor's *gendang* player, performing at Kresikars 2000.

groups I observed in that it included in its lineup a traditional musician—a Sundanese *kendang* (barrel drum) player—who added his own parts to the Western pop and rock songs performed by the band. Often the rock instruments in the ensemble (the band also had a drummer, a guitarist, a bassist, and a keyboardist) completely drowned out the *kendang,* though Tor did play one song—a departure from their usual repertoire of Jimi Hendrix covers—that featured it prominently: a humorous version of the New Kids on the Block song "Step by Step." Not only was it unusual for a group specializing in classic rock covers to play a song made famous by the quintessential 1980s "boy band," this particular rendition featured a lengthy and virtuosic *jaipong*-style *kendang* solo in the middle of the song that garnered an enthusiastic response from the audience.

But why were the students cheering? The answer is no doubt complex; certainly the audacious aural and visual juxtaposition of traditional drumming with a song regarded as a paragon of Western pop commercialism appeared to be an undeniable source of pleasure for audience members. In Tor's performance, the "local," represented by an "ethnic" musical tradition, could be heard and seen "colonizing" a globally hegemonic music product, and the response was laughter and applause. Significantly, Tor *chose* to incorporate traditional music—they were not "resorting" to ethnic sounds because of an inability to perform global popular music correctly. In fact, the band's ability to master Western rock was well demonstrated elsewhere in their set by their energetic and tight renditions of the Jimi Hendrix compositions "Crosstown Traffic" and "Purple Haze."

Tor, like most other cover bands, aspired to write original material and record an album, though by their own admission they had not yet begun taking steps to achieve this goal. In fact, many successful Indonesian rock and pop groups began as cover bands on the live performance circuit, and many remain strongly associated with the Western groups whose songs they used to play. For example, the rock group The Fly was well known among Jakarta students as a U2 cover band before they began to record their own material, which, not surprisingly, resembles the Irish band's music.

Deena Weinstein's sociological analysis of heavy metal concerts in the West divides participants into three spatially and socially distinct groups: performing artists, "backstage workers" (technicians, roadies, stage managers, etc.), and audience (1991, 199–205). I found that a distinguishing feature of live rock and pop music performances at Indonesian student-organized events is the lack of a strict separation between classes of participants, in particular the visibility of backstage personnel and audience members onstage—on the performer's turf, so to speak. Although some distinctions between groups of participants persist, they are blurred in the course of the concert event. The committee (*panitia*) plays a special mediating role. Its members generally lack technical roles in the proceedings but are free to watch from the stage, sharing space with performers in full view of the audience, their matching, custom-made T-shirts setting them apart from other participants. I took photographs of performers onstage at most of the *acara* I attended, and I noticed that I always had difficulty photographing bands' drummers. Due to their customary position toward the back of the stage, drummers were often completely surrounded by *panitia* members who preferred to watch the show from that position. Often these nonperformers completely or partially blocked the drummer from the audience's view, especially if he or she was playing with an especially popular group. No one ever asked these onstage onlookers to move out of the way. One band photographer, Helvi from Bandung, solved the problem by shooting pictures while standing atop a riser at the rear of the stage in order to gain an unobstructed, bird's-eye view of the drummer.

The Economics of Student Music Festivals

An important task of the *panitia* is to obtain sponsors for the event; this is usually not difficult. A number of companies—both international and Indonesian—that target their products at affluent youth have sponsored music *acara*. Major sponsors for musical events I attended included Close-Up toothpaste, Sprite, Arby's, McDonald's, Zevit-C vitamins, Teh Kita ("Our [inclusive] Tea," a national bottled tea beverage), Chips Ahoy! cookies, Bisik.com (a student-oriented Web site [*bisik* = whisper]), *Hai* (a youth-oriented pop culture magazine), Baskin-Robbins ice cream, and the national dairy-product company Indomilk.

Although not usually involved with school-affiliated concerts, Indonesian *kretek* (clove cigarette) brands such as Djarum Super, Gudang Garam, Bentoel, and Sampoerna frequently sponsored other youth-oriented live musical events, and audience members often received a free pack of cigarettes with the price of admission. Sponsors' products were heavily promoted at *acara*. Fast food companies operated well-staffed booths selling refreshments during the event, banners and posters advertising the sponsors' wares decorated the stage and the surrounding area, and television advertisements for the products were played repeatedly on large projection video screens between acts (recall the *Mildcoustic* event discussed in chapter 7).

Televisual images were an integral part of most pop and rock *acara*, and not just those that were broadcast for a home television audience. In addition to showing sponsors' advertisements, *acara* video screens were also used to project Western rock videos and concert footage during the breaks between bands. These sequences of imported videos, which were painstakingly assembled beforehand in a video editing studio, generally received a positive response from the audience, often far more positive than that generated by most of the local bands. Also, many *acara* screened their own custom-made computer animation sequences, which incorporated the event's logo and the list of event sponsors. These multimedia presentations were not "supplements" to the live performances but were an integral part of the *acara*. In fact there is no reason to assume that the bands' presentations were any less "mediated" than the video sequences, since their performances were often themselves self-conscious replications of the sounds, movements, and images of imported concert videos.

Acara Expresi: "Noceng Nodrugs"

The following is description of an *acara* organized by the Faculty of Communications at Moestopo University, Jakarta. The title of the *acara*, "Noceng Nodrugs" (No Drugs 2000), was created by a combination of Jakartanese (*Noceng* means "two thousand," a term borrowed from Hokkien Chinese) and English words; together they described the main theme of the event.[2] Many youth-organized *acara* of the time shared the "say no to drugs in the new millennium" theme, as awareness of the problems of drug abuse grew more widespread among Indonesian youth in the late 1990s.

12:30 p.m., July 30, 2000

It is a sweltering afternoon in the Senayan Sports Complex in Central Jakarta.[3] Student rock bands have been playing since morning, but very few audience members have arrived to watch them. A tent covers the stage; the unprotected, sun-drenched concrete basketball courts in front of the stage are still devoid of people. Behind the basketball courts is a larger tent housing a series of booths: food stands, a student photography exhibit, a display of leftist books and T-shirts run by the Universitas Moestopo School of Communications, an exhibit advertising a drug rehabilitation facility, and a large stand operated by a store called Underground, which has branches in Bandung and Bintaro, South Jakarta. The stand is selling pirated Western recordings and videos and a few nonpirated Indonesian underground cassettes. Also on sale are T-shirts, wool hats, jewelry, bandanas, sunglasses, and other accessories, as well as a row of large posters, mostly of popular Western bands like Blink 182, Slipknot, Rancid, and the Beastie Boys. There is even a colorful Che Guevara print.

The student photo exhibit provides a fascinating glimpse into middle-class Indonesian student culture. The display includes several photographs of the November 13, 1998, "Semanggi Tragedy," a notorious incident during which as many as eight unarmed student protesters were killed by soldiers during a demonstration in Central Jakarta.[4] The photographs include a violent confrontation between protesters and riot police, a group of student protesters observing evening prayers (*syolat maghrib*), a profusely bleeding student being carried off by his comrades, and a large picture of cars set ablaze in front of Atma Jaya University, which is located in the Semanggi area.

Another category of photographs portrays typical scenes from Indonesian life: schoolchildren in uniform, a young *kampung* mother and child, a garbage-strewn Jakarta cityscape. Finally, there is a still life, an abstract figure study, and two pictures of Indonesian rock singers performing (Armand Maulana from Gigi and Andy from /rif). I conclude that the exhibit combines some recurring themes in student life: a somewhat detached and aestheticized view of the life of ordinary Indonesians, the desire for artistic self-expression, and at least a sentimental attachment to politics. The day's performances provide further examples of these central themes.

The headlining "guest stars" at this particular *acara* included alternative rock band Netral, veteran Jakarta hardcore group Step Forward, alternative pop band Padi (which would later release one of the most commercially successful recordings in Indonesian history), Balcony, a Bandung-based "emo-core" (emotional hardcore punk) band, and a cover band specializing in the music of the 1960s American rock group The Doors. But these bands would not take the stage until long after sundown. Until evening arrived, a more eclectic than usual assortment of ensembles performed in the hot sun for a small but growing crowd.

3:30 p.m.–10:00 p.m.
The musical offerings at the start of the day are rather predictable. The stage is occupied by a succession of high school–and university student–aged bands covering songs by contemporary Western rock groups. Their audience consists of a mere ten people huddled under the shade of an umbrella below the stage. To the right of the performers the event planning committee (*panitia*), all dressed in matching white T-shirts emblazoned with the *acara*'s name, gather under the shade of a small grove of trees. They drink from their own water cooler, off-limits to regular audience members.

As the day progresses, there is greater variety in the performances. A group of young women in traditional, folkloric dress sing and perform an Acehnese dance. I later learn that the members of the troupe are students from SMA 70, a Jakarta high school, and that none are actually from Aceh, a province in northern Sumatra that has long been the site of a separatist rebellion against the Indonesian government. There is also a clown (*pelawak*) act, a demonstration by a *silat* (Indonesian martial arts) troupe, a cheerleading routine complete with pompoms, and a male a cappella group that performs songs from a number of different genres, from a Bob Marley reggae composition to 1970s American soft rock to 1950s rock and roll. Their clever all-vocal arrangements of two dangdut songs receive an especially positive reaction, and a few audience members even begin to *joget* enthusiastically in response. The group performs a rhyming, spoken passage in the middle of their second dangdut song, the ever-popular "Kopi Dangdut," in an aggressive American rap style, to the audience's amusement.

By sundown, after the break for evening prayers (which, as usual, I see no one actually performing), the audience has grown to around 250 people. As the evening progresses, the emcees—one man and one woman—stage dancing contests, quiz the audience, and give out prizes provided by the event's sponsors in the intervals between band performances. They also spend a considerable amount of time speaking with a mentally handicapped audience member, their gentle teasing eliciting laughter from the audience while at the same time establishing his significance as a participant in the event.

This description captures some of the basic patterns of the *acara* and highlights its juxtaposition of folkloric performance, humor, Western rock music, and consumerism. At the event described above, regional music from Aceh was appropriated in the name of the nation, aspects of global youth culture were appropriated in the name of trendiness and fashion, and national cultural forms were performed, parodied, cele-brated, and hybridized.

Women and Performance Revisited

At student-organized *acara*, the gender roles that predominate at dang-dut concerts, in which women are dangerous objects of desire and men exhibit their mastery over their passions as a way of relieving stress, are largely absent. In their place are equally complicated constellations of gendered meanings saturated by class differences and global popular culture influences. Women musicians were a small minority at *acara* I attended, but women's contributions to the event often took forms other than musical performance. Between bands there were sometimes "fashion shows" during which young models wearing student-designed outfits strode across the stage to the sound of loud, prerecorded, usu-ally Western, music. In Jakarta, student events often featured troupes of young women in tight-fitting, matching outfits who, much like cheerleaders at an American athletic event, performed precisely choreographed dance routines to a prerecorded soundtrack. These troupes collectively composed their own choreography, and their internal organization seemed to parallel that of the male-dominated rock bands. "Women are soft/graceful" (*wanita lembut*) was the reason one male audience member offered to explain why women formed dance troupes, but I suspect that another reason was that, like the mostly male members of cover bands, they too wanted to experience embodying the icons of Western popular culture through mimetic performance.

The women's moves and costumes were extremely suggestive and risqué by Indonesian standards, and for that reason their performances often received an enthusiastic response from male audience members. The soundtrack for their dances was usually a cassette containing a homemade montage of electronic dance or R & B songs, each segment usually lasting less than a minute before an abrupt transition to the next. The dance moves occasionally drew on traditional sources (many middle-class Indonesian girls take classes in Balinese and Javanese traditional dance in a manner similar to the way many Western girls study ballet) but were clearly mostly inspired by the dancing in Western hip hop and R & B music videos. Unlike dangdut singers or the "women without husbands" who dance at dangdut clubs, the young women's performance did not seem to signal a lack of virtue or sexual availability. Their cosmopolitan style resulted from a playful, collective impersonation of global divas. In a sense, the "truth value" of their impersonations was analogous to that of a cover band playing a Western pop song.

One composition frequently performed by both café and student cover bands was Sting's "An Englishman in New York." When the vocalist sang the line in the refrain, "I'm an Englishman in New York," the audience was well aware that the singer was neither British nor residing in New York City. Similarly, the sensual moves of the Indonesian dancers were not intended to permanently liken their (assumed to be virginal) bodies to the dancing, sexualized bodies of the virtual (but not virtuous) Western women who originally performed these movements. This mimetic relationship differs somewhat from that between the Acehnese song and dance and the non-Acehnese performers at the Noceng No Drugs concert event. In the latter case, the women in the ensemble were not members of the Acehnese ethno-linguistic group, but they shared the same nationality as the Acehnese. Appropriating the expressive culture of Aceh was therefore an example of the folkloricization that accompanies nation-building projects (Bruner 2001), though in this instance it appeared to be the product of a grassroots initiative, rather than a direct intervention by the state.

Marc Schade-Poulsen (1999) describes male Algerian *raï* fans' perceptions of women as divided into three categories: "good" Muslim women; "bad" Muslim women who only want money; and Western women, who are perceived as attractive and offering unconditional love and devotion, standing somehow outside the moral standards and expectations of reciprocity that characterize Algerian society. The third category existed largely in the imagination of Schade-Poulsen's informants, yet it nonetheless had powerful effects on their attitudes toward the opposite gender. These three categories correspond remarkably to those discussed by contemporary Indonesian youth. The women in the dance troupes temporarily inhabited the roles of Western women—like those on MTV—whose sexuality was not subject to the moral reprobation of Islam or of "traditional" Indonesian values. As a result of this cultural mimesis, they had a freedom of expression that women in other parts of Indonesia, even in other cities, lacked.

The relative flexibility of gender roles at student-organized events indicates the presence of more westernized and flexible notions of masculinity and femininity, whereas dangdut concerts exhibit traditional gender understandings as mass, commodified entertainment. However, the differences between dangdut performance and the performance of women dance troupes are less the product of cultural differences between the more conservative lower classes and the more cosmopolitan middle-to-upper classes than they are the result of *class difference itself*. The young women onstage were not *janda* (divorcées/widows), and they were not performing for economic survival. When asked, their members explain that their troupes were formed "just for fun" (*iseng-iseng aja*), and that they, like amateur rock musicians, were merely pursuing a "hobby" (*hobi*), with all the wholesomeness that term implies in both English and Indonesian usage.

The privileged status of these middle-class, educated teenagers gives them an "obtuse purity," even when they choose to become "experimental girls" (*perempuan eksperimen* or *perek*) from the middle or upper class who engage in premarital sex for money or kicks (Hull, Sulistyaningsih, and Jones 1999, 18; see also Murray 1991, 119–20). According to a published study of prostitution in Indonesia, "[t]he behavior of these [experimental] girls, many of whom are middle class and still at school, represents a considerable challenge to official norms. It is strongly influenced by materialism and rising expectations fuelled by the media and advertising; it stresses individualism, [and] having sexual relations with whomever they like, whether paid or unpaid" (Hull, Sulistyaningsih, and Jones 1999, 18).

While female dangdut singers display themselves on stage for economic reasons, and because of their impoverished condition may be available for paid sexual encounters, becoming an experimental girl is a *lifestyle choice*, albeit an extreme (and probably rarer than commonly reported) one. Dangdut singers and professional prostitutes are driven by economic necessity, but middle-class adolescents and postadolescents possess the economic security and cultural capital to play with the sexual and social identities made available through "the media and advertising." Although most do not become sexual adventurers, some young middle-class women may choose to perform borrowed cosmopolitan identities in the safety of a student-oriented event that celebrates the ability of upwardly mobile young Jakartans to make their own temporary identity choices in a boisterous cultural marketplace of heterogeneous commodities, images, styles, and sounds.

10

Underground Music

IMAGINING

ALTERNATIVE COMMUNITY

Underground music is the third genre category in our discussion of live musical performance. While the rock and pop festivals discussed in chapter 9 frequently included underground groups, this chapter investigates the social meanings of *acara* that were exclusively devoted to underground music and the communities those *acara* purported to represent. These events resemble the more heterogeneous rock and pop events in many ways, but interestingly, though they seem to offer youth greater autonomy from the dominant adult-controlled mainstream, the range of gendered subject positions underground concerts allow are, if anything, more restrictive. Young men wear similar uniforms depending on the genre of choice and a portion of them partake in specific, predictable dance behaviors. Women audience members, who usually make up a small minority at underground shows, seem freer to defy the unofficial dress code, but on the other hand are likely to refrain from dancing or other forms of active participation in the proceedings. Female performers are likewise rare, and generally are relegated to supporting roles.

My analysis of underground music events further extends my general argument that popular music performances in Indonesia are important loci of playful contestation over alternative modernities based on different articulations of local, national, and global forms. Nonetheless, despite this contestation, the desired outcome of live performance, regardless of the particular genre(s) being played, is a positive feeling among the participants, one of experiential "sharedness" that suspends, at least temporarily, the preexisting social differences that impede the production of solidarity. Underground concert events, despite their often overtly oppositional stance toward the national mainstream, are not exceptions to this general aim. What makes underground concerts distinctive is the *imagined alternative community* such solidarity evokes, a community based on belonging to a global subculture of musical production and consumption.

Daniel Miller, an innovator in the anthropology of consumption and consumers, argues that contemporary consumption practices can and do generate novel forms of identity and community around the world. He suggests the phrase "a posteriori diversity" to describe the condition resulting from this process and argues that it is qualitatively different from "a priori diversity," which is created by separate local histories that predate the consumption practices of modernity. Miller describes a posteriori diversity as "the sense of quite unprecedented diversity created by the differential consumption of what had once been thought to be global and homogenizing institutions" (1995, 3). He adds, "The idea of a posteriori diversity allows for the possibility of more radical rupture under conditions of modernity, but does not assume that homogenization follows. Rather it seeks out new forms of difference, some regional, but increasingly based on social distinctions not easily identified with space. It treats these, not as continuity, or even syncretism with prior traditions, but as quite novel forms, which arise through the contemporary exploration of new possibilities given by the experience of these new institutions" (ibid.).

In Indonesia, underground rock music has become a remarkable source of a posteriori diversity among young people, especially as increased globalization of the music industry has precipitated a proliferation of musical alternatives to established national genres (see Baulch 2002a, 2002b). Indeed, the unprecedented rise of an Indonesian music underground dedicated to performing a diverse array of specialized imported genres is a most dramatic example of new identities and solidary communities forged in response to the new consumption possibilities opened up by global institutions such as MTV and the Internet. These "communities" may be short lived and temporally confined to a single generation, but they are nonetheless powerfully present in the lives of their participants. To understand a bit more about these communities, we take a short detour to an analysis of the printed acknowledgments found in the liner notes of underground album releases.

Representing Community:
Thank-You Lists in Underground Cassettes

Although writing thank-you lists in album liner notes is a textual practice that originated in the West, in the hands of Indonesian musicians these lists have become more elaborate and inclusive. Globalizing forces themselves are manifested in many thank-you lists, which include expressions of gratitude toward international recording artists cited as influences and sources of musical inspiration. These groups are not members of the Indonesian music community but are nonetheless included and praised, their appearance in the text indexing the globalization-influenced "unbounded seriality" of underground identities (Anderson 1998, 29–45). Thank-you lists can be written in a variety of styles, but usually underground bands divide them into acknowledgments written by the entire band followed by separate lists from each individual band member. Often there is an additional section expressing gratitude to fellow bands, and another acknowledging the support of underground fanzines, production companies, distributors, and other scenic institutions involved with the promotion of underground music.

In almost every case, regardless of the particular underground subgenre (including those preoccupied with satanic and occult themes), the first thanks is to God. References to God vary depending on the religion of the musicians: sometimes Allah S.W.T. (Arabic, Allah Subhanahu Wa Taala, "Allah the Almighty and Most Worthy of Praise"), sometimes Tuhan Y.M.E. (Tuhan Yang Maha Esa, "God the All-Powerful"), and sometimes Tuhan Yesus Kristus (Lord Jesus Christ). In Java, Muslims and Christians often play together in the same band; thus in their individual thank-you lists they thank their own version of the deity while the bands' collective thanks is to Tuhan Y.M.E., a generic title compatible with both religions. Individual thank-you lists generally acknowledge family members after God, then proceed to thank friends and colleagues, and end with a final apology to "anyone whose name was not mentioned." Here is a typical, though relatively short, example from the album *Abandon* [*sic*], *Forgotten, & Rotting Alone* (1999) by the extreme metal band Grausig:

> *Ricky* [the band's lead guitarist] *thanks to:*
> Allat [*sic*] SWT, my parents, Wike Sulasmi, Sony, My Wife Asri &
> Shena "Altaf," Bogor family, "Pai," Iksan, Adi, Ade, Niko "Bandung,"

Dwi "uwi" Farabi, Ki Sulaiman, Ustad Allul, Oele Patisilato, Kadek, Hendry, Chery, KH Kiansantang, Peggy, Ute, Windi, My brother band Benkel Seni, Sidick Rizal para bandit Tanjung Priok, Drs. Kasmianto and family, all Farabi gank, Deden Tobing, prumpung and the gank, Heru, Tanduk, Astreed gank, Didi, "usuf," Alex Lifeson of Rush.]

This list includes the names of friends (referred to by nickname), adults (referred to by formal titles), places (Bandung, Tanjung Priok, the Farabi music school), and collectivities (Farabi *gank* [gang], Astreed *gank*), as well as the name of the guitarist from the Canadian progressive rock band Rush. Most thank-you lists follow this pattern, though many are far more elaborate.

Much like the acknowledgments section of a book, thank-you lists assert the existence of a community of friends and colleagues; hence, it is not surprising that underground music cassettes contain quite elaborate lists—more extensive than those found in the liner notes of cassettes of other genres—since underground music relies on a national network of local, self-supporting scenes for its survival outside the commercial music industry. "In order to study the underground you need to study the places where we all hang out," Wendi Putranto, the editor of *Brainwashed,* a Jakarta fanzine, told me. He emphasized that the activities of socializing and sharing ideas at specific hangouts located in Blok M and other places were essential to the development of the Jakarta scene. The thank-you lists textualize this web of voluntary association and support, and by addressing the reader directly, explicitly include him or her in this expanding musical community. The purchaser of an underground cassette thus strengthens and supports the local scene and furthers its goal of existence outside the official channels of commerce. Many thank-you lists conclude with a message directed at the reader; in underground liner notes, this message is frequently an exhortation to support Indonesian underground bands and "your local scene" or a general expression of thanks to all the band's enthusiasts, such as this example from an underground industrial cassette:

Dan untuk seluruh fans Koil yang super setia: Top of the morning to you, kids.

 Cheers.

[And for all the *super*-faithful Koil *fans: Top of the morning to you, kids. Cheers.*][1]

As mentioned, a separate section in the acknowledgments is frequently reserved for fellow bands. Band names often appear followed by their city of origin in parentheses or preceded by the name of one of their members. Such lists assert the existence of a national musical community by indexing an extended network of interdependent relationships founded on shared enthusiasm and cooperation. This network is not only the conduit through which underground music flows but is also the underground's crowning achievement: the subculture's ideological commitment to musical independence finds fruition in a nationwide web of like-minded individuals dedicated to cultural production outside the sphere of the mainstream commercial entertainment industry. The significance of thank-you lists is evidenced by the many underground bands whose cassette inserts include extensive thank-you lists on behalf of the band as a whole and from each individual band member and yet omit printed lyrics.

An interesting variant of the thank-you list is the "no-thank-you" list, which sometimes appears at the end in a separate section or is incorporated into thank-you lists. In these lists, various parties are singled out as particularly undeserving of thanks of any sort and are instead targets of the musicians' ire. Frequently included in no-thank-you lists are ex-president Soeharto, the Indonesian military, "poseurs," and the police. The following is from the liner notes of metal band Purgatory's 2000 (major label!) album *Ambang Kepunahan* (Threshold of Extinction):

> *No Thank To: Political Clowns Who Gots The Double Face and also To Indonesian Army Who Repressing The Students and Indonesian People since 30 years ago until NOW!!!*

More comprehensive still is the following vivid excerpt from the album notes for *Systematic Terror Decimation* (1999), by the Jakarta-based underground band Vile, which establishes the musical underground as a source of oppositional consciousness:

> *WE ALSO WOULD LIKE TO VENT OUR ANGER AND REVENGEFUL HATRED TO THESE FEW FUCKING ASSHOLES:*
> *Fuckin' Suharto & his crony bastards, Fuckin' [General] Wiranto & TNI [Indonesian Armed Forces] (brainless psychopathic mass murderers), Habibie, Golkar, facist & Racist, Fuckin' Provocators, False Religious Fucks (don't use a holy religion to mask any fucking decayed purposes!), Money Suckers, Fuckin' Big Mouth, Traitors, Backstabbers, Meaningless*

bastards whom doesn't know how to appreciate of what we've done,
Fuckin' Rip Offs,... etc... your life is worthless than your fucking shits!!!...
huahahaha...!!!

Benedict Anderson's seminal discussion of "print capitalism" ([1983] 1991) provides a way of tracing how textual production and mass reception encourages the imagining of translocal social entities. Cassette liner notes help listeners imagine concentrically organized musical interpretive communities—local, national, and global. The imagined social entities indexed by thank-you lists help to contextualize the music for the listener.

The origin of underground music in a particular interpretive community is supposed to be an essential feature of the listener's encounter with that music. In the underground's "jargon of authenticity" (Adorno 1973), a poseur is someone who consumes underground music but does not participate in the life of the underground community and does not interpret the music primarily as an extension of a particular scene. The occasional discursive presence of "poseurs" in cassette liner-note texts helps define the boundaries of the underground community. The community boundaries nevertheless always implicitly include the reader of the texts.

One consistent feature of thank-you lists is multilingualism. The majority of underground cassette thank-you lists are written in English with some Indonesian. Regional languages are also used—usually for personal messages included in parentheses after someone's name. Thank-you lists thus express the multilayered identities of their authors—local, national, and global—to a national audience. They demonstrate how underground scenes, examples of consumption-generated a posteriori cultural diversity, do not embrace radical individualism (exemplified by the "cruel" capital city of Jakarta) but rather reject it in their utopian quest for an authentic music-based youth community that is both profoundly rooted in local realities and potentially global in scope.

Underground Concert Events

Underground *acara* provide the context in which the imagined alternative community of the musical underground—constructed textually through sound recordings and print culture—coalesces into a palpable reality. All-day concert events featuring underground music bands representing a single subgenre or related subgenres were an important type of student-organized *acara*. Such events tended to have colorful titles that sometimes revealed their featured subgenre (*aliran*), sometimes not. In Jakarta and Bandung, these included "Nocturnis Orgasm" (underground metal), "Bumi Satoe" ("One Earth," punk and hardcore), "Independent Youth" (various, more melodic underground styles classified as *indies*), "Jakarta Meraung" ("Jakarta Roars," metal), and Jakarta Bawah Tanah ("Underground Jakarta," metal). The following is an excerpt from my field notes written while attending this last event:

Poster Café, South Jakarta, October 4, 1997
The air is thick with perspiration, despite the air-conditioning. The entire crowd is wearing black concert T-shirts, many long-sleeved and double-layered despite the heat outside. (Nino, the lead singer of Trauma, explained that the long-sleeved, layered look was *keren*, "cool.") Most of the overwhelmingly male audience members have long, flowing hair that they flail around wildly to the rapid beat of the music. Hundreds of long-haired, black-clad Jakarta metalheads stream in and out of the concert hall, splitting their time between watching the bands onstage and hanging out outside on the wooden benches set up by the front entrance. Many of the bands performing have two alternating vocalists: one is responsible for low growls, the other for the songs' high shrieks. Was this yet another example of unequally sized paired instruments in Indonesian music? When I ask an audience member why so many groups have two vocalists, the response is that it is *lebih rame* (more crowded, noisy, fun) that way. Two of the day's headliners are grindcore group Tengkorak (Skull) from Jakarta and death metal band Slowdeath from Surabaya, East Java. The members of Slowdeath tell me they have traveled twenty hours by train to play at this concert event. (The slower trains were cheaper.) The concert starts around ten in the morning; headliners take the stage around five, and lesser-known bands play to a dwindling crowd afterward until the event's conclusion around seven in the evening. Later that night, the Poster Cafe (named for the posters of Anglo-American rock icons, from Jimi Hendrix to Kurt Cobain, that decorate its walls) will revert to a mainstream rock club catering to a slightly older, more upscale clientele.

Underground *acara* tended to be organized by smaller committees than those featuring mainstream pop and rock groups. They were also less likely to be officially affiliated with schools or universities and hence were often sponsored by cigarette companies. Although profit was certainly a motive for some *panitia* (committee) members and not all organizers were fans of underground music, for many committee members money was not of paramount concern. Although there were potential economic windfalls, these *acara* could also lose money or barely break even.

A 2001 concert report from the city of Pontianak in West Kalimantan (Indonesian Borneo) posted on a now-defunct underground music Web site (bisik.com) tells the story of a *panitia* that unexpectedly lost a cigarette company's sponsorship for an on-campus concert because of the regulation against promoting cigarettes on university grounds. As a result, the *panitia* members faced a substantial financial loss, yet they decided to persevere, and they mounted a major concert event featuring a wide variety of musical genres titled "Pontianak Bersatu" (Pontianak United). According to the author, afterward the organizers felt the concert was well worth the effort and the financial loss they sustained. The conclusion of the article reads:

> *Pontianak Bersatu! Akhirnya digelar juga, hal yang menarik memang melihatnya. Dimana perbedaan Genre musik tidak lagi menjadi persoalan. Semuanya terlihat satu, dan memang ini kami namakan musik Pontianak.*
>
> *Indah saat Punk melaju, kemudian musik etnik mengalun, grunge, pop, sampai khasidahan berdendang dan disambut teriakan death, grind, hardcore yang mengalun kencang. Saatnya bersatu, idealis bermusik-mu untukmu, Idealisme-ku untuk-ku!*
>
> *Semuanya satu diatas panggung, tidak ada lagi perbedaan. Hal ini kami mulai sebagai yang pertama di Pontianak. Dengan total kerugian 6 juta lebih, panitia masih bisa tersenyum. Kita kaya! Kita damai! Kita bersatu! Karena kita adalah satu, Pontianak Bersatu! Support Your Local Musicians!!! Apapun itu.*

[Pontianak United! In the end, it was really staged, something indeed interesting to behold. There the differences of musical genre were no longer a problem. They all appeared as one, and indeed this we (exclusive) could truly call "Pontianak's music."

Beautiful the moment when *punk* music played rapidly, then ethnic music moved steadily; *grunge, pop,* to *qasidah* sang happily and were answered by the screams of *death* (metal), *grind,* and *hardcore* at a rapid tempo. The moment of unity, your musical idealism for you, my idealism for me!

All was as one onstage; there were no more differences. This phenomenon we (exclusive) began as the first in Pontianak. With a total financial loss of over six million (rupiahs), the committee could still smile. We (inclusive) are rich! We are at peace! We are united! Because we are one, Pontianak is united! *Support Your Local Musicians!!!* No matter what.] (Mallau 2001)

This remarkable text exemplifies the underground rhetoric of scene unity, which here appears to extend to all the musical genres present at the *acara* and to the entire imagined musical community of the city of Pontianak. In the text, the author shifts back and forth between exclusive and inclusive first-person plural pronouns. The former appears to refer to the *panitia* members, while the latter's reference extends outward to all the participants present at the concert, who at the concert's end celebrate their newfound unity. Also significant is the slippage between different forms of unity: musical, social, geographical. While some underground musicians view their music as antithetical to dangdut, the anticipated effects of underground *acara* are perhaps not very different from those of dangdut concerts, except that the erasure of social divisions operates along different lines.

Moshing and Other Underground Dance Practices

Like dangdut performances, underground concerts involved dancing and embodied exchanges between performers and audience members. But instead of *joget, goyang,* and *nyawer* behavior, underground audiences engaged in less-"indigenous" practices such as moshing and stage diving.[2] Dance behavior at underground concerts was strongly influenced by the conduct of underground audiences in the West. Music videos and videotaped live performances by Western groups were readily available in Indonesia, and they provided models for concert behaviors that have become widely diffused. However, significant differences in dancing behavior nonetheless existed.

In general, I found that Indonesian concert audiences were somewhat more restrained than those in the United States. Their applause and dancing tended to be more subdued, though on occasion they would enthusiastically sing along with the performers (usually on-key) when popular songs were played. Even at underground events, the majority of the crowd would stand or sit nonchalantly while the music played, and a relatively unknown band with limited performing skills often faced an audience of disengaged, passive, seated listeners. When a better-known underground band, especially one of the "guest stars," took the stage, the crowd's actions would change dramatically. A "pit" would form in the space in front of the stage as members of the audience (no more than a third of the total, often much less than that) surged forward and began engaging in the three characteristic pit activities, which were known in Indonesian by their English names: *moshing, stage diving,* and *crowd surfing.*

Moshing, also called slamming, is an aggressive dance familiar in underground scenes the world over. While occasionally taking the form of a slow-moving circle dance (cf. Weinstein 1991, 228), moshing generally involves a group of individuals crowded together in an enclosed space (the pit) intentionally colliding with and shoving one another. Stage diving refers to the practice in which an audience member climbs up to the stage, sometimes interacting with the performers, sometimes not, and then after a short interval dives face first into the crowd (this practice resembles the ascending-the-stage behavior of some audience members at dangdut concerts, though underground music fans do not generally acknowledge this resemblance). If he (women stage divers are extremely rare in Indonesia) is fortunate, he is caught by the people standing below him and is then held aloft and passed from hand to hand, a practice known as crowd surfing. Stage diving, even more than moshing, can result in injuries, both to the audience members beneath the diver and to the diver himself, particularly when the crowd is too thin to support the diver's weight and he falls to the floor (I occasionally witnessed this occurrence). Nonetheless, serious injuries were uncommon in Indonesia as elsewhere.

While it is certainly a hazardous activity, stage diving is celebrated in underground scenes not only as a show of daredevil skill but also as a corporeal way of breaking down the separation between performer and audience (Goshert 2000, 99). Overcoming the separation between musicians and audiences is an important goal of underground concerts the world over, with their explicit rejection of an alienating media star system that places a wedge between performers and fans. In addition to audience members' stage diving, some singers onstage occasionally cross over from the other direction, diving into the crowd from the stage, with microphone in hand and microphone cable trailing behind. Hariadi "Ombat" Nasution, the lead singer of Tengkorak, was notorious for doing this during his band's performances.

At first moshing, stage diving, and crowd surfing might appear to be antithetical to the stereotypical Indonesian traditional values of order,

social harmony, consideration for others, and self-restraint. Such practices instead seem to epitomize violent individualism, as audience
members engaged in them appear to be heedless of the possibility of
hurting those around them. The mosh pit also exemplifies a darker aspect of Indonesian cultural life: the dissolution of individual responsibility in collective actions (see the discussion in chapter 5 about the
breakdown of the steel cage in Netral's video). Dancers are seemingly
unconcerned with the consequences of their violent actions because
they are acting not as individuals but as members of a collective body,
yet I believe that it is this feeling of collective belonging that mitigates
the individualism of the pit participants. While appearing to valorize
violent egoism, the dancing in fact celebrates membership in a larger
whole: the ephemeral collective consisting of those onstage, those in the
audience, those straddling the line between stage and crowd, and, by
extension, the whole underground scene itself. Indeed, although they
sometimes result in the infliction of unintentional harm, stage-diving
and crowd-surfing activities embody a collectivist ethos: the diver places
his physical well-being in the hands of his compatriots, whom he trusts
to catch him and keep him aloft.

As mentioned previously, while the characteristic underground
dance practices originated in the West, in Indonesia they have been
indigenized to a degree and differ in some ways from Western practices. For instance, dancers at concerts commonly coordinated their
movements with others around them. A row of metal enthusiasts, arms
around each other's shoulders, performing the up-and-down "head-
banging" movement in unison (looking like a heavy metal version of the
Rockettes) was a common sight at Indonesian metal concerts but virtually unknown in the United States. (As mentioned in chapter 8, characteristic ska dance moves were also executed in this fashion; the result resembled a chorus line.) Indonesian mosh pits often took on a collective
character and ebbed and flowed as a unit. Thus dance moves thought to
signify violent individualism and alienation in the West are communal-
ized in the Indonesian context and appear to index intense collective
sentiment more than individual angst.

Dangdut Underground?
The Emergence of Student Dangdut Bands

This book has focused on the ideological contrasts that exist between
different popular music genres in Indonesia. Of all these contrasts,

Pemuda Harapan Bangsa (Youth, Hope of the Nation) performing in Bandung, West Java.

arguably that between dangdut and underground is the most stark—the former indigenous, mass-market oriented, proletarian, and musically accessible; the latter imported, selective in its appeal, associated with university students and middle-class youth, and musically challenging. Yet an equally salient theme in the current study has been the self-conscious creation of musical hybrids, a process that often playfully transgresses historically and discursively constructed boundaries between genres and by metonymic extension, social categories as well. Perhaps it was inevitable, then, that some student musicians would begin to experiment with playing dangdut songs with the attitude and musical trappings of underground music.

Like the café bands discussed in the previous chapter, these ensembles played dangdut songs with rock instrumentation. None had the full complement of musicians found in dangdut groups, nor did any of the groups at the time I met them have a *suling* player. I found representatives of this unusual genre in a few Indonesian cities; they included Sekarwati (from Jakarta), Soekarmadjoe (Yogyakarta), Kuch Kuch Hota Hai (Surabaya), and Pemuda Harapan Bangsa (Bandung). While student dangdut was clearly a transregional phenomenon, the small number of student dangdut bands hardly constituted a movement—and for the most part the bands were not even aware of one another's existence. Nevertheless, the bands had certain characteristics in common:

1. The groups' members were often art students at prestigious institutions such as the Institut Kesenian Jakarta (Jakarta Art Institute), Yogyakarta's Institut Seni Indonesia (Institute of Indonesian Arts), or Bandung's Sekolah Tinggi Senirupa dan Desain (High School of Art and Design).

2. All the groups were extremely popular and received many invitations to play at *acara*. During their performances, members of the audience, both men and women, would *joget*, cheer, and applaud, and sometimes even offer money to the performers in a parody of the practice of *saweran*.

3. Band members who had previous performing experience had played rock and/or underground music; I spoke to no one who had prior experience or training playing dangdut music. Indeed, for the most part these bands exhibited very little musical mastery of the genre.

4. Band members claimed to dislike contemporary dangdut, which they saw as corrupted by disco and house music, and preferred older, "pure" dangdut songs from the 1970s and 1980s by established artists like Elvy Sukaesih, Rita Sugiarto, Rhoma Irama, and Meggi Z.

5. Onstage costumes resembled those of underground ensembles rather than the usual uniforms of dangdut musicians (see chapter 8).

In addition to dangdut, two of the groups played songs from other working-class-identified genres: the Surabaya group Kuch Kuch Hota Hai played the Hindi film song from which it took its name and a few songs from another *kampungan* imported genre, Malaysian *slowrock* (see appendix B). When Soekarmadjoe added a popular *campur sari* song to their repertoire, they received an enormously positive crowd response.

Student dangdut groups may turn out to be part of a short-lived trend in a larger and longer history of humorous student performances, but I contend that the synthesis they represent is motivated by specific and important cultural agendas. In essence, student musicians appropriating dangdut music are suggesting an alternative to the elitism and foreignness of underground music, while at the same time making a provocative claim about conspicuous formal musical similarities between ideologically opposed genres. After all, dangdut and underground music use similar electrified and electronic Western instruments and technologies, share common minor-key chord progressions, and are strongly influenced by hard rock, heavy metal, and reggae.

Soekarmadjoe (Difficult to Advance) performing in Yogyakarta. Note the members' facial expressions.

But why dangdut? A conversation with Nedi Sopian, the lead singer of the sarcastically named group Pemuda Harapan Bangsa (Youth, Hope of the Nation) suggests a concern for national authenticity in response to global musical influences. This excerpt is from an interview held backstage after a performance conducted in the rowdy presence of more than a dozen of the band's fans.

Nedi Sopian: *Saya influence artisnye . . .*
JW: *Ya?*
Nedi: *Smashing Pumpkins . . .*
JW: *Smashing Pumpkins, ya . . .*
Nedi: *Eh . . . Rotor . . .*
JW: *Rotor? Grup Indonesia ya?*
Nedi: *Grup Indonesia, ya, Indonesia. Terus, Biohazard. . . . Saya nggak suka dangdut sebenernye . . .*
JW: *Tidak suka?*
Nedi: *Tidak suka dangdut saya.* Tapi karena jiwa saya Melayu . . .
        [uproarious laughter and applause from onlookers]
Nedi: *Semua di sini juga Melayu, cuman sok bule gitu . . .*
                [more laughter]
Nedi: *Bener gak? Bener gak? Bener, khan?*

[Nedi Sopian: My (recording) artist *influences* are . . .
JW: Yeah?
Nedi: Smashing Pumpkins (American alternative rock group) . . .
JW: Smashing Pumpkins, okay . . .
Nedi: Um . . . Rotor (Indonesian thrash metal/industrial group) . . .
JW: Rotor? That's an Indonesian band, right?
Nedi: Yeah, an Indonesian group, Indonesian. Also, Biohazard
    (American hardcore/metal/rap group). . . . I don't like dangdut
    actually . . .
JW: (You) don't like (it)?
Nedi: I don't like dangdut. *But because my soul is Malay* . . .
          (uproarious laughter, applause from onlookers)
Nedi: Everyone here is also Malay; they're only wannabe whites!
                (more laughter)
Nedi: Right? Right? Am I right or what?]

In this brief but telling exchange, Nedi disavows his attachment to dangdut music only to reassert it for racialistic reasons. Rather than pretend to be "white" (*bule*), like certain others among his peers, his music expresses his "soul's" true identity as a "Malay"—a biological category that every Indonesian schoolchild learns encompasses the indigenous populations of Indonesia, Malaysia, Singapore, Brunei, and the Philippines. This is the case despite his inclusion of "white" American rock bands (and one Indonesian industrial metal group) in his list of influences. Such ambivalence toward the compelling aesthetic pull of global rock music and the contrasting musical and ideological attractions of dangdut are perhaps what made Pemuda Harapan Bangsa's hybrid music so appealing to its middle-class student audience. Both band members and fans interviewed at the concert expressed the opinion (not particularly facetiously) that dangdut was *nasionalis,* an Indonesian word that is generally synonymous with "patriotic." In any case, the popular response to student dangdut bands also illustrates how the most socially transgressive musical hybrids are often the most successful.

Dangdut and Student Culture

The appropriation of classic dangdut music by Indonesian postsecondary students parallels certain revivalist phenomena in other times and regions, such as the 1950s and 1960s popularization of American "folk" music by college students in the United States, and the *nueva canción* student movement in Latin America, in which appropriated Andean folk music became a vehicle for social protest (Manuel 1988, 68–72). But in several important respects the rise of student dangdut bands differs from these earlier movements. Although the student dangdut musicians' preoccupation with "pure" dangdut songs from earlier decades may resemble the folk revivalists' concern with authenticity, no rhetoric of a pure, precapitalist past or of preservation accompanies their performances. Such a discourse would be fairly absurd in that context, given dangdut's tremendous popularity and commercial origins, and such thinking was clearly not reflected in the impure, hybridizing habits of student dangdut bands.

More importantly, while popularized folk music was often promoted as an austere, not very danceable alternative to mindless mass-market pop music, dangdut played by student bands appeared to be an antidote to the austerity and nondanceability of imported underground rock music, with its "serious" themes and jagged, lunging rhythms. Dangdut music appeared to free the audience from its inhibitions, and the atmosphere at student dangdut concerts combined the exuberance of the mosh pit with the intense pleasures of a neighborhood dangdut show. Thus the appropriation of dangdut bears a certain similarity to the appropriation of different types of working-class music by middle-class youths in the United States in the second half of the twentieth century, which was accompanied by the appealing notion that the sensual enjoyment of organic grooves from below would dismantle structures of repression in middle-class American life.

Performing Relationships to Global and National Musical Commodities

The rise of student dangdut groups can been further illuminated by comparing it to analogous developments in Western rock music history. In an essay titled "Concerning the Progress of Rock & Roll," Michael Jarrett addresses what he views as a central problem with accounts of the development of Anglo-American rock music, namely, how the genre has been able to periodically revitalize itself despite the ongoing commercialization and dilution of rock music, which he likens to "an aesthetic version of entropy as heat-death" (1992, 169). Jarrett locates innovation in rock music in a particular cultural dynamic of growth out of entropic decay, which he compares to mushrooms growing on a compost heap. He writes that the popularization and subsequent banalization of rock music "fosters artistic renewal by generating conditions that allow for aberrant readings" (174). Thus he reads a series of canonically innovative moments in rock and roll history—the emergence of Elvis Presley, the rise of the 1960s counterculture, and the late 1970s punk rebellion—as the result of musicians perversely "misreading" the musical compost heap created by all the pop music that had come before. In Jarrett's view, American rock legends such as Little Richard, Bob Dylan, and the Ramones were great because they played inept and refracted versions of rhythm and blues, country, American folk music, and the 1960s girl-group sound. (And perhaps I should note parenthetically that, like many student dangdut group members, numerous Anglo/American rock innovators, from John Lennon to Eric Clapton to the Talking Heads, happened to be students of the visual arts.)

Though Jarrett does not acknowledge this explicitly, the cultural dynamic he describes relies on the materiality and circulating capabilities of music recordings. Recordings from remote times, places, and cultures make up the cultural "compost heap" on which, according to Jarrett, innovative rock music developments thrive funguslike on an eclectic diet of decontextualized sonic objects. Thus one does not have to be from a particular place or have a specific cultural background in order to innovate within the rock "tradition" as long as one has access to recordings. Indonesian student dangdut groups in performance replicate the sounds of twenty-year-old dangdut cassettes and three-year-old imported Western rock music compact discs. Their relationship with these sounds is mediated by the recorded musical artifact, which through its very materiality flattens the temporal, geographical, and social distance that separates its producers from its consumers. The members of Soekarmadjoe, Pemuda Harapan Bangsa, and their compatriots thus perform an inspired hybrid from the jumble of heterogeneous national and global artifacts that comprise their musical biographies. I would venture to say that in doing so they demonstrate that Indonesian musicians have mastered the art of creating original and innovative rock music.

But which genre is being revitalized here? When Pemuda Harapan Bangsa was signed to a major label in 2001, it was promoted not as a rock band but as a dangdut group, appearing on dangdut-oriented television music variety shows and producing an album in which their stripped-down song arrangements were filled in with the standard multitracked instrumentation of dangdut recordings. In an April 2001 e-mail, Temtem, Pemuda Harapan Bangsa's rhythm guitarist, expressed some ambivalence about his record company's class-based promotion strategy.

Kita juga lagi berjuang buat diterima di masyarakat. Kita udah bikin videoclip, tapi stasiun TV cuman mau nayangin di program2 dangdut, terus terang, kita gak suka dikotak2in begitu. Mungkin mereka nganggap kami musik dangdut, it's o.k ... tapi selanjutnya kita malah susah untuk bergerak, karena sebagian masy. Ind masih beranggapan bahwa dangdut itu milik masy kelas B, C (low class). Kita pengen musik kita diterima seluruh masy — tanpa terkecuali. Selain itu kami juga meramu musik — bukan hanya dangdut, tapi ada keroncong, pop, arabian, rock dan macem-macem deh.

[We are also struggling to be accepted in society. We made a *video clip,* but the TV stations only want to screen it on dangdut programs; frankly, we don't like being boxed in like that. Maybe they consider us dangdut; *it's ok* . . . but then it follows that it's quite difficult for us to maneuver, because a segment of Indonesian society still considers dangdut the property of the society of classes B and C (*low class*). We want our music to be accepted by the entire society, without exception. Besides that, we also mix music together — not only dangdut, but *keroncong,* pop, Arab music, rock, and really all sorts of things.]

As mentioned in chapter 3, the Indonesian music industry classifies the record-buying public into socioeconomic classes labeled A to D, in which class A includes young professionals and the coveted affluent teenager demographic. (In Edy Singh's words, "Teenagers don't think about how money is hard to come by!" [*Remaja sich kagak pikirin duit susah di cari!*].) Using record-company terminology, Temtem protests that PHB's music is for everyone, not just people from classes B and C (categories roughly corresponding to lower-middle class and working class). While his protest may reflect a desire to reach the most lucrative market segment (class A consumers), it may also hint at an underlying nationalist idealism that motivates musicians like the members of Pemuda Harapan Bangsa to attempt to forge a hybridic music accessible to all Indonesians regardless of class position. One could argue that by enthusiastically embracing dangdut, Indonesian students, both onstage and in the audience, are embracing the old nationalist dream of a modern, unified Indonesia and (symbolically) rejecting the tyranny of class hierarchy. But although it is true that with the demise of Soeharto's regime came a new round of negotiations between modernity's "warring possibilities," the glaring social inequality that characterized New Order society persists, as does the Indonesian elite's need to blame modernity's troubling failures in their country on the "backward" village culture of ordinary citizens (which dangdut music supposedly exemplifies) rather than on economic and political injustice.

Conclusions:
Lifestyle versus Inclusionary Community

Acara perform a variety of functions, from the most humble student-sponsored event to the most polished televised award show, from the local dangdut ensemble playing a neighborhood gig to the *pop Indonesia* star performing at a concert in a five-star Jakarta hotel. All *acara*, however, provide a space for the negotiation of meanings from local, national, and global sources. Participants—emcees, performers, audience, organizing committee members, and so on—take part in this process through musical, linguistic, sartorial, iconographic, televisual, and kinesthetic channels. These different media present performed hybridities of foreign, local, and national elements—juxtapositions often accompanied by self-conscious humor. In the context of this study, musical *acara* remind us that *hybridity does not necessarily equal synthesis.* Totalizing syntheses of genres do not occur in Indonesia or anywhere else. The reality is that in *acara*, "foreign," "Indonesian," and "regional" genres coexist with various hybrids of those genres—hybrids that rarely, if ever, entirely subsume their constituent elements.

One key concept that can help us distinguish between pop/rock and underground concerts, on the one hand, and dangdut concerts, on the other, is "lifestyle."[3] Indonesians occasionally translate this term into Indonesian (*gaya hidup*), but in Jakarta the English term is used most often. In Jakarta, *lifestyle* connotes exclusiveness, a voluntarily chosen set of behavioral and consumption practices that presumably cohere and identify the individual as differentiated from the mass public. Youth are particularly interested in *lifestyle,* and industries such as the cassette business cater to this interest by creating products that construct and reinforce youth identities based on trends. In Indonesia, lifestyle choices are thought not necessarily to express an individual's uniqueness, but rather to underscore his or her allegiance(s) to a particular desirable societal subgroup. "Coolness" therefore is defined less by character traits and personality than by one's ability to socialize (*bergaul*) with the right people and therefore keep abreast of what is "currently trendy" (*lagi nge-trend*).

In early twenty-first-century Indonesia, dangdut represents a refusal of the logic of *lifestyle* and by extension a rejection of the individualizing logic of global consumer culture. In contrast to *lifestyles* promoted in

Lifestyles vs. a life of struggle: "Which Kid Are You?" Cartoon by Mice. See page 297, note 3, for a translation.

youth-oriented popular culture (including pop/rock and underground *acara*), dangdut bridges generations, from the smallest child to the oldest grandparent, and the imaginary ideal audience for dangdut is a community without distinctions of class or status. This is perhaps one reason why performed music recognizable as "dangdut" has such powerful and immediate social effects, whether it takes place in an upscale café, a student-organized underground event, or at more-conventional dangdut concert venues.

The contrasts that separate pop/rock, underground, and dangdut *acara* illustrate the tensions that exist among conflicting modernities, all of which revolve in different ways around desire, social prestige, and the project of identity in a globalizing world. In examining the different trajectories of popular music genres in Indonesia, it does not suffice to simply reiterate the argument that local agents appropriate global cultural products for their own purposes. This phenomenon certainly occurs, but it is also true that *the purposes themselves are changed in the encounter.* Nor is it sufficient to claim that meanings at *acara,* and in Indonesian popular culture more generally, are "contested," thereby implying that the ultimate condition of these cultural performance events is incoherence and fragmentation. Anthropologist Edward Bruner writes, "I maintain that culture can be conceptualized as both contested and shared, in part because *in the contestation there is sharing*" (1999, 474, emphasis mine). In all popular cultures, an important component of what is shared is an awareness of the interpretive arena in which struggles over meaning and power take place. This overarching framework resembles Urban's (1993) notion of "omega culture," a system of meanings that governs the relationships between "alpha cultures" — the various subcultures that together constitute contemporary multicultural societies. I would argue that the *acara* acts as a physical manifestation of national "omega culture," an arena in which the competing sociomoral visions of music genres, cultures, nationalities, classes, genders, and taste publics are displayed, parodied, and juxtaposed. It is the role of the performers, the audiences, and the mediators to collaboratively make sense of this exuberant cacophony of "alpha cultures" and in the process to forge an ephemeral but deeply gratifying solidary community of participants. In this process, social differences and power differentials are not dissolved but instead are made into objects of play through the reflexive performance of musical hybridities that bring together local, global, and national cultural forms in new and unforeseen constellations.

Conclusion

INDONESIAN YOUTH, MUSIC, AND
GLOBALIZATION

Obviously critical study should retain self-doubt, especially about the
status of knowledge. But for anthropologists to wait around until
someone gets epistemology right would be like Sisyphus waiting for
Godot.

D. Miller 1995

Fieldwork is practical, messy, empirical, difficult, partial, step-by-step,
but it grounds our explanations in the dialogue between self and other.
It counteracts the intellectual tendency to theorize the world without
living in it.

Titon 1997

Our journey is nearly at its end. In this book I have attempted to capture
the musical life of young urban Indonesians at a unique historical moment. Through ethnographic accounts of various musical practices—
recording, performing, listening, purchasing—I have also tried to reveal
some fundamental dynamics in contemporary Indonesian national culture and to explore their implications for the identity projects of contemporary Indonesian youth.

In this final chapter, I return to four main themes of this study—
globalization and the nation, sociality, social class, and hybridity—and

discuss my major findings in each category. I close with some tentative predictions about the future evolution of Indonesian popular music genres and suggest how the disciplines of anthropology and ethnomusicology can benefit from ethnographic studies that take popular musics seriously as meaningful loci of cultural contestation and consensus in modern complex societies.

The Global Sensorium

The Indonesian archipelago has a centuries-long history of absorbing and indigenizing foreign cultural influences, from Hinduism, Buddhism, and Islam to the ideology of modern nationalism. It is therefore hardly surprising that the current wave of worldwide cultural globalization has had a dramatic impact on Indonesian society and culture. The United States of America has emerged as a geographically distant center of power with a palpable impact on the fantasy life of Indonesian youth, and global institutions, from fast-food chains to MasterCard, have become familiar presences in urban daily life. Global (predominantly Anglo-American) popular culture enjoys great prestige and exerts a formative influence on developments in Indonesia's "national culture-under-construction" (Suryadi 2005, 131). Thus globalization in Indonesia has transformed not only the physical and visual landscapes of settings such as Central Jakarta but also the cognitive and emotional landscapes of acting subjects (cf. Greene and Henderson 2000; Liechty 2003; Mazzarella 2003). A key indicator of this change can be found in recent innovations in the milieu of Indonesian popular music, the most grassroots-derived and populist branch of the mass media, and in the ways those innovations (re)configure relationships between local, national, and global cultural forms.

Following Urban (2001), I view the local and the global as metacultural constructs. In Indonesia, "global culture" is culture that is present in the form of particular signs and objects perceived to have come from a distant "elsewhere" (cf. Baulch 2003), while "local culture" originates in particular, proximate, physically accessible places, or at least appears to do so. Recognizing "the global" in everyday life always requires a leap of faith aided by "the work of the imagination" (Appadurai 1996, 5). An example in Indonesia is the Kansas brand of cigarettes, the motto of which is (in English) *Taste the Freedom*. Kansas is actually not a common brand in the United States (if it exists there at all), but its advertisements in Jakarta would lead one to think so, and the Kansas advertisement poster affixed to an outer wall of the Warung Gaul (see chapter 6) generated much curiosity about "American" cigarettes among the *warung* regulars. Yet identifying "the local" *also* requires a leap of faith—though it is not always recognized as such—since products that seem to come from nearby places may actually originate in a distant elsewhere or contain conspicuous elements that come from other locales.

Consumption of global cultural forms may discipline and channel desire (toward Western women, for instance) and reinforce hegemony (for example, the seemingly undisputed ontological superiority of Western popular music), but it may also open up new ways of making sense of the world. The explosion of new youth-oriented musics in Indonesia appears to have had little impact on either family relationships or religious belief or practice. Indeed, as conspicuous as cultural globalization seems in Jakarta and in other major Indonesian cities, many of its effects could be viewed as limited primarily to the ephemeral patterns of youth culture. These patterns are not inconsequential, however. In the words of "Monster," an underground metal musician in Surabaya, explaining the typical age range of underground music fans, "The years between fifteen and twenty-five are the time to search for one's identity [*mencari jatidiri*]!" The identities forged in social encounters with the products of global culture can carry implications for the way one chooses to live one's life, not only during adolescence but also throughout one's adulthood.

Local, National, Global

The Indonesian nation-state is not only postcolonial but also multi-ethnic—an ambitiously synthetic and syncretic, irrevocably modern and modernist project.

Ang 2001

In this book I have explained how the national level of cultural production mediates between the local and the global (see also Armbrust 1996; Sutton 2003; Turino 1999, 2000). In Indonesia, where the appropriate content of its modern national culture has long been a subject of intense debate (Frederick 1997) and national consciousness is generally well developed even in remote areas, the national level of cultural production nearly always plays a role in the ongoing dialectic between local and global entities. (Indeed, it may make more sense to speak of a "trialectical" dynamic when discussing macrosocial cultural processes in Indonesia.)

Local, national, and global are intertwined and interact in complex ways. Global cultural forms can be mobilized to resist the nation-state, as in the rise of politicized underground music during the Soeharto period. Similarly, local forms can be mobilized against national culture (for example, the rise of *campur sari,* a hybrid Javanese-language style that has competed successfully against Indonesian-language dangdut among Javanese listeners), and national or global forms can overwhelm local genres (as evidenced by the displacement of Betawi folk music by dangdut, or by the wild popularity of rock music in Surabaya). National and local forms can likewise become agents of resistance to the global, as was the case with the popularization in the 1980s of *jaipongan* (a nationalized West Javanese regional genre) as an indigenous alternative to Western dance music.

The Indonesian musicscape abounds with nationalized local forms (such as *keroncong* and *jaipongan*), nationalized global forms (*pop Indonesia*), globalized local forms (world beat, ethnic jazz), localized national forms (*dangdut Jawa* and *campur sari*), globalized national forms (dangdut's popularity in East Asia, the successful marketing of *keroncong* in Europe as "world music"), and even localized global forms (Minangkabau ska, Sundanese punk rock). Each of these combinations promotes a particular orientation toward each of the three levels. This study has demonstrated the importance of popular music in negotiating between local, global, and national appeals to affective allegiance in the lives of Indonesians. In the process, popular music genres contribute to the phenomenological realness of these levels, which are at base *imagined entities* constituted through metacultural discourses and specific social practices.

Sociality and Experiential Context

We have explored how Indonesian popular music circulates through Jakarta and the rest of the nation in the form of recordings, video clips, and live performances, through broadcast media and through social pathways that the circulating music itself creates and reinforces (Urban 2001). Traveling with the sonic artifacts and performances are a variety of metacultural constructs—some imported, some indigenous, some indigenized—that render the music comprehensible and relevant to its audiences.

Yet I contend that to simply analyze the cultural forms themselves and the explicitly articulated metacultural constructs that accompany them is insufficient and falls short of the epistemological goal of music ethnography: to understand the complex, multilayered meanings of music in the lives of actual people. This study has therefore also focused on the experiential context of Indonesian popular music. That is, in addition to analyzing the artifacts themselves and common verbal discourses about them, I have attempted to illuminate the cultural spaces, the social relationships, and the shared experiences of participants that frame the production and reception of popular music in Jakarta and other large cities in Java and Bali. Thus we have learned how musical objects and performances acquire particular meanings through specific activities and interactions, from shopping in a record store to hanging out with friends to performing onstage. These and other experiences of musical encounter are often overlooked by textualist approaches to popular culture. As theorists of popular music have pointed out (e.g., Frith 1981; Wicke 1990), the significance of mass-mediated music derives from everyday life and its variable rhythms of work, leisure, socializing, resting, and dreaming. What is important to keep in mind is that these mundane aspects of existence are not the same everywhere. For example, in general Indonesians prefer to spend more time in groups and less time alone than do Americans. There is evidence to suggest that this aspect of daily life is manifested in Indonesian popular musics by a lyrical preoccupation with combating loneliness, by the common practice of singing popular songs at social gatherings, by the importance of collective participation and dancing at concerts, and by a willingness to combine different music genres.

The topical concerns of song texts, the "busy" musical textures, and the strikingly hybridic elements found in Indonesian popular musics are inseparable from the ethic of sociality, which creates an experiential context for daily life that includes sociability, tolerance of difference and contradiction, and the attempt to elide or suspend hierarchy and status for the sake of unity and social harmony. I have concluded from my research that it is more appropriate to view Indonesian popular musics, from dangdut to underground, as soundtracks for "hanging out" with others than as facilitators of private, contemplative listening. In other words, in Indonesia, musical encounters are usually social affairs, and they derive their meanings and emotional resonance from intersubjective experiences.

Popular Music Genres and Social Class: Bridging the Gap?

The ethic of sociality—the necessary and desirable copresence of others and the valuing of social intercourse above solitary activities—appears to be nearly constant across the social boundaries that otherwise divide Indonesian youth. Nevertheless, these boundaries play a central role in the cultural politics of popular music genres. Although Indonesia's multiethnic character has attracted considerable interest among scholars concerned with the ways in which different ethnic, regional, and religious identities are reconciled in the name of national unity and integration, it is really class hierarchy that most threatens the Indonesian national project in the post–Soeharto age—and that factor, not coincidentally, most consistently divides the music audience.

For most of Indonesian history, especially since the beginning of the New Order, the working- and lower-class national majority—the *rakyat kecil* (little people)—have had little voice in national public discourse (Weintraub 2004, 127). As a consequence, the most prominent expression of their identities, aspirations, and sufferings in the public sphere has been through popular music, especially in the form of the celebrated but highly controversial dangdut. The sociological fact of dangdut's vast nationwide audience (though its appeal is far from universal) makes it the de facto popular music of Indonesia, even if the majority of its disparate sonic ingredients are easily traceable to exogenous sources in India, the wider Muslim world, Latin America, and the West.

The problem of dangdut's acceptance by the middle class has existed from the origins of the music in urban folk styles such as *orkes melayu,* and it has been further complicated by the music's obvious borrowing from prestigious Western popular musics such as rock (Siegel 1986, 215–17). I assert that the continuing conflict between dangdut and the more middle-class-oriented and westernized *pop Indonesia,* not to mention Western imported music itself, can be viewed as nothing less than a battle between competing visions of Indonesian national modernity: the collectivist, egalitarian national vision of the Sukarno era versus the individualist, status-obsessed developmentalism of Soeharto's New Order. Arjun Appadurai writes, "The megarhetoric of developmental modernization (economic growth, high technology, agribusiness, schooling, militarization) in many countries is still with us. But it is often punctuated, interrogated, and domesticated by the micronarratives of film, television, music, and other expressive forms, which allow modernity to be rewritten more as *vernacular globalization* and less as a concession to large-scale national and international policies" (1996, 10, emphasis mine). In precisely this way, New Order discourses of development were "interrogated" by dangdut and other hybridic Indonesian popular music genres appealing to the nonaffluent; *pop Indonesia* "domesticated" such discourses for its assumed-to-be-middle-class audience, Indonesianizing the globally circulating "megarhetoric" of developmental modernization; while the "vernacular globalization" represented by the Indonesian musical underground suggests possible alternatives to that megarhetoric.

The demise of the Soeharto regime and Indonesia's subsequent democratic transition brought about a period of cultural dynamism and experimentation that challenged received New Order wisdom about class, modernization, development, and nationalism. These New Order–era values, which had become orthodoxy for the middle class and the elites, had never been fully absorbed by the *rakyat kecil,* who largely held on to Sukarnoist notions of self-sufficiency and community. The current popularity of dangdut music among members of the middle class, albeit hardly a new phenomenon, stems in part from a reevaluation of New Order ideology vis-à-vis the future of the nation. That some student rock bands accustomed to playing hardcore, metal, and other imported genres have begun to play dangdut songs might hint at a growing resistance to the idea that stark social inequality is a necessary fact of life in a developing nation-state.

Those who continue to play Western-derived underground music increasingly view their activities in terms of a national, cross-class community of enthusiasts, and in doing so many have turned to singing in Indonesian instead of in English (see Wallach 2003a). The most striking aspect of this process of musical indigenization is the ease with which middle-class underground participants have assimilated the imported underground ideologies of "Do It Yourself" (*D.I.Y.*), cultural autonomy, grassroots populism, and scene unity to the parallel rhetoric of the early days of Indonesian independence—rhetoric that praised national self-sufficiency, national unity, and egalitarianism. Rather than diminishing a sense of national identity in favor of the imaginary global identity marketplace, the rise of the underground may thus represent nothing less than a modest revival of Sukarnoist nationalism among educated, middle-class Indonesian youth in the guise of a global musical movement.

Dangdut music—as manifested in the hybridizing practices of cassette producers, the multigenerational collective effervescence at concerts, and its presence in informal roadside performances—erases social boundaries and attempts to create a utopian community in which identity is reduced to the inclusive ideological category of "Indonesian-ness," with gender as the sole remaining divide. Just as Sukarno tried to encompass the contradictory streams of communism, nationalism, and political Islam within a larger, integrated whole (Anderson 1990, 73–75), dangdut music attempts to encompass the entire gamut of popular sounds: the polished production techniques and sweet timbres of pop; the sensual, ornamented singing of the Islamic world; the tantalizing dance rhythms of Indian film music; the energy and power of Western hard rock; and the "ethnic nuances" of Indonesia's regional musical traditions. Indeed, there is very little in the contemporary Indonesian popular music scene that has *not* been introduced and incorporated into the dangdut sound. Even hip hop and electronic dance music have found their way into *dangdut trendy,* as has an unprecedented array of traditional instruments and sonic textures recreated through digital sampling.

Like Sukarnoism, however, dangdut ultimately fails in its totalizing mission, unable to fully engulf the individualistic, xenocentric orientation and cosmopolitan longings of the elite and middle classes within its stylistic boundaries. The developmentalist ideologies held by members of the Indonesian middle class justify the persistence of the social gap as the inevitable consequence of the perceived cultural backwardness of the poor. This mentality ensures that dangdut music, a cultural form that exemplifies this backwardness, will never lose its associations with the "village," that perpetual site of ignorance, stasis, and stubborn resistance to the project of modernity. The fact that even the urban poor are considered "villagers" (*orang kampung*) reinforces the stereotype and conflates the traditional/modern dichotomy of old-fashioned modernization theory with the persistent economic inequalities produced by uneven and corrupt patterns of national development. Dangdut's obvious deviations from the sound and style of global pop music genres make it an "abject" form, neither traditional nor modern, that to its critics expresses nothing more than the nonaffluent majority's cultural inauthenticity and lack of cultivation. The modern must be defined by what it is not—this holds as true for followers of modernist Islam as for developmentalist technocrats—but dangdut music does not exclude any possibilities. Instead, it incorporates them all into an unruly and impure hybrid formation that elicits disgust and disavowal from modernists even as it invites them to join the dance.

Pop Indonesia's ideological role in the Indonesian class structure is distinct from that of dangdut or that of the underground, and this role seems to be the most conflicted of the three. The attempt by members of the underground music scene to construct an independent, autonomous cultural and economic system outside the corporate entertainment industry echoes Sukarno's defiant stance toward international aid organizations and the agents of world capitalism. *Pop,* by contrast, can be seen as representing acquiescence to global corporate hegemony. As a national genre, *pop Indonesia* must confront the "spectre of comparisons" (Anderson 1998) that haunts all such institutions. The point of *pop Indonesia* music is neither to be distinctively "Indonesian" nor to be an exact copy of Western popular music, but rather to be a style comparable to the westernized popular music of other nations sung in national vernaculars. Thus, despite conspicuous musical differences between "pop" and "rock" and the recent proliferation of Indonesianized Western genres from R & B to ska, *pop Indonesia* remains an undifferentiated category on record-store shelves. Its particular musical content is less important than its place of origin and the fact that it is sung in the national language, unlike international or regional pop.

Moreover, unlike regional pop, which frequently incorporates elements of local musical traditions, *pop Indonesia* is supposed to sound like a national version of international music, which is nearly always assumed to be Western music. As such, *pop Indonesia* must be musically interchangeable with Western pop, or it risks falling short of a transnational ideal. Like the national bank or the national anthem, *pop Indonesia* must unproblematically fit into the international grammar of national institutions. Any deviation risks compromising the nation's modernity. It is no wonder, then, that attempts by Krakatau and other Indonesian jazz and pop musicians to create Indonesian "world beat" music, no matter how high-minded and tasteful, have met with limited popular success in Indonesia, whereas completely Western-sounding pop (such as the slick jazz-pop music Krakatau played in the 1980s) enjoys a large audience. As a result of these stylistic restrictions, the Indonesian pop audience is composed primarily of middle-class and elite listeners.

Pop Indonesia also poses a problem for working-class music fans precisely because it participates in the generic fiction of the modern nation-state, which entails an assumption of a relatively affluent audience of consumers comprised of atomized individuals separately navigating the cultural marketplace. This is why *pop Indonesia* is the music of malls and businesses—it is the music of capitalist consumption, of *homo economicus.* But neither the assumption of prosperity nor the ideal of the isolated, consuming subject resonates with the experiences of Indonesia's nonaffluent majority. Thus *pop Indonesia* is viewed by many members of this majority as egoistic (*egois*), and as fundamentally belonging not to "the people" but to an exclusive elite excessively concerned with its country's image abroad. Hence *pop Indonesia*, unlike dangdut, can never be *musik kita-kita* (all of our music) because it is a product of the artful domestication of global musical sounds by talented individuals, rather than a collectively owned and celebrated musical heritage.

In the course of my research, I encountered a great deal of anxiety among fans, record producers, and musicians about whether Indonesian pop was of comparable quality to pop music from the West. No one ever entertained the notion that it might be superior. This is because it is in the very nature of *pop Indonesia* to be derivative, so by definition its artistic value can never surpass Western pop, no matter how well-produced or well-played the music, and no matter how talented the singer or the songwriter. This does not mean that Indonesians prefer Western to Indonesian pop music. Quite the opposite is the case. Yet many Indonesians interpret the preference for *pop Indonesia* songs as resulting from the Indonesian public's lack of sophistication, their need for mediation between the global musicscape and their local sensorium. As this perceived need diminishes for a new generation raised on MTV and the Internet, *pop Indonesia* will need to reinvent itself to survive.

If to place *pop Indonesia* on equal footing with *pop Barat* (Western pop) is to deconstruct the entire concept of nationalized pop, the crisis *pop Indonesia* faces is caused by its growing parity with Western pop, made possible by increasing flows of knowledge, capital, and technology to the developing world. *Pop Indonesia*'s internal differentiation threatens to rival the West with regard to stylistic diversity, and the equalizing effects of computer-driven record production make it harder than ever to distinguish domestic from imported musical products on a purely sonic level.

Pop Indonesia must adapt to the changing conditions of the global musicscape. Global youth music genres such as rap, metal, and alternative rock are stylistically (and sonically) opposed to the saccharine and innocuous music that was once the mainstay of Indonesia's popular music industry, and it is unlikely that these new forms of music will comfortably fit under the *pop Indonesia* rubric for long. Nor do they conform to the ideal national popular culture of banal love songs meant to accompany affluence and consumption, the longing of romance metamorphosing into the longing for commodities. One significant threat posed by the new pop genres is linguistic in nature, because they disrupt the previous hegemony of poetic Standard Indonesian in song lyrics. Rock and rap styles have introduced heteroglossia (Bakhtin 1981) into *pop Indonesia*, adding Indonesian colloquialisms, Jakartanese, youth slang, regional languages, and even English to the range of linguistic possibilities employed by pop songwriters (cf. Bodden 2005). No longer the monologic voice of an imaginary affluent society, *pop Indonesia* has become increasingly responsive to the aspirations and multiply articulated identities of the nation's youth, and in the process it may cease to resemble "pop" altogether.

Pop producers and artists long for the prestige, wealth, and global stature of their Western counterparts, while dangdut producers and artists long for the prestige enjoyed by *pop Indonesia*. They dream of a day when dangdut music assumes its rightful place as the proud musical representative of a fully modern, self-possessed nation. Young working-class dangdut fans long for the cosmopolitan glamour of global popular culture that they experience through dangdut music, while some progressive middle-class students view dangdut as the authentic voice of the Indonesian people. Indonesian underground artists, for their part, yearn for a transnational community that provides an alternative to a national one stratified by class and ethnicity. They are all, in their own way, united by a longing for a truly modern, culturally authentic community—national or otherwise—that grants recognition to all its members.

Hybridities: Techno, Performative, and Postcolonial

> Hybridity is not like a cocktail that you can recompose back to its parts. . . .
> It's something that comes about when you're not even sure where your origins
> are coming from.
>
> Srinivas Aravamudan, discussing the work of Homi K. Bhabha
> (quoted in Eakin 2001)

Indonesia's diverse, vibrant, and innovative popular musicscape is characterized by a willingness on the part of producers to combine and hybridize musical forms in order to create music that is simultaneously local, national, and global. Such musical practices claim a kind of modernity that is recognizably Indonesian and contest the notion that cultural modernization must be synonymous with an uncompromising westernization. For example, it is significant that the polyvocal sonic texture and rhythmic organization of Indonesian dance musics such as *house jaipong* and *dangdut house*, with lower-pitched instruments moving at a proportionally slower rate than higher ones, strongly resembles gamelan and other indigenous Indonesian musics. This resemblance is intensified by the frequent use of *bonang* (kettle gong) and *suling* (bamboo flute) samples and complex interlocking synthesizer lines that evoke the characteristic patterns of high-pitched Indonesian metallophones in traditional ensembles.

Hybridity has become one of the principal concepts of postcolonial theory (e.g., Ang 2001; Bhabha 1994). Yet despite the aggressive theorizing that has surrounded the concept, there has been very little research, ethnographic or otherwise, into the range of possible forms that hybridity can take and the significance of that variation. The integrationist ethic of hybridization found in dangdut and regional pop—in which instruments, sounds, genre labels, and production techniques are juxtaposed to create multitextured hybrid musical artifacts—has its roots in Sukarnoism and perhaps in traditional Indonesian notions of power and incorporation (see Anderson 1990). Such an approach differs markedly from the seamless, disciplined techno-hybrid fusions of Eternal Madness and Krakatau. Yet another type of hybrid cultural production—one with its own separate set of motivations—is the use of Indonesian-language song lyrics by Indonesian underground rock musicians playing otherwise Western-sounding music.

What I have attempted to demonstrate in this study is that musical hybridities are *strategic,* subject to the artistic, commercial, and social purposes of their producers (see Berger 1999). "Sound engineering" (Greene 1999) practices in recording studios and performative gestures onstage at *acara* combine elements of the local, the national, and the global in order to attract new audiences (dangdut remixes), comment on the nature of Indonesian musical hierarchy (student dangdut groups), make bold political statements (Indonesian-language hardcore punk), and generate alternative ways to be global cosmopolitan subjects (Krakatau, Eternal Madness).

Ironies abound with musical hybridity: Moel from Eternal Madness; Dwiki, Pra, and Trie from Krakatau; and Edy Singh and his production staff are all far more familiar with Western music than with the traditional music that they incorporate into their work. Likewise, the student rock bands that cover dangdut songs often have little grasp of dangdut vocal and instrumental techniques (though this does not seem to diminish these bands' popularity and perhaps even enhances it), and underground bands that sing in Indonesian bring their music closer to the cultural location of underground music in English-speaking societies—as carriers of powerful messages in clear, direct language that listeners do not need a dictionary to decipher.

The heterogeneity of styles and sounds found in Indonesian popular music is usually the result of conscious calculation; very rarely does it result from a failure to master a particular global genre (a possible exception being some Indonesian songwriters' difficulty with writing lyrics in grammatically correct, idiomatic English). Rather, the creation of musical hybrids results from the desire to move beyond the conventions of established forms, to add an "ethnic accent" (*logat etnis*) that emerges not from the inability to speak without one (an unintended and undesirable consequence of what Greg Urban [2001, 15–33] calls "inertial culture") but from a conscious effort to introduce "local" elements into a global form—*to add something new* and thus to participate in the replication of culture characteristic of the metaculture of modernity. Often this effort is facilitated by the additive sonic logic of the multitrack recording studio. For this reason I have identified "techno-hybridity" as an important subcategory of self-conscious musical mixing. It is also fortuitous that multitrack recording techniques are remarkably compatible with the Indonesian aesthetic of *rame* (crowded, noisy, fun), characterized in the sonic realm by overlapping, layered sounds originating from multiple sources, and with the interlocking colotomic structures of gamelan and other indigenous musical traditions.

The Future of "Indonesian" Music

In the current uncertain political and social climate of Indonesia, it is difficult to set forth predictions about the fate of the three main musical genres discussed here. Nonetheless, a few tentative projections are possible.

Pop

Earlier in this chapter, I discussed the possible future of *pop Indonesia*, along with the threat of obsolescence it faces. I now add my assessment that Indonesian youth will increasingly demand Indonesian pop music that not only is musically competitive with global styles but also addresses their everyday experiences and aspirations. Members of the most recent generation of pop and rock artists record songs about their lives and, by extension, those of their fans, combining social observations, depictions of everyday life, topical humor, and of course romantic relationships. The fact that the music of *pop Indonesia* artists can address the specific experiences of Indonesian youth better than imported popular music and does so in comprehensible language will continue to constitute a competitive advantage. On the other hand, music falling under the category of *pop Indonesia* is increasingly likely to be produced by global rather than national recording companies, and this particular form of musical globalization will no doubt produce unintended effects for the recording industry. It is possible that in reaction to the slick, up-to-date global sounds of current *pop Indonesia,* older pop styles, such as *pop nostalgia,* may even enjoy a revival. (Such an occurrence would greatly benefit the national companies that hold the copyrights to *pop nostalgia* songs.)

Regardless of the eventual fate of *pop Indonesia* as a genre, I am certain that the creativity and skill of Indonesian musicians and producers will ensure that commercial music produced in Indonesia, no matter how it is labeled, will remain a vital form of expression and will likely continue to outsell Western imports in the national market.

Underground

The Indonesian underground scene began with groups of urban middle school and high school students covering songs by their favorite Western bands. This was followed by the formation of bands that wrote their own songs and recorded them, usually singing in English. Gradually more and more of these groups began to record songs in Indonesian, and occasionally in regional languages, instead of in English.

Although the lyrics and social context of underground music have been indigenized to some extent, musically underground bands have generally remained within the stylistic parameters set by Western artists. The writing of lyrics in Indonesian, therefore, has been more an attempt to approximate the Western underground ideal of music capable of unmediated communication than a desire to "Indonesianize" underground rock (Wallach 2003a). Nevertheless, many members of rock and underground bands with whom I spoke did express a willingness to combine Indonesian traditional genres with their music. For example, Bagus from Netral told me he hoped one day to form a collaboration with Javanese gamelan/ethnic fusion composer Djaduk Ferianto, and Jerry, the lead singer of the hardcore band Bantal (Pillow), once mentioned he had the idea to add *angklung* (pitched bamboo shakers) and other traditional instruments to his band's songs and call the result *art-core.* Nevertheless, Indonesian underground rockers remained generally hesitant about actually attempting to "ethnicize" their music, claiming (inaccurately) that "it had not yet been tried" (*belum dicoba*).

In short, the Indonesian underground seems quite a long way from achieving any kind of grand synthesis between "Indonesian" and "Western," as genres continue to fragment (newly introduced subgenres during my fieldwork included *crustcore, brutal death,* and *hyperblast*) and as musical approaches ranging from ethnic techno-hybridization (Eternal Madness) to austere purism (punk rock) continue to coexist and compete. It is likely, however, that the popularity of underground music will continue to increase, especially among rural and working-class young men, and that the number of bands that "cross over" and record on major labels also will continue to rise. This trend will no doubt create controversy in the underground community, but as long as the scene is composed of university students and other young people who for a time do not have to worry about earning a living, musical "idealism" will live on, and the grassroots, anti-commercial networks that sustain independently produced rock music in Indonesia will not wither.

Dangdut

The metacultural controversies surrounding dangdut—its contested status as a truly "Indonesian" music, its disreputable class associations, its connection with sexual immorality, and so on—cannot be separated from the fact that so many Indonesians find the music a compelling source of undeniable pleasure, whether they admit it or not.

Andy Atis, the Christian Ambonese R & B producer whose studio I describe in chapter 4, once told me that *"dangdut is dead."* His two reasons for this claim—that the rising costs of cassettes put legitimate (nonpirated) dangdut recordings out of reach of the music's nonaffluent core audience, and that the cross-class youth market was becoming more oriented toward MTV and global pop—seemed sound, yet in the course of my research I uncovered no evidence that the dangdut genre was in serious decline. Although the economic crisis did devastate sales of dangdut cassettes, the enthusiasm of ordinary Indonesians—male and female, young and old—for this music has persisted. Furthermore, a growing number of middle-class listeners have embraced dangdut (albeit with a frequent dose of irony), perhaps, as I have proposed, as part of a general process of rethinking the pro-Western developmentalism of the New Order. Although this tentative embrace may yet lead to new, inspired hybrids (such as *dangdut underground* and various cross-fertilizations with *pop Indonesia*), the continued mass appeal of dangdut music will most likely perpetuate the relative stylistic conservatism that has typified the genre since the early days of Rhoma Irama's career.

MTV Indonesia itself featured a dangdut program, *Salam Dangdut,* which became one of its most popular offerings. The following listing appeared on MTV Asia's English-language Web site:

Get one hour of the best and most popular Dangdut music videos. Catch VJ Arie Kuncoro on MTV Salam Dangdut every Sunday at 10:00 a.m. and a repeat viewing on Wednesday at 2:00 p.m.

To capture the essence of Dangdut, the show is hosted from a mock disco Dangdut set, complete with flashing disco lights. On each episode VJ Arie gets in touch with the fans of Dangdut by reading their letters and gives us information on the lives and music of the biggest Dangdut stars around. If you are a Dangdut fan or someone who never really gave Dangdut a listen—MTV Salam Dangdut will get you saying "asik" [intense, cool, pleasurable]. (MTV Asia)

Although clearly begun as a way to exploit dangdut's preexisting popularity, *Salam Dangdut,* as this text implies, may well have won over skeptical middle-class youth to dangdut fandom as a result of MTV's unparalleled cultural authority in the sphere of youth fashion (Sutton 2003, 326).

A 2001 article in the Singaporean *Straits Times* describes dangdut's growing popularity among middle-class Indonesians. According to the article, global major label Sony Music Indonesia (which I had been told two years earlier was unwilling to produce its own dangdut music) recently started an ambitious dangdut division (Kearney 2001). One of the division's first acts was to sign artist Ikke Nurjanah, who sang one of the first dangdut songs to catch on with middle-class audiences, "Terlena." This state of affairs may indicate a sea change in Indonesian middle-class perceptions of dangdut music, but it is more likely merely the latest in a series of well-hyped attempts to expand the music's audience that nonetheless fail to completely disassociate dangdut from its *kampungan* reputation.

Anthropology, Music, Modernity, and the Creative Side of Culture: A Polemic

Even in an anthropology that is now "embodied," too rarely do we find bodies at play or sounds that set grooves in our ethnographies.

Shannon 2004

Anthropologists tend to be ambivalent about the study of music. On the one hand, they consider it as worthy an object of study as any other

meaningful human endeavor. On the other, the study of music is generally believed to entail mastering an esoteric technical vocabulary, and
many nonmusician anthropologists conclude that the kinds of cultural
insights that potentially can be gained from a cultural study of music
and musicians can be obtained just as easily (if not more so) from investigating other areas of "expressive culture" that do not require such
technical training. Such an attitude overlooks the tremendous body of
academic literature on popular music that does not make use of the analytical techniques of musicology; indeed, some of the best-known writ-
ers on the subject, such as Simon Frith, do not engage in technical musical analysis at all. This view also overlooks the fact that investigating
musical phenomena opens up vital fields of inquiry inaccessible by other
means (Monson 1999). These areas of investigation often extend far beyond the preoccupations of the anthropology of aesthetics to matters of
central anthropological concern, such as the development of political
consciousness, the cultural correlates of social change, and the ethical
basis of social relationships.

Musical expression, a panhuman universal, has taken on a special
importance in modern societies. Its ability to channel affect, open possibilities for self-expression, and foster communal solidarity (in both
imagined and realized-in-the-moment communities) stimulates various
attempts to control music and/or harness its power to promote ideology.
In Indonesia, powerful but abstract concepts such as nationalism, modernity, unity, and "Indonesian-ness" itself are made palpable and affectively compelling through music, but they rarely take on the monovocal-
ity and semantic specificity of ideology in the process. Anthropologists
of modern complex societies thus ignore music at their peril if they wish
to access the heteroglossic and ambivalent social reality behind the
dominant representations produced by the state and by the commercial
print and visual media, or hope to enter the realm of private subjectivities and their affect-laden responses to actual social conditions.

Greg Urban's concept of "the metaculture of modernity" directs
anthropological attention to the fact that innovations in cultural forms
are just as "cultural" as their perpetuation and conservation through
time (the orientation Urban calls "the metaculture of tradition," which
is more characteristic of small-scale societies). The creative side of culture becomes all the more important in changing societies that metacul-
turally identify themselves as modern or modernizing or even as "backward" yet hopeful. Urban describes the production of "new" cultural
forms in the metaculture of modernity as a process of combining preexisting forms and genres. This ethnography has depicted many examples

of this process at work in recording studios, at video shoots, onstage, and at other sites of cultural production. It is important, however, to note that Urban's insights do not rob artistic creation of its "originality," even if they do demystify the process somewhat. Rather, in this book I have argued that in order to be intelligible to an audience, cultural forms must contain aspects of the familiar; furthermore, the creation of cultural objects occurs through the expressive agency of social actors, not as a result of an automatic, subconscious process of combination and recombination. In fact, the high level of technological mediation in contemporary cultural production encourages a certain reflexivity among both producers and listeners regarding the nature of popular forms and the intentional manipulation and juxtaposition of preexisting templates.

Popular music is a vital means through which Indonesian youth creatively explore identity and their position in the modern world and the nation. The inclusive Sukarnoist collectivism of dangdut, the oppositional consciousness of underground music, and the cosmopolitanism of Indonesian pop all in their own way address the urgent concerns of contemporary young people and the relative appeal of each of these forms to different groups of young Indonesians tends to be mediated in important ways by class, gender, and other social categories. Thus popular music, more than any other branch of the Indonesian mass media, registers the ambivalences, allegiances, and emotional attachments different segments of society feel toward the Indonesian nation and the wider world.

The world of Indonesian popular musics is one part of a larger project of national cultural production in which the "product" is a fully modern, culturally distinctive nation. The precise composition of this hybrid cultural form-in-process has yet to be determined, but I would argue that popular music is an excellent starting point for investigating the future contours of such an imagined entity. Although the Indonesian national utopia does not (yet) exist, it can still be powerfully evoked in performance.

To conclude, I hope that the research and analysis contained herein have not only added to our understanding of how struggles over national modernity are played out in Indonesian music and culture but also contributed to an emerging type of anthropological inquiry that combines the insights of popular culture studies with an examination of lived experience in specific social settings. For only through sensitive ethnographic investigation can we understand what is truly at stake in the contestatory field of public culture.

APPENDIX A

Notes on Language in This Book

Throughout this study, direct quotations in the body of the text that are translated from the Indonesian appear in Roman characters, while quotations from Indonesian sources originally in English appear in italics, as do individual English words used in Indonesian passages. Grammatical and other errors in the original are preserved in the text. Thus, the sentence *Katanya musik dangdut udah go international* would be translated as "They say dangdut music has already *go international*," and the sentence *I no good English* (I'm not good at speaking English) would appear as "*I no good English.*" All translations of lyrics and quotations are by the author.

The primary language used by the participants in this study is the Jakartanese nonstandard variant of Indonesian (see appendix C). Much of this language is based on the Javanese-, Sundanese-, and Hokkien-influenced Malay dialect spoken in colonial Batavia, and its grammar, pronunciation, spelling, and lexicon may appear strange to those familiar only with Standard Indonesian. For instance, many common words in Indonesian are pronounced with an *e* sound instead of an *a* sound. Jakartanese grammar, though far from standardized, generally has the following characteristics:

- The standard Indonesian active verb forms *meng*-[root]-*kan* and *meng*-[root]-*i* are both replaced with [root]-*in* or *nge*-[root]-*in*. This form is used for transitive and benefactive verbs and for verbs that use nouns and adjectives as roots.
- Similarly, passive -*kan* and -*i* verbs use the -*in* suffix.
- Active verbs with roots that begin with *c*- are pronounced with *ny*- as the beginning consonant, similar to verbs in Standard Indonesian that begin with *s*.

Examples:
> *membelikan* (to buy something for someone) becomes *beliin*
> *merepotkan* (to inconvenience; to impose) becomes *ngerepotin*
> *mencari* (to search for) becomes *nyariin*
> *mencoba* (to try) becomes *nyoba*

- *Nge-* can also be used to create intransitive verbs from nouns, particularly from English loanwords.
  Examples:
      nge-band (to play in rock groups).
      nge-chat (to engage in online chatting)
      nge-drink (to imbibe alcoholic beverages)
      nge-drugs (to take illegal pharmaceuticals)

Unmarked foreign terms in the text are Jakartanese, colloquial, and/or formal Indonesian. Words in other languages or dialects, such as Javanese, Sundanese, Betawi, and Arabic, are followed by parentheses in which their origin is stated before the gloss, unless they have entered general Indonesian or Jakartanese usage.

    Examples:
        nepsu (Javanese, "desire")
        awewe (Sundanese, "young woman")
        nemuin (Betawi, "to tell")
        magrib (evening prayers)
        gendruwo (demonic village spirit)
        angklung (pitched bamboo shaker)

One final note: this book's spelling of the names of former presidents Sukarno, Soeharto, and Megawati Soekarnoputri follow the post–New Order conventions of the *Jakarta Post,* Indonesia's leading English-language newspaper.

APPENDIX B

Other Indonesian Popular Music Genres

Although this book focuses primarily on dangdut, *pop Indonesia,* and under-ground music, these are not the only major popular music genres in Indonesia. The reader may find the following descriptions helpful, as the genres listed below appear occasionally in the text.

Rock

Indonesian *rock* music is often conceptually separated from Indonesian pop even though it usually appears as a subset of *pop Indonesia* in record-store shelf displays. The label refers to loud, electric guitar–based music, what in America would usually be called "hard rock" and in Indonesian is sometimes referred to simply as *musik keras,* "hard/loud music." Mainstream Indonesian rock bands sing in both English and Indonesian, mostly the latter, and their music is influenced by a variety of Anglo-American groups, from the Rolling Stones to Limp Bizkit to Wilco. This music has a large, primarily male audience usually described with the phrase *menengah ke bawah* (middle to lower [class]). This is also the term used to describe dangdut's audience, but unlike dangdut, *musik rock* does not usually carry the stigma of being *kampungan.*

The popularity of "power ballads," songs sung by hard rock and heavy metal bands that combine distorted guitars and virtuosic solos with slower tempos and heartfelt sentiment, encouraged the development of *slowrock,* a rock subgenre that originated in Malaysia and has successfully crossed over into the Indonesian market (Indonesian and Malay are mutually intelligible). *Slowrock,* with its emotional excess, is considered *kampungan.* There is no separate category of "soft rock" in Indonesia, as such music is classified under pop.

Jazz, Jazz-Pop, and *Jazz Etnik*

Jazz is considered the most prestigious popular music in Indonesia, and Indonesia is home to a number of world-class jazz musicians, including Bubi Chen, Candra Darusman, Dwiki Dharmawan, Indra Lesmana, Pra Budidharma, Syaharani, Gilang Ramadhan, Tohpati, and Donny Suhendra. Indonesian jazz is dominated by keyboardists, guitarists, drummers, bassists, and vocalists;

accomplished horn players are relatively uncommon, perhaps due to the scarcity of high-quality brass and reed instruments in the country. Because the audience for instrumental jazz is extremely limited, many Indonesian jazz players perform on pop albums or form bands of their own that play jazz-inflected, sophisticated *pop Indonesia*.

Indonesian jazz musicians have also experimented with combining jazz with traditional Indonesian music; arguably this has as much to do with reaching an international audience (and thus overcoming the limits of the domestic market) as it does with national or ethnic pride. Nevertheless, such cross-cultural fusions are often quite compelling, and a small overseas audience has taken notice. The best-known of these "progressive ethnic" groups is Krakatau, a multiethnic band from Bandung, West Java, that makes occasional appearances in this study.

Keroncong

Celebrated as the music of the generation of Indonesians who won Indonesia's independence, *keroncong*'s complex origins are even more disreputable than dangdut's. Brought to colonial Batavia (now Jakarta) and other port cities by freed slaves from the Portuguese colonies, *keroncong* was an Iberian-sounding urban folk music enjoyed by members of the Netherlands East Indies' native working and lower classes (Becker 1975). The word *keroncong* is the name of a ukulele-like instrument that is part of this music's customary ensemble, which also includes cello (played pizzicato style), guitar, and *suling*. During the Indonesian war for independence (1945–49), *keroncong* songs sung in Indonesian with nationalist themes became popular, and the style gained a measure of respectability. Unlike dangdut—Indonesia's other major hybrid popular music genre—modern *keroncong* is slow, stately, and refined music more suited to contemplative listening than to dancing.

Keroncong's centuries-long presence in parts of Indonesia has led local musicians to combine this style with local idioms. This led to the emergence of highly syncretized *keroncong* subgenres such as *cilokaq* music in Lombok. The best known of these is *langgam Jawa*, an extraordinary hybrid in which the stringed instruments of the *keroncong* ensemble are tuned to a Javanese scale and play colotomic rhythmic patterns resembling those found in indigenous music of the region (Yampolsky 1991). The refined Portuguese bel canto singing style of original *keroncong* is also merged with traditional Javanese vocal techniques, creating a distinctive hybrid timbre. *Langgam Jawa* was foundational to the development of *campur sari* music, the highly successful genre combining traditional Javanese folk and classical styles, *keroncong*, and dangdut that emerged in the late 1990s.

As for original *keroncong* (*keroncong asli*), it remains a marginal but significant recorded genre. As an exotic yet familiar-sounding acoustic music, *keroncong* has even enjoyed modest success abroad as "world music." *Keroncong* songs are still an active part of the live performance repertoire of Indonesian street musicians and other local, small-time ensembles (Ferzacca 1997). Young Jakartans consider *keroncong* music less than modern but not especially low-class and associate the genre mainly with their grandparents' generation.

Religious Music

Indonesia is the world's largest predominantly Muslim nation, and popular music with Islamic themes plays a significant, if limited, role in the national music scene. *Gambus* and *qasidah* are Middle Eastern–influenced syncretic genres often sung in Arabic. *Pop Muslim,* also known as *nasyid,* includes conventional pop with Islamic themes and Muslim male vocal groups that sing R & B–influenced songs with or without instrumental accompaniment in Indonesian, Arabic, and English (Barengdregt and Zanten 2002, 76–80). Rhoma Irama's songs often contain a moralistic, Islamic message, though his music is still classified as dangdut—a genre many strict Muslims condemn as immoral.

Christian pop music is also recorded and sold in Indonesia, though musically most *pop Rohani* (music of the spirit) does not differ significantly from secular pop genres. There are even a few *dangdut Rohani* recordings in existence; these are usually performed by Muslims who have *masuk Kristen,* converted to Protestant Christianity. In many music retail outlets, the *pop Rohani* section is the only part of the store where domestic and foreign music are mixed together—Indonesian *pop Rohani* recordings share shelf space with international Contemporary Christian albums. Most of this imported music is from the United States.

Musical Imports from Malaysia, China, Japan, and India

Popular music recordings from other Asian countries occupy different positions in the Indonesian musical status hierarchy, in part determined by their specific country of origin. Indonesian and Malaysian Malay are similar languages, and Malay-language popular music has successfully penetrated the large Indonesian market. Malaysian varieties of pop, dangdut, rock, Muslim pop, and heavy metal are widely available and more or less correspond to their Indonesian counterparts with regard to prestige and audience.

Japanese, Mandarin, and Cantonese pop can be found in some medium- to large-sized record stores. This music has a small but significant middle-class following in Indonesia, among both *pribumi* (native) and Chinese Indonesians. The pop music from these countries often resembles *pop Indonesia;* indeed, there appears to be a pan-Asian sentimental pop song style that varies solely by language. This is perhaps one reason why Indonesians find this music an accessible and appealing, if somewhat less prestigious, alternative to Western pop.

Lowest on the scale of prestige is music from India, primarily film song, which is on the opposite end of the spectrum from Anglo-American music in terms of both class associations and price (Indian cassettes cost about half as much as Western imports and about 40 percent less than *pop Indonesia* cassettes). Indian pop music shares many characteristics in common with dangdut, and it is not unusual for a local dangdut ensemble to include a Hindi film song or two in its repertoire. In early 2000, the theme song from the Indian film *Kuch Kuch Hota Hai* (Hindi, "Something, Something Generally Happens") was enormously popular among working-class Jakarta residents. One young Betawi man told me that there were families in his *kampung* (poor urban neighborhood) who owned a copy of the song even though they could not even afford rice to feed themselves!

APPENDIX C

More on Nonstandard Speech Variants

The following ethnographic investigation of Jakarta's speech variants, an update of sorts to Errington's landmark study (1986), reveals the fluidity, multiple subject positions, and intense sociability of life in the city, and provides an important backdrop for understanding Jakartans' speech about popular music and its interpretation.

Bahasa Betawi

I once asked a taxi driver where he was from, and he smiled and replied, "*Batavia.*" He was identifying himself as an *orang Betawi,* a descendant of the original "native" working class of Jakarta during the Dutch colonial period (1619–1942), when the city was known as Batavia (*Betawi* is the Malay pronunciation), the capital of the Dutch East Indies. The Betawi people came to be as the result of a Dutch strategy of importing labor from distant parts of the East Indies in order to prevent the formation of an anti-Dutch alliance between the "native" residents of Batavia and the local Sundanese people of the surrounding countryside (Abeyasekere 1987, 65). The Betawi language that evolved as a medium of communication between the migrants was a dialect of Malay, the language used as a lingua franca by Asians and Europeans alike during the colonial period. Separate dialects of Betawi are still spoken in different Jakarta neighborhoods, and *kampung* dwellers on the outskirts of the city speak dialects strongly influenced by Sundanese.

Betawi is very likely the only language in the world that uses Arabic for its formal first- and second-person singular pronouns (*ane* and *ente*) and Hokkien Chinese for the informal (*gua* and *lu*). Non-Betawi Jakartans (and Betawi speaking to non-Betawi) tend to use the Standard Indonesian *saya* for the formal first-person singular pronoun, while for the informal "I," "me," and "my" they use *gua,* from the Hokkien. *Gua* can also be pronounced *gue,* and when it appears as the subject of a sentence, the pronunciation is sometimes shortened to *go.* This informal Betawi pronoun, and its second-person singular counterpart *lu,* are the quintessential markers of Jakartan speech and by extension, of trendy, cosmopolitan youth culture. In 2000, Pepsi Cola's main slogan for all of Indonesia, *Kalo gue, pilih Pepsi* (As for me, I choose Pepsi), relied on this association to attract a status-conscious youth market for its product. (Actually the slogan would probably read *kalo gue* milih *Pepsi* in truly idiomatic Jakartanese.)

In practice, fully distinguishing between Betawi (a fully recognized regional language, with the same status as Javanese and Sundanese) and Jakartanese is nearly impossible, akin to attempting to separate Black English Vernacular from hip American slang. The linguistic basis of Jakartanese has been identified as Modern Betawi, a loose entity that differs systematically from Old Betawi and is closer to Standard Indonesian (Muhadjir 1999, 69–70). Contemporary Jakartanese words come from a variety of languages—Javanese, Old Betawi, Sundanese, Hokkien, Dutch, Japanese, and English—and their etymologies are sometimes unclear and often unknown to speakers. Jakartanese terms, even those that have entered common usage throughout the archipelago, are always italicized in the official mass media, where they frequently appear in quotations of spoken language and are occasionally used to add flavor or emphasis to a writer's prose. (Non-Indonesian words, such as English business-management jargon or humorous Javanese expressions, also appear frequently in the Indonesian mass media and are similarly italicized.)

The discourse on language use in Jakarta does not address the urban rich/poor dichotomy explicitly, though it is clear that English is considered the most modern and most powerful language choice, while regional languages are deemed the most traditional and solidarity oriented, with both formal and colloquial Indonesian somewhere in the middle. Jakartanese (*bahasa Jakarta*) is seen *not* as an ethnic/regional language (despite its Betawi origins) but as a way of speaking that connotes trendiness, almost like English in particular contexts.

Unlike other forms of language that are considered *kasar* (coarse, low), Jakartanese does circulate publicly on a national level in the mass media. Jakartanese is especially common in youth-oriented popular culture such as student Web sites; the lyrics on some rock, rap, and *dangdut disco* cassettes; and popular magazines. Colorful uses of Jakartanese can also be found in the work of many Indonesian cartoonists, notably Muhammad "Mice" Misrad, whose "Rony" cartoons chronicle, with incisive social satire, the adventures of a working-class Betawi man. The title of a book of collected Rony cartoons (1999), *Bagimu Mal-mu, Bagiku Pasar-ku* (For You, Your Mall; For Me, My Market), is an apt illustration of one of the central themes of this ethnography. The cartoon on the book's cover features the scruffy protagonist talking (in fractured English, no less!) into a banana as though it were a cellular telephone, startling a nearby well-groomed, necktie-wearing man conversing on a real cell phone.

In addition to Jakartanese, Jakarta is home to a number of other, more specialized speech variants developed in response to the conditions of a multiethnic, cosmopolitan milieu.

Bahasa Prokem

Bahasa Prokem, also called *bahasa Okem*, is based primarily on a simple formula involving the infix *-ok-*. The infix is usually added behind the first consonant in a word, and the last syllable is dropped. For example, *duit* (money) becomes *doku*, *gila* (crazy) becomes *gokil*, *sepatu* (shoe) becomes *spokat*, and so on. The word *prokem* is actually Prokem for *preman* (criminal, thug); young criminals are supposedly the originators of this speech style, though it has more often been associated with Indonesian high school and university students (Wijayanti 2000, 129; Chambert-Loir 1990). Now considered passé by the student culture that first popularized it, Prokem is still used by some working-class youth in Jakarta, and a few words, such as *bokap* (father), *nyokap* (mother), *pembokat* ("servant"—considered extremely derogatory), *bokin* (wife), and *toket* (breast) have entered general usage in Jakarta. Like Jakartanese itself, Prokem appears to have originated to fill a need for an informal alternative to Standard Indonesian (*bahasa Indonesia baku*) that could be used to promote solidarity and intimacy within groups of people who do not share the same regional (ethnic) language. In 1990, a Prokem-Indonesian dictionary was published in Jakarta (Rahardja and Chambert-Loir 1990).

Singkatan

A feature of *bahasa Prokem* that survives into the present is the habit of creating humorous acronyms and abbreviations (*singkatan*). The Prokem word for *orang tua* (parents), for example, is *ortu*. Hundreds of these *singkatan*, which appear to parody the New Order bureaucracy's penchant for Orwellian neologisms, circulate throughout Jakarta. Popular abbreviations frequently acquire multiple, often contradictory glosses. For example, *ABG* (pronounced *abege*) stood originally for *anak baru gede* ("child just grown," literally "child newly big"), a phrase referring to young adolescents, usually women. It can now also mean *awas babe galak* ("beware, angry father"—a warning to those men who associate with *ABG* girls), *anak Betawi gedongan* (Betawi who live in mansions, i.e., Betawi nouveau riche), or, the opposite of the original gloss, *angkatan babe gue* ([from] my father's generation, i.e., old). Another common slang expression, *BT* (*bete*), used by young people to describe a subjective state of either boredom or irritation, is glossed in numerous ways by different speakers: *bad trip*, *boring time*, and by its opposite meaning, *binahi tinggi* (high arousal). These examples result from the grassroots creativity of young people from different social classes, and coming up with *singkatan* is a common pastime, particularly for young men (see chapter 6).

Indonesian Gayspeak and *Bahasa Gaul*

Sometimes associated erroneously with the language of male transgendered cross-dressers (known as *waria* or the less polite *banci* or *bencong*), gayspeak is primarily spoken in *gay* and *lesbi* communities in Jakarta and other Indonesian cities. (For a valuable study of the emergence of *gay* and *lesbi* identities in Indonesia, see Boellstorff 2005; see Murray 2001, 43–61, for a discussion of the heavily marginalized lesbian subculture of Jakarta and the ways in which its members are deeply divided by class differences of the sort discussed in this book.) Various terms and expressions from gay speech have been adopted by members of Jakarta's entertainment industry and by young, hip Jakarta professionals. José Capino notes a similar phenomenon in the Philippines, where urban Tagalog gayspeak, known as "sward speak," has become the in-group language of celebrities and entertainment talk-show personalities (2003, 271–72).

In the 1980s the argot spoken by gay Indonesians was known for its multiple use of the infix *-in-*, so that *cewek* (young woman) became *cinewine,* and *bule* (white person) became *binuline* (Chambert-Loir 1990). In the 1990s a new speech style emerged in the gay community that, rather than adding infixes to common words, was based on the principle of *plesetan* (puns), replacing common Indonesian words with less common ones or with the names of countries, ethnic groups, celebrities, brand names, and so on that formally resemble the original word. For example, *sudah* (already) becomes *sutra* ("silk"; also a major brand of condom in Indonesia); *malas* (lazy, to not feel like doing something) becomes *Malaysia*; *minum* (drink) becomes *Minahasa* (the name of an ethnic group from Sulawesi); *ke kiri* (to the left) becomes *ke Chrissye* (to a famous Chinese Indonesian pop singer); and *belum* (not yet) becomes *Blue Band* (a brand of imported margarine). Other words are created by adding infixes in a variety of ways (for a detailed, formalistic inventory of the different techniques of word coinage in Indonesian gayspeak, see Wijayanti 2000). For example, *apa* (what) becomes *apose* or *apipa,* and *aku* ("I"/"me" in informal Standard Indonesian) becomes *akika.* The following hypothetical sentence illustrates the word-substitution principle at work:

> Colloquial Indonesian: *Aku lapar banget. Kamu mo makan di warung ini aja?*
> English: I'm really hungry. Do you wanna just eat at this food stall?
> Gayspeak: *Akika lapangan bola. Kawanua mawar Macarena di Warsawa indang anjas?*
> Literal meaning in Indonesian: [*Akika*] soccer field. Fellow countryman rose Macarena in Warsaw winnow [*anjas*]?

Thanks in part to a best-selling dictionary compiled by a Jakarta entertainment figure (Sahertian 2000), gayspeak has rapidly spread outward from its originary speech communities, becoming a source of trendy youth slang. The dictionary, rather confusingly titled *Kamus Bahasa Gaul* (Dictionary of

Cool/Social Language), makes very little reference to the language's origins in the gay community except in a brief foreword written by an Indonesian folklorist; rather it represents the argot as part of the affluent lifestyle of young, fashionable Jakartans hanging out at *warung,* eating, gossiping, and, of course, getting caught in traffic jams. (The *bahasa gaul* expression *macan tutul* [literally "leopard"] means traffic gridlock [*macet total*].) From an etic point of view, gayspeak is linguistically distinct from *bahasa gaul,* which for most Jakartans simply denotes the slang-filled language of everyday socializing, which is not based on such an involved system of phonetic transformation. Therefore, the title of Sahertian's dictionary is somewhat misleading.

Regional Languages and Regional Slang

Jakarta is a city of many languages in addition to those based on the national vernacular. Immigrants bring to the capital city their regional languages, which have their own versions of *bahasa gaul.* The following is a brief survey of youth slang forms among speakers of Java's other two main regional languages: Javanese (Central and East Java) and Sundanese (West Java).

The majority of Jakarta's immigrants and residents are native Javanese speakers. Unlike Indonesian, Javanese has a complicated system of politeness registers. Each language level resembles a language unto itself, with different lexical items for most common words and phrases. Although all spoken Javanese is hierarchical in this way, parts of Java have a reputation for either more or less refined speech, ranging from the highly refined formal linguistic register spoken in the Central Javanese courts of Yogyakarta and Surakarta to the extremely coarse (*kasar*) informal dialects spoken in less celebrated locales like Tegal and Madiun.

The language Javanese young people employ for informal socializing among friends is *ngoko* or *jawir,* Low Javanese. Although the ability to speak refined forms of Javanese varies considerably depending on region, class, and personal inclination, the youth of Central and East Java all speak *ngoko* and Indonesian, a language they study in school beginning at a very young age. Not surprisingly, the slang spoken in Javanese cities is a combination of Indonesian and very coarse Low Javanese. In many cases, words with fairly mundane meanings such as *nguntal* (Javanese, "eat rice") and *kencot* (Javanese, "hungry") are considered so vulgar they cannot be uttered in mixed company. Such language is unlikely to ever be used in popular music or any other publicly circulating texts.

The university town of Yogyakarta has its own variant of *Prokem* in which Indonesian and Low Javanese words are transformed according to a system of consonant substitution that, I was told by some Yogyanese students, was used by Prince Diponogoro's spies in the nineteenth century. With this code, *cewek* (young women) becomes *jethen, motor* (motorbike) becomes *dogos, mangan*

(Javanese, "eat") becomes *dalak,* and *ibu* (mother) becomes *pisu.* Dagadu, the T-shirt and accessory manufacturer based in Yogya, got its name from the *Prokem* for *matamu* (literally "your eyes," a mild expletive in Indonesian). Students at Yogyakarta's several universities speak to one another in Low Javanese regardless of their island of origin or ethnic background; Indonesian is reserved for the classroom. A friend told me a story about a university colleague from Sumatra who visited his *kampung* in East Java and made the mistake of addressing the friend's parents in the *kasar* Javanese he had learned from hanging out on campus. This was a grave breach of etiquette, since elders in Java should always be addressed in more elevated forms of Javanese. Though my friend came from a progressive family and usually addressed his parents in *madya* (the middle level of politeness) rather than *krama* (High Javanese), it was still unacceptable to address them in *ngoko.* His Sumatran companion would have been far better off just using Indonesian.

Bandung, another important university town in Indonesia, is the capital of the Sundanese-speaking province of West Java. The city is close enough to Jakarta to be strongly influenced by Jakartan speech, and the language of everyday socializing among Bandung youth is a combination of Jakarta-inflected Indonesian and a very *kasar* form of Sundanese, identified by the first-person singular pronoun *aing.* Sundanese has fewer politeness levels and is less rigidly hierarchical than Javanese, but *kasar* words such as *lebok* (Sundanese, "eat") are also considered inappropriate for public speech.

Pronominal Strategies

Even if one only speaks Indonesian and/or Jakartanese, the choices among possible pronouns to refer to oneself and others are daunting, and they depend on several sociolinguistic factors. Often personal pronouns are omitted in colloquial speech; when this is not possible, the speaker must choose among the following options, which can be used in different combinations:

> First-Person Singular
> *Saya* (Formal Indonesian)
> *Aku* (Informal Indonesian)
> *Gue/Gua* (Jakartanese)
>
> Second-Person Singular
> *Anda* (Formal Indonesian)
> *Kamu, Kau* (Informal Indonesian)
> *Lu* (Jakartanese)

A more neutral alternative to all these pronominal options is to refer to oneself by one's proper name and refer to others by their names. Students in

Jakarta occasionally use this construction when speaking to peers with whom they are not well acquainted.

Which Indonesian pronouns a young Jakartan uses in a given situation with a given interlocutor depends not only on immediate contextual factors but also on ethnicity. Javanese, for example, are more likely to use *aku* in informal conversations. One reason for this is that *aku* is also the first-person pronoun in Low Javanese. Some Sumatran groups find *kamu* offensive and prefer to use *kau*, which most other Jakartans consider somewhat coarser than *kamu*. Sundanese young people are more likely to use *saya* for both informal and formal speech, sometimes using *saya mah* for the former, the Sundanese/Jakartanese particle adding a colloquial familiarity. Betawi people, and many non-Betawi Jakartans, use *gue/gua* and *lu* with friends.

Pronoun choices are also conditioned by more personal, autobiographical factors. Some residents of Jakarta, particularly Javanese who originated from other parts of the country, find *gue/lu* coarse and offensive (*kasar*) and try to use only *aku/kamu* or *saya/kamu*. The informal Jakartanese pronoun *lu* (sometimes spelled *elo* or *elu* or *loe* but pronounced the same) in particular is considered the height of *kasar*, far coarser than the informal Indonesian pronouns *kamu* and *kau*. Other newcomers to the city immediately adopt the Jakartanese pronouns. In the relatively individualistic environment of Jakarta, many variations in pronoun use exist. I met a Jakarta-born middle-class Sundanese graphic designer who used only *saya*, even with his wife, and a Jakarta-born Chinese Indonesian record producer who used *gua* in staff meetings with his employees. I have also observed several figures in the entertainment industry switch first-person pronouns in midstream, sometimes in the course of a single sentence, when being interviewed by journalists. In general, they used *saya* when discussing career-related matters or opinions on serious subjects, *aku* when commenting on their personal aspirations or feelings, and *gue/gua* for humorous asides and when joking around with the reporters. In fact, it is quite common for speakers from all walks of life to switch between pronominal options when speaking to the same person, depending on what is being said.

GLOSSARY OF INDONESIAN AND JAKARTANESE TERMS

Many of the following terms possess several meanings; the definitions below are limited to those relevant to their specific uses in the text.

acara	organized event, often featuring musical performances
aliran	literally "stream," music genre or subgenre
anak gaul	fashionable rich kid
anak jalanan	"street child," child beggar
bajaj	three-wheeled motorized buggy found in Jakarta, a cheaper alternative to taxis
banci	male transgendered cross-dresser (derogatory)
becak	pedal-powered trishaw, pedicab
begadang	to stay up all night, usually for social reasons
belagu	arrogant, proud, self-important
bencong	see *banci*
Betawi	ethnolinguistic group descended from the native laborer class of colonial Batavia, now Jakarta
Blok M	fashionable shopping and entertainment district in South Jakarta
bonang	set of tuned kettle gongs, part of a gamelan ensemble
bule	literally "albino," colloquial term for white person
cengeng	weepy, sentimental, mawkish
cengkok	melismatic ornaments characteristic of dangdut vocals
cinta	love, especially the romantic variety
daerah	region, countryside
D.I.Y.	"Do It Yourself," punk-derived ethos of autonomous artistic production
gaul	cool, social
gendang	(1) tablalike pair of drums used in dangdut music; (2) double-headed barrel drum used in traditional and ethnic music
genit	flirtatious
gicik	crude, tambourine-like percussion instrument used by street-side ensembles and child beggars

goyang	to sway, undulate; the main dance movement of female dangdut performers
jago	champion, virtuoso
jaipong	Sundanese popular dance music played on traditional instruments
janda	a woman without a husband as a result of death, divorce, or abandonment
joget	dance step performed by audiences at dangdut nightclubs and concerts
kampung	village or poor urban neighborhood
kampungan	low-class, repellently characteristic of backward village life
kendang	see *gendang* (2)
keroncong	Indonesian national popular music genre derived from Portuguese-influenced urban folk songs and performed on Western stringed instruments
kesepian	loneliness, isolation
macet	clogged, congested
menengah ke atas	middle to upper [class]
menengah ke bawah	middle to lower [class]
nongkrong	to squat; to socialize, hang out
ngobrol	to talk, chat
nyawer	to publicly bestow money on a performer during a performance
pasar	market, bazaar
pengamen	itinerant street musician
pinggir jalan	the side of the road
plesetan	a play on words, a pun
rakyat	the people, the folk
rakyat kecil	"the little people," the nonaffluent masses
ramai or rame	crowded, noisy, active, fun
saweran	money presented to an onstage performer
selingan	contrastive musical interlude, interpolation
sepi	lonely, deserted, quiet
singkatan	abbreviation, acronym
sombong	arrogant, self-important; Standard Indonesian synonym of *belagu*
suling	Indonesian bamboo flute, end-blown or transverse
waria	"ladyboy," a polite term for male transgendered cross-dresser that combines *wanita* (woman) and *pria* (man)
warnet	cyber café; from *warung internet*
warung	roadside or market stall
wong cilik	Javanese equivalent of *rakyat kecil* (see above)

NOTES

Introduction

1. For a more detailed explanation of the sonic materialist approach, see Wallach 2003b. I use this notion to establish the materiality of popular music products, as objects that intervene in and shape social life. Moreover, perceiving musical sounds as audiotactile material culture invites researchers to trace their distribution through a cultural field and examine their various uses by different social agents.

2. Multigenre ethnographic studies of popular music in the West include Finnegan 1989 and Berger 1999. These two studies have provided valuable models for the present work.

3. My notion of "musicscape" is derived from Arjun Appadurai's famous essay on the various overlapping "scapes" of the global cultural economy (1990) as well as R. Murray Schafer's influential concept of the environmental "soundscape" (1977, 1994). The musicscape is thus both a fluid, translocal and a localized, immediate phenomenon.

4. Gus Dur was appointed by the elected representatives of the People's Consultative Assembly. Susilo Bambang Yudhoyono, who became the country's sixth president in 2004, was the first Indonesian president chosen directly by the Indonesian people in a nationwide general election widely praised by international organizations for its transparency and high voter turnout.

5. In order to address translocal cultural phenomena, Ulf Hannerz divides the contemporary "social organization of meaning" into four "frameworks of flow": state, market, movement, and "form of life" (1992, 46–52). The first two frameworks are characterized by relative asymmetry of resources between producers and consumers of meaning, while the second two are characterized by more-egalitarian forms of organization (60). (I would add that popular musics are shaped by all four frameworks, often simultaneously: they are subject to state control, market forces, appropriation by grassroots social movements, and incorporation into communal lifeways.) Though the four frameworks can be separated analytically, Hannerz notes that they "do not work in isolation from one another, but it is rather in their interplay, with varying respective strengths, that they shape both what we rather arbitrarily demarcate as particular cultures, and that complicated overall entity which we may think of as the global

ecumene" (47). In 1988, the journal *Public Culture* was launched to analyze macro-level cultural "flows" (Appadurai 1990) at the local, global, and national levels.

6. The accompanying illustration on the T-shirt depicts a student protesting for Reformasi confronting a corpulent, smiling man in a suit holding a bag of money labeled *uang negara rakyat* (the people's state money). The man is holding a sign on which is written (in English) *The Best Corruptioner*; a caption pointing to his head reads *cueq aja* (just blowing it off). T-shirts like this one were sold all over Jakarta in traditional markets for 11,000 rupiahs (less than US$2 at the time). See figure on page 10.

7. Daniel Ziv, a longtime expatriate resident of Jakarta, notes sardonically, "Each year in Jakarta we optimistically repeat the same stupid joke: that this coming December *krismon* will finally be over because it becomes 'krismas'. . . . Christmas still hasn't arrived" (2002, 80).

8. See Widjojo et al. 1999 for a collection of detailed firsthand accounts of the student movement that helped topple the New Order. For an examination of the role of song in the Indonesian movement for Reformasi (and in Southeast Asian politics more generally), see Dijk 2003.

9. The Indonesian rupiah slid from 2,450 to the U.S. dollar in July 1997 to 15,000 to the U.S. dollar in January 1998; in May 1998, the month Soeharto stepped down, the exchange rate was 14,000 rupiahs to the dollar (Dijk 2001, 71, 130, 193).

10. For a fascinating, if hardly impartial, insider's account of the political machinations behind Gus Dur's ouster, see Witoelar 2002. An Indonesian TV personality and Wahid's former presidential spokesman, Wimar Witoelar sums up the ordeal as follows: "From the beginning, President Wahid was doomed because he was made president by an unholy alliance whose only purpose in electing him was to block Megawati from becoming president. And that alliance had hoped that Gus Dur would play according to their tune. But when he asserted his independence and basic values of humanism and democracy, he lost the political support" (193–94).

11. Throughout this study, English loanwords, such as *social gap*, used by Indonesians are italicized. See appendix A for more information regarding how foreign terms and translations appear in the text.

12. In later statements, this phrase *ngak-ngik-ngek* became *ngak-ngik-ngok* (Sen and Hill 2000, 186n8).

13. Inspired by the work of feminist theorist Judith Butler (1990), which highlights the constitution and/or subversion of gender identity in performance, a wide range of studies that critically examine the performance of gender in popular music have appeared since the early 1990s. Notable examples of this type of inquiry include Auslander 2006; Schippers 2002; and Walser 1993.

Chapter 1. Indonesian Popular Music Genres
in the Global Sensorium

1. See Pioquinto 1998 for a more detailed consideration of dangdut's history. One example of the pervasiveness of dangdut music throughout the Indonesian archipelago can be found in Anna Tsing's ethnography of a remote region of Kalimantan (Indonesian Borneo), where she encounters a mountain-dwelling spirit medium who claims to be possessed by the spirit of dangdut star Rhoma Irama (Tsing 1993, 245–46).

2. Addressing the earlier style, Margaret Kartomi writes, "In *orkes Melayu*, a soloist sings Malay poetry to Malay melodies, usually accompanied with thin Western harmonies on both Malay and Western instruments, including a flute, acoustic guitar, bass, harmonium, and Malay percussion—drums and optional gongs" (2002, 148 n40).

The repertoire of *orkes Melayu* ensembles often came from Malay *bangsawan* folk theater productions (popular since the late nineteenth century), and early recordings by *orkes Melayu* groups were marketed to ethnic Malays in both Sumatra and peninsular Malaysia (Barendregt 2002, 421).

3. This *suling* is distinct from the end-blown bamboo flute found in Javanese gamelan, which is also called a *suling*. Charles Capwell has pointed out that while the physical instrument itself may be indigenous to Indonesia, the *suling*'s characteristic timbre and playing style in dangdut music more closely approximate those of the South Asian *bansuri* flute heard on thousands of Indian film soundtracks than they resemble anything found in traditional Indonesian music (personal communication, December 2003).

4. Tom Goodman, an American historian who spent time in the strife-torn Maluku province in the late 1990s, reports that musical taste in the most religiously polarized region in Indonesia was indeed split along religious lines. Christians for the most part denied liking dangdut music, while Muslim Moluccans embraced it. On the other hand, Muslims were more willing to admit they liked *dansa*, a local popular music genre with roots in Christian hymnody (personal communication, June 2000).

5. The rise and influence of *pop daerah* variants have attracted the notice of ethnomusicologists and other scholars who work in various parts of Indonesia. See, for example, Williams 1989/1990 for a discussion of New Order Sundanese popular music and Laskewicz 2004 and Harnish 2005b for investigations of the influence of popular music technology and aesthetics on the traditional performing arts in Bali. Useful analyses of Javanese *campur sari* can be found in Perlman 1999; Sutton 2002b, 23–24; and Supanggah 2003. For historical accounts of *pop Minang* and reflections on its cultural significance in contemporary Indonesia, see Barendregt 2002 and Suryadi 2003; see Jones 2005 for an exploration of the popularity of national and regional popular music genres on

public transportation vehicles in the West Sumatran capital of Padang. Sutton 2002a (196–228) provides information on *pop Makassar* and a historical overview of the commercial music industry in South Sulawesi, and Suryadi 2005 gives an illuminating account of local radio and regional pop music in Riau. The growth of increasingly robust regional pop scenes throughout Indonesia has coincided with movements for more regional and cultural autonomy in the post–New Order period.

6. In fact, regional music from Sunda (West Java) has historically demonstrated the most "crossover appeal" in the national market. R. Anderson Sutton notes, "[I]n the past 20 years the music of this one region has, unlike those of any other Indonesian region, found a receptive audience in various parts of the country, due primarily to its infectious drum rhythms and also to the haunting and enticing sound of Sundanese female singers" (2002b, 23). I would add that Sundanese music's access to national media exposure as a result of the West Java province's proximity to Jakarta, and the fact that it constitutes an "ethnic" alternative to the regional music of the culturally dominant (and resented) Javanese, are likely also important factors influencing Sundanese popular music's reception among non-Sundanese listeners.

7. Although numerically few and occasionally the object of envy by the impoverished majority, university students in Indonesia have long been a vanguard of social and political change (see Geertz 1960, 307–8; Anderson 1999, 3). At the beginning of the twenty-first century, there were approximately 2.4 million postsecondary students in Indonesia, out of a total population of roughly 225 million (Arnold 2002, 89). Interestingly, Indonesia ranked eighth, right after Canada, among countries of origin for foreign nationals enrolled in U.S. universities during the 2000–2001 academic year, with a total number of 11,625 students (Secor 2002, 37). After the terrorist attacks on September 11, 2001, it became more difficult to obtain a visa to study in the United States, particularly for Muslim men, and this number went down considerably.

8. The music that became known as ska evolved out of imported American rhythm and blues and indigenous Jamaican influences in the working-class neighborhoods of Kingston in the years after Jamaican independence in 1962 (Bilby 1995). By the late 1960s, ska had been largely superseded in Jamaica by newer genres like rock steady and reggae, but ska, with its infectious, upbeat-stressed rhythms, subsequently caught on in Great Britain, where it was performed by "two-tone" bands composed of black and white musicians for multiracial youth audiences. The so-called third wave of ska bands emerged in England and the United States in the 1980s, many of which, such as Berkeley, California's Operation Ivy, combined ska's characteristic rhythms with the noisy aggression and socially conscious lyrics of punk and hardcore, forging a hybrid style known as "ska-core," which would later become the dominant ska variant in Indonesia. The next phase in ska's development brought the genre to the attention of large numbers of Indonesian music fans for the first time: for a

brief period in 1996–97, segments of the transnational music industry attempted to turn ska into "the next grunge" by introducing a rash of major-label, heavily promoted, and mostly white ska and ska-influenced groups like Sublime, No Doubt, and Reel Big Fish. Ultimately, ska lacked the staying power of what came to be known as "alternative rock," and after producing a handful of modest hits, the style sank out of sight, at least in the American mainstream. However, this relatively brief but far-reaching exposure brought the ska sound to Indonesia, and a number of rock bands in underground music scenes there subsequently began to play in that style.

9. Waiting Room took its name from a song by Fugazi, a seminal band from Washington, DC that has long championed progressive political causes and an ethos of "do-it-yourself" independence. Fugazi has never recorded with a major record label, and I was surprised and impressed that Fugazi was so well known among members of the Indonesian underground movement.

10. The purist attitude toward independent production in the Indonesian underground is summed up in the following text from the liner notes for *Human's Disgust* (1998), an independently released cassette EP by Bandung metal band Fear Inside: *"WHO SAID MAJOR LABELS IS THE SOLUTION / MAJOR LABELS MAKE ME SICKS! / DO IT BY YOURSELF OR DIE."*

11. O. M. Ranema's Web site is home.att.ne.jp/orange/Raj_Hikomar/dangdut/omrE.html. By contrast, the limited but positive attention dangdut has received from Western researchers does appear to affect middle-class Indonesian perceptions of the music. For example, Alison Murray claims that the publication of William Frederick's groundbreaking article "Rhoma Irama and the dangdut style" (1982) actually led to increased middle-class acceptance and "mainstream appropriation" of dangdut music in Indonesia (1991, 120–21n2; see also Pioquinto 1998, 74). If this is indeed the case, it illustrates the important lesson that the work of the researcher can create unforeseen consequences for the subjects of his or her research, and that works of scholarship, no less than popular music recordings, are cultural interventions with multiple social effects in various arenas.

Chapter 2. In the City

1. Poorer *kampung* tend to be especially crowded places. The population density of Jakarta as a whole reported in the 1995 census was an astonishing 13,786 people per square kilometer (Forbes 2002, 410).

2. According to Daniel Ziv, "[a]n estimated 20,000 *bule* [colloquial Indonesian for white foreigners] call Jakarta home. . . . They are diplomats, journalists, consultants, bankers, artists, teachers, and NGO activists" (2002, 27). Although glamorous, mass-mediated images of the Western world play a central role in the fantasy lives of many young urban Indonesians (see chapter 6), real-life Westerners working and residing in Jakarta tend to have a rather negative

reputation for drunkenness, profligate spending, and lasciviousness. In my limited interactions with expatriate businessmen living in Jakarta, I often found this stereotype to be sadly right on the mark. See Leggett 2005 for an ethnographic account of expatriate businessmen at one transnational corporation in Jakarta and their arrogant, colonialist perceptions of their Indonesian coworkers.

3. Often the two economic sectors literally overlap in space. An example is the widespread phenomenon of the *pasar kaget* (surprise market), a name given by locals to a cluster of food stalls that mysteriously springs up in empty store and office parking lots at night and is gone by morning.

4. In everyday youth parlance, a common discursive construction for indexing the social gap involves food, namely, the opposition between the *anak singkong* (cassava kids) and the *anak keju* (cheese kids). In many parts of Indonesia, cassava is used as a dietary starch for those too destitute to afford rice, while cheese remains an exotic imported foodstuff associated with expensive Western-style cuisine (such as cheeseburgers and pizza). A well-known Indonesian *pop nostalgia* song written by composer Arie Wibowo, "Cassava and Cheese," places this opposition in the context of a failed cross-class romance:

> "Singkong dan Keju" (refrain)
> *Aku suka jaipong*
> *Kau suka disco oh . . . oh . . .*
> *Aku suka singkong*
> *Kau suka keju oh . . . oh . . .*
> *Aku dambakan seorang gadis*
> *Yang sederhana*
> *Aku ini hanya anak singkong.*
>
> [I like *jaipong*
> You like disco *oh . . . oh . . .*
> I like cassava
> You like cheese *oh . . . oh . . .*
> I desire a girl
> Who is simple
> I'm just a cassava kid.]

5. Alison Murray relates the following quote from Tomo, a middle-aged Sundanese *becak* driver working in Manggarai, South Jakarta, in the 1980s: "There's no-one like Bung Karno. He was a man of the people and cared for the poor. In those days [during the Sukarno presidency] you were free to do any job; it didn't depend on your connections. Before I used to ride my trishaw all over Jakarta, even up to Pasar Ikan. Things are much harsher now; all the riders are scared of the police" (quoted in Murray 1991, 92).

6. Those responsible for the rapes and murders during the May 1998 riots were commonly thought to be hired goons, working for whoever originally orchestrated the violence and chaos—in most accounts, a faction in the

Indonesian military or Soeharto himself. Yet I heard several accounts from eyewitnesses of the riots that suggest that at least some of the violent acts were committed by ordinary people, just as there is evidence civilians participated enthusiastically in the military-backed mass slaughter of suspected Indonesian Communists and Communist sympathizers that took place in 1965–66 (see Rochijat 1985; Report from East Java 1985).

7. For an American expatriate anthropologist's firsthand account and interpretation of the riots, see Leggett 2005, 289–94.

8. Ethnomusicologist David Harnish describes *rame* as "a magnified aesthetic state of liveliness" (2006, 4). While he is defining the term in the context of a multiethnic religious festival in Lombok, I would contend that his characterization applies equally well to the performance of everyday life in Jakarta.

9. One popular *warnet* is located in a corner of the spacious twenty-four-hour McDonald's restaurant adjoining the Sarinah department store in Central Jakarta. Here customers willing to pay three times the usual hourly *warnet* rate can experience two paradigmatic symbols of globalization—the Internet and American fast food—under the same roof.

10. At the same time, even humble roadside food stalls began to offer "*internet*" in their list of specialties. But in such establishments, the term was used as a humorous abbreviation for a popular late-night Jakarta snack: hot soup containing In*domie* (instant ramen noodles), te*lur* (egg), and *kor*net (canned corned beef). Such linguistic play constitutes a symbolic appropriation of an aspect of "modern" lifestyle by working-class Indonesians who lack the educational skills and financial resources to take advantage of the "real" Internet.

11. See appendix C for a survey of nonstandard speech variants in Jakarta.

Chapter 3. Cassette Retail Outlets

1. An exception is Marc Perlman's survey of cassette stalls in Solo, Central Java (1999), which describes a bewildering spectacle of diverse musics on display, both strange and familiar to Western readers.

2. For an investigation of how music genre is indexed by cover graphics, liner notes, and sonic features of Indonesian cassette recordings, see Wallach 2002, 114–31.

3. Xenocentric attitudes regarding religion are common in Indonesia: Muslims look to the Middle East, Christians look to the West, and Hindus increasingly look to India (see Harnish 2005a) for the proper modes of religious conduct and belief.

4. Prices for recorded music rose steadily during the period of my fieldwork, a consequence of rising production costs and Indonesia's weakened currency.

5. Jazz musician and music industry figure Candra Darusman estimates that the cassette format accounted for 95 percent of Indonesian music sales in 1999 (n.d., 1).

6. Darusman, in a discussion of "creativity" in Indonesian popular music, writes, *"Reservations should be mentioned in the field of Dangdut Music which is experiencing a stagnant output in terms of creativity. Maybe the cause of this is the fact that the major decrease in cassette sales is vastly effecting* [sic] *this type of music"* (n.d., 2-3). While dangdut cassette sales did plummet as a result of the *krismon*, I do not agree with Darusman's statement that this caused the creative stagnation of the genre. Instead his words could be viewed as yet another elitist dismissal of dangdut music by a musician specializing in a more prestigious genre. For an earlier example of this tendency, see Piper and Jabo 1987.

7. Jakarta megamalls are expensive places in which to open a music store. According to Daniel Ziv (2002, 88), in 2002 monthly rent for a medium-sized shop in ultra-trendy Plaza Senayan was approximately US$10,000, and there was a six-month-long waiting list to obtain a spot.

8. In mid-2000, another playback device was installed near the entrance to the smaller room. This was a listening booth that played a limited assortment of new releases on compact disc, both Indonesian and Western, through an accompanying set of headphones. The listener was able to operate the controls in order to hear particular albums and tracks stored in the machine. Similar digital listening booths have become popular fixtures in large Western record stores; thus, rather than constituting an extension of the Indonesian practice of trying out cassettes before purchasing, the presence of this particular playback device in the Aquarius store is better viewed as an example of transnational influences in record-store commerce.

9. Puppen's 2000 self-titled cassette was a notable exception: Guitarist/manager Robin Malau decided to pay the value-added tax required by law in order to sell the album in mainstream retail outlets like Aquarius. Puppen was one of the few underground bands to take this bold and costly step, which in the end proved to be a wise investment: during one week in May 2000, Puppen's cassette was ranked at number 38 in the Aquarius store's Top Forty list, outselling the then-new album by Sting.

10. According to Robin Hutagaol, the store's proprietor, the name is an irreverent pun on *ishkabibble*, an obscure Yiddish-American colloquialism he encountered once in a dictionary of American slang. In addition to running Ish-Kabible, Robin played drums and sang with the underground band Brain the Machine, which described its sound as *industrial hardcore progressive*.

Chapter 4. In the Studio

1. Remixes of dangdut songs, which rerecord the analog tracks of the original and import them into a totally digital domain, are a different matter. See Wallach 2005 for a discussion of dangdut remix recordings.

2. Some recording companies have used other *gendang* players on their recordings besides the top three. At an ethnic fusion concert event in a Jakarta

hotel featuring the Sundanese group Krakatau, I met an Indian classical tabla player affiliated with Jakarta's Indian Cultural Center who claimed that while living in Indonesia he frequently recorded rhythm tracks on commercially released dangdut songs. He mentioned that he found playing dangdut rhythms to be easy and that playing on dangdut cassettes was a lucrative side venture for him.

3. The function of chordal polyphony in dangdut music resembles its role in Indian film song, about which Peter Manuel asserts, "The role of harmony in a song may ultimately derive from the nature of the melody, especially since almost all film songs consist of a solo vocal melody with accompaniment. In most songs using harmony [that is, employing chordal polyphony], the conception of the melody is clearly modal, such that the chordal accompaniment functions in an ornamental rather than structural manner" (1988, 183).

4. In his study of the Papua New Guinea recording industry, Malcolm Philpott includes this quotation from Mike Wild, an Australian sound engineer who worked in a major Papuan recording studio. It is worth requoting here: "One thing any newcomer notices right away [about Papuan popular music] is the melody line. They don't just sit there and set a beat, then do a melody line over the top. They set about it in reverse. They set the melody and then work out the beat underneath. Most musicians I've ever worked with played a drum beat, then they went for a chord structure over that, and finally sang a melody line over the top of that. Up here [in Papua New Guinea] it's a bit like building a house starting with the roof first, and finishing up with the basement and the foundations. Whatever, it sounds great" (quoted in Philpott 1998, 119). I reproduce this text not in order to posit a primordial connection between Indonesian and Melanesian music but to point out that the architectonic model of musical composition that Wild assumes to be normative is in many ways culturally specific. Such a model is in fact derived from historically situated rock music compositional techniques and multitrack studio practices that are far from universal. Wild's "house" metaphor reveals an ethnocentric bias; the notion that musical composition should start with a rhythmic foundation over which a melody is layered like a "roof" does not take account of the diversity of world musics, nor does it acknowledge that different sound-engineering practices, such as those described here for dangdut, might accompany this diversity.

5. Not everyone was happy with the producer's arrangement. I attended a birthday party sing-along in a working-class neighborhood where the participants made a point of adding a *gendang* and bass-guitar rhythm track on the synthesizer (*organ tunggal*) when performing a rendition of this song.

6. For considerations of the production/simulation of "liveness" with studio technology and its importance for establishing genre-specific expectations of musical authenticity, see Auslander 1999, 61–111; and Meintjes 2003, 109–45. New cassette releases are usually easily adapted to live instrumentation by

local dangdut performing ensembles, despite the complexity and polish of their arrangements.

7. Edy's advice notwithstanding, I would argue that the rise of *pop alternatif* in Indonesia in fact transformed expectations of how women singers should sound. Although some artists in that genre, such as Potret lead singer and solo artist Melly Goeslaw, specialized in breathy, girlish vocalizing (in Goeslaw's case, inspired in part by Icelandic recording artist Björk), female-led groups like Bandung's Cokelat have achieved significant commercial success with more assertive, less sexualized vocal personae.

8. Sadly, this recording was never released.

9. In addition to combining English, Indonesian, and Spanish in his songs, Andy Atis added one more, even riskier language: Hebrew. For complicated reasons, Hebrew has become a language of church worship for many Indonesian Christians, whose pro-Jewish and Zionist leanings appear to be a reaction against the anti-Jewish and anti-Zionist sentiments attributed to the more powerful and numerous Muslim population. Andy inserted a partially masked Hebrew phrase, *heveinu shalom aleichem* (we bring peace unto you), into the introduction of one of his songs on the theme of peace and brotherhood between Indonesians of different religions—an act he regarded as rather subversive, given Indonesia's Muslim majority. The phrase is sung by an ethereal, electronically processed voice similar to that employed by Patty for the strange-sounding English-language phrase at the beginning of one of her songs. It may not be coincidental that these two uncanny vocal performances, with their use of foreign tongues and wraithlike timbres, appear to index the limits of acceptable expression in the Indonesian national music market in the same way that strange (*aneh*) Javanese spirits index the limits of the human cultural and linguistic order (Geertz 1960, 28–29; Siegel 1986).

10. Music video programs, on the other hand, often alternated freely between Indonesian and overseas artists; perhaps this strategy of presentation will gradually erode the conceptual barrier between domestic and foreign music products, and Andy's prediction of a truly globalized Indonesian music market will come to pass.

11. Such dismissive attitudes appear to have changed very little. While researching the Balinese metal scene for a forthcoming documentary, filmmaker Sam Dunn was told repeatedly by prominent figures in the Jakarta underground metal world that Bali was "backward" and that he would find little of interest there (Sam Dunn, personal communication, September 2006).

Chapter 5. On Location

1. See Williams 2001 (115–16) for a description of similar visual and narrative conventions in the making of *tembang Sunda* video clips.

2. For useful analyses of this emblematic cultural product of the Soeharto regime, see Anderson 1990, 176–83; Hendry 2000, 99–104; and Pemberton 1994a, 1994b.

3. After viewing the finished video clip of "Cinta Hanya Sekali" at a Bowling Green State University Popular Culture departmental colloquium, Marilyn Motz alerted me to the ways in which the camera's gaze invites the viewer to empathize with Iyeth's character. Instead of eroticizing and objectifying the image of the woman singer (a characteristic visual strategy in Western music videos), the camera focuses on Iyeth's face and its expressive features—lips, (tearful) eyes, and mouth—rather than on other body parts (personal communication, October 2003). This filmic technique—typical of dangdut videos featuring women singers—corresponds to the female-centered nature of the clip's narrative as well as to the woman's point of view expressed in the song itself.

4. In fact, Iyeth went on to become a major dangdut star in the early 2000s, with several hit songs to her credit and frequent mentions in the Indonesian tabloid press.

5. In 1996 Netral, Nugie, and Pas opened for American groups Sonic Youth, the Beastie Boys, and the Foo Fighters (a group founded by Nirvana's former drummer) at a concert in Jakarta. This event provided a rare moment of face-to-face contact between three well-known Western "alternative" bands and the Indonesian groups they inspired.

6. *Nurani*, from the Arabic, means "innermost, pure, and radiant." One of Netral's most poignant compositions, according to Bagus, the band's vocalist, the song "Nurani" expresses a longing for a vanished era when people in Jakarta were less "individualist" and selfish, and when there was a greater level of caring and solidarity within the communities that made up the city. One Betawi fan of the song suggested that it was also about "peacemaking" (*perdamaian*) in the aftermath of the 1998 Jakarta riots, when people involved in the violence and looting refused to heed the voice of their "inner conscience" (*hati nurani*). The timing of the song's initial 1999 release bolsters this interpretation, as does the Indonesian television network's decision to broadcast its video clip during televised coverage of an event many feared would result in a renewed outbreak of citywide rioting and chaos.

7. The theme of the moon as sympathetic companion and cure for nocturnal feelings of loneliness recurs in Indonesian pop texts. "Hujan" (Rain), a song by Bandung-based *heavypop* band Cherry Bombshell, contains these lyrics:

> *Ooooooh . . . rembulan malam*
> *Temani aku dalam lamunan*
> *Ooooooh . . . rembulan padam*
> *Jangan aku kau tinggalkan*

Jangan kau bersedih, jangan kau menangis
Bulan kau kembali temani dirimu

[Ooooooh, night's moon
Befriends me in my dreaming
Ooooooh, extinguished moon
Do not leave me

Don't you be sad, don't you cry
Your moon returns to be your friend and keep you company.]

(From the album *Luka Yang Dalam*
[A Deep Wound], 2000)

Cherry Bombshell and Netral both worked with the same producer, Jerry Bidara of Bulletin Records, though this was probably not a factor in the lyrical convergence of "Hujan" and "Cahaya Bulan." More likely, I would argue, is that both songs convey a preoccupation with loneliness (experienced as the absence of sociality, of companionship) typical of Indonesian middle-class youth culture in general (see Wallach 2002, 143–47).

Chapter 6. Offstage

1. This song can be found on *Music of Indonesia, Vol. 2: Indonesian Popular Music* (Yampolsky 1991). Another Warung Gaul favorite, "Sengaja" (Intentionally) performed by Elvy Sukaesih, is also on this compilation.

2. This definition of *bahasa gaul* should not be confused with the trendy, playful speech variant based on Jakarta gayspeak discussed in appendix C. The regulars at the Warung Gaul were unaware of the existence of that language, which at the time was spoken mostly by celebrities, *gay* and *lesbi* Indonesians, and hip Jakarta yuppies, and they did not themselves understand it.

3. I employ pseudonyms throughout the discussion of the three *warung*. In the section on the university I use real names, as I do everywhere else in the book.

4. Creambaths are actually an Indonesian salon specialty with an English name. Years later, I came across the following definition: "A few remarks on the famous Indonesian 'creambath.' First, it's not a bath in cream, or anything quite so sensual. It is basically a thorough hair wash followed by a head, neck and shoulder massage using an herbal conditioning cream. Eventually, with the cream fully rubbed in, a steamer is applied so that the cream seeps into the pores and revitalizes the hair and scalp" (Ziv 2002, 124).

5. Beautiful Western women, to borrow a phrase from James Siegel (2000), have a "ghostly presence" in Indonesia, where for many young men they are the elusive embodiments of male sex and power fantasies. One secret of their allure, I suspect, is that *cewek bule* (white chicks) represent the possibility of a sexual

and romantic relationship that exists magically outside the normal exchanges and obligations of everyday life and the strictures of Islamic religious morality (cf. Schade-Poulsen 1999, 182–87, and chapter 9 of the present volume). A contemporary Indonesian urban legend is the story of the ugly, dark-skinned *becak* (pedicab) driver with whom a Western woman falls in love. She then devotes her life to him, and her considerable wealth saves the man from destitution.

An East Javanese friend of mine once lamented the decline of the *hitam manis* (black sweet) ideal of feminine Indonesian beauty in favor of westernized notions that stressed light skin and Caucasoid features. Although I suspect that *hitam manis* has long been a counteraesthetic in Indonesia, he may have a point when so many contemporary Indonesian actors, models, and singers happen to be *Indos*, Indonesians of partial European descent.

6. For an enlightening interpretation of "dubbing culture" in the Indonesian context, see Boellstorff 2003.

7. Marc Schade-Poulsen notes a strikingly similar phenomenon in a description of informal performances of *raï* music in Algeria. He states that in Arab and Algerian music, vocal melody and drum rhythm "cannot be dissociated from each other": "This became clear to me when I took my guitar along to beach trips or drinking sessions outside Oran. When I played songs from the local repertoire, not many seconds would pass before I had someone in the group playing the rhythm on the wood of my guitar; we were two persons playing the same instrument" (1999, 70). Dangdut music seems to follow a similar musical logic, and this leads to analogous behaviors in Indonesian informal performance settings (see figure on page 157).

8. At the time of this writing in late 2006, Wendi is a writer for the Indonesian *Rolling Stone* and is a major figure in the Jakarta rock scene as a journalist, concert promoter, and band manager.

9. American communications scholar Kembrew McLeod (2005, 60–61) notes that the United States frequently violated European intellectual property laws during its early history as a struggling new nation.

10. These radicalized university students belong to a tradition of cultural and political avant-gardism dating back to the years before Indonesia's independence. In his 1960 monograph on Javanese society, Geertz describes the members of what he terms "the emerging 'youth culture'" in the Indonesia of that time:

> [A] group of restless, educated, urban young men and women possessed of a sharp dissatisfaction with traditional custom and a deeply ambivalent attitude toward the West, which they see both as the source of their humiliation and "backwardness" and as the possessor of the kind of life they feel they want for themselves. . . . Painfully sensitive, easily frustrated, and passionately idealistic, this group is in many ways the most vital element in contemporary Indonesian society. . . . They are the Republic's hope and its despair: its hope because their

idealism is both its driving force and its moral conscience; its despair because their exposed psychological position in the avant-garde of social change may turn them rather quickly toward the violent primitivism of other recent youth movements in Europe whose inner need for effective social reform was greater than the actual changes their elders were capable of producing for them. (1960, 307–8)

Many of the young idealists Geertz describes were to succumb to this "violent primitivism"; hundreds of thousands of young Indonesians went on to participate in the horrific events of 1965–66 as perpetrators or victims of mass murder. More than three decades later, student activism emerged once again in Indonesia as a more positive source of social change, and the activists I encountered in Jakarta fit Geertz's description—written about members of their grandparents' generation—remarkably well.

11. It is difficult, but not impossible, for Chinese Indonesians to gain acceptance into *pribumi* ("native") male hangout groups. Gus, a Chinese noodle-cart vendor in his midthirties, explained to me how through hanging out he was able to develop rapport with the local toughs in the North Jakarta neighborhood where he worked and thus to ensure his safety against harassment. Gus knew well the destructive power of anti-Chinese sentiment among the *pribumi:* the multistory building that housed the bakery he once owned was destroyed in the 1998 riots, during which Gus himself was pursued and nearly killed by a rampaging mob. For a discussion of the poignantly conflicted subject positions of Chinese Indonesians, see Ang 2001, 52–74.

Chapter 7. Onstage

1. This interpretation of the /rif song is certainly open to question. Am I being a bit too idealistic here? Probably. Although I would maintain that the musical and emotional emphasis /rif placed on the line *Ku hanya orang biasa* (I'm just an ordinary person) during its performance encouraged audience members to sing along and identify with this lyric, experiencing the "ordinariness" of the protagonist as being not that different from their own. Moreover, *orang biasa* was a phrase that I often heard Indonesians use to describe themselves in contrast to the *pejabat* (officeholders) and the *koruptor*s of society, and it seemed in those contexts to contain more dignity than related expressions such as *orang miskin* (poor person), *orang kampung* (village/slum person), or *wong cilik* (little person). Following this usage, in this book I often describe working-class and underclass people as "ordinary Indonesians."

2. Badjuridoellahjoestro is a poet based in Yogyakarta who writes verse inspired by the plight of various types of working-class Indonesians. I am greatly indebted to Benedict Anderson for his suggestions on how to translate and interpret this poem. He alerted me to the fact that the speaker in the first

stanza is intended to be an irritated motorist, unwilling to listen to the street musician's song. The second stanza is the *pengamen's* reply (which in real life he would never get a chance to voice), in which he asks the speaker from the first stanza when he will listen to his song through to the end (instead of presumably cutting him off with a token payment of spare change) and join in the singing, for without openness toward one's fellow man, both musician and listener are doomed to sing forever of the "stifling deadness" of their individual lives (B. Anderson, personal communication, October 2002). In addition to its poignant portrayal of the humble street busker, the poem also expresses a central value of Indonesian sociality: the desire to *bergaul*, to interact with others, as a way to ward off loneliness and "deadness."

3. Krakatau was the only group that used electronic keyboards during their set despite the evening's "acoustic" theme. This was necessary because Krakatau's music employs a customized gamelan-based tuning system that cannot be played on an acoustic piano tuned to the standard Western equal-temperament scale.

4. See Sen and Hill 2000, 108–36, and Sutton 2003 for a historical overview of the Indonesian television industry and the controversial place of "foreign content" in national network programming.

5. TPI specialized in dangdut-related programming, which earned it the mean-spirited nickname Televisi Pembantu Indonesia (Television for Indonesian House Servants) among members of the middle and upper classes.

6. Music producer Edy Singh told me that the King of Dangdut himself, Rhoma Irama, was originally supposed to participate in the Three Tenors sequence but had bowed out.

Chapter 8. Dangdut Concerts

1. In Indonesia, the sight of two men dancing together does not carry the same homoerotic overtones as it might in the West.

2. Dangdut performer and media superstar Inul Daratista, whose controversial rise to prominence took place after the period of time this book covers, provides an obvious example of the power of erotic onstage dance moves. In the beginning, her sole claim to fame, which caused her to be targeted by religious moral watchdogs even as it won her fans from around the archipelago, was a technique known as the "drilling dance" (*goyang ngebor*). As a result of the notoriety this dance caused, Inul was able to rise from obscurity and become a multimedia celebrity, appearing on VCDs (initially bootlegged recordings of live performances), TV specials, and even an Indonesian soap opera (Mulligan 2005). For articles about Inul in the Western media see, for example, BBC News 2003; Lipscombe 2003; Walsh 2003; and Wilde 2003. For a more academic study that perceptively situates the Inul controversy in the context of contested gender ideologies in post–New Order Indonesia, see Wichelen 2005.

3. Susan Browne's (2000) monograph distinguishes between *"dangdut kampungan"* (trashy, low-class dangdut) and dangdut that is *"sopan dan rapi"* (which she translates as "respectable and orderly," though "polite and neat" is perhaps a closer approximation). Browne associates the former with live performances in *kampung* settings and the latter with recording artists, televised concerts, and nightclubs (though she also confusingly asserts that dangdut nightclub performances may be considered *kampungan* [28]). I did not encounter either phrase during my fieldwork, and the first, with its blatantly pejorative tone, would be unlikely to be used as the name of a musical category by enthusiasts (who would find it offensive) or critics (for whom it would be redundant). Though they make use of Indonesian words, the two categories appear to be entirely etic, and Browne acknowledges that the phrase *dangdut kampungan* is not specifically employed by dangdut fans or detractors (31). Although it is true that the staging and dance moves of televised dangdut events often bear little resemblance to those of outdoor dangdut concerts, the distinction that Browne claims exists between the two types of dangdut she identifies seems for the most part not to be recognized by the music's fans and producers, who generally regard dangdut as a holistic phenomenon that belongs to the common people whatever form it takes.

4. Dangdut clubs belong to a category of male-dominated leisure spaces found in many East and Southeast Asian societies that feature hostesses, alcohol consumption, and myriad forms of paid female companionship. For an informative ethnographic investigation of the cultural and psychosexual dynamics of "hostess clubs" in Japan, see Allison 1994.

5. Similar techniques of instrumental substitution were used by dangdut bands to perform Lilis Karlina's dangdut/ethnic fusion hit "Cinta Terisolasi" at live concerts. For instance, the *suling* player usually performed the song's violin parts. See chapter 4 for a description of "Cinta Terisolasi" and its nonstandard rhythm and instrumentation.

Chapter 9. Rock and Pop Events

1. An intriguing, perhaps related, example of elite appropriation of this song: in October 1998, an Indonesian all-star jazz group (tenor saxophone: Trisno; piano: Bubi Chen; upright bass and trombone: Benny Likumahuwa; drums and percussion: Cendi Luntungan) recorded a multitracked jazz instrumental version of "Moliendo Café" ("grinding coffee" in Spanish) that is included on the album *Wonderful World* (1999). Accomplished jazz vocalist Syaharani, who sang on the album but did not perform on this particular track, insisted to me it was *not* an attempt to cover "Kopi Dangdut," though the recording's prominent use of a tambourine might suggest otherwise, since this instrument is unusual in both Latin popular music and acoustic jazz but ubiquitous in dangdut music. Moreover, the tambourine is playing a dangdut rhythm!

2. Sean Williams (personal communication, February 2005) suggests that *noceng* could also be short for "no *cengeng*" (nonweepy), which would highlight the hard rock orientation of the event.

3. This sports complex was also the location of the Netral video shoot described in chapter 5.

4. See Dijk 2001, 347–50, for a detailed account of this incident and its aftermath.

Chapter 10. Underground Music

1. The inclusion of these salutes to groups' fans in cassette liner notes may stem partially from commercial motives. Carol Muller discusses a thank-you list in a South African Nazarite hymn cassette insert and suggests that with the final message to the "fans," the worship community the cassette indexes "is commodified and redefined as a potential market" (1999, 144). While in this particular South African religious sect the tension between community and market is often cast in terms of sacred and secular, in the Indonesian underground movement the opposition is between "idealism" and "capitalism," the latter concerned with commercial viability and the former with artistic expression. Both the Nazarite religious sect discussed by Muller and the Indonesian underground movement have had to confront new commercial opportunities in a postauthoritarian, market-driven society that, while widening the movements' potential reach, also threatens their integrity as cohesive interpretive communities.

2. See Weinstein 1991, 228–30, for a helpful, unsensationalized description of moshing and stage-diving activities at live concerts.

3. A memorable cartoon by Muhammad "Mice" Misrad satirizes middle-class youth's preoccupation with lifestyle choices (see figure on page 245). The cartoon depicts the Rony character asking, "*Anak mana loe?*" (Which kid are you?). The four panels that follow depict possible choices, all middle-class youth subcultural types: *anak punk* (punk kid), *anak rap* (rap kid), *anak metal* (metal kid), and *anak gaul* (trendy rich kid), but the final panel depicts a saddened Rony and a rather different social type: an *anak jalanan* (street kid) playing a *gicik* and singing mournfully of his hardship: *Betap maling nasib ku . . . gara-gara Orde Baru*, "How unfortunate is my fate . . . all because of the New Order" (1999, 29). The cartoon's incisive social satire underscores the difference between "lifestyle" and a life of struggling to survive. Mice's cartoon portrays the underground music movement, for all its earnestness and its progressive politics, as little more than an affectation for westernized, privileged kids indifferent to the suffering of the impoverished majority of Indonesians, who do not have the luxury of making lifestyle choices.

WORKS CITED

Literature Cited

Abeyasekere, Susan. 1987. *Jakarta: A history*. Singapore: Oxford Univ. Press.

Adorno, Theodor. 1973. *The jargon of authenticity*. Evanston, IL: Northwestern Univ. Press.

Allison, Anne. 1994. *Nightwork: Sexuality, pleasure, and corporate masculinity in a Tokyo hostess club*. Chicago: Univ. of Chicago Press.

Anderson, Benedict R. O'G. [1983] 1991. *Imagined communities: Reflections on the origin and spread of nationalism*. London: Verso.

——. 1990. *Language and power: Exploring political cultures in Indonesia*. Ithaca, NY: Cornell Univ. Press.

——. 1998. *The spectre of comparisons: Nationalism, Southeast Asia and the world*. New York: Verso.

——. 1999. Indonesian nationalism today and in the future. *Indonesia* 67:1-11.

Ang, Ien. 2001. *On not speaking Chinese: Living between Asia and the West*. New York: Routledge.

Appadurai, Arjun. 1990. Disjuncture and difference in the global cultural economy. *Public Culture* 2 (2): 1-24.

——. 1996. *Modernity at large: Cultural dimensions of globalization*. Minneapolis: Univ. of Minnesota Press.

Armbrust, Walter. 1996. *Mass culture and modernism in Egypt*. Cambridge: Cambridge Univ. Press.

Arnold, Wayne. 2002. Young Indonesia. *DoubleTake* 8 (1): 88-90.

Atkins, E. Taylor. 2001. *Blue Nippon: Authenticating jazz in Japan*. Durham, NC: Duke Univ. Press.

Auslander, Philip. 1999. *Liveness: Performance in a mediatized culture*. New York: Routledge.

——. 2006. *Performing glam rock: Gender and theatricality in popular music*. Ann Arbor: Univ. of Michigan Press.

Austin, J. L. 1975. *How to do things with words*. Cambridge, MA: Harvard Univ. Press.

Badjuridoellahjoestro. 1994. *Kudengar tembang buruh, puisi pilihan lima tahun: 1987-1991*. Yogyakarta: Media Widya Mandala.

Bakhtin, Mikhail M. 1981. *The dialogic imagination: Four essays*. Ed. Michael

Holquist. Trans. Caryl Emerson and Michael Holquist. Austin: Univ. of Texas Press.

———. 1984. *Rabelais and his world*. Trans. Hélène Iswolsky. Bloomington: Indiana Univ. Press.

Barendregt, Bart. 2002. The sound of "Longing for Home": Redefining a sense of community through Minang popular music. *Bijdragen tot de Taal-, Land- en Volkenkunde* 158 (3): 411–50.

Barendregt, Bart, and Wim van Zanten. 2002. Popular music in Indonesia since 1998, in particular fusion, indie and Islamic music on video compact discs and the Internet. *Yearbook for Traditional Music* 34:67–113.

Bass, Colin. 2000. Indonesia: No risk—no fun. In *World music: The rough guide*, ed. Simon Broughton and Mark Ellingham, rev. ed., vol. 2, 131–42. London: Rough Guides.

Baulch, Emma. 1996. Punks, rastas and headbangers: Bali's Generation X. *Inside Indonesia* 48. http://www.insideindonesia.org/edit48/emma.htm (accessed June 18, 2003).

———. 2002a. Alternative music and mediation in late New Order Indonesia. *Inter-Asia Cultural Studies* 3:219–34.

———. 2002b. Creating a scene: Balinese punk's beginnings. *International Journal of Cultural Studies* 5 (2): 153–77.

———. 2003. Gesturing elsewhere: The identity politics of the Balinese death/thrash metal scene. *Popular Music* 22 (2): 195–215.

Bauman, Richard. [1977] 1984. *Verbal art as performance*. Prospect Heights, IL: Waveland Press.

Bauman, Richard, and Charles L. Briggs. 1990. Poetics and performance as critical perspectives on language and social life. *Annual Review of Anthropology* 19:59–88.

BBC News. 2003. Indonesian cleric adopts "erotic" dancer. *BBC News*, March 6, 2003. http://news.bbc.co.uk/go/pr/fr/-2/hi/asia-pacific/2825529.htm (accessed May 2, 2003).

Beazley, Harriot. 2000. Street boys in Yogyakarta: Social and spatial exclusion in the public spaces of the city. In *A companion to the city*, ed. Gary Bridge and Sophie Watson, 472–88. Malden, MA: Blackwell.

———. 2002. "Vagrants wearing make-up": Negotiating spaces on the streets of Yogyakarta, Indonesia. *Urban Studies* 39 (9): 1665–83.

Becker, Judith. 1975. Kroncong, Indonesian popular music. *Asian Music* 7 (1): 14–19.

Berger, Harris. 1999. *Metal, rock, and jazz: Perception and the phenomenology of musical experience*. Middletown, CT: Wesleyan Univ. Press; Hanover, NH: Univ. Press of New England.

Bhabha, Homi. 1994. *The location of culture*. New York: Routledge.

Bilby Kenneth. 1995. Jamaica. In *Caribbean currents: Caribbean music from rhumba to reggae,* ed. Peter Manuel, 143-82. Philadelphia: Temple Univ. Press.

Bodden, Michael. 2005. Rap in Indonesian youth music of the 1990s: "Globalization," "outlaw genres," and social protest. *Asian Music* 36 (2): 1-26.

Boellstorff, Tom. 2003. Dubbing culture: Indonesian *gay* and *lesbi* subjectivities and ethnography in an already globalized world. *American Ethnologist* 30 (2): 225-42.

———. 2005 *The gay archipelago: Sexuality and nation in Indonesia.* Princeton, NJ: Princeton Univ. Press.

Bourdieu, Pierre. 1984. *Distinction: A social critique of the judgment of taste.* Trans. Richard Nice. Cambridge, MA: Harvard Univ. Press.

Breese, Gerald. 1966. *Urbanization in newly developing countries.* Englewood Cliffs, NJ: Prentice-Hall.

Brenner, Suzanne. 1998. *The domestication of desire: Women, wealth, and modernity in Java.* Princeton, NJ: Princeton Univ. Press.

Browne, Susan. 2000. *The gender implications of dangdut kampungan: Indonesian "low-class" popular music.* Monash Univ. Institute for Asian Studies Working Paper no. 109. Melbourne: Monash Univ., Centre of Southeast Asian Studies.

Bruner, Edward. 1999. Return to Sumatra: 1957, 1997. *American Ethnologist* 26 (2): 461-77.

———. 2001. The Maasai and the Lion King: Authenticity, nationalism, and globalization in African tourism. *American Ethnologist* 28 (4): 881-908.

Butler, Judith. 1990. *Gender trouble: Feminism and the subversion of identity.* New York: Routledge.

Capino, José. 2003. Soothsayers, politicians, lesbian scribes: The Philippine movie talk show. In *Planet TV: A global television reader,* ed. Lisa Parks and Shanti Kumar, 262-74. New York: New York Univ. Press.

Chambert-Loir, Henri. 1990. Prokem, the slang of Jakarta youth: Instructions for use. *Prisma* 50:80-88.

Chow, Rey. 1993. Listening otherwise, music miniaturized: A different type of question about revolution. In *The cultural studies reader,* ed. Simon During, 382-402. New York: Routledge.

Chun, Allen, Ned Rossiter, and Brian Shoesmith, eds. 2004. *Refashioning pop music in Asia: Cosmopolitan flows, political tempos and aesthetic industries.* New York: RoutledgeCurzon.

Cooper, Nancy. 2000. Singing and silences: Transformations of power through Javanese seduction scenarios. *American Ethnologist* 27 (3): 609-44.

Crafts, Susan, Daniel Cavicchi, Charles Keil, and the Music in Daily Life Project. 1993. *My music.* Hanover, NH: Univ. Press of New England.

Danesh, Abol Hassan. 1999. *Corridor of hope: A visual view of informal economy.* Lanham, MD: Univ. Press of America.

Danu. 2000. Ditekan Sedikit, Ahh . . . *Kompas,* July 9, 2000. http://www
.kompas.com/kompas-cetak/0007/09/latar/dite14.htm (accessed July 12,
2000).

Darusman, Candra. n.d. The current and future outlook of popular music in
Indonesia. Seminar paper.

Davis, Sara L. M. 2005. *Song and silence: Ethnic revival on China's southwest
borders.* New York: Columbia Univ. Press.

Dijk, Kees van. 2001. *A country in despair: Indonesia between 1997 and 2000.*
Leiden: KITLV Press.

——. 2003. The magnetism of songs. *Bijdragen tot de Taal-, Land- en Volkenkunde* 159 (1): 31–64.

Doyle, Peter. 2005. *Echo & reverb: Fabricating space in popular music recording,
1900–1960.* Middletown, CT: Wesleyan Univ. Press.

Durham, Deborah. 1999. Predicaments of dress: Polyvalency and the ironies of
a cultural identity. *American Ethnologist* 26 (2): 389–411.

Eakin, Emily. 2001. Harvard's prize catch, a Delphic postcolonialist. *New York
Times,* November 17, 2001, A15, 17.

Errington, J. Joseph. 1986. Continuity and change in Indonesian language development. *Journal of Asian Studies* 45 (2): 329–53.

Feld, Steven. [1982] 1990. *Sound and sentiment: Birds, weeping, poetics, and song
in Kaluli expression.* Rev. ed. Philadelphia: Univ. of Pennsylvania Press.

——. 1988. Notes on world beat. *Public Culture* 1 (1): 31–37.

——. 1996. Pygmy pop: A genealogy of schizophonic mimesis. *Yearbook for Traditional Music* 28:1–35.

——. 2000. A sweet lullaby for world music. *Public Culture* 12:145–71.

Ferzacca, Steve. 1997. *Keroncong* music in a Javanese neighborhood: Rehearsals
with spirits of the popular. Paper presented at the Society for Ethnomusicology, 42nd annual meeting, October 24, 1997.

——. 2001. *Healing the modern in a Central Javanese city.* Durham, NC: Carolina Academic Press.

Fikentscher, Kai. 2000. *You better work! Underground dance music in New York
City.* Hanover, NH: Univ. Press of New England.

Finnegan, Ruth. 1989. *The hidden musicians.* Cambridge: Cambridge Univ.
Press.

Forbes, Dean. 2002. Jakarta. In *Encyclopedia of urban cultures: Cities and cultures
around the world,* ed. Melvin Ember and Carol R. Ember, vol. 1, 410–18.
Danbury, CT: Grolier.

Frederick, William. 1982. Rhoma Irama and the dangdut style: Aspects of contemporary Indonesian popular culture. *Indonesia* 32:103–30.

——. 1997. Dreams of freedom, moments of despair: Armijn Pané and the
imagining of modern Indonesian culture. In *Imagining Indonesia: Cultural
politics and political culture,* ed. Jim Schiller and Barbara Martin-Schiller,
54–89. Athens: Ohio University Center for International Studies.

Frith, Simon. 1981. *Sound effects: Youth, leisure, and the politics of rock'n'roll.* New York: Pantheon Books.

——. 1996. *Performing rites: On the value of popular music.* Cambridge, MA: Harvard Univ. Press.

Frith, Simon, Will Straw, and John Street, eds. 2001. *The Cambridge companion to pop and rock.* New York: Cambridge Univ. Press.

Geertz, Clifford. 1960. *The religion of Java.* Chicago: Univ. of Chicago Press.

——. 1963. *Peddlers and princes: Social development and economic change in two Indonesian towns.* Chicago: Univ. of Chicago Press.

——. 1995. *After the fact: Two countries, four decades, one anthropologist.* Cambridge, MA: Harvard Univ. Press.

Goffman, Erving. 1974. *Frame analysis: An essay on the organization of experience.* Cambridge, MA: Harvard Univ. Press.

Goshert, John Charles. 2000. "Punk" after the Pistols: American music, economics, and politics in the 1980s and 1990s. *Popular Music and Society* 24 (1): 85–106.

Goodwin, Andrew. 1993. Fatal distractions: MTV meets postmodern theory. In *Sound and vision: The music video reader,* ed. Andrew Goodwin and Simon Frith, 45–66. New York: Routledge.

Greene, Paul. 1999. Sound engineering in a Tamil village: Playing audiocassettes as devotional performance. *Ethnomusicology* 43 (3): 459–89.

——. 2001. Mixed messages: Unsettled cosmopolitanisms in Nepali pop. *Popular Music* 20 (2): 169–88.

Greene, Paul, and David Henderson. 2000. At the crossroads of languages, musics, and emotions in Kathmandu. *Popular Music and Society* 24 (3): 95–116.

Greene, Paul, and Thomas Porcello, eds. 2005. *Wired for sound: Engineering and technologies in sonic cultures.* Middletown, CT: Wesleyan Univ. Press.

Grijns, Kees, and Peter J. M. Nas, eds. 2000. *Jakarta-Batavia: Socio-cultural essays.* Leiden: KITLV Press.

Guinness, Patrick. 2000. Contested imaginings of the city: City as locus of status, capitalist accumulation, and community; Competing cultures of Southeast Asian societies. In *A companion to the city,* ed. Gary Bridge and Sophie Watson, 87–98. Malden, MA: Blackwell.

Hannerz, Ulf. 1992. *Cultural complexity: Studies in the social organization of meaning.* New York: Columbia Univ. Press.

Harnish, David. 2005a. Defining ethnicity, (re)constructing culture: Processes of musical adaptation and innovation among the Balinese of Lombok. *Journal of Musicological Research* 24 (3–4): 265–86.

——. 2005b. Teletubbies in paradise: Tourism, Indonesianisation, and modernisation in Balinese music. *Yearbook for Traditional Music* 37:103–23.

——. 2006. *Bridges to the ancestors: Music, myth, and cultural politics at an Indonesian festival.* Honolulu: Univ. of Hawai'i Press.

Hatch, Martin. 1989. Popular music in Indonesia. In *World music, politics, and social change,* ed. Simon Frith, 47–68. Manchester, UK: Manchester Univ. Press.

Hendry, Joy. 2000. *The Orient strikes back: A global view of cultural display.* New York: Berg.

Herbst, Edward. 1997. *Voices in Bali: Energies and perceptions in vocal music and dance theater.* Hanover, NH: Univ. Press of New England.

Hill, David, and Krishna Sen. 1997. Wiring the *warung* to global gateways: The Internet in Indonesia. *Indonesia* 64:67–89.

Hull, Terence, Endang Sulistyaningsih, and Gavin Jones. 1999. *Prostitution in Indonesia: Its history and evolution.* Jakarta: Pustaka Sinar Harapan.

Hymes, Dell. 1975. Breakthrough into performance. In *Folklore: Performance and communication,* ed. Daniel Ben-Amos and Kenneth Goldstein, 11–74. The Hague: Mouton.

Ivy, Marilyn. 1995. *Discourses of the vanishing: Modernity, phantasm, Japan.* Chicago: Univ. of Chicago Press.

Jakarta Post. 2000. Leave cars at home on Earth Day: Official, Friday, April 14. http://www.thejakartapost.com/Archives/ArchivesDet2.asp?FileID= 20000414.A07 (accessed March 28, 2002).

Jarrett, Michael. 1992. Concerning the progress of rock & roll. In *Present tense: Rock & roll and culture,* ed. Anthony DeCurtis, 167–82. Durham, NC: Duke Univ. Press.

Jellinek, Lea. 1991. *Wheel of fortune: The history of a poor community in Jakarta.* Honolulu: Univ. of Hawai'i Press.

Jones, Tod. 2005. *Angkutan* and *bis kota* in Padang, West Sumatra: Public transport as intersections of a local popular culture. Paper presented at the Arts, Culture and Political and Social Change since Suharto Workshop, Launceston, Australia, available from http://www.utas.edu.au/indonesia _workshop/abstracts.htm (accessed August 13, 2006).

Kaplan, E. Ann. 1987. *Rocking around the clock: Music television, postmodernism, and consumer culture.* New York: Methuen.

Kartomi, Margaret. 2002. Debates and impressions of change and continuity in Indonesia's musical arts since the fall of Suharto, 1998–2002. *Wacana Seni* 1:109–49.

Kartoyo, D. S., and Uki Bayu Sedjati. 1997. *Biografi satria bergitar: Rhoma Irama.* Jakarta: Limo Pendowo Karyaindo.

Katz, Mark. 2004. *Capturing sound: How technology has changed music.* Berkeley: Univ. of California Press.

Keane, Webb. 1997. *Signs of recognition: Powers and hazards of representation in an Indonesian society.* Berkeley: Univ. of California Press.

——. 2003. Public speaking: On Indonesian as the language of the nation. *Public Culture* 15 (3): 503–30.

Kearney, Marianne. 2001. Dangdut hits it big in Indonesian music industry. *The Straits Times,* November 5, 2001, 46.

Keil, Charles, and Steven Feld. 1994. *Music grooves: Essays and dialogues.* Chicago: Univ. of Chicago Press.

Kesumah, Dloyana. 1995. *Pesan-pesan budaya lagu-lagu pop dangdut dan pengaruhnya terhadap perilaku sosial remaja kota.* Jakarta: Departemen Pendidikan dan Kebudayaan Republik Indonesia.

Khudori, and Paulus Winarto. 2000. Virtual office plus. *Virtual* suppl. no. 8, *Gamma* 2 (25): 16.

Kramer, A. L. N., and Willie Koen, eds. 1995. *Tuttle's concise Indonesian dictionary.* Rev. ed. Rutland, VT: Charles E. Tuttle.

Labrousse, Pierre. 1994. The second life of Bung Karno: Analysis of the myth (1978–1981). *Indonesia* 57:175–96.

Laskewicz, Zachar. 2004. Pop music and interculturality: The dynamic presence of pop music in contemporary Balinese performance. In *Refashioning pop music in Asia: Cosmopolitan flows, political tempos and aesthetic industries,* ed. Allen Chun, Ned Rossiter, and Brian Shoesmith, 183–97. New York: RoutledgeCurzon.

Leggett, William H. 2005. Terror and the colonial imagination at work in the transnational corporate spaces of Jakarta, Indonesia. *Identities: Global Studies in Culture and Power* 12 (2): 271–301.

Liechty, Mark. 2003. *Suitably modern: Making middle-class culture in a new consumer society.* Princeton, NJ: Princeton Univ. Press.

Lipscombe, Becky. 2003. Indonesia's controversial star. *BBC News,* May 1, 2003. http://news.bbc.co.uk/go/pr/fr/-2/hi/asia-pacific/2992615.stm (accessed May 2, 2003).

Lockard, Craig. 1998. *Dance of life: Popular music and politics in Southeast Asia.* Honolulu: Univ. of Hawai'i Press.

Mallau, Dion. 2001. Pontianak Bersatu. http://www.bisik.com/underground/Beritadetail.asp?idw=139&page=1&choi=1&pr=1 (accessed January 16, 2001; page no longer active).

Manuel, Peter. 1988. *Popular musics of the non-Western world: An introductory survey.* New York: Oxford Univ. Press.

———. 1993. *Cassette culture: Popular music and technology in North India.* Chicago: Univ. of Chicago Press.

Manuel, Peter, and Randal Baier. 1986. Jaipongan: Indigenous popular music of West Java. *Asian Music* 18 (1): 91–110.

Mahon, Maureen. 2004. *Right to rock: The Black Rock Coalition and the cultural politics of race.* Durham, NC: Duke Univ. Press.

Mazzarella, William. 2003. *Shoveling smoke: Advertising and globalization in contemporary India.* Durham, NC: Duke Univ. Press.

McLeod, Kembrew. 2005. *Freedom of expression™: Overzealous copyright bozos and other enemies of creativity.* New York: Doubleday.

McVey, Ruth. 1982. The Beamtenstaat in Indonesia. In *Interpreting Indonesian politics: Thirteen contributions to the debate,* ed. Benedict Anderson and Audrey Kahin, 84–91. Ithaca, NY: Cornell Univ. Press.

Meintjes, Louise. 2003. *Sound of Africa! Making music Zulu in a South African studio.* Durham, NC: Duke Univ. Press.

Merriam, Alan. 1964. *The anthropology of music.* Evanston, IL: Northwestern Univ. Press.

Middleton, Richard. 1990. *Studying popular music.* Philadelphia: Open Univ. Press.

———. 1999. Form. In *Key terms in popular music and culture,* ed. Bruce Horner and Thomas Swiss, 141-55. Malden, MA: Blackwell.

Miller, Daniel. 1995. Introduction: Anthropology, modernity, and consumption. In *Worlds apart: Modernity through the prism of the local,* ed. Daniel Miller, 1-22. New York: Routledge.

Miller, Flagg. 2005. Of songs and signs: Audiocassette poetry, moral character, and the culture of circulation in Yemen. *American Ethnologist* 32 (1): 82-99.

Misrad, Muhammad "Mice." 1999. *Rony: Bagimu Mal-mu Bagiku Pasar-ku.* Jakarta: Kepustakaan Populer Gramedia.

Moehn, Frederick. 2005. "The disc is not the Avenue": Schizmogenetic mimesis in samba recording. In *Wired for sound: Engineering and technologies in sonic cultures,* ed. Paul Greene and Thomas Porcello, 47-83. Middletown, CT: Wesleyan Univ. Press.

Monson, Ingrid. 1999. Riffs, repetition, and theories of globalization. *Ethnomusicology* 43 (1): 32-65.

Muhadjir. 2000. *Bahasa Betawi: Sejarah dan perkembangannya.* Jakarta: Yayasan Obor Indonesia.

Mulder, Niels. 2000. *Indonesian images: The culture of the public world.* Yogyakarta: Kanisius.

Muller, Carol. 1999. *Rituals of fertility and the sacrifice of desire: Nazarite women's performance in South Africa.* Chicago: Univ. of Chicago Press.

Mulligan, Diane. 2005. The discourse of Dangdut: Gender and civil society in Indonesia. In *Gender and civil society: Transcending boundaries,* ed. Jude Howell and Diane Mulligan, 117-38. New York: Routledge,

Murray, Alison. 1991. *No money, no honey: A study of street traders and prostitutes in Jakarta.* Singapore: Oxford Univ. Press.

———. 2001. *Pink fits: Sex, subcultures and discourses in the Asia-Pacific.* Clayton, Victoria, Australia: Monash Univ. Press.

Nass, Martin. 1971. Some considerations of a psychoanalytic interpretation of music. *Psychoanalytic Quarterly* 40 (2): 303-16.

Nelson, Angela. 1999. Rhythm and rhyme in rap. In *This is how we flow: Rhythm in black cultures,* ed. Angela Nelson, 46-53. Columbia: Univ. of South Carolina Press.

Ong, Aihwa, and Michael Peletz, eds. 1995. *Bewitching women, pious men: Gender and body politics in Southeast Asia.* Berkeley: Univ. of California Press.

Ortner, Sherry. 1995. Resistance and the problem of ethnographic refusal. *Comparative Studies in Society and History* 37 (1): 173-93.

Peacock, James. 1968. *Rites of modernization: Symbols and social aspects of Indonesian proletarian drama.* Chicago: Univ. of Chicago Press.

Pemberton, John. 1994a. Recollections from "Beautiful Indonesia": Somewhere beyond the postmodern. *Public Culture* 6 (2): 241–62.

——. 1994b. *On the subject of "Java."* Ithaca, NY: Cornell Univ. Press.

Perlman, Marc. 1999. The traditional Javanese performing arts in the twilight of the New Order: Two letters from Solo. *Indonesia* 68:1–37.

Philpott, Malcolm. 1998. Developments in Papua New Guinea's popular music industry. In *Sound alliances: Indigenous peoples, cultural politics, and popular music in the Pacific,* ed. Philip Hayward, 107–22. New York: Cassell.

Pickles, Jo. 2000. Punks for peace: Underground music gives young people back their voice. *Inside Indonesia* 64. http://www.insideindonesia.org/edit64/punk1.htm (accessed June 18, 2003).

Pioquinto, Ceres. 1995. Dangdut at Sekaten: Female representations in live performance. *Review of Indonesian and Malaysian Affairs* 29 (1–2): 59–89.

——. 1998. A musical hierarchy reordered: Dangdut and the rise of a popular music. *Asian Cultural Studies* 24:73–125.

Piper, Susan, and Sawung Jabo. 1987. Indonesian music from the 50's to the 80's. *Prisma* 43:25–37.

Porcello, Thomas. 1998. Tails out: Social phenomenology and the ethnographic representation of technology in music-making. *Ethnomusicology* 42 (3): 485–510.

Putranto, Wendi, with Krisna Sadrach. 2002. Mengupas sejarah metal Jakarta dengan Sucker Head! http://musickita.com/news/detail.php?id=1010480068 (accessed January 9, 2002; link no longer functioning).

Qureshi, Regula. 2000. How does music mean? Embodied memories and the politics of affect in the Indian *sarangi. American Ethnologist* 27 (4): 805–38.

Rahardja, Prathama, and Henri Chambert-Loir. 1990. *Kamus Bahasa Prokem.* Jakarta: Pustaka Utama Grafiti.

Report from East Java. 1985. *Indonesia* 41:135–49.

Rochijat, Pipit. 1985. Am I PKI or non-PKI? Trans. with an afterword by Benedict Anderson. *Indonesia* 40:37–56.

Rofel, Lisa. 1999. *Other modernities: Gendered yearnings in China after socialism.* Berkeley: Univ. of California Press.

Roseman, Marina. 1987. Inversion and conjuncture: Male and female performance among the Temiar of Peninsular Malaysia. In *Women and music in cross-cultural perspective,* ed. Ellen Koskoff, 131–49. Westport, CT: Greenwood Press.

——. 1991. *Healing sounds from the Malaysian rainforest: Temiar music and medicine.* Berkeley: Univ. of California Press.

Ross, Andrew, and Tricia Rose, eds. 1994. *Microphone fiends: Youth music and youth culture.* New York: Routledge.

Sahertian, Debby. 2000. *Kamus bahasa gaul.* Rev. ed. Jakarta: Pustaka Sinar Harapan.

Schade-Poulsen, Marc. 1999. *Men and popular music in Algeria: The social significance of raï.* Austin: Univ. of Texas Press.

Schafer, R. Murray. 1977. *The tuning of the world.* New York: Knopf.

———. 1994. *The soundscape: Our sonic environment and the tuning of the world.* Rochester, VT: Destiny Books.

Schippers, Mimi. 2002. *Rockin' out of the box: Gender maneuvering in alternative hard rock.* New Brunswick, NJ: Rutgers Univ. Press.

Sears, Laurie, ed. 1996. *Fantasizing the feminine in Indonesia.* Durham, NC: Duke Univ. Press.

Secor, Laura. 2002. Foreign relations. *New York Times,* January 13, 2002, Education Life, 36–37.

Seeger, Anthony. 1987. *Why Suyá sing: A musical anthropology of an Amazonian people.* Cambridge: Cambridge Univ. Press.

Sembiring, Ita. 1998. *Catatan dan refleksi: Tragedi Jakarta 13 dan 14 Mei 1998.* Jakarta: PT Gramedia.

Sen, Krishna, and David Hill. 2000. *Media, culture, and politics in Indonesia.* Melbourne: Oxford Univ. Press.

Shank, Barry. 1994. *Dissonant identities: The rock 'n' roll scene in Austin, Texas.* Hanover, NH: Univ. Press of New England.

Shannon, Jonathan. H. 2004. Knocking some sense into anthropology. Review essay for Meintjes 2003. *American Anthropologist* 106(2): 395–96.

———. 2006. *Among the jasmine trees: Music and modernity in contemporary Syria.* Middletown, CT: Wesleyan Univ. Press.

Siegel, James. 1986. *Solo in the New Order: Language and hierarchy in an Indonesian city.* Princeton, NJ: Princeton Univ. Press.

———. 1998. *A new criminal type in Jakarta: Counter-revolution today.* Durham, NC: Duke Univ. Press.

———. 2000. *Kiblat* and the mediatic Jew. *Indonesia* 69:9–40.

Sovani, N. V. 1964. The analysis of "overurbanization." *Economic Development and Cultural Change* 12:113–22.

Spiller, Henry. 2001. Using music video to conflate old and new in West Java, Indonesia: "Goyang Karawang" by Lilis Karlina. Paper presented at the Society for Ethnomusicology 46th Annual Meeting, Southfield, Michigan.

———. 2004. *Gamelan: The traditional sounds of Indonesia.* Santa Barbara, CA: ABC-CLIO.

Stallybrass, Peter, and Allon White. 1986. *The poetics and politics of transgression.* London: Methuen.

Steedly, Mary. 1999. The state of culture theory in the anthropology of Southeast Asia. *Annual Review of Anthropology* 28:431–54.

Sterne, Jonathan. 1997. Sounds like the Mall of America: Programmed music and the architectonics of commercial space. *Ethnomusicology* 41 (1): 22–50.

Stocker, Terry. 2002. *It happened so fast! Changing Korea, critical years 1994–1997.* Daejon, South Korea: Heliot House.

Stokes, Martin. 1992. *The arabesk debate.* New York: Clarendon/Oxford Univ. Press.

Stone, Ruth. 1982. *Let the inside be sweet: The interpretation of music event among the Kpelle of Liberia.* Bloomington: Indiana Univ. Press.

Sujatmoko, Bambang Hamid, and Paulus Winarto. 2000. Angkot Dunia Informasi. Virtual suppl. no. 8, *Gamma* 2 (25): 4–7.

Sumarsono, Tatang. 1998. *Sajadah panjang Bimbo: 30 tahun perjalanan kelompok musik religius.* Bandung: Penerbit Mizan.

Sun Yung Shin. 2004. Economic miracles. *Mid-American Review* 24 (2): 183–87.

Supanggah, Rahayu. 2003. Campur sari: A reflection. *Asian Music* 34 (2): 1–20.

Suryadi. 2003. Minangkabau commercial cassettes and the cultural impact of the recording industry in West Sumatra. *Asian Music* 34 (2): 51–90.

——. 2005. Identity, media and the margins: Radio in Pekanbaru, Riau (Indonesia). *Journal of Southeast Asian Studies* 36 (1): 131–51.

Suseno, Dharmo Budi. 2005. *Dangdut musik rakyat: Catatan seni bagi calon diva dangdut.* Yogyakarta: Kreasi Wacana.

Sutton, R. Anderson. 1996. Interpreting electronic sound technology in the contemporary Javanese soundscape. *Ethnomusicology* 40 (2): 249–68.

——. 2002a. *Calling back the spirit: Music, dance, and cultural politics in lowland South Sulawesi.* New York: Oxford Univ. Press.

——. 2002b. Popularizing the indigenous or indigenizing the popular? Television, video, and fusion music in Indonesia. *Wacana Seni* 1:13–31.

——. 2003. Local, global, or national? Popular music on Indonesian television. In *Planet TV: A global television reader,* ed. Lisa Parks and Shanti Kumar, 320–40. New York: New York Univ. Press.

——. 2004. "Reform arts"? Performance live and mediated in post-Soeharto Indonesia. *Ethnomusicology* 48 (2): 203–28

Taylor, Charles. 1991. *The ethics of authenticity.* Cambridge, MA: Harvard Univ. Press.

Taylor, Timothy. 1997. *Global pop: World music, world markets.* New York: Routledge.

——. 2001. *Strange sounds: Music, technology, and culture.* New York: Routledge.

Tenzer, Michael. 2000. *Gamelan gong kebyar: The art of twentieth-century Balinese music.* Chicago: Univ. of Chicago Press.

Théberge, Paul. 1997. *Any sound you can imagine: Making music/consuming technology.* Hanover, NH: Univ. Press of New England.

Theodore, K. S. 1999. Industri Musik Indonesia di Ujung Abad Ke 20. *Buletin ASIRI* 5 (November): 10–11.

Thornton, Sarah. 1996. *Club cultures: Music, media, and subcultural capital.* Hanover, NH: Univ. Press of New England.

Titon, Jeff Todd. 1997. Ethnomusicology and values: A reply to Henry Kingsbury. *Ethnomusicology* 41 (2): 253–57.

Tsing, Anna L. 1993. *In the realm of the diamond queen: Marginality in an out-of-the-way place*. Princeton, NJ: Princeton Univ. Press.

Turino, Thomas. 1999. Signs of imagination, identity, and experience: A Peircean semiotic theory for music. *Ethnomusicology* 43 (2): 221–55.

——. 2000. *Nationalists, cosmopolitans, and popular music in Zimbabwe*. Chicago: Univ. of Chicago Press.

Turner, Victor. 1967. *The forest of symbols: Aspects of Ndembu ritual*. Ithaca, NY: Cornell Univ. Press.

Urban, Greg. 1993. Culture's public face. *Public Culture* 5 (2): 213–38.

——. 2001. *Metaculture: How culture moves through the world*. Minneapolis: Univ. of Minnesota Press.

Wallach, Jeremy. 2002. Modern noise and ethnic accents: Indonesian popular music in the era of *Reformasi*. PhD diss., Department of Anthropology, University of Pennsylvania.

——. 2003a. "Goodbye my Blind Majesty": Music, language, and politics in the Indonesian underground. In *Global pop, local language*, ed. Harris M. Berger and Michael T. Carroll, 53–86. Jackson: Univ. Press of Mississippi.

——. 2003b. The poetics of electrosonic presence: Recorded music and the materiality of sound. *Journal of Popular Music Studies* 15 (1): 34–64.

——. 2004. Dangdut trendy. *Inside Indonesia* 78:30.

——. 2005. Engineering techno-hybrid grooves in two Indonesian sound studios. In *Wired for sound: Engineering and technologies in sonic cultures*, ed. Paul D. Greene and Thomas Porcello, 138–55. Middletown, CT: Wesleyan Univ. Press.

Walser, Robert. 1993. *Running with the devil: Power, gender, and madness in heavy metal music*. Hanover, NH: Univ. Press of New England.

Walsh, Bryan. 2003. Inul's rules: A new idol is putting some sex and sizzle into Indonesia's pop-music scene. *Time Asia* 161 (11) (March 24), www.time.com/time/asia/magazine/article/0,13673,501030324-433338,00.html (accessed May 2, 2003).

Waterman, Christopher. 1990 *Jùjú: A social history and ethnography of an African popular music*. Chicago: Univ. of Chicago Press.

Waters, Malcolm. 1995. *Globalization*. New York: Routledge.

Waxer, Lise A. 2002. *The city of musical memory: Salsa, record grooves, and popular culture in Cali, Colombia*. Middletown, CT: Wesleyan Univ. Press.

Weintraub, Andrew. 2004. *Power plays: Wayang golek puppet theater of West Java*. Athens: Univ. of Ohio Press.

——. 2006. Dangdut Soul: Who are "the people" in Indonesian popular music? *Asian Journal of Communication* 16 (4): 411–31.

Weinstein, Deena. 1991. *Heavy metal: A cultural sociology*. New York: Lexington Books.

Wichelen, Sonja van. 2005. "My dance immoral? *Alhamdulillah* no!" *Dangdut* music and gender politics in contemporary Indonesia. In *Resounding international relations: On music, culture, and politics*, ed. M. I. Franklin, 161–77. New York: Palgrave Macmillan.

Wicke, Peter. 1990. *Rock music: Culture, aesthetics, and sociology.* New York: Cambridge Univ. Press.

Widjojo, Muridan S., et al. 1999. *Penakluk rezim Orde Baru: Gerakan Mahasiswa '98.* Jakarta: Pustaka Sinar Harapan.

Widodo, Amrih. 1995. The stages of the state: Arts of the people and rites of hegemonization. *Review of Indonesian and Malaysian Affairs* 29 (1–2): 1–35.

Wijayanti, Sri Hapsari. 2000. Bahasa gaul: Fenomena kehidupan bahasa. *Atma nan Jaya* 13 (1): 128–36.

Wilde, Craig J. de. 2003. Inul Daratista: An Indonesian concert idol. *Music Business Journal* 3 (1). http://www.musicjournal.org/03inuldaratista.htm (accessed May 12, 2003).

Williams, Sean. 1989/1990. Current developments in Sundanese popular music. *Asian Music* 21 (1): 105–36.

——. 2001. *The sound of the ancestral ship: Highland music of West Java.* Oxford: Oxford Univ. Press.

Witoelar, Wimar. 2002. *No regrets: Reflections of a presidential spokesman.* Jakarta: Equinox.

Wong, Deborah. 1989/1990. Thai cassettes and their covers: Two case histories. *Asian Music* 21 (1): 78–104.

Wong, Deborah, and René T. A. Lysloff. 1998. Popular music and cultural politics. In *The Garland encyclopedia of world music*, vol. 4: *Southeast Asia*, ed. Terry Miller and Sean Williams, 95–112. New York: Garland.

Yampolsky, Philip. 1987a. *Lokananta: A discography of the national recording company of Indonesia, 1957–1985.* Bibliography Series no. 10. Madison: Center for Southeast Asian Studies, Univ. of Wisconsin.

——. 1987b. Liner notes to Idjah Hadidjah's album *Tonggeret.* Icon Records 79173.

——. 1989. "Hati Yang Luka," an Indonesian hit. *Indonesia* 47:1–17.

——. 1991. Liner notes to *Music of Indonesia*, vol. 2, *Indonesian popular music: Kroncong, Dangdut, and Langgam Jawa.* Smithsonian/Folkways SF40056.

——. 1995. Forces for change in the regional performing arts of Indonesia. *Bijdragen tot de Taal-, Land- en Volkenkunde* 151 (4): 700–725.

Yano, Christine. 2002. *Tears of longing: Nostalgia and the nation in Japanese popular song.* Cambridge, MA: Harvard Univ. Asia Center.

Zak, Albin. 2001. *The poetics of rock: Cutting tracks, making records.* Berkeley: Univ. of California Press.

Ziv, Daniel. 2002. *Jakarta inside out.* Jakarta: Equinox.

Zuberi, Nabeel. 2001. *Sounds English: Transnational popular music.* Chicago: Univ. of Illinois Press.

Internet Sites

Note: References to Internet Web sites (URLs) were accurate at the time of publication.

Periodicals

www.thejakartapost.com (*The Jakarta Post*)
www.jawapos.co.id (*Jawa Pos*)
www.tempointeraktif.com (*Tempo Interactive*)

Music-Related Sites

www.bisik.com
http://members.tripod.com/~IrvKa/index.html (Irvan's dangdut page)
www.iwan-fals.com (official Iwan Fals Web site)
www.k5.dion.ne.jp/~ranema/logo_e.html (O.M. Ranema [Japanese dangdut group] Web site)
www.angelfire.com/nm/eternalmadness (official Eternal Madness Web site)
www.geocities.com/SunsetStrip/3817/bio.htm (official Trauma Web site)
www.krakatau.net (official Krakatau Web site)
www.mellygoeslaw.com (official Melly Goeslaw Web site)
www.mtvasia.com (MTV Asia)
http://netral.hypermart.net (official Netral Web site, now defunct)
www.NewsMusik.net (NewsMusik magazine)
www.not-a-pup.com (Puppen's official Web site, now defunct). For more current information about the group (now disbanded), see www.robinmalau .net/category/puppen (accessed May 20, 2008).
www.rileks.com
www.tembang.com

Discography

Note: Catalog numbers and years of publication are provided when available. All albums are cassette format unless otherwise noted.

Balcony. *Terkarbonasi.* Harder Records H-004. 1999.
Bubi Chen and Friends. *Wonderful World.* Compact disc. Sangaji Music SM 005. 1999.
Burgerkill. *Dua Sisi.* Riotic Records. 2000.
Cherry Bombshell. *Luka Yang Dalam.* Bulletin BUI 0290700. 2000.
Cokelat. *Untuk Bintang.* Sony Music 497753-4. 2000.
Cucun Novia. *Ska Bon Versi 2000.* Inti Suara Production/PT Sani Sentosa Abadi. n.d.
Eternal Madness. *Bongkar Batas.* PT Resswara Rodakreasi. 2000.
Evie Tamala. *Kasmaran.* Blackboard/Polygram Indonesia IND-1148. n.d.

Fear Inside. *Human's Disgust.* Extreme Fear Terror/Extreme Souls Production. Independent 008. 1998.

Grausig. *Abandon, Forgotten, & Rotting Alone.* Independen (Aquarius Musikindo) P9916/APC IND 16-4. 1999.

Ikke Nurjanah. *Best of the Best '99.* MSC Plus/Polygram Indonesia MC.034-9. n.d.

Iyeth Bustami. *Cinta Hanya Sekali.* Maheswara Musik/Musica MS.0245. n.d.

Koil. *Kesepian Ini Abadi (Maxi Single).* Apocalypse/Karat Rekord. 1998.

Krakatau 2000. *Magical Match.* Compact disc. Kita Music/HP Records/Musica HPCD-0099. 2000.

Kremush. *Deadly Consience* [*sic*]. Independent 060997. 1997.

Lilis Karlina. *Cinta Terisolasi.* Maheswara Musik/Musica MS.0227. n.d.

Lirra Zanni. *Ska Minang India.* Tanama Record. n.d.

Melly Goeslaw. *Melly.* Aquarius Musikindo AQM9187-4. 1999.

Netral. *Paten.* Bulletin BUI 0220699. 1999.

Netral. *Netral Is the Best.* Bulletin BU-0280700. 2000.

Pas. *Psycho I.D.* PT Aquarius P9216. 1998.

Patty. *Dulu, Mimpi & Kini.* Maheswara Musik/Musica. 2000.

Puppen. *S/T.* Distorsi. n.d.

Puppen. *Mk II.* Self-released. n.d.

Rage Generation Brothers. *Our Lifestyle.* Independen (Aquarius Musikindo) P9919/APC IND19-4. 2000.

Rhoma Irama. *Euphoria 2000.* Blackboard/Polygram Indonesia IND.1179-5. 2000.

/rif. *Radja.* Sony Music 489091-4. 1997.

Sheila on 7. *Self-Titled.* Sony Music 494042.4. 1999.

Slowdeath. *Learn Through Pain.* Independent 007. 1998.

Slowdeath. *From Mindless Enthusiasm to Sordid Self-Destruction.* Independent 001. 1996.

Suckerhead. *10th Agresi.* Aquarius Musikindo AQM9219. 1999.

Various artists. *20 Lagu Dangdut Terseleski Terpopular,* vol. 15. Maheswara Musik/Musica MS 0226. n.d.

Various artists. *Metalik Klinik 3.* Rotorcorp/Musica MSC.8346. 2000.

Various artists. *Pesta Rap.* Compact disc. Musica MSCD 0095. n.d.

Various artists. *Tembang Pilihan 5 Jagoan Dangdut.* PT Anggada Irama Melodi/Wilhan AIM-00141. n.d.

Vile. *Systematic Terror Decimation.* Dementia Records DR002. 1999.

Waiting Room. *Self-Titled.* Tropic. 1997.

INDEX

Since Indonesian nomenclature does not always follow the same rules as those used in the Western world, for the sake of convenience all Indonesian personal names, even those that include Western-sounding first names, are alphabetized here by the first word. A few select names have been listed in two places, under both the first and last elements (for example, B. J. Habibie appears both as "B. J. Habibie" and as "Habibie, B. J."). Names beginning with the honorific "Pak," however, are alphabetized by the second word. An italicized page number indicates a picture, while a page number followed by the letter "t" indicates a table. "CD" as a reference locator is used to identify artists and song titles that are featured on the accompanying compact disc.

NEW PERSPECTIVES IN
SOUTHEAST ASIAN STUDIES

From Rebellion to Riots: Collective Violence on Indonesian Borneo
Jamie S. Davidson

*Pretext for Mass Murder: The September 30th Movement and Suharto's Coup
d'État in Indonesia*
John Roosa

Việt Nam: Borderless Histories
Edited by Nhung Tuyet Tran and Anthony Reid

Modern Noise, Fluid Genres: Popular Music in Indonesia, 1997–2001
Jeremy Wallach

CD Track Listing

1. Dangdut. "Hanya Cinta Yang Kupunya" (I Have Only Love) written by Sonny JS. Performed by the group Manis Manja. From the album *20 Lagu Dangdut Terseleski Terpopular,* vol. 15. Courtesy of Maheswara Musik.

2. Dangdut/Combination ethnic. "Cinta Terisolasi" (Isolated Love/Love Stuck Like Cellophane Tape) written by Hawadin and Lilis Karlina. Performed by Lilis Karlina. From the album *Cinta Terisolasi.* Courtesy of Maheswara Musik.

3. *Pop alternatif.* "Mungkin" (Maybe) written and performed by Patty. From the album *Dulu, Mimpi & Kini* (Then, Dreams, and Now). Courtesy of Maheswara Musik.

4. Dangdut/*Pop Melayu.* "Cinta Hanya Sekali" (Love [Happens] Only Once) written by Dino Sidin and Iksan Arepas. Performed by Iyeth Bustami. From the album *Cinta Hanya Sekali.* Courtesy of Maheswara Musik.

5. Underground: Balinese gamelan-influenced death metal. "Bunuh Diri" (Suicide) written and performed by Eternal Madness. From the album *Bongkar Batas* (Break Down Boundaries). Courtesy of the artists.

6. Underground: Metallic hardcore. "Hijau" (Green) written and performed by Puppen. From the album *S/T.* Courtesy of the artists.